THE
KING
SLAYER

A SEQUEL TO THE WITCH HUNTER

VIRGINIA BOECKER

LITTLE, BROWN AND COMPANY
New York Boston

Copyright © 2016 by Virginia Boecker
Map art © 2016 by James Madsen

Little, Brown and Company

Hachette Book Group
1290 Avenue of the Americas, New York, NY 10104
Visit us at lb-teens.com

Little, Brown and Company is a division of Hachette Book Group, Inc.
The Little, Brown name and logo are trademarks of Hachette Book Group, Inc.

The publisher is not responsible for websites (or their content) that are not owned by the publisher.

First Edition: June 2016

Library of Congress Cataloging-in-Publication Data

Names: Boecker, Virginia, author.
Title: The king slayer : a sequel to The witch hunter / Virginia Boecker.
Description: First edition. | New York : Little, Brown and Company, 2016. | Summary: "Set in an alternative 16th-century England, former witch hunter Elizabeth Grey is hiding out in the magical town of Harrow, avoiding the price put on her head by Lord Blackwell, and gearing up for a war that will test her both physically and emotionally"— Provided by publisher.
Identifiers: LCCN 2015038825| ISBN 9780316327237 (hardback) | ISBN 9780316327206 (ebook) | ISBN 9780316327251 (library edition ebook)
Subjects: | CYAC: Fantasy. | Love—Fiction. | Great Britain—History—16th Century—Fiction. | BISAC: JUVENILE FICTION / Action & Adventure / General. | JUVENILE FICTION / Fantasy & Magic. | JUVENILE FICTION / Love & Romance.
Classification: LCC PZ7.B6357175 Ki 2016 | DDC [Fic]—dc23
LC record available at http://lccn.loc.gov/2015038825

10 9 8 7 6 5 4 3 2 1

RRD-C

Printed in the United States of America

For Holland
and
for August

Harrow-On-The-Hill

Cambria

Galfion's Reach

River Wye

The Mudchute

Whetstone

Rochester

High Street

Hatch End

Hexham

Anglia

62 miles to
Upminster

1

I SIT ON THE EDGE of the bed waiting, the day I've feared for months finally here. I look around the room, only there's not much to distract me. Everything is white: white walls, white curtains, white stone fireplace, even the furniture— bed, wardrobe, and a small dressing table set below a looking glass. On cloudy days, this lack of color is soothing. But on the rare sunny winter day, such as today, the brightness is overwhelming.

There's a gentle rapping on the door.

"Come in," I call.

The door squeaks open on its hinges and there's John, standing in the doorway. He leans against the frame and watches me a moment, his brows creased in a frown.

"Are you ready?" he finally asks.

"Would it matter if I'm not?"

John crosses the room to sit beside me, somewhat gingerly. He's dressed well today, in stiff blue trousers and matching blue coat, and a white shirt that somehow isn't wrinkled. Hair that manages to be curly but not unruly. He looks like he could be going to a masque or a ball, someplace festive. Not where we're really going.

"You're going to be fine," he says. "We're going to be fine. And if they make you leave, well"—he smiles then, but it doesn't quite reach his eyes—"Iberia is beautiful, even this time of year. Think of the fun we'll have."

I shake my head, feeling a rush of guilt at his being forced to make light of what's about to happen: the council hearing. To face my crimes, to answer to the charge of treason against Harrow.

When I was first summoned to attend, it was the week after Blackwell's masque, after John and Peter brought me to their home. After we'd learned of Blackwell's plan to steal the throne, to turn the hundreds of witches and wizards I helped capture into his army; after I gave John my stigma—the inky-black, elegantly scrawled XIII on my abdomen, the mark that healed me and gave me strength—and nearly died myself.

I wasn't conscious then, nor was I conscious when I received the second summons, nor the third. I received a total of six before I even opened my eyes, six more before I could take a step unassisted. They were coming at a rate of one or two a week before Nicholas put an end to it, assuring the council I would meet with them when I was ready.

It took two months.

And for two months, I've lived in the shadow of this hearing, wondering what will become of me. It's unlikely the council will allow me to remain living here, not without a price attached. Becoming their assassin is Peter's guess; their spy, John's. But mine is exile: given an hour to collect my things, then an escort to the boundaries of Harrow, ordered never to return.

"If they make me leave, you're not coming with me," I say. "Fifer, your father, your patients... you can't leave them."

John stands up. "We talked about this."

Actually, John did all the talking; I did all the protesting.

"I don't want to leave them, but I refuse to leave you," he continues. "And anyway, it won't come to that. Nicholas won't allow it." He takes my hand, gives it a gentle tug. "Come on. Let's get this over with."

I get to my feet, reluctant. I'm dressed well, too, today, in a gown Fifer gave me. Shimmery, pale blue silk skirt, the bodice a darker blue brocade, trimmed with silver thread and white seed pearls. It's the prettiest gown I've ever owned. It's the only gown I've ever owned. She even plaited my hair, pulling it into an elaborate rope that falls over my shoulder. I wanted to wear it down, like I usually do. But Fifer insisted.

"With your hair like this, you look about fourteen," she said. "The younger you look, the more innocent you look. It'll make the council think twice about exiling a child."

John reaches forward and gently grasps my plait, running his fingers down the length of it. I close my eyes against the sensation, against the feel of him standing so near. When I open them, he's watching me carefully, and I know I'm looking back the same way.

The sound of someone clearing his throat in the hallway

3

breaks the spell. John steps away just as Peter appears at the door, concern etched into every line on his weathered face. Like John, he doesn't quite look himself today. Dark curly hair, carefully combed. Dark beard, closely cropped. He's clean, ironed, and starched, and if it weren't for the sword at his side—broad, curved handle, a pirate's blade—I might not recognize him.

He gives us a quick once-over.

"Good, good. You both look good. Proper but not prim. Well-groomed but not overly so." Peter leans in closer, taking in whatever he sees on our faces. "Mind, you might want to try and look a bit more somber. Save the celebration for after, hmm?"

I step back, away from John, but he only laughs and rolls his eyes.

"We should start out," Peter continues. "Best to be there early. We don't know what kind of crowd we might run into."

At the word *crowd*, my stomach seizes into a knot. It's something else I've feared since I was summoned to this hearing. Facing the people of Harrow, hearing their stories. Learning how I, or someone I know, have killed someone close to them; how I, or someone I know, have ruined their lives.

Downstairs, John helps me into my coat. Long, made of blue wool and lined in rabbit fur—another gift from Fifer—and the three of us slip from the cottage into the bitter late-February air, the wind biting our faces and numbing our cheeks.

John and Peter's home, nicknamed Mill Cottage for the enormous waterwheel built into the attached barn, lies outside the village of Whetstone in northern Harrow, tucked at the end of a narrow dirt road that runs alongside a slow-moving river. It's peaceful here, and quiet today as usual. Nothing but the sound of the water mill splashing softly in the banks and a pair of mallards swimming along the edge, squawking at us for food.

Mill Cottage is a funny, charming little place, once three separate smaller homes that, over time, Peter combined into one larger one. It still maintains a rather haphazard look: The front house is long and low, brown stone with a weathered blue door and large, blue-paned windows. The middle house is red brick and the tallest of the three, the façade lined with small windows and a brick-columned smokestack. And the back house, where my bedroom is, dark gray brick with a thatched roof, surrounded by John's lush physic gardens. He says they'll be full of birds come spring, building nests and hatching chicks; nearly unlivable for all the noise.

Not for the first time, I wonder: *Will I still be here come spring? Will Mill Cottage? Will Harrow?*

It's just over an hour's walk from Whetstone to Hatch End, where the hearing will be. Peter says it's tradition for every council meeting to be held at the residence of the head councilman—no longer Nicholas, not after his illness kept him from performing his duties, but a man named Gareth Fish. I met him once, at Nicholas's home after I'd first arrived: tall and cadaverous in black, taking dictation. Peter said he's a fair man, if a bit ardent; John and Fifer said nothing, their silence telling me all I needed to know.

Our path runs across sloping, grassy terrain, marked occasionally by weather-logged signposts with arrows that point to the nearby hamlets that make up Harrow's settlement: THEY-DON BOIS, 3.2 MILES. MUDCHUTE, 17 MILES. HATCH END, 3.7 MILES. The sign reading UPMINSTER, 62 MILES has been crossed out and now reads in untidy scrawl beneath it: *Hell lies this way.*

Winter has settled in everywhere I look. The grasses in the meadows and distant rolling hills brown and dotted with unmelted snow; the trees barren and lifeless. Farmhouses dot the landscape, smoke from fireplaces seeping from chimneys, sheep and cows and horses huddled in quiet, shivering masses under the brightness of the heatless sun. The scene is peaceful but with an underlying current of tension: a village lying in wait.

"Nicholas will be there already, along with Fifer." Peter's voice breaks the frigid silence. "We debated whether Schuyler should come, but decided it was too much of a risk. We don't want to draw any comparisons between his somewhat... capricious past and yours."

Schuyler. A revenant, lifeless and immortal but with almost unimaginable strength and power. He saved Nicholas's life by helping me break the curse tablet that Blackwell used to try to kill Nicholas; he saved all our lives by pulling us out of Blackwell's palace and onto Peter's ship, bound for safety. But for all that, he's still a thief and a liar, a goad and a miscreant, and despite Peter's delicacy what he really means to say is that Schuyler's past is violent, unpredictable, and untrustworthy. Just like mine.

"As for George," Peter says, "he wrote a lovely letter, which will be entered into evidence on your side."

In the days that followed Blackwell's usurpation of the throne and Malcolm's subsequent imprisonment, and before

Blackwell closed Anglia's borders, George—a spy once in the guise of the king's fool—took a ship bound for Gaul. He was to meet with their king in a bid for troops and supplies, knowing that sooner or later, probably sooner, Blackwell would attack Harrow. There are too many people here who have the power to oppose him. And as long as Harrow exists, it will be a threat to him: an unsteady king on an unsteady throne.

"Then there's Nicholas," Peter continues. "While it's true he's a bit diminished, politically speaking, after everything that's happened"—he waves his hand vaguely, but it's clear he means me—"he's still influential among the older Reformists. Of course, there are some in the council who argue that Nicholas is complicit in Blackwell's takeover. That if he hadn't been intent on helping you, on making sure your life was spared"—a glance at John, who scowls—"we could have somehow stopped him."

The idea, it's so absurd I almost laugh.

"Blackwell has been planning this for years," I say. "Decades, even. Since he started that plague that killed the king and queen. My parents. Half the country."

Peter holds his hands up, a conciliatory gesture. But I go on.

"Even if you'd known, you couldn't have stopped it. I would have said that even before I knew he was a wizard." I think of the man I knew—the man I thought I knew. The man who was once Inquisitor, devoting his life to rooting out and destroying magic. Who spent his life plotting in secret and lying in attendance; who used me, Caleb, the rest of his witch hunters to capture witches and wizards so he could build an army, overthrow the king—his own nephew—and take over the country. "You don't know Blackwell the way I do. You don't know what he's capable of."

I've stopped walking, and now instead of shivering I'm sweating beneath all this rabbit fur. John gives my hand a slight squeeze, and only then do I realize I was shouting.

"I do know," Peter says. "And the council needs to know, too. What Blackwell's done, everything he's done. With any luck, it will tell us something about what he plans to do next."

We've been over this strategy countless times. Nicholas wants to put me on the stand and have me tell them what I told him, things I've never told anyone else before. About my training, about how I became a witch hunter, about Caleb.

Caleb.

My stomach twists into a tight, painful knot the way it does every time I think of him. And I think about him often—too often. The way I raised my sword to try to kill Blackwell, the way Caleb threw himself in front of him. The way I killed Caleb instead.

He needed me out of the way, I know that now. He saw me as an obstacle, as something keeping him from the ambition he so desperately needed to reach. But knowing that is still not enough to quell the guilt that eats at me, that has eaten at me every single day in the two months since his death.

"...and that's it," Peter finishes. "That's all you have to say. I realize we've been over it a hundred times. But it's important to be prepared." I nod again, even though I didn't hear a word he said. I never do. Every time he starts to talk about it, my thoughts drift to Caleb and I don't hear anything else.

We travel the rest of the way in relative silence. I'm too

nervous to talk, Peter too tense, John too worried. John walks alongside me, brows furrowed, running a hand through his hair until his once-neat curls are nearly standing on end. It makes him seem boyish, younger than his nineteen years.

The path before me begins to narrow, passing through a squeeze of trees lining the road. The trunks are high and twisted, their leafless branches curling and intertwining like fingers, forming a dense canopy to throw shade on the damp dirt beneath our feet and obscuring the view ahead.

"Mind your step." Peter points to the felled trunk blocking our path in the center of the road. "These trees, they're quite lovely in summer. But after the first of the winter rains, it seems as if half of them come down, quite a pain in the—*God's blood.*"

I hear John's sharp intake of breath, and I look up and see them. Hundreds, maybe even a thousand people, lining the road to Gareth's. For a moment, we stand there, the three of us rooted to the ground, staring at the faces of the men and women before us, who wear expressions ranging from curiosity to disgust to hatred.

We push past them, shivering beneath wool cloaks and hats and scarves and gloves. I don't recognize any of them but I recognize the look they give me, the way their eyes sweep over my too-fine gown and too-fine coat, and all at once the effort Fifer put into making me look respectable, into making me look innocent, all of it seems at best a farce, at worst an insult. I don't belong here, and they all know it.

"Head up," Peter whispers. "You look hangdog. Worse, you look guilty."

"I feel guilty," I say. "I do feel guilt."

"Feeling guilt and looking guilty are two very different things," Peter says. "Now look, there's Gareth ahead. He'll lead us inside."

The endless sea of people ends at the low stone wall surrounding Gareth's home. Sand-colored brick two stories high, surrounded by an expanse of manicured gardens, trimmed low for winter. It's bordered by a hill on one side, thick with dark, winter-hardy trees, and on the other, a cathedral. Separate from the home but built from the same sand-colored brick, it's fenced by a tall iron gate and fronted by a crumbled cemetery, full of irregularly planted slabs and crosses, mossy and weatherworn.

Gareth, dressed in black council robes, the red-and-orange badge of the Reformists emblazoned on the front, strides toward us. He's as I remember him: spindly and gray, pale blue eyes flashing behind wire-rimmed spectacles. He offers his hand to Peter and then to John, who shakes it without enthusiasm.

"I trust you found your way here without incident?" Gareth says.

"We're here, aren't we?" John mutters.

Peter throws him a sharp look; John ignores it.

"No incident," Peter replies. "Though that's down to luck more than intent, I reckon. I seem to recall your wanting to keep this a private affair? Looks like half the northern hamlets showed up."

Gareth offers a thin smile, a glint of an apology. "News travels fast in Harrow, you know that. Especially news of this magnitude." He looks to the crowd, now pressed in so close they're nearly surrounding us. They've fallen silent, those in the back craning their heads, trying to hear him speak. "For many, this was the first they'd heard of Nicholas's illness. It's natural for them to be concerned for his well-being. He is a popular figure, of course." Gareth's smile wavers just a bit. "I'm sure many here are grateful to Elizabeth for sparing his life."

"She didn't spare it, she saved it." John's voice is sharp, irritated. Peter lays a hand on his shoulder but John ignores that, too. "And if people are so grateful to her, then why are we having this hearing at all?"

"I'm afraid it doesn't work that way." Gareth spreads his hands, as if he himself is helpless to the machinations of the council, as if he himself is not the head of it. "The council calls the hearings, not the populace. Although I am sure the vote will bring their gratitude into consideration."

Of all the looks leveled in my direction, not one could pass for gratitude.

"In any event, the council is convened inside, waiting for your arrival. Shall we?" Gareth gestures not at his home but at the neighboring cathedral. "With the crowd such as it is, we had to move the hearing there. I assume there are no objections?"

"Would it matter if there were?" John snaps.

"None at all," Peter says cheerfully. "Shall we?"

Gareth leads us down the short path to the cathedral's gate, the crowd pressing close behind. He opens it and waves us inside, striding quickly toward the front door, black cloak billowing behind him like a storm cloud. Peter steps through but I hesitate, feeling a sudden shiver of foreboding at my surroundings. The gates: like those at Ravenscourt, tall and forbidding. The crowd: like the one that protested in front of them, angry and demanding. The spire atop the cathedral: a judge pointing an accusatory finger. The tumble of tombstones: a jury waiting to pass sentence.

"It will all be over soon," John whispers in my ear, his hand steady on my back.

I turn to him and that's when I see it: a split second of movement, a man in a blur of black, and that familiar sound, the creaking of wood, the sound yew makes when strung with hemp; a bow with an arrow nocked and ready to fly.

The scream tears out of my mouth just as the arrow tears through the neck of the man standing right beside John.

2

THE MAN'S MOUTH OPENS WIDE, in shock as much as horror. Blood fountains from the wound in his neck, saturating his shirt even before he drops to the ground with a heavy thump, like an overstuffed sack of turnips.

The crowd around us erupts in screams. Another arrow, two, zing through the air. Another man goes down, then a woman.

Peter yanks his sword from the scabbard with one hand, points toward the cathedral with the other. "Go! Get inside. Both of you. *Now.*" He charges past us, back out the gate, and disappears into the crowd.

John grabs my arm, viselike, and pushes me down the path ahead of the people who push and scream behind us. He shoves open the cathedral door and Fifer stands on the threshold, pale and pretty in an emerald velvet gown, her hair pulled back tightly from her face.

"What's happening?" Her normally gravelly voice is thin with fear. "I heard screams—"

"We're under attack." John thrusts me through the door. Throngs of people crowd behind him, push around him, come between us. He's released me and is now disappearing from sight, back out the door again. "Stay inside," I hear him call. "Don't come out, no matter what."

"John!"

"Don't come out!" he repeats. I hear his voice but I don't see him. I call his name again, but he's gone.

I skirt along the back wall of the cathedral and down the side aisle toward the transept, Fifer on my heels. People crowd the nave, fill the pews, all of them screaming and pushing.

"Where's Nicholas?" I shout.

"With the rest of the council," she shouts back. "They convene in the crypt before hearings; they hadn't come up because you weren't here yet."

I stop before a tall arched window overlooking the grave-yard. A dozen or so men, John and Peter among them, stand huddled beyond the gates. Peter presses a sword in John's hand and before I can make sense of what's happening, before I can reconcile the sight of John holding a weapon, they scatter.

I slip off my rabbit coat, let it slide to the ground. Lift up the outer skirt of my gown, tear off the kirtle underneath.

Fifer's mouth drops open in horror. "What are you doing?"

"What does it look like?" I kick the fabric aside. "I'm going to help."

"I see that," Fifer snaps. "I meant, what are you doing to that gown?"

I shoot her a look.

"You can't go out there." She changes tack. "You could get hurt." She casts a furtive glance around, but the people crushed around us aren't paying attention; even if they were, they couldn't hear us above the fray. "You could die."

"Which is why I need weapons," I say. "Some of the men here must be armed. A sword, or knives, preferably, but I'll take anything."

Fifer hesitates, scowling. Finally, she picks up the hem of her heavy velvet skirt and pushes into the crowd. I turn back to the window. Arrows fly indiscriminately; men—I can't see who—dart behind trees, hedges, headstones. There's shouting inside, shouting outside; I can't make sense of anything. Moments later, Fifer reappears behind me, carrying a handful of silver-handled knives. She passes them to me one by one, handle first.

"I don't know if they're what you want," she says, "but I had to steal them, so I don't want a word of complaint."

A grin slides across my face at the feel of their cool, comforting weight. I pick up my discarded kirtle, slice off a strip with one of the knives, tie it around my waist into a makeshift belt. Shove the rest of my weapons inside, then step to the small door beside the window and unbolt the latch.

"Lock it after I leave," I tell her. "Don't open it again, not for anyone."

"Don't do anything stupid," she replies before shutting the door and sliding the heavy bolt back into place.

Before me, the cemetery and the surrounding gates. Beyond that, trees, and then an expanse of brown rolling hills. To my right, men fighting and shouting, Peter among them. I don't see John but I do see two others, not archers in black but townsmen in simple winter robes, lying faceup in the grass, arrows lodged in their chests. Dead.

I edge my way toward the front of the cathedral. I don't make more than a few feet before an arrow sings by me, lodging itself in a crack in the stone. It's followed by another, then another. They arrange themselves in a neat little row, not six inches in front of my face. The aim is not a mistake, it's a warning. I crash to the ground. Crawl on my stomach across the dirt and grass, take refuge behind a crumbled slab pocked with lichen and moss. Arrange my thoughts as neatly as the arrows messaged before me.

First, find the shooter. The arrows came in high, landed low; somewhere in the trees, then. Second, kill the shooter. I slide a knife from my belt and dart from behind the headstone to another, my eyes on the shadowed branches above me, inviting him to show himself.

Where are you? I think.

A reply comes in the form of yet another arrow, this one skimming the space between my third and fourth fingers, wrapped around the corner of the stone. I jerk my hand away, the smallest yelp escaping my lips as a stream of blood runs down my fingers, a crimson streak against pale skin. Out of habit, I wait for it, but it doesn't come. Not the flash of heat in my abdomen, not the sharp, prickling sensation. Because out of habit, I forget I no longer have my stigma.

I duck behind the slab again and assess. I'm bleeding, I'm cornered. I'm armed but not as much as I'd like, and I can't spot my attacker. I have no advantage. But I didn't survive two years of witch-hunter training without knowing how to make the most of a disadvantage. Unbidden, Blackwell's voice rings through my head: *In order to regain lost advantage, you must always do the unexpected.*

So I do the one thing I shouldn't do when surrounded by a hidden enemy: I stand up. I hear it then, the tiniest sound—a ruffle of leaves, a barely suppressed grunt of surprise. It's enough. I spot him perched in a low branch of an oak tree, camouflaged by the boughs of a nearby evergreen. I slide one of the heavy silver knives from my belt. Pull back my arm, take aim, throw.

And I miss.

Damnation.

A short, derisive laugh; the soft thud of feet hitting ground. Whoever was in the tree is out of it now, and he's coming for me. Footsteps. The rustle of fingers on fletching, the drawing back of an arrow. So I do the only other thing I can do when surrounded by a hidden enemy:

I turn. And I run.

The arrow whistles over my head, just barely and by mistake—my foot gets tangled in the hem of my gown and I tumble to the ground. Roll to my back, scrabble for another knife, but it's too late: The archer is standing over me. Dark hair, stocky build, early twenties. I don't know him, but he seems to know me. He regards me with a half-suppressed smirk, a shake of his head.

"From everything I've heard about you, I'd hoped for a better fight than this."

"Who are you?" I ask.

The archer doesn't bother to reply. He pulls another arrow from his quiver, slowly nocks it in place, never taking his eyes from mine.

"I like a good sport," he says. "Blackwell assured me you'd be one. He'll be disappointed to hear he was wrong." He cocks his head to the side, considering. "Perhaps not *that* disappointed."

I shuffle back and away from him, from the arrow now aimed directly at my face. I don't get far, backing into another headstone, the rough surface digging into my spine.

The archer swings his bow back and forth, slowly, as if taking inventory of my features. "You have pretty eyes," he says. "Seems a shame to shoot you there, but it's the best place, you know. It'll only hurt for a moment."

I notice it then: the badge stitched on the front of his black wool cloak. It's a grotesque thing: a red rose strangled by its own thorny green stem and pierced through the top with a green-hilted sword. I've never seen it before now, but I know exactly what it is: Blackwell's new emblem.

"He won't win," I whisper. They're my last words; I should make them count. "Blackwell. He thinks he'll win. But he won't."

A shrug. "He already has."

I don't reply; I only wait. For the arrow to pierce my skull, my brain; wait for death. I close my eyes, as if it will hurt less that way.

Then, in the space between one moment and the next, it happens. A footfall, the tread of boots on the soft grass, the snap of a twig. My eyes fly open as the archer whirls around but not in time, not before the blade lands hard across his neck and down his back, nearly slicing him in two.

His dark eyes go blank. A spray of blood spurts from his mouth onto my face, my arms, my dress. The archer sways

18

once, twice, then topples to the forest floor like a felled tree. Behind him is John, his blue jacket and trousers no longer stiff but wrinkled and torn, his white shirt no longer white but red with blood.

He drops to his knees beside me. "Are you all right?" He cups my face in his hands, turns it gently from side to side. "He didn't get you, did he?"

My eyes dart from the downed archer, his blood spattered all over the tombstones and pooling crimson beneath him, to the sword in John's hand, also dripping blood.

"Elizabeth." John tilts my head toward his with a finger on my chin.

"He got my hand," I finally reply. "But I'm fine."

John swipes his thumb over the still-bleeding cut. "It's not deep, but I should take a closer look at it later anyway." He pulls me to my feet. "I saw him watching you. He was in the tree, firing at us, then he stopped as soon as you stepped from the cathedral. Why did you do that? I told you to stay inside. You could have been killed."

A look passes between us, and in it is the unspoken realization of how different things are now. I am not the person I was when we met, not the person I was three months ago. A witch hunter then, invincible; bearer of a stigma and the subject of a prophecy: the most wanted person in Anglia.

I don't know who I am now.

"You shouldn't be out here," he goes on. "It's too dangerous. You're not well enough, and you're not..." He stops himself, but I seize on his words anyway.

"I'm not what?" I pull away from him. "Not strong? Not useful? That I'm not able to fight anymore so I should just stay away since I'm not wanted anyway?" The words pour out of me before I can think better of them.

"That's not what I meant and you know it."

"I'm sorry," I reply quickly, because I do know it. "I shouldn't have said that, and—" I fall silent as it hits me then, what John has done. He used a weapon, and he killed someone. The boy who has done nothing but save lives has now gone and taken one. "You killed him." I glance at the archer at our feet.

"Yes," John agrees. "But I'm not sorry for it. I would do it again if I had to, if it meant protecting you, or anyone else."

I blink at the sudden vehemence in his voice.

"I don't want you to do that," I say. "That's not what you do."

"I think we're all going to do things we don't want to before this is all over," he says. "Let's go. We got them all, at least I think we did. But we'll want to do a head count inside, make sure everyone's accounted for."

We thread through the cemetery to the front of the cathedral where a huddle of men gather—Peter, Gareth, a handful of others I don't recognize. They stand beside a line of bodies, a trail of blood leading up to and soaking the ground beside them.

"How many?" I ask. "I saw one man down when I came out, one of ours. Did they get anyone else? Did we get any more of theirs?"

"Five." John shoots me a grim look. "Four men, one woman, all of them ours. Of theirs, we only got the one. The others—we counted four more—disappeared as soon as we gave chase."

Harrow is a ten-mile-long stretch of land surrounded

by a magical protective barrier, allowing in only those who reside here or, like me, are accompanied by those who reside here. But with Blackwell's claim to the throne, and the revelation that he, too, possesses magical ability, Harrow has become exposed and vulnerable. With hundreds of witches and wizards missing since the Inquisition began four years ago, there's no telling who are dead and who may have turned traitor, either by choice or by force. But someone has, and now they're letting Blackwell's men inside Harrow.

The first breach happened a month ago. A single man—he was thought to be a spy or scout—was caught in the village of More-on-the-Marsh, about halfway between John's house in Whetstone and Gareth's in Hatch End. He was discovered quite by accident: He fell out of the tree he'd been sleeping in, frightening a pair of wizards fishing in a nearby pond at dawn, and ran away before they could catch him.

The second breach was more sinister. Three men were caught creeping through the Mudchute, a desolate area full of patchwork fields that stretch south, from the populated settlements in northern Harrow to the border. They weren't after anything, they weren't armed, and they didn't run away when they were caught. They simply disappeared into thin air.

Despite the fear running through Harrow that Blackwell's men are being allowed through, there's a contrary undercurrent of hope. Because for many, the idea that someone they love, someone they thought was dead but is instead traitorous and alive, is a seductive one. But since John watched his own mother and sister burn to death on the stake in front of him, it's not one he can indulge in.

Over a year on, he still struggles with it. Although I may

not be responsible for their capture, I am complicit. And I know he struggles with that, too.

"Where did you learn how to use a sword?" I ask.

"I've known how to use a sword since before I could walk," John replies, a wan smile on his face. "A benefit of having a pirate for a father, I suppose."

"You use it well," I say cautiously.

He nods, noncommittal. "I've never had much use for it, but I'm glad for it now. Especially after today."

I want to tell him to be careful. I want to tell him how it goes. That first you kill for a reason, then you kill for an excuse. Then you kill for neither, and bit by bit the lives you take begin to steal from your own. I saw it happen to Caleb just as I felt it happen to me. I can't watch it happen to John.

But before I can say this, before I can get out a word, Nicholas rounds into sight. I feel a rush of relief to see him alive, unharmed, but that relief quickly turns to dread the moment he joins the other men, all of them pointing at me, at the cathedral, Gareth nodding, adamant.

Peter breaks away as we approach, Nicholas following close behind. Peter grasps John in a tight embrace before turning to me and doing the same. Nicholas regards me closely, his clear, dark-eyed gaze moving from the blood on my clothes to the blood on my hand. We both say nothing as the others descend upon us, still in rapid conversation.

"What's going on?" John says.

"I wanted to gather the women and children into small groups, escort them back to their homes," Peter replies. "Set up a revolving perimeter, armed men to patrol the barrier around Harrow day and night to ensure no further breaches."

"To which I agreed," Nicholas says. "I also agreed that the hearing can wait. With what's happened today, we have more important matters to attend to."

I breathe a sigh of relief at this stay of execution, that I can have a few more days, a week, perhaps, to prepare. Until Gareth says, "On the contrary. I think now is the perfect time to hold the hearing."

3

JOHN STEPS IN FRONT OF ME, as if to shield me from the idea. "No. We don't have to hold the hearing today. It can be postponed."

"Unfortunately, that isn't how it works," Gareth says. "The council has been convened, the font to tally the votes has been readied. Neither can be adjourned until a resolution is met." He looks to Nicholas. "These were the rules you yourself instated, when you set up the council."

"The rules were put in place to prevent treachery within the jury, as you well know," Nicholas replies. "It's to prevent threats from within the council, not without."

"Precisely," Gareth says. "Which is why they do not apply. The people in Harrow came today for answers. That is what they will get."

"They came for answers, but instead they got an assault," Peter says. "They're frightened. Let them go home."

"If you're asking me to reconvene the council in order to give our enemies yet another chance to attack us en masse, I must decline," Gareth says. "It's no coincidence the attack happened today, that it happened here. Blackwell's men knew where we would be. Where *she* would be." He glances at me, whatever ease he felt toward me earlier now gone. "They're looking for her, there is no doubt about that. And we need to decide what to do about that. Today.

"However, I will not stop you from leaving if you feel you need to," Gareth continues, looking to Nicholas. "Bylaws state that the head of the council can enter in a vote for an absentee member. I would be more than happy to do that for you."

Nicholas doesn't reply, but the anger in his dark eyes speaks for him.

The first time I saw Gareth, I thought he was a clerk. That night, Peter told me he was actually a member of the council, and now he's the head of it. Something about that reminds me of Blackwell, gaining advantage at the expense of someone else's disadvantage. And that's when I decide. While it might be to my benefit to put the hearing off until another time, I don't want Harrow to suffer.

"Gareth is right." I turn to Nicholas. "We should have the hearing today. There's no sense in putting it off any longer."

Perhaps Nicholas expected I would say this, perhaps he hoped I would; either way, his only response is a crisp nod.

"Excellent." Gareth claps his hands, then gestures back toward the cathedral. "Shall we?"

"Can she change clothes, at the very least?" John says. "She's covered in blood. There's no need for anyone to see her like this." He doesn't say it but he doesn't have to—all the effort Fifer went through to dress me and make me look like a young girl, an innocent girl, it's undone, and now I'll stand in front of the council looking like the very thing they're trying to hide.

A killer.

"I'm afraid that's not possible." It's Nicholas who replies this time. "If the council has been called to session and the subject of that session is physically within the grounds, they may not leave until it has been adjourned."

Gareth nods. "Those are indeed the rules."

John throws me a quick glance, then peels off his jacket and drapes it around my shoulders. My once-beautiful blue silk-and-brocade gown is now ripped and stained with dirt and grass and blood, my once-carefully plaited hair tumbles in disarray over my shoulders. John's coat covers some of it. But more than what it covers is what it uncovers: my reliance on him, his allegiance to me, our connection to each other that hurts him as much as it helps me.

The doors creak heavily on their hinges as Gareth pushes them open. Inside, in the relative calm, I see things I didn't before. A font of water in an elaborate stone vessel standing in the narthex, the water swirling around of its own accord. Rows of shining oak pews, bloodred kneeling cushions hanging from tiny hooks along the back. The red, blue, and white Anglian flag draping from the timbered ceilings alongside the Reformist flag in black, red, and orange. The entire space smells sharply of incense—frankincense, benzoin, myrrh. Soothing scents, though not today.

As before, the pews are filled with people, so many that they spill into the aisles, along the back and the sides. And they're all looking at me.

Maybe it's the dim, kaleidoscopic light, maybe it's the chill inside the cathedral, maybe it's fear, but the edges of my vision go dark and I'm seized with an urge to run. Out these doors, through that tree-felled tunnel, across the sloping meadows and past the borders of Harrow. But where would I go? It's been a constant question ever since those herbs spilled from my pocket, branded me a witch and landed me in jail, turned me into a traitor and changed my life forever.

A hand grasps my shoulder, spins me around. Nicholas steps in close, his tall, dark figure towering above me.

"You'll be tempted, but do not lie." His voice is low. "They will ask you questions you will not want to answer but if you do not tell the truth, they will know it. Tell them what you know, how you know it, just the way you told me. The rest," he adds, "will take care of itself."

The rest will take care of itself. Everything else will follow. These words, these catechisms, they continue to demand an audience of me. First Nicholas asked me to allow someone else's prophecy to be my guide, now he asks me to let someone else's judgment be my fate. His faith is meant to be encouraging, I know. But this same faith is asking me to put my life in someone else's hands, and so far, experience has shown me that's the worst place for it to be.

Gareth steps forward and takes my arm. John releases me and reluctantly, I walk up the aisle with Gareth. Everyone else remains seated as I pass. I can feel their eyes on me, hear their whispers. I feel like a bride in the most ill-conceived, ill-fated marriage ever imagined.

We reach the pulpit, scrolled and elaborate and painted gold, the stand carved into the shape of a raven: a messenger of truth but also a symbol of misfortune and deception. Lined up before it is a row of chairs, all of them plain but for the one in the center. It's large and uncomfortable-looking, all sharp angles and battered wood, the back spiked to a point. All four of the fat wooden legs are carved into the shape of a lion.

A door behind the altar opens. Out walk a line of men, all dressed identically to Gareth and Nicholas. Plain, floor-length robes, hooded and velvety black, adorned with the Reformist herald: a small sun surrounded by a square, then a triangle, then another circle, a snake devouring its own tail: an Ouroboros. The councilmen. My judge and jury.

Gareth leads me to the chair in the center, gestures for me to sit. Immediately, a set of chains spring from the arms and legs, bracketing themselves around my wrists and ankles. The carved wooden lions roar to life, snapping their jaws, growling, flexing splintery-sharp wooden claws. I jerk away but go nowhere as John, seated in the front row beside Fifer and Peter, clambers to his feet in protest. Peter grabs his shoulder and pulls him down.

Gareth steps to his place behind the pulpit—the seventeenth councillor but the only one who counts—and clears his throat.

"Before we begin, I think it's only appropriate to observe a moment of silence, in honor of those killed in the attacks today."

He reads the names of Harrow's four dead men and one dead woman, then turns and addresses the crowd.

"As you all know, we have convened here today to determine whether Elizabeth Grey should be allowed the privilege of remaining within the protective borders of Harrow, or whether she should be banished, never to return."

There's a low murmuring from the pews.

Gareth continues. "Today's attacks mark the third breach of security, the third time Blackwell—the new ruling king of Anglia—has managed to infiltrate Harrow. But it is the first time he has sent his men to retrieve what I believe he sees as his property. While it is our policy—that is to say, a Reformist policy—to offer protection to those who seek it, we must determine whether this protection can and should be offered at the expense of our own safety."

"The attacks on Harrow are no fault of Elizabeth's," Nicholas says. "Whether she is here or not, Blackwell's men would come."

"We have lived in Harrow in safety for many years without incident," Gareth replies. "I find it impossible to believe that her arrival and these attacks are mere coincidence."

"I imagine we all found it impossible to believe that the former Inquisitor would turn out to be a wizard," Nicholas responds. "Yet so it is."

"The girl is dangerous," begins one councilman. He's the oldest of the men, even older than Nicholas, his pale skin and wispy white hair stark against his black robe. "I cannot discount that. But she saved Nicholas's life and I cannot discount that, either. Were it not for her, he would be dead."

A pair of men sitting side by side nod in unison. "Indeed, she did save a life," one of them says. "Of course, one could argue that saving one life is not quite recompense for the lives she has taken." He fixes me with a pair of mismatched eyes: one deep brown, the other canary yellow. "And how many lives would that be, Miss Grey?"

I pause a moment, considering a lie. As if on cue, I catch the minute shake of Nicholas's head. I feel the weight of a thousand pairs of eyes on me, and I start to sweat beneath John's heavy blue coat. And I look away as I answer the question that not even he has dared to ask me.

"Forty-one," I murmur.

"What's that?" The man's single yellow eye gleams with malice. "I don't think the people in the back can hear."

"Forty-one," I say again, a little louder.

The man gives a grim nod. "As I say. Forty-one lives gone, one life spared—"

"Saved." Nicholas corrects the man, the same way John corrected Gareth. "She did not spare my life, she saved it. And she has saved others." Nicholas looks to Fifer but not to John. No one on the council knows what I did to save him. "Given the opportunity, she may save far more."

"You're not suggesting we allow a witch hunter—"

"Former witch hunter," Nicholas interrupts quietly.

"To fight with us? For us?" The two councilmen look at each other, puffed as a pair of crows. "How are we to believe this isn't all part of a trap? A plan she concocted with Blackwell to get inside Harrow and do away with us all?"

Silence falls as the whole of the cathedral considers his words. Considers the idea that I might be playing my part in a trap, one set by Blackwell and that results in my killing everyone inside Harrow. It's impossible.

Except that it's not.

"It isn't." I grip the hard, square armrests, hating the tremulous sound of my voice but afraid to raise it any higher. "I would never help Blackwell. Not anymore."

The councilmen look down the line to one another, exchanging glances that range from surprise to disbelief. Mainly disbelief.

"I don't want to hurt anyone. I never did, not really," I say. "When I became a witch hunter, I was just a child. I didn't realize what it meant—what it would mean. But I didn't know what else to do." It's a pitiful excuse, the worst. But it's the truth.

"But whether I stay or go, whether I am here or not, Blackwell is coming after you," I continue. "He wants Harrow. Under his thumb or gone, but he will not stop until he gets what he wants. That is something you have to know about him—he always gets what he wants."

The councillors look down the row at one another again.

"If you do allow me to stay, I can help you," I say. "I can help keep him away. I can help try to do away with him." I purposely avoid the word *kill*. "I worked with him for three years, lived under his roof for two. I know him."

"Not well enough, I'd say," the yellow-eyed councillor retorts. "Otherwise you'd have known he was a wizard. Despite everything you say you know about him, somehow the most important thing managed to escape you completely. It was right in front of you."

"I thought he was using one of you!" My voice rises to a pitch; the lions at my feet bare their teeth at me in warning. "I thought he was using a wizard to perform magic for him. He told me he hated magic. I didn't know it was a lie!"

"How could you not know?" This from the old white-haired man. He doesn't sound angry, just bewildered. "Nicholas assured us you were an educated, intelligent girl."

"But that's just it," I say, and my voice is quiet again. "I'm just a girl. Or, I was when I went to live with him. I was thirteen years old. I was looking for him to be a teacher, a mentor." I almost don't say the next word, but then I do. "A father, after I lost my own. Not a wizard."

That's when I tell them everything: the truth the way Nicholas wanted me to tell it. How I was the king's mistress. How I was arrested for carrying herbs that prevented me from conceiving his child, then sentenced to death, only to be saved by Nicholas. How I discovered Blackwell was a wizard before setting out to find the tablet Blackwell cursed in order to kill Nicholas, that the only reason I could find it, resting in that dark, dank, moldy, and deathly tomb, was that Blackwell wanted to kill me first.

"He betrayed me, too," I finish. "I believed the things Blackwell told me. I didn't have any reason not to. I didn't go around looking for lies, like I do now. But I know now, and I can help you stop him." I look at John then, his hazel eyes going wide as he guesses what I'm about to say next: "I will fight for y—"

John is on his feet before I finish the sentence.

"She can't fight," he says. "She's still recovering. She's still not strong enough. And she doesn't—" John cuts himself off as he catches himself, about to announce to the whole of Harrow that I no longer have my stigma.

It was Nicholas's idea to keep this a secret from the council. His fear was that if they knew I didn't have it, the threat today wouldn't be exile; it would be execution.

"She nearly died," John finishes, and it's a long moment before he sits again, resistance giving way to resignation.

"I'm afraid I have to agree." A councilman, quiet up until now, speaks from his chair to my right. "She's a child. And as Mr. Raleigh points out, an unwell child at that." His eyes, a deep cornflower blue, sweep over me, observant but not unkind. "I fail to see what she can do for us that we cannot do for ourselves."

I bristle a little at this: at being called a child, at being underestimated.

"She was one of Blackwell's best witch hunters," Gareth points out. I feel a rush of gratitude at his defense, until I realize it is most likely an offense. "And there is the inarguable truth that she did manage to infiltrate Blackwell's fortress, fight her way from that tomb, and destroy the curse tablet."

The line of councilmen erupts with comments.

"She showed a tremendous amount of courage—"

"—went back into that tomb after nearly being buried alive the first time—"

"She managed to get into his palace once before, perhaps she can do it again—"

"Aside from fighting," Nicholas interrupts, "there are many other ways in which Elizabeth can help. She can help train an army. She can provide us with information. About Blackwell's strategy, his home, his defenses. His witch hunters. Of course, you understand this is why he is intent on hunting her down. He knows that in the wrong hands, this information could be a weapon."

"You speak of training an army," another councilman says to Nicholas. "What army? All we've got assembled are guards, a handful of pirates, and some noblemen." He glances into the pews. "We don't have strength, and we don't have numbers. Not unless we want to start requiring men to fight. Men who have no experience fighting."

"We will get troops," Nicholas says. "But negotiating for them is not a straightforward matter. Gaul has offered men but understandably, they're wary. They've got their own borders to protect, and while they certainly do not side with Blackwell, they also do not want to risk his animosity. What happened with King Malcolm is not something the Gallic king wishes to repeat."

The night of the masque, after Peter came for us and we disappeared from Greenwich Tower, Malcolm and Queen Margaret were arrested and thrown into the depths of Fleet, the most notorious prison in Anglia. Their arrest frightened everyone in Harrow. To orchestrate the incarceration, and possible murder, of a monarch is something not even the staunchest Reformist would consider.

"And in the meantime?" The blue-eyed man addresses Nicholas. "You can't expect Blackwell to wait until we manage to recruit troops. He won't wait for them to arrive before he attacks. That's weeks from now at the earliest. What do we do until then?"

"Prepare," Nicholas says. "Assemble our guards, recruit more men. Men who are willing and able to train, men who are not able but who are willing. Open our borders to outsiders willing to fight for us."

He turns to the pews. Makes eye contact with those sitting toward the front.

"It's not enough to wait; it's not enough to deny. Nor is

it necessary to place blame, point fingers, punish." Nicholas looks to the councilmen then, at each of them in turn. "We've hidden long enough. The fight has not just been brought to our doorstep, it's through the threshold and it stands inside and it carries a sword. Sending Elizabeth into exile will not close that door, nor will turning her over to the enemy. We must show Blackwell that he cannot simply take what he wants, that Harrow will not fall as long as we are here to defend it. And Elizabeth can help us do that."

The men and women in the pews, moved by Nicholas's words, murmur and nod to one another. Gareth looks from Nicholas to me, to the councilmen.

"Let us prepare to vote."

4

THE COUNCILMEN RISE FROM THEIR chairs and start down the aisle toward the entrance, stopping beside the water-filled font I passed on my way in. The man at the front holds up a hand, index finger pointed to the sky. Holding back his velvety, bell-shaped sleeve with the other hand, he plunges his finger into the bowl.

From where I'm seated, I can see the water, a slow, tepid swirl before, begin to pick up speed, a few droplets splashing into the air. After a moment, a small puff of steam erupts and he removes his hand from the bowl. Then, one by one, each councilman repeats the process.

As the last man steps from the font, the water stops swirling, turning placid and still as a mirror, silvery and beckoning. It's not a font of holy water, as I first thought when I saw it. It's a scrying bowl.

I've found a few inside the homes of wizards I've arrested, but I've never seen one in use before. They're used to read the thoughts of many people instead of only one, the way a scrying mirror does. Water is a conductor, and an element of truth: impossible to lie to, no doubt to prevent votes from being fixed or made under duress. This must be part of the council rules that Nicholas instated; the magic bears his hallmark: simple, honest, resolute.

Each councilman steps forward and peers inside. Some give a quick glance; some take a longer look. But they each, after seeing whatever it is they see, nod before proceeding back up the aisle and settling into their chairs again, their velvet cloaks a sigh against the wood.

Gareth steps behind the pulpit. Before I can swipe my damp palms against the wooden armrests, he speaks.

"It's a tie."

Fifer looks to me, then John, a grim smile of solidarity passing her lips. Peter's face shows alarm; he knows it's likely I will be sent away and his only son with me. Because eight against eight, a tie, must be broken, and only Gareth, as head of the council, can do it.

"To stay or to go." Gareth's voice holds the tone of a man who revels in every eye being on him—which they are—and having the fate of someone in his hands—which it is. "It's clear some of you see Elizabeth Grey as a danger. Someone untrustworthy, someone violent, someone disloyal."

Fifer opens her mouth to object, but closes it quickly. She can't object, because it's true. If I were loyal, I'd still be with Blackwell. The way Caleb was, until the very end.

"By that same token, because we are up against someone

untrustworthy, violent, and disloyal, I see that many of you consider that an advantage."

Nicholas watches Gareth as he speaks. His dark eyes harden, obsidian, and I know that look well. It's the look he gave me when his seer, Veda, told him I was a witch hunter. That I was not the wronged innocent girl he believed me to be. I feared him then, and despite everything he's done for me, I fear him still.

"Despite my initial misgivings, I, too, see this as an advantage," Gareth continues. "But the condition by which you will be permitted to remain in Harrow is not only that you fight. It is not enough for you to train our army, not enough to catalog what you know. I want you to use your training to turn against the man who trained you." A pause before his words, hard as steel, clash through the silent cathedral. "I want you to kill him."

Here I sit: chained to a chair in a blood-soaked gown with a blood-soaked past, being asked once more to trade on violence for the sake of peace. I look to John. He holds my stare, the weight of it telling me what he wants me to do. He wants me to decline, to refuse, to be exiled so that we can leave Anglia together, for somewhere he believes we will be safe.

But I was never one to do what others wanted me to.

"Yes," I say. "I will fight for you. I will"—I stop on the word before pronouncing it with more force than I feel—"I will kill him."

Gareth nods at me, satisfied; he gets the response he wants. But John startles me with one I don't when he climbs to his feet and says, "Then I will fight for you, too."

The pews erupt with voices but one, more musical than the rest, cuts through them all.

"You can't. He can't."

I—along with everyone else—turn to see Chime, that pretty dark-haired girl from the Winter's Night party who laid claim to John before I came along, on her feet. She glares at the councilman to my left, the one with the same cornflower-blue eyes as hers. At once, I know who he is; Fifer told me all about him. Chime's father, Lord Fitzroy Cranbourne Calthorpe-Gough.

"I really must object." He glances at his daughter, then back at Gareth, his handsome face etched in a scowl. "I don't see how allowing a healer to fight will help us."

"I don't see how it can hurt," Gareth says. "You yourself said we had no army, no men. Now we have one more." He flashes a brittle, indulgent smile at John, who doesn't smile back.

"This is war," Lord Cranbourne Calthorpe-Gough continues. "There will be injuries. John Raleigh is a healer. He saves lives. He does not take them."

"Yet he took one today with very little hesitation," Gareth responds. "And from what I saw, he did it very well. He's already in this fight."

There's nothing to say to this, because Gareth is right. For better or worse, John was in this fight the moment we met. But Chime's father is right, too: Taking lives isn't what John does.

"It simply makes no sense," Lord Cranbourne Calthorpe-Gough says. "We need a healer to attend—"

Gareth waves it off. "We have other healers."

"Surely there are other—"

"Enough." John's voice, deep and sure, rings through the cathedral. "I appreciate your objections, but they're unnecessary. I already said I'll fight, and that's final." He shifts his attention to Gareth. "Are we done here?"

I wait for Gareth to reprimand John's disrespect, maybe to deny his pledge. Instead, he only smiles.

"The council is adjourned."

The chains around my wrists and ankles snap open, falling to the floor with a loud clank. The lions cease their restless prowling, wrap themselves around the wooden legs of the chair, and become inanimate once more. The crowd is silent as they file from their pews, row by row into the aisle and out the front door.

Gareth gathers his book from the pulpit and exits through the side door along with the rest of the councilmen, the same way they came in. John rises from his seat and pushes his way toward me, but he's stopped every few feet by men and women who approach him, shaking his hand and offering their thanks.

Harrow has suffered since the rebellions in Upminster— Anglia's capital and the seat of Blackwell's new power—began two years ago. Witches and wizards from all over the country sought refuge here, safe from the Inquisition and from witch hunters, from prison and torture, flame and death. But more people meant less to go around, and there have been rations for food, land, supplies, and weapons.

John is well liked here, of course he would be. He helps

people when they're ill, often for very little money, more often for free. Now he's going into battle on my behalf, many of those here no doubt assuming he won't return.

It's Fifer who reaches me first, emerging from the crowd in front of my chair.

She pulls me to my feet and, together, we make our way to the door that opens into the cemetery, to avoid the stares of the men and women still idling in the hall. We step into a patch of shade beneath a tree, not far from where Blackwell's archer had me cornered against a headstone, not far from where his blood still stagnates sticky in the bright sun. Then she turns to me, her hands crushed against the hips of her green velvet gown.

"Have you gone completely mad?" she demands. "Fighting? Killing Blackwell? Why would you agree to that?"

"I had no other choice."

"Yes, you did," she says. "You could have, oh, I don't know, not agreed."

"If I still had my stigma, it's the first thing I would have done," I say. "Not fighting would have created more problems. The council would have asked questions, and one way or another, the truth would have come out."

Fifer casts about, to make sure no one is nearby, listening. There isn't, but she lowers her voice anyway.

"You could die."

"I won't die," I say. Empty words: It's not a promise I can make and she knows it. "But I also won't sit back and do nothing." I search the people spilling from the cathedral, looking for one in particular. "I don't know what John was thinking, telling the council he would fight, too."

41

"I do," Fifer says. "He was thinking of you."

"It doesn't matter. He still can't do it."

"I know you think that," she says. "But if I'm being honest, they could do worse. He has your stigma, so he can't be hurt. And he's pretty good in a fight. Peter trained him well."

"I saw."

"At least you didn't make an utter fool of yourself like Chime, the whey-faced thing," she continues. "What right does she have speaking up for John? But there she was, on her feet before the whole of Harrow, bellowing like a fishwife guarding her bucket."

"She was hardly bellowing," I say. "She was just defending him. She did what I should have done."

"He's not her bucket to defend," Fifer says with finality. "And speaking of." She jerks her head toward John, at last making his way out of the cathedral.

The blood has dried on the front of his white shirt, stiff and dark. He has his sleeves pushed up past his elbows, hands and forearms stained red. His hair is unruly and sweaty, his face harried and unsettled. When he reaches us, he wraps an arm around me and pulls me to him.

"I'm in dire need of a bath," he whispers before kissing me.

I smile against his lips; Fifer makes a retching noise.

John pulls back then. "You shouldn't have agreed to fight," he says to me.

"That's what I said," Fifer says.

"No choice," I say again. "Council's orders."

"I know. But I still don't want you—"

"I don't want you fighting, either," I interrupt. "I know

you can, but that doesn't mean you should. You're a healer. I already said this, but fighting isn't what you do."

"And I told you before, things are different now," he replies, an edge slipping into his voice. "I will do what I have to."

"But it doesn't make any sense."

"Things stopped making sense a long time ago. I don't see why they should start now."

"John—" It's all I manage before a familiar voice interrupts.

"John, may I speak with you?" Chime stands off the dirt path, under a tree by the gates. She's dressed in a cerulean-blue silk-and-velvet gown, the same color as her eyes. Real, live butterflies adorn the shoulders, their wings blue and edged with black, fluttering softly. Her jet-black hair is pulled off her face into a loose knot and adorned with blue-jeweled butterfly-shaped pins.

The whole effect is beautiful, ethereal, just as she is. I can easily see what John saw in her, even though he says when they were together he was too drunk to see much of anything. Fifer says she's trouble and while that may be so, I can't imagine she's more trouble than me.

"Of course." John arranges his irritated expression into something resembling calm.

"In private, please?" Chime glances at Fifer, then me. "If you don't mind." Her voice is high and soft, warm and melodic, the sound of a summer's day.

"Not at all," I say. John gives me a small smile before the two of them turn and walk down the path together.

"We'll be waiting," Fifer coos. I shoot her a look; she jabs

43

me with her elbow. "Why'd you let them go off together?" she hisses when they're out of earshot.

"She just wants to talk," I say. "There's no harm in that."

Fifer purses her lips but doesn't reply.

John and Chime stop under the tree at the end of the path. She appears to be doing most of the talking; John watches her intently, and every now and again he nods. Seeing them together, I feel a sharp pang of jealousy, but there's something else, too: inevitability.

Chime touches her hand to John's, says something in parting. She glances at me, those deep blue eyes sweeping over me, her face carefully neutral. She ignores Fifer entirely. Then she turns and walks away to join her father. Lord Cranbourne Calthorpe-Gough nods at me, then John, before taking Chime's arm and leading her away.

John walks back to us, his face expressionless.

"What did she want?" Fifer demands.

"Nothing," he says. "Well, not nothing. She wanted to talk to me about her grandmother. She's very ill." John turns to me. "She's my patient; I've been treating her for years. It's actually how I know her. Chime, I mean."

Fifer purses her lips again.

"Anyway, she was asking me if I could come by and spend some time with her grandmother before things got under way."

Fifer makes a noise partway between a scoff and a snort. "Can't it wait until it's all over?"

"Fifer," I say, my voice reproachful.

"It really can't," John says. "And it's better if I do it now anyway, just in case."

44

"In case what?"

"In case something happens to me."

"Nothing is going to happen to you," Fifer says.

John smiles a little, but it doesn't reach his eyes. "I don't think anyone can promise that."

5

THAT EVENING, PETER AVOIDS LOOKING at me during supper, too busy beaming at John as if his son had managed to fulfill all the fatherly dreams he'd held for him, all in one afternoon. In turn, John avoids his gaze, too intent on trying to catch mine, the echo of our earlier disagreement still hanging between us. I want to fight; John doesn't want me to. Peter wants John to fight; I don't want John to. John is angry with me, for reasons I understand, and I'm angry with him, too, for reasons I don't.

I avoid looking at both of them entirely, staring down at my trencher of beef stew and bread, which goes largely untouched.

"You'll wait for your summons, but I expect it'll be here within the week." Peter waves his glass of brandy around, his third—a celebration—and continues. "You're to report in when you do. Straight to Rochester Hall."

Rochester Hall. Lord Cranbourne Calthorpe-Gough's home, Chime's home. Where camp is to be set up, where training is to take place, where the troops from Gaul, when they arrive, are to be stationed. Where John and I, as new recruits in the fight to protect Harrow, are to live for the foreseeable future.

"Is Rochester Hall well suited for a camp?" I pick up my bread, tear off a piece. "Does it have adequate grounds? Spaces for people to live? To train?"

I think of Blackwell's home at Greenwich Tower. Hidden behind forty-foot walls, guarded day and night, protected on one side by the Severn River, on all sides by a moat. And I think of all the magic inside: As much as inside Harrow, I realize now. Magic used to train us, to frighten us, to harden us into soldiers, all done by the hardest and most frightening man I know.

John and Peter exchange amused glances, and I feel my irritation grow.

"Quite so," Peter says. "Fitzroy's grandfather, the Fourth Earl of Abbey, he was a prophetic man. Not a seer, mind, just observant. He foresaw trouble with magic, foresaw that it would no longer be tolerated. He founded Harrow, you see. Most of the land we're living on belongs to the Cranbourne Calthorpe-Goughs."

I'm surprised, though perhaps I shouldn't be, that Chime is heir to all of Harrow.

"Some of it he sold to Nicholas, some to Gareth, and I own some, of course," Peter continues. "But the majority of the men who live in Harrow are tenants. Fitzroy, he's a hard man, but he's a good man. He won't conscript them to fight if they do not wish it."

"Unlike Gareth," John mutters.

Peter nods. "Even so, conscription isn't necessary. We've got plenty of volunteers. Messages have been pouring in all afternoon, since the trial." He gestures to his desk at the stack of letters half a foot high. "Men to hold the line, to stop the attacks until the troops arrive." Peter touches his snifter to John's goblet, a toast. "And a girl, too, of course," he says to me, as if I'm an afterthought.

Finally, it settles into me, with clarity, what I'm angry about: I'm an afterthought in my own fight.

"Of course" is all I can manage.

To an outsider, this exchange is innocent. Pleasant, even. But with the intuition John has, part of that healer's magic he possesses, I know he senses the tension simmering beneath the surface. He's on his feet, a beat before me.

"It's late," John says to Peter, but his eyes are on me. "It's been a long day, and I'm tired. I'm sure Elizabeth is, too."

"I'm fine," I say. "I want to clean up first." Since I arrived at Mill Cottage, and since I've been able to, I've helped Peter and John with the cleaning and cooking. They don't do it, not well anyway, and though they don't ask and most of the time they try and stop me, I do it anyway.

"Leave it," John says. I throw him a sharp look and he adds, "At least until tomorrow. All right? You need to get your rest."

I snatch the dishes off the table and stomp into the kitchen with them, ignoring John's advisement completely. I don't need to rest. What I need to do is to get strong again, to start training. I need to learn how to fight—and to fight well—without my stigma. I can't do any of that if I'm resting.

Peter and John give me a wide berth, doing and saying nothing as I grab up linens, rattle around cutlery. Finally, I finish. The dining room is clean now, and awkward in its silence. Nothing but the crackle of the fire in the hearth, the ticking of the clock on the mantel, the rustle of branches on the trees against the mullioned windows. I can almost feel the weight of the pair of matching dark eyes on me, watching me.

I don't know what to say to either of them. I'm embarrassed by my outburst, but not enough to apologize for it. Angry, but too much to ask for forgiveness. After a moment I settle on "Good night," pushing past them both, out of the dining room and into the foyer, then upstairs to my room. Soon enough I hear the creaking of footsteps on the wood staircase, the careful shutting of John's door across the hall from mine. The sound of it is somehow lonely.

I'm not tired, but I change into my nightdress anyway. Something else Fifer gave me: pale green linen with a square neckline and wide sleeves, both trimmed with dark green ribbons. Almost too pretty to sleep in. I move to the dressing table in the corner of the room, sit in front of the mirror. Pull a brush from the drawer and begin to run it through my hair.

Once again, I don't recognize myself. Six weeks ago, I was deadly. Today, I am cautionary. My reflection confirms it: Pale. Fragile. Weak. The loss of my stigma took more than just my strength and my ability to heal—it took away my identity. I don't know where to find it, or even where to begin looking.

I cram the brush back into the drawer, slam it shut. As I do, a piece of parchment slips from the bottom, flutters to the floor.

After I woke up but before the weather cleared enough for us to spend our days outside, John and I spent all night writing notes and passing them to each other beneath our closed doors. Peter was adamant we not see each other after dark; he still is. But to John's way of thinking, it didn't mean we couldn't speak to each other.

It was simple. He fashioned a loop of twine, one end slipped under my door frame. He had the other end. He'd write me a note, fold it around the twine, then give his end a little tug. I'd reel it around, read it, and write back, then give my own end a little tug. Back the note went. Sometimes we'd have several pieces going at once, so neither of us was waiting on the other.

I pick up the note, unfold it. The page is filled with a series of botanicals, carefully etched and labeled in Latin. *Angelica sylvestris,* a fine-petaled plant with a spray of white blossoms. *Salvia officinalis*, a gray-leafed shrub full of deep purple flowers. *Berberis vulgaris*, another plant marked by spiked leaves and fat red berries. The delicate beauty of each rendering is a stark contrast to John's crooked, nearly illegible scrawl.

He drew them for me, in part, after I teased him about his penmanship. The other reason, he said, was that these were some of the plants he used to heal me. They were beautiful to him, he said, because they brought me back to him.

I drop my head into my hands, the parchment fluttering to the floor. I don't have a lot of experience with what it means to be with someone the way I am with John. None, in fact. I don't know how to navigate waters in which half the time I feel as if I'm drowning. But I do know there are better ways of treating someone who loves you than by flinging beef stew at them, falling into stony silence, then storming out of the room.

A cool breeze snaps in through the open window, rattling it against the frame. I get up to close it, glancing at the dimly lit gardens below. Most of John's carefully cultivated plants are dormant now, pruned back for winter. But the trellis that snakes up the stone wall is choked with winter honeysuckle, wild and flowering, the scent heady even in February.

The trellis.

In less than a minute I'm out the window and over the edge, down the wall and on the ground. A quick glance through the blue-paned window of the front house shows Peter at his desk, busy with his letters. I duck beneath it and pass to the other side, my bare feet crunching in the narrow gravel pathways until I'm standing in the garden beneath John's window. There's a trellis here, too, full of the same winter honeysuckle.

I start to climb.

Within seconds I'm at the top, peering into his window. John is sitting at his desk, propped up on one elbow, his head resting in his hand, reading. He's tired, I can tell; his eyes are at half-mast and even as I watch him, they slide shut and his head bobs forward.

I tap on the window.

His head snaps up, eyes wide. He glances toward the door.

I tap again.

John whips his head around, catches sight of me outside his window. I smile at the way his jaw drops open, shocked. He's on his feet in an instant, crossing to the window, pulling it open, and tugging me inside. I clamber over the sill, clutching my nightgown around my legs so it won't tangle.

His eyes travel from my hair, loose and hanging around my shoulders, down to my bare, mud-stained feet then back to my face, but not before lingering slightly on the low, square neckline of my nightgown that shows more than it should.

I really should have changed.

"Elizabeth," he starts.

"Before you say anything, I need to talk to you." I step away from him, out of reach of his arms, of the way his shirt is unbuttoned too low, his hair that looks like it's had my hands in it. The way he looks at me, a half smile bordering on a smirk, and the way he smells, lavender and spice and something unmistakably him. My insides do a long, slow twist.

He takes a step closer.

I hold my hand up. "You stay right there. I can't have you distracting me."

John sighs, running a hand through his already-disheveled curls. Then he points at the chair at his desk, the one he was sitting and almost sleeping in moments ago.

"Please, sit."

I do.

"I'm sorry," I say. "For how I acted today. Earlier. Downstairs. You know." I shake my head at the ineptness of my apology.

"It's all right."

"No, it's not," I say. "I was terrible. You didn't do anything. And I never even thanked you for what you did do. Standing up for me at the trial. Agreeing to fight with me. I know it couldn't have been easy."

"You're wrong." John sits on the edge of his mattress facing me, resting his bare feet along the dark wooden bed frame. "It was very easy."

"I know that's what you think now," I say. "But nothing about this is going to be easy."

"I only meant that the decision was."

"You say that only because you have the stigma," I say.

"It has nothing to do with that." John considers. "No, you're right. It has everything to do with it."

"I don't regret giving it to you," I say quickly, before the seed of the idea can take root. "I never regret that."

"But you do regret not having it," he says.

"Yes," I say. And there it falls: the truth. "I would be lying if I said I didn't. It would make what I have to do...doable. Because right now it isn't. Right now it seems impossible."

John falls silent, in the way that tells me he's thinking something he doesn't want to say. So I wait for it. For him to tell me I can't kill Blackwell. To tell me, as he's done so many times before, that it's too dangerous, that I'm not strong enough.

"I know you think I'm going to try to stop you from doing what you want with this," he says finally. "But I'm not."

"You're not?" I enjoy a second of relief before it falls into distress. "Oh. Is that because...you don't want, you know, you, and me, and..."

"No!" He gets to his feet, takes my hand, and pulls me off my chair and onto the bed to sit beside him. "Of course not. That isn't it at all. Do I wish I could lock you away until this is all over? Yes. But you would hate me for it, and anyway, that's not who you are. And I never want you to be anything different."

I blink. "No?"

"No."

"And…that's it?" I say. "No arguments, no fighting?"

John huffs a quiet laugh. "Would you prefer I pull a sword on you? Duel it to the death?" I smile, and he goes on. "I've got your stigma, but I'll be damned if I'm not going to protect you with it. As much as I can, however I can. I won't stop you. But I don't want you to try to stop me, either."

I hesitate, but only for a moment. The conditions of the truce he's offering aren't ideal, but they're unlikely to get any better.

"I guess we're in this together, then."

He grins. "That's what I've been trying to tell you."

I laugh at that. I can't help it.

John shifts a little, moving closer to me. The light in the room is dim, the tired candle on his desk having already extinguished itself. The last one sits on the table beside the bed, the flame bobbing softly in the night breeze. He slides his hand into my hair, cupping my neck, his thumb skimming across my cheek. I lean into him and I don't know who kisses who first but it hardly matters.

We half push, half pull each other down onto the bed. We're tangled together on the sheets, kissing and fumbling and tugging at each other's clothes. I don't remember deciding to take off his shirt but there it is, off. His hand moves to my bare leg, sliding up to my hip and taking my nightgown with it. I let out a little gasp; he kisses me harder.

The feel of his hands on my skin, of mine on his. His lips on my neck, his hair tangled between my fingers, his breath in my ear. I can't think. Maybe it's the control we spent staying apart while living so close in this house, maybe it's the control spent keeping ourselves together today, but it's falling apart now. My heart is racing, my breath is coming fast, we're doing what we've done before but it's never felt like this: all urgency and carelessness and need, and I want it all to carry me as far as it will take me.

A flurry of wind blows through the window then; the candle on the bedside goes out with a hiss. The room plunges into darkness. The sharp, opaque scent of sulfur from the extinguished flame; the mattress creaking under our weight; the feel of his bare skin pressed against my own. At once, I'm not in John's room, kissing him, feeling his body on top of mine. Instead, I'm in Ravenscourt Palace, in Malcolm's room. I'm coerced, I'm unwilling, and I'm frightened.

The heat I felt just moments before gives way to a sudden snap of cold. I push him off and away from me. Scurry to the head of the bed, pulling my nightgown down to cover my bare legs. My breath is still coming fast.

I can't see through the darkness in the room, not really, but I can make out John's silhouette as he sits up. His breath is still coming fast, too.

"Hold on a minute." John gets up, fumbles around for his shirt, pulls it on. Makes his way to the table. I hear the scratch of a match, watch as he relights the candle in front of him. He glances at me, then crosses the room and lights three more, set into brackets at intervals along the wall. Light floods the room.

"I'm sorry," I say, before he can say anything. "I don't know what happened. I don't know why I did that."

"You don't have to know," he replies. "And you don't have to apologize."

"I guess it was the dark," I continue. "It reminded me of being somewhere else, with someone else—"

"Elizabeth." John moves to the bed again and sits at the very end of the mattress, as far away from me as he's able. "You don't have to explain it to me."

He slides his hand forward across the mattress until his fingertips touch mine, tentative.

I'm reminded of the way he did that on the morning after we first went to Veda's, after I reacted the way I did in the tunnel beneath her cottage, remembering my final test, filled with so much fear I couldn't stand, couldn't walk, couldn't do anything but curl into a ball. Reminded of how he carried me in his arms back to Nicholas's, stayed with me all night. How, even then, he cared for me in a way no one else had before.

I'm also reminded of how none of this is easy for him. Nothing about me, or him and me, is simple. I know it would be easier if I had never come into his life at all. If he had stayed with Chime, if he'd preferred her over me. The guilt eats at me, but I can't tell him this. Because if I do, it will be just one more burden he will take on for me, when he's already taken on so many.

"I should go." I swing my legs over the edge of the mattress.

"Wait." He catches my arm. "Please, stay. I'll sleep on the floor," he adds quickly. "You don't have to if you don't want to. But I don't want you to go."

I start to say no, that it's best for me to leave. But just like every other day, when I stay when I know I should go, I don't.

"All right," I say. "But you're not sleeping on the floor." I turn back to the bed, sliding under the clean, lavender-scented linen sheets.

John pauses, then slides in beside me, pulling the bedcovers over both of us. He's careful not to touch me, too careful. But after a moment I roll over to face him, wrap an arm around his waist. He pulls me closer, my head resting on his chest, his face buried in my hair.

And we sleep.

6

COUGH.

The sound cuts through my slumber, pulling me awake. I open one eye, then the other, taking in the dark paneled walls, the deep blue bedcovers, John's arm slung around my waist. We're still in the same position we fell asleep in, curled up in each other.

Cough.

Peter.

"God's nails," John murmurs into my hair.

"How long do you think he's been out there?" I whisper.

Cough. A pause, then a horrible choking sound of Peter clearing his throat. *Cough.*

"Judging by that noise he's making, I'd say awhile."

I press a hand to my mouth to smother a laugh.

"Shh, you'll make it worse," John says, only he's laughing,

too. "I guess I'd better talk to him." He pulls away from me and climbs out of bed. His warmth goes with him, leaving me cold.

"Wait." I sit up. "You can't go out there looking like that."

"Why?" John looks down at himself. At his wrinkled trousers, his rumpled shirt that looks exactly what it is: slept in. What he can't see is his tousled hair, or the smirk on his face that makes him look as if he's been up to no good—or quite a bit of good, depending on the one looking.

"Because you look as if you've been doing exactly what your father thinks we've been doing."

"Ah." John grins. "Here's the thing: If I go out there with neat hair and proper clothes, he'll think I've got something to hide. Because if I were really guilty of something, there's no chance I'd go out there looking like this."

"Oh." I think about this a moment, then scowl. "Done this before with other girls, have we?"

"I've never done this with other girls. Only you." He dips his head, brushes his lips against mine. "You'll always be the only girl."

My lips curve into a smile as I kiss him back.

Cough.

"Into the breach." John crosses to the door, flinging it open with a flourish. "Sounds like you've got the croup," he announces, stepping into the hall. "That's quite a feat, you know. Croup is almost exclusively a child's illness, and exceedingly rare in old men."

John closes the door then, but I hear Peter's response anyway.

"I'll give you the croup, young man."

I press my hand against my mouth again to stifle my giggles.

John and Peter continue talking, their voices muffled through the wood so I can't hear what they're saying. I can't exactly leave and go back to my room, not with them standing in the hallway. I could climb back out the window, but there's no point in that now. May as well wait until John returns, to hear our punishment.

I climb out of bed, examine the tangled sheets and coverlet before pulling them over the mattress, smoothing them tight. Then I remember what John said about looking guilty and pull them back down again.

The window is still slightly open, the cold morning breeze slipping inside. I pace the room, and in the light of day I can see just how transparent this linen nightgown is, how you can see nearly everything underneath. So I sit down at John's worktable and tuck myself in as far as the chair will allow.

It's a mess. Books, parchment, ink, and quills scatter the surface. Scales, mortars and pestles, strainers and stirring sticks made from wood and glass and metal. Half the drawers in the table are open, spilling forth with herbs and powders, roots and leaves. I'm overcome with an urge to clean it all up, but I leave it all be. I've seen enough of the way John works to know there's some sort of method in his madness.

A familiar scent hits me then, drifting in with the breeze. It's deceptively soft and sweet, like scented talcum, but with a bite that lingers in your nose afterward—a warning. I peer into drawer and there it is: *Aconitum*. Also called wolfsbane, or devil's bane, it's extremely poisonous. It can cause paralysis; it can stop someone's breathing; it can stop a person's heart.

While devil's bane is recognizable by scent in its raw

form, it can be mixed with other herbs to become neutralized, making it odorless, tasteless, untraceable: the perfect poison. There's no use for it except to kill.

I look through a few more drawers. Dig through more sachets, more jars, more bottles. Find more poisons. Belladonna. Mandrake. Foxglove. Why does John have them? More than that, how did he get them? Even in Harrow, where magic is allowed, these herbs are banned. Fifer said that Harrow's prison, Hexham, was once filled with wizards who tried to settle one grudge or another using poison: a salting of devil's bane in someone's soup or a dusting of deadmen's bells on a letter.

I set the poisons on the table, thinking to ask John about them. Then I reconsider. If he hasn't told me about them, there's a reason for it. So with the skill born of years spent ransacking wizards' homes—finding things they didn't want me to, rearranging them back the way I found them before leaving and filing a formal report with the office of the Inquisitor, and eventually, inevitably, returning to arrest them—I tuck them back into the drawers.

When John returns moments later, I'm sitting in his bed on top of the blue coverlet, smoothed tight over the mattress again. I've plaited my hair down my back, securing it with a piece of twine I found on his table. My hands are folded in my lap. John stops on the threshold, takes one look at me, and starts to laugh.

"I've never seen anyone look guiltier than the way you look right now."

I don't reply, not right away.

"What did your father say?" I finally manage.

John shuts the door and leans against it. He's grinning.

"He says I'm to remember my manners, and your modesty. I'm also to consider my future instead of my present, weigh my intentions against my impulses, eschew vagary and vulgarity, caution against capriciousness, reject foibles, and embrace virtuosity."

"Those are a lot of words."

"There were a lot more besides that."

"He talks a lot, doesn't he?"

"You have no idea." He tilts his head, his grin fading into a look of sympathy. "You look so glum. Don't be. If this were at all a problem, I would tell you. It's not. It's just his way of showing he cares. It's odd, I know. But believe me, if he didn't act this way there would be a problem."

"If it's not a problem, then why are you still standing there instead of over here?"

John's grin is back. "Because he's on the other side of the door, waiting for me to escort you back to your room."

"Oh."

I get up, cross to the door. Stop in front of him. He looks down at me, his eyes full of warmth and amusement and something else, too: love. When he leans down to kiss me, I push down my guilt, as far as it will go. Wrap my arms around his neck and kiss him back.

"Vagary," he whispers.

"Vulgarity," I whisper back.

The following day, Harrow is hit with another attack. Five more archers, just like last time. Only this time they get farther, all the way to Gallion's Reach, the very center of Harrow. Where the high street is, where the shops and taverns are, where a hundred or so people were when they came roaring through in a swirl of inky-black cloaks and arrows and violence. They fired at random, killing two unarmed men, a horse when they missed, one of Peter's pirate brethren when they didn't.

The archers escaped as quickly as they invaded, before what little guard we have could rally a chase. Our men spent the morning picking through the surrounding villages but came up empty, the attackers no doubt returning to Upminster to fill Blackwell's ears with yet more information on Harrow: the layout, the security and lack thereof, where people congregate, where people do not.

Nicholas and the other council members spend the week increasing and adding to the spells around Harrow. Before, only those without sovereignty were disallowed. Now there are three veils of magic: sovereignty, sanction, and intent. Three chances to pass, three chances to fail.

But as Blackwell's men are armed with magic, magic is not enough. So within that same week, the Watch was formed—a group of two hundred armed men patrolling the thirty-odd miles of Harrow's borders, day and night, determined to prevent another breach. Peter and John were among the first to volunteer. Not wanting to disrupt the fragile peace that's settled between us, I encouraged it. And when they packed their bags and stowed their swords and left Mill Cottage, I hid my reservations beneath a smile and a bid of good luck for Peter, a kiss and a whisper of care for John.

While Peter and John and every other able-bodied person

inside Harrow either guards the border or assists in setting up camp inside Rochester, Schuyler and Fifer decide to use the time to try to make me battle ready.

They come for me one morning at dawn, the pair of them striding into my room with a bang of a door and the knock of a boot on my bedpost.

"On your feet, bijoux."

I sit up, squinting at Schuyler's tall, pale frame at the end of my bed. Fifer stands beside him, a fiery contrast.

"What time is it?" A glance at the window shows no light behind the curtain.

"Time to take a little pounding." Fifer tosses a handful of clothes in my direction. A pair of trousers, a tunic, a pair of boots, and a steel-buckled belt nearly hit me in the head.

"Watch it," I grumble.

"Blackwell didn't coddle you during training, so neither will we." She yanks the covers off me, the cold predawn air an assault.

"At least give me a minute to wake up," I say. "Or eat? You can't expect me to work on an empty stomach."

Schuyler tosses me something, and I snatch it out of the air just before it hits my face. It's bread. "According to my sources"—he taps his forehead, reminding me of the power he has to hear my thoughts—"this is what you ate, the only thing you ate, every morning before training. Any more and you'd vomit it up, any less and you couldn't finish. So get it down and let's get going."

"We'll wait for you in the hall," Fifer adds, then shuts the door.

I climb out of bed, a sick sense of dread roiling in my

64

stomach. It's the same feeling I had every morning of every day spent at Blackwell's. Wondering what I would face, how much I would be hurt, if I might die. I stare at the piece of bread in my hand. It even looks the same. Not white manchet bread made from fine flour but coarse, gray wheaten bread. I take a bite; it tastes like gravel.

I pick up the clothes Fifer tossed my way, starting a little when I see what they are. Black trousers, white shirt, tan coat, black boots. The belt I thought was for my trousers is for weapons instead. Witch-hunting clothes.

Damned Schuyler.

I pull them on. Tie my hair back the way I used to, twisted into a knot at the nape of my neck. Walk to the dressing table, look at myself in the mirror mounted above it. Freckles standing in relief against pale skin, pale blue eyes made paler by uncertainty. I'm wary and I'm afraid but I cling to it, comforted somewhat by the familiarity.

As promised, Fifer and Schuyler wait for me in the hallway. Without a word they lead me downstairs, past the dining room and through the kitchen, out the back door. The sun is just now creeping over the horizon, the sky gray and cold, the air misty with dew. I hurry after them, past John's physic gardens and the low stone fence that surrounds them, into the rolling meadows, the frozen grass crackling under our feet.

"Where are we going?"

Fifer points ahead, where the meadow begins sloping upward into a hill. "We need privacy," she says. "We thought about doing this at Nicholas's, but Gareth is always popping in and out like some damned spying specter. But he never comes out this way, and neither does anyone else, really."

"Privacy?" I repeat. "What are you doing that you need privacy for?"

Fifer turns to face me, now walking backward. "Scared?" She smirks.

"You wish." But I am, and she knows it.

We reach the top of the hill, and there, in the flat ground below, I see what they've got planned for me. It's a tiltyard. No sand, stands, or crowds, but a tiltyard nonetheless. Long and narrow, measured and marked by small flags and lined with weapons. Rows of targets, racks of polearms, crossbows, and swords, and a large wooden chest that I can only presume holds even more. Despite my fear, I feel a little thrill rush through me.

The pair of them walk to the edge of the tiltyard and I follow. Schuyler kicks open the lid on the chest and pulls out a mace, a battle-ax, and a handful of knives. One by one he tosses them to the ground; they land on the grass with a wet thud. Finally, he pulls out a set of mail—a hood and a long-sleeved tunic, the small iron rings tinged red with rust.

I pull a face. "Mail? Only pageboys wear mail. I never wore it, not even when I was a recruit. Not even when I knew nothing. Not even the time I got sick and could barely—"

In a blur, Schuyler whips a knife off the ground and flings it at me. It spins end over end, heading straight for my heart. I dive to the ground as it whistles overhead, lifting my head just as the blade buries itself in a birch sapling ten feet behind me. The trunk is barely three inches wide.

"Have you lost your mind?" I wipe mud from my face in a furious swipe. "You could have killed me."

"Better wear the mail, then."

66

I haul myself to my feet. My trousers are already stained and wet, my hands and face dirty, and we haven't even begun. Fifer holds up the offending mail; I pull off my coat and slip it on over my shirt.

"Headpiece, too." Schuyler flips his wrists, miming the motion of putting on a hood.

I pull the hood over my head, cursing the way the metal rubs against my ears, the way it blocks my hearing, the way it tugs on my hair, cursing Schuyler with every profanity I can think of.

"Stop complaining." Fifer pulls out a necklace, one I recognize—brass chain, ampoules filled with salt, quicksilver, and ash—and slips it around my neck. "So he can't hear you during the fight." She grins. "Don't say I never did anything for you."

Schuyler watches me, his face impassive. Then he snatches a sword off the ground, tosses it to me. Walks to the rack, snatches up a swallow: a long, double-sided sword. Spins it around and around, the blade a flashing blur.

We step into the center of the field. Schuyler circles me, slow; I match his movement step for step. He strikes. Once, twice. I parry the first two; the second he lands a hit, knocking the sword out of my hand and sending it skittering along the grass.

"Point." Fifer raises a hand.

"You're scoring?" I retrieve my sword.

She nods. "If you win, you choose your next test."

"And if Schuyler wins?"

"He does."

"Again, bijoux." Schuyler steps toward me.

I lunge forward and attack, but he's ready. He blocks,

then blocks again. Frustrated, I drop to the ground and swipe my leg under his. He's not expecting this; he stumbles and I throw up my other leg, kick him in the groin.

Schuyler falls to one knee, groaning a catalog of curses. I toss my sword aside and jump him; he's not expecting this, either. We hit the ground, rolling over and over. He hooks an arm around my throat, throws me to my back, pins me there. I jam a thumb into his eye, an old trick. He yelps like a child, rushes at me with a roar. Slams on top of me, reaching for my wrists, trying to pin me. But before he can, I yank a dagger from my belt, thrust it against his throat. The blade pierces his skin, a drop of curiously black blood bubbling to the surface.

"Point," Fifer calls. I glance at her. She's grinning.

Schuyler gets to his feet, a shadow of pain etched across his face. He swipes at the blood on his neck, glances at it, then at me. His blue eyes glitter with antagonism.

"Again."

7

AS IT DID THE FIRST time around, training exhausts me.

Most days I fall asleep before the sun sets, only to wake with the kick of a boot against my door at dawn, Schuyler and Fifer bidding me to rise, to get dressed, to follow them to whatever new test they've devised for me. Day after day the tests get harder, more painful, draw more blood. But day by day I get stronger, more confident, less afraid.

In the week since I began training and John left with the Watch, he's written to me twice, both letters delivered in the bony clutches of his falcon, Horace. He tells me about the patrol along the border: uneventful. He tells me how he is: tired. Horace perches on my windowsill, patiently preening his feathers as I write back, telling John about my training with Fifer and Schuyler. I don't mention how hard it is, I don't mention how I ache. In reply, he doesn't tell me to stop; he only tells me he misses me.

On the evening John is due to return home, I'm determined to stay awake long enough to see him. I lost today's scrimmage with Schuyler and he sentenced me to a ten-mile run, fully armed, through the hills of Whetstone. My muscles scream for rest, but I manage to stay awake.

I lie in my white bed, the quartered moon shining through squared panes, sending pale shafts of light along the floor and up the darkened walls. The cottage is quiet tonight: There's no patter of rain on the roof, no winged rustle of an odd barn owl or the soft tapping of branches against the window. I've got an ear half cocked, listening for the door to finally open, for the familiar thud of footsteps on creaky stairs. The only thing that breaks the silence is the clock on the mantel downstairs, softly chiming out the hours.

Twelve. One. Two.

I don't remember hearing the clock chime three, so I suppose I drifted off. But then I hear the smallest whisper of noise, hovering just above me. I feel a smile work its way across my face.

"You're back." My voice is sleepy, half dreaming. "I tried to stay awake for you, but..." I trail off, wait for his hand in my hair, for the familiar weight of him as he sinks into the mattress beside me.

"Playing cottage with a new paramour, are we? How sweet." The voice is oily, dripping with sarcasm, and it's not John's.

My eyes fly open.

Looming above me, a figure in all black. Black hooded cloak, black heavy boots, and a black, stupid smile. And it's a figure I recognize: Fulke Aughton. A witch hunter.

I lurch to sit up, but Fulke slams his hand around my throat, forcing me back down.

Fulke was the lowest-ranked of all Blackwell's recruits. The slowest, the clumsiest, the most fearful. Caleb and the others called him Fluke Naughton—they reckoned he made it through training by a combination of sheer accident and luck. To see him here, in my bedroom, my first feeling isn't fear, nor is it dread. It's outrage.

I jam my thumb into his eyeball. Fulke bites back a grunt of pain, then snatches my hand, twisting my thumb back so far I hear a pop as the bone dislocates from the joint. I let out a gasp, but I refuse to scream. Not for him.

I reach up, grasp the back of Fulke's head with both my hands, and slam my forehead into his. Fulke, the idiot, bites his tongue, hard, and lets out a strangled cry. He backs away from the bed and I leap on top of the mattress and launch myself at him. He's caught off guard and the two of us stagger backward into the white brick fireplace. We hit the hearth and I jump off him, grab his head again, and slam it into the brick. Fulke lets out another cry and drops to his knees. I snatch a poker from the fireplace, hold the sharp end to the vein on the side of his neck. He's trapped between the wall and me, and neither of us is yielding.

There aren't a lot of ways to kill a witch hunter. But a broken neck or a knife to the jugular or a sword to the eye or ear, something that penetrates to the brain, that's something not even a stigma would be able to heal.

"What are you doing here?" I keep my eyes on his. As long as he's looking at me, he won't try anything. It's another reason Fulke isn't a good witch hunter. He's not smart enough to

71

plan a move without first shifting his eyes to the target, alerting them to his next move.

"I don't have to tell you anything."

"I hold the weapon, I make the rules," I say. "If you want to see the sun rise, tell me why you're here."

"No."

I thrust the poker into his neck and with a tiny popping noise, the point breaks the skin. I can just see his blood in the pale moonlight, a running rivulet down his neck.

"Stop!" His voice is a high-pitched whine.

"Why are you here?" I repeat.

"Why do you think?" Fulke's brown eyes are steady on mine. "We're here to bring you back to Blackwell."

A pause, then it sinks in. *"We?"*

Fulke's eyes flick to the window. I whirl around just as it slams open and there, sitting on the ledge, is another witch hunter in all black: Griffin Talbot. Short blond hair, dark blue eyes, handsome and charismatic, a friend of Caleb's and a favorite of Blackwell's. Unlike Fulke, Griffin isn't slow. Nor is he stupid, or clumsy, or fearful. He's everything a witch hunter should be: Smart. Strong. Fast.

Deadly.

"Fluke, you idiot." Griffin slides off the ledge, his heavy boots a menacing thud against the floor. He saunters toward us, his gaze traveling from Fulke, still on his knees with his back against the fireplace and my poker in his neck, to me crouched beside him in a thin white linen nightdress, low cut and trimmed with pale pink ribbons, my hair spilling down my back.

Griffin smirks.

"You're looking well these days, Elizabeth," he says. "I was never one for your particular brand of charm, but perhaps I was wrong." His eyes roam the length of my body; I'll gouge them out given half a chance. "Being a traitor becomes you."

I fire off a string of obscenities.

"Enchanting, as always." Griffin switches his attention to Fulke. "You had one job," he says. "Watch a sleeping girl while I checked the house. Jesus, Fluke. She had you against the wall in under a minute, and she's not even dressed. Nor was she armed. Unless she sleeps with a fire poker under her pillow."

Fulke pouts. "You know who she is."

Griffin shrugs and turns back to me. "I didn't know you had it in you, Grey. Your healer gets killed and you go and cozy up with his father?"

Fulke lets out a sycophantic laugh. "That's right. Who do you think you are? Myrrha?"

"No, that's not Myrrha," Griffin says. "Myrrha was in love with her own father. Not her lover's father."

"Jocasta, then?"

"No, she's the one who married her son."

I tune out their bickering as my stomach drops. John? Killed? But that's not possible. He's got my stigma, they couldn't have killed him. He can't be dead, he can't be...

That's when it occurs to me, with a sigh of relief they don't hear: The night of the masque, Blackwell stabbed John—but Blackwell left before Fifer transferred my stigma to him. They think John is dead, and they think I'm still what I was.

I think fast. Two witch hunters in my room, one I could easily kill, another who could easily kill me. John and Peter

73

are still gone, but that could change any minute. John could hold his own in a fight, at least for a while. Peter, too. But Griffin is good—too good. He's an excellent strategist; his only weakness is he gets too aggressive in the heat of battle and makes stupid mistakes. But this won't be a battle, it'll be a massacre. Unless…

Schuyler. I think his name in my head; I shout it. *They're here. Witch hunters. Two of them, inside my room, they're here…*

"…no, Nyx and Erebus were siblings. Jesus, Fluke. Remind me to tell Blackwell to send you back to remedial—"

"Shut it, Griffin."

"Blackwell must be hard-pressed for help if he's sending Fulke to do his dirty work." I break into their ridiculous conversation. Maybe if I get Griffin talking, I can buy time for Schuyler to reach me.

"Not hard-pressed at all," Griffin says. "It's an honor to serve the king. The rightful king."

"Blackwell is not the rightful king."

"He's the one sitting on the throne. That seems rightful enough to me."

"What are you doing these days, now that Blackwell's a wizard and witchcraft isn't against the law?" I ask. "Do you call yourself witch hunters still?"

"We're knights now," Griffin replies. "Knights of the Anglian Royal Empire."

"Fulke is a knight?" I glance at the motto stitched beneath the herald on their cloaks. In Gallic it reads *Honte à celui qui ne peut pas atteindre.* Shame be to him who achieves less.

I scoff then. I can't help it. "They got the shame part right anyway."

Griffin doesn't reply.

"How many of you are there?" I continue. "Is it just witch hunters? Or is Blackwell recruiting new members?"

"Nice try, Grey," Griffin says. "I'm not telling you a damned thing."

"What are you going to do, then?" I say. "Try to kill me? Because I'll tell you right now, that won't end well for you."

"Always picking a fight, aren't you?" Griffin tuts. "No, we aren't here to kill you. But then, we don't kill. We never did. Just you. You're the one who kills."

I'm the one who kills.

"I saw Caleb's body," he continues. "When Blackwell brought it back. You know, I always thought you had a thing for him. Caleb, that is. The way you followed him around, made sheep's eyes at him. We all saw it. Then we saw his body. The way you flayed him open, eviscerated him, really. You must have hated him. Deep down, you must have. Maybe because he didn't care for you back. Not in that way, anyway."

Griffin's trying to rattle me, and it's working. I can feel Fulke beside me, loosening his posture, about to make a move. I can feel myself disconnecting from this moment and moving into another, into the past where I see Caleb coming, where I stay my hand, where I don't kill him...

"Grab her, Fluke."

Before Fulke can make a move, I shove the fire poker into his neck until the point thrusts out the other side.

Blood hurls itself across my face with a sickening splash. Fulke slumps to the boards, thrashing and jerking, pawing at the poker with his hands, trying to stem the flow of his own blood spurting from his neck.

I'm on my feet but Griffin is on me in a second, his dagger raised, steel flashing like lightning in the moonlight. I dodge it once, duck from it twice; he won't miss a third. I back across the room, stumble into the wardrobe. Griffin lunges for me; I throw open the wardrobe door, hear a crunch as his face meets wood, then his muttered curse. I scramble over the bed, snatching my bedsheet as I go, balling the white linen in my fist. Rush to the window, smash my fist through it. The broken glass falls in satisfyingly large shards and I snatch them up, holding them in front of me as if they were knives.

Griffin wipes the smallest smear of blood from beneath his nose. It must have broken on the wardrobe door, but it's healed now. He's watching me as he prowls around the bed, his eyes glittery with anger and the thrill of the hunt. I know that feeling, or I did: part nerves, part fear, part excitement.

I don't feel it now.

He starts for me again and I pull back, narrowly miss stepping on a shard of the broken window glass. I stumble from it, but the delay is enough. Griffin tosses his dagger to the floor, snatches my wrists, and hauls me across the bed. I slash at him; he twists my arm, hard, to get me to release the glass. I don't. We scuffle around on the mattress, him on top of me, me thrashing beneath him. I knee him in the groin and he grunts in pain, rolling off me and onto the floor, dragging me with him. Somehow in the tumble the glass gets loose again, raking across my forearm, the cut smooth and sharp.

I slap my hand over my skin but it's too late: Blood leaps from my veins and seeps between my fingers, running fast down my arm to join the rest of the blood—both mine and Fulke's—on my nightdress.

Griffin pushes me off him and scrambles to his feet. He stands there a moment, silent, pointing at my arm. "You... your arm. It's not healing," he says finally. His eyes are wide. "Why isn't it healing?"

Before I can think of what or how to reply, he grabs me by the throat, lifts me off the floor, and slams me into the wall.

"Where is it?" Another slam, then another. "What happened to it?"

My head is spinning, and not just from Griffin throttling me like a rag doll. He knows I don't have my stigma; this is nothing but trouble for me. So why is he acting as if he's the one hard put by it? If he's here to bring me back to Blackwell, he's got me right where he wants me.

A creak of a window frame. Another rumble of boots on the floor. A *tsk* of impatience, amusement, irritation, or all three, and there's Schuyler standing in front of the window, arms crossed, eyebrows raised. He takes in the bloody scene before him and shakes his head.

"Isn't this a treat, then? A witch hunter inside Harrow." Schuyler's eyes, alight with anticipation, lock on to Griffin. "Managed to evade the Watch, did you?"

Griffin releases me and I slump to the floor, gasping for air. "Your watch leaves much to be desired."

Schuyler glances at Fulke, drained of blood and pale as moonlight, sprawled out beside the fireplace, the poker still crammed in his neck.

"I wouldn't go that far." Schuyler shrugs. "As they say, it's the end that counts, not the beginning. And so far, your side isn't making a very good end."

Griffin yanks the fire poker from Fulke's neck with a

sickening squelch and steps toward Schuyler. He swings it slowly in front of him, droplets of blood falling onto the floor, dark as ink.

"Pyrrhic victory," Griffin says. "Whatever small wins your side manages to achieve, they'll never outweigh your losses." He looks Schuyler up and down, cold and appraising. "But let's be honest. When I kill you, I'm not sure they'll consider that a loss."

And here it is: Griffin's aggression, his overconfidence, his inability to see what's really happening. He doesn't see what I do—the malice lurking beneath the surface of Schuyler's calm demeanor, the shine of violence that in a revenant is never truly tarnished.

Griffin hurls the fire poker at Schuyler as if it were a javelin. Schuyler bats it away just as Griffin yanks a sword from his scabbard, so fast it's a silver blur. He lunges toward Schuyler, blade flying. He swings the sword toward Schuyler's neck while simultaneously reaching into the bag knotted by his side, full of salt, sending a spray of it directly into Schuyler's face. It's a move Blackwell taught us: The salt is meant to blind and confuse a revenant, allowing the blade to land somewhere, anywhere. It's not meant to kill, just to stun long enough to allow for escape. Much like what I did to Schuyler the first time I met him, inside the Green Knight's tomb.

Only escape isn't Griffin's plan.

Schuyler ducks the shower of salt, evades most of it. By this time Griffin's got a dagger, a weapon in each hand now. He jabs at Schuyler, but Schuyler knocks the dagger away with ease; it flies from Griffin's hand and skitters across the floor. Then he grabs the sword with the other, wraps his fingers around the blade. I wince as it cuts into his hand, that curious black blood flooding to the surface, watch as he bends—*bends*—the shaft of the sword. Griffin lets go and it, too, clatters to the floor.

Schuyler holds out his palm, then squeezes it into a fist, as if wringing himself of his own blood. He steps toward Griffin, weaponless. But not powerless.

Griffin pulls out another dagger.

To watch them is to watch a game of cat and mouse. A cat swiping at the mouse, over and over, toying with it, making it think it's on equal footing just for the sport of it when you know—even if the mouse doesn't—that it never even stood a chance.

It happens so quickly then.

The dagger, knocked from Griffin's hand. A futile reach for another fireplace tool, missed. A thrown punch, also missed, a tossed piece of furniture, the dawning recognition on Griffin's face that he's out of options.

Hands on either side of the head, a quick and savage snap, and Griffin is gone. Slumped to the floor, his eyes and mouth both open, the defeat on his face a surprise, even in death. For a moment, the room falls back into the silence of before. No patter of rain, no rustling barn owl, no brushing branches. Not even the chime of the clock downstairs to break the sound of my ragged breathing.

Schuyler crosses the room, his boots crunching on the glass, and looks me over, his nostrils flared slightly at the heavy, iron scent of blood in the air.

"You all right?"

"I think so." I hold up my arm. "I'm cut, but I don't think it's serious."

Schuyler snatches the blood-spattered bed linen from the floor, tears off a piece, and hands it to me. "Don't get up. You'll cut yourself again if you can't see where you're standing." He starts for the door. "I'll be back."

Schuyler returns a moment later with a handful of candles and a bundle of matches. In seconds, the room comes alive with light and the sight of carnage. He looks around, shakes his head. "This is a damned fine mess you made."

I almost laugh.

"Witch hunters, eh?" Schuyler nudges Griffin's body with his toe, then glances at Fulke. "You know, I rather thought Blackwell's men were after Harrow in general, but this time it seems as though they're actually after *you*." A pause. "D'you have any idea why?"

"'Course not," I say, irritable. The cut on my arm stings like hell. "If I did I'd do something about it. If for no other reason than to keep idiots from breaking into my bedroom and making this happen."

Schuyler looks around. "What do you want to do, then? If you want to get rid of them before the guard arrives, you'd better do it quick, because—*ah*."

Seconds later the door to the bedroom slams open and Peter and John stand on the threshold, broadswords in hand. The emblem of the Watch, a simple orange triangle, is embroidered on the front of their short gray cloaks: a symbol for stability. Almost in unison, their eyes go round as they take in the scene. Griffin, lying on the floor, eyes wide open to the ceiling, his head set in an unnatural angle. Fulke, who has emptied every bit of his blood onto the floor, like a sponge that's been wrung dry.

"What happened here?" Peter rushes to the window, looking out as if he's expecting men to come pouring in at any moment. "They left the front door open, then we saw footsteps leading up the stairs. Mud," he adds. "What the hell happened?"

Schuyler gives them a rapid rundown.

John crouches beside me. It's only been a week since I saw him, but somehow he looks different. His hair seems tamer than usual, curls pushed back instead of falling into his eyes. He's unshaven by more than a few days, he's got deep circles under his eyes, and the furrow in his brow now seems etched there, as if it belongs. He drops his sword and picks up my arm, gently peeling off the strip of linen. He hisses a swear at the sight of it.

"It's not as bad as it looks," I say. "It's just a scratch."

"It's more than a scratch." He flings aside the bloody fabric. "I don't think you'll need stitches, but I'll need to attend to it anyway. Can you stand?"

John helps me to my feet. Schuyler rummages around in the wardrobe and pulls out my black leather boots and passes them to John. He looks confused for a moment, until Schuyler points at the shards of glass scattered along the floor.

"What else did they say?" Peter turns from the window to face me. "Did they say why they were after you?"

"No." I tug the boots from John's hand and slip them on. "It's as Schuyler said. They broke in, said they were here to take me to Blackwell. We fought, I got cut. But then he said something, I don't know…"

81

"What did who say?" Peter is beside me then. He plucks a clean handkerchief from somewhere beneath the folds of his cloak and presses it against my arm, which has begun to bleed again. I look to John, but his attention has drifted back to the bodies on the floor.

"Griffin." I point to the feet sprawled on the floor at the end of the bed; it's all I can see of him from here. "When he saw I was injured and didn't heal, he knew I didn't have my stigma. He wanted to know what happened to it."

"Not to worry, love." Peter pats my hand. "He won't be able to tell anyone about it now, will he?"

"That's not it," I say. "It's that I expected him to be glad, when he found out. To taunt me for being weak. Or to get in a few punches on me, knowing I couldn't retaliate. I expected him to do anything but what he did."

"Which was?"

"Act afraid," I say. "You don't know, because you don't know Griffin, but he's not afraid of anything. Anything except Blackwell. But he acted as if he were the one in trouble, not me."

"Elizabeth, what are you saying?"

Schuyler and I exchange a rapid glance, a look of surprise settling into his face as he hears my thoughts before I say them out loud.

"I'm saying I think they were after my stigma."

8

PETER SLIDES HIS SWORD INTO his scabbard. "I want you to get cleaned up," he says to me. "And then I'm going to take you to see Nicholas."

"Now?" John says. "Why?"

Peter makes a gruff noise. "Because Elizabeth was attacked in her bed by a pair of witch hunters and nearly killed," he replies. "Because she thinks Blackwell sent them after her stigma, which she doesn't have, which you do. I expect that's reason enough?"

"We've got more pressing concerns at the moment, don't you think?" John says. "Elizabeth's arm. And these two." He looks back at the bodies on the floor. "We can't just leave them here. What if there are more of them on the way? Shouldn't we be out there, looking for them?"

"The area was clear when I arrived," Schuyler says.

"Obviously it wasn't that clear," John snaps.

Schuyler raises an eyebrow but doesn't reply.

"I'll take care of matters here," Peter says. "John, you take Elizabeth to Nicholas's once you've got her cleaned up. Schuyler, if you don't mind going ahead to let him know what's happened, and that we're on our way? You can check for more men on your way out."

Schuyler nods, then turns back toward the window, going up and over the sill in a flash. But John doesn't move, nor does he respond.

"John." Peter turns to him and, finally, John wrenches his gaze from the massacre on the floor. "Did you hear what I said, son?"

"Don't you need help moving them?"

A brief scowl crosses Peter's face, then he steps forward and grasps John by the shoulder. Gives it a little shake. "I'd like you to help Elizabeth," he says, his voice gentle. "Fetch some hot water. Prepare some medicine, and some bandages for her arm. She'll meet you across the hall in your room."

John looks to me, his eyes at once going wide at the sight of Peter's handkerchief, damp and crimson with blood, still pressed against my forearm.

"Of course. Yes. I'll do that right now." He moves toward the door, then back to me, an uncertain dance. Finally, he leaves, his footsteps creaking on the staircase as he makes his way downstairs.

Peter offers me a wan smile. "He's upset, of course. This evening might have gone differently, and you might be lying on the floor instead of them. It's a lot for him to take in. I daresay he's in shock."

I don't know if that's it at all, but I nod anyway.

"And you? Are you all right?" Peter pulls me into a fatherly embrace.

"I'm fine," I reply, my voice muffled against his shoulder. "A little shaken, but otherwise fine. And I'm sorry about all this."

He releases me. "Don't apologize. I should apologize for leaving you alone. But please. Let John take care of you now; I'll manage the rest."

As Peter sets about wrapping up the bodies, I take a stack of clothing from the wardrobe and step across the hallway. I haven't been in John's room since I spent the night there, shortly before he left for the Watch. But something seems different. Last I saw, it was untidy to say the least: wrinkled clothing in a heap on the floor, the table under his window a riot of herbs, powders, and sachets. His desk scattered with books and parchment, pens and ink.

Now it's clean. Books stacked neatly on the desk, the table surface clear, everything tucked neatly into the drawers and shelves below. The room even smells different—what was once a heady mix of spices, herbs, and him—is gone. Now the air is crisp, clear, sterile.

I pull out a chair at the desk and sit, waiting for John to return. A moment later he does, bumping in through the door, lugging a pail of water. Wordlessly, he walks to the basin on the stand beside his bed and starts to empty water into it. But he's not paying attention, not really, and the water spills over the rim and splashes onto the floor.

He doesn't seem to notice his boots getting wet, nor does he seem to notice me watching him. And when the bucket is

85

empty, he doesn't seem to notice that, either; he's still holding it aloft, faint dripping the only sound in the room.

"John." The word comes out a whisper.

He jerks his head around to look at me and, at once, his expression both lifts and crumples, as if he's just now seeing me for the first time.

"Are you all right?" I say.

"You shouldn't be asking me that. I should be asking you that." He drops the bucket with a clatter. "This shouldn't have happened at all. If I'd been here, it wouldn't have. I could have fought them off. Kept them from hurting you."

John pushes away from the basin and makes his way to the table under the window. He rummages around in his drawers, pulls out a small amber bottle. I can just make out his untidy scrawl on the label. *Oil of jasmine.* He crosses back to the basin and taps a few drops of the scented oil into the water.

"Jasmine is good for a lot of things, such as soothing a cough or stopping snoring," he says. "Which you don't need, of course. It also helps with a woman's labor pains, which you don't need, either. Really, you don't need it at all, only I like the scent of it. It makes me think of you."

I blink at his rapid change of topic, at his nervous stream of chatter. Both are unlike him in every way.

"Thank you." I manage something between a frown and a smile. "I like the smell of it, too." Finally, I rise from the chair and move to stand beside him at the basin.

There are no bathing sheets or cloths to wash or dry myself with, but I dunk my arm in the water anyway, hissing a little as the jasmine oil burns into my cut. I recall the first time John tended to a cut on my hand, after I learned Caleb was the new Inquisitor and squeezed my wineglass so hard it shattered. I remember the scent of mint, the pleasant way my skin tingled when he set my hand in the bowl of water. The way he held my hand in the water, his long fingers wrapped around my smaller ones with his careful touch.

It wasn't like this at all.

John stares unseeing into the basin, the water now swirled through with blood and stained pink. Perhaps Peter is right; perhaps John is in shock. He's been on watch for a week, he's tired and thought he was coming home to rest, but instead he came home to bloodshed—and the possibility that Blackwell's men may be after the stigma—and him.

"If they really are after the stigma, I won't let them find it," I say. "I won't let them find you. I will protect you."

This jerks him out of silence. "I don't need you to protect me. I need you to show me what to do if they do find me. How to use it." His gaze is sharp. "You were asleep. You had no weapons. You weren't even dressed and you still managed to hold them off. You even managed to kill one of them. How did you do it?"

This is so unlike anything John would ever say, or even think, that I'm nearly struck dumb.

"I did what I was trained to do," I finally manage. "Knowing how to do that, it doesn't only come from the stigma. It came from three years of training, from facing danger every single day. From facing death every single day."

"I haven't been facing death every day?"

"You have," I say. "But this is different. You know it is."

John makes a dismissive noise.

"My stigma wasn't handed to me," I say. "I earned it. It may not belong to me any longer, but it is still a part of me that will never go away. I earned it." I repeat it because it needs to be repeated.

"I never said you didn't."

"You didn't need to," I say. "You've made it clear—you and your father both—that you think my value rests on it. You think I cannot do what the council wants me to do, what they kept me here to do." The anger I've felt since the trial flares up once more. "I suggest you go back into that bedroom and take a look at what I'm capable of doing."

I regret the words as soon as they're out of my mouth. John recoils, his face going dark.

"I know full well what you're capable of." He backs away from me. "Not a day goes by that I don't know that."

"John—"

"I'll wait out in the hallway for you to finish." He slams the door behind him, so hard it rattles the frame.

My hands begin to tremble, ruffling the surface of the water. It's not until now that I realize it's cold. Not because it's gone cold, but because it was cold to begin with.

I pull them out of the basin, shake them dry. Walk to John's table, search the drawers until I find a simple paring knife. I remove my nightgown and set about slicing it into strips to wrap around my arm. It's no longer bleeding, but it's still angry, red, and weeping. Unhealed. And my thumb. Swollen and blue and bent, gone nearly numb with pain. I take a breath, press down on the bone, and bite back a groan as it snaps back into joint. I use the last of the linen strips to bind it tight, then slowly dress, pulling on simple brown trou-

88

sers, a pale blue tunic, and a long dark blue cloak. Run my damp fingers through my hair, pulling it into a knot.

When I step into the hall I don't expect to see him, but he's there, leaning against the wall, arms folded, eyes on the floor. But he doesn't look up when my footsteps creak against the floorboard, nor when I pull his bedroom door shut with a click.

"John."

He pushes off the wall and makes his way downstairs. I'm tempted to call after him, to apologize, to tell him I didn't mean what I said.

Only I did mean it.

I trudge down the stairs after him. I can just make out the imprint of a pair of muddy boots on the threshold where Fulke made his entrance. They lie beneath scattered droplets of blood: his exit.

I step through the front door into the cold, moonlit night. Across the river from Mill Cottage, in the meadow that stretches for miles behind it, Peter stands beside Griffin's and Fulke's bodies, spade in hand. John stands motionless, watching. He's changed into his old black coat, the gray cloak of the Watch left behind. The collar is flipped up so I can't see his face, but I'm warned by his posture—still, stiff, intractable—to keep my distance.

I pause to watch Peter at work. Take in the sound of iron hitting dirt, the sight of sheets stained with blood and the limp, lifeless limbs splayed beneath them. It hits me then, all the trouble I've caused since coming into John's life. Not just for him, but for everyone around him, everyone he knows and loves. They took me in and stood by me when they could have tossed me aside. It would have been easy enough; it was for Blackwell and Caleb.

I turn to tell him this, to once again apologize for once more failing to understand what he's done for me. But without a word and without waiting for me, he starts down the path that leads from Mill Cottage into town, toward Nicholas's house.

Reluctantly, I follow.

9

IT'S THREE MILES TO NICHOLAS'S house in Theydon Bois, a walk we take entirely in silence—John leading, me following. He does not ask me how I am, he does not try to comfort me. I don't know what to say to this John who says nothing to me, who stares ahead in stony silence, wielding a sword before him as if he's about to be attacked.

So I say nothing at all.

We walk along an open, uncomplicated road over gently rolling meadows, the fractured moon helping to guide a path John already seems to know well. Eventually, it ends at an arched wooden bridge, the water beneath dark and still. On the other side is a house I presume belongs to Nicholas.

It's different from his home in Crouch Hill, where Nicholas first brought me after rescuing me from Fleet. That house was large, grand, built to impress. This house is smaller, cozier; a country home. Rough-hewn stone walls, slatted wood roof, the front lined with a dozen square shuttered windows.

John leads me down the narrow path to the front door. Dozens of rosebushes in every color, enchanted into bloom even in winter, line the walk. Red ivy and pink honeysuckle crawl their way up the walls, lavender bushes bursting beneath them. I turn to say something to him about it; the delicate wildness of it all is something I know he would appreciate. But he walks inside without even a glance at them, or at me, pushing past Schuyler as he appears in the doorway.

Schuyler walks out to meet me. He's dressed in the same black clothing he wore earlier but his hands, face, and hair are clean of blood. I find myself wondering if Fifer helped him, if she brought him warm water and bath sheets, or if she stood by while he washed up with cold, stinging water and strips of dirty, bloodied fabric.

"I've seen better nights, haven't you?" he says.

"I've seen better months," I mutter in reply.

Fifer hurtles out the door then, throwing herself at me in an embrace that nearly knocks me over. "Schuyler told us everything. You're not hurt too badly, are you?" She pulls back to inspect me. "I can't believe it. Witch hunters inside Harrow! Rather, what do they call themselves now?"

"Knights of the Anglian Royal Empire," Schuyler and I reply in unison.

Fifer pulls a face. "Nicholas is inside, waiting for you. And John." She pauses, considering. "Why didn't he wait for you out here?" She peers at me closely, green eyes narrowing. "Everything all right with him? And you?"

"He's fine," I lie. "It was a long week on watch. I think he's just tired and a little shaken up. I'm fine, too."

Fifer tugs me inside the house through a short entrance hall into the drawing room. It's cheerful and inviting: Upholstered chairs and settees are scattered over rugs, woven with flowers and vines in vivid shades of yellow, orange, and green. Tapestries of woodland scenes cover the white plaster walls, and the ceilings are open to the rafters in the country style. A stone fireplace takes up nearly an entire wall, crackling flames throwing light and warmth into the room.

Nicholas crosses the room to greet me. He clasps me by the shoulders, his eyes creased with concern.

"Schuyler told us what happened. I'm relieved to see that you're safe, and on the mend." He says this last part almost as if it's a question.

He settles me in a plush seat beside Fifer, then looks to John, sitting beside the fireplace and staring into the flames as if he can read them.

"John?"

He turns his head.

"I wondered if you'd be so kind as to make Elizabeth a tonic?" Nicholas smiles, but it doesn't quite reach his eyes. "She's a bit pale and appears to have a chill."

The room falls quiet, and I feel as if everyone in it is watching me, watching us; trying to piece together what's happening while it's still falling apart.

"You can help yourself to my stores," Nicholas prompts. "They're right where you remember them."

John rises from his chair and finally—finally—looks at me. "Of course I'll make you something. I won't be long."

Fifer jabs her elbow into my side. We both watch as he walks from the room, his hands jammed in the pockets of his coat, the one he still hasn't removed despite the warmth in the room, almost as if he hopes he won't be asked to stay long.

Nicholas turns back to me.

"The Knights of the Anglian Royal Empire." This is how he begins. No questions. "They were after you. They knew where you were. They knew you'd be alone."

"They didn't know I was alone," I say. "Not for certain. Fulke—he's the one I killed, the one who came in first—was sent to watch over me while the other one, Griffin, searched the house. And they were only looking for Peter. They thought John was dead."

Fifer starts to speak, but Nicholas holds up a hand to stop her. "Go on."

"Fulke said they were ordered to bring me back to Blackwell," I continue. "I didn't ask why; I didn't think I needed to. I know too much, both about him and about you. I thought that was why he wanted me back, just as you said at my trial. But now I'm not so sure."

I pause, thinking again about Griffin. About the look on his face when he saw me cut, when he saw me bleed.

"Griffin, he acted the way he always does," I say. "He didn't seem worried that he was here, in Harrow, surrounded by enemies. He didn't seem worried that he could be caught. He didn't seem worried about anything, not until he cut me. Until he knew I didn't have my stigma." I recall the way Griffin threw me against the wall, over and over, demanding to know what happened to it. "Why? It should be nothing to him if I don't have my stigma."

Nicholas steps to the window overlooking the front of the house, moonlight falling through the panes and illuminating his expression. There's a world of difference in the way he appears now compared to when I first met him, alone in my cell at Fleet. Thin and haggard and gray then; now bright and full of life. Even so, there is a gravity in his face that hasn't changed.

Finally, he speaks. "Elizabeth, I want you to tell me about Blackwell."

I open my mouth to say—I don't know what—but shut it as John steps into the room, carrying a copper goblet. He's flushed and disheveled, his coat finally gone, the sleeves of his blue cambric shirt pushed up past his elbows. His eyes are bright and he's grinning. He looks and acts so much like the John I know that I'm able to manage a brief smile in return.

"I'm sorry it took me so long." He hands me the quietly smoking cup. A scent drifts from the top and there's something about it that makes my stomach curdle. "It's wormwood, dill, and horehound boiled in wine," he tells me. "It's nice, and I think you'll like it. At the very least, it should warm you up."

Wormwood. I know enough from his notes that while wormwood is used in soothing tonics, it's also the primary ingredient in absinthe—which is also the primary ingredient in the ale I drank too much of the night I dropped witches' herbs in front of the king's guard, got arrested, and nearly lost my life.

Another jab from Fifer.

I nod my reluctant thanks but John doesn't acknowledge it, already moving back to his chair beside the fire. After a long moment, I turn back to Nicholas.

"What about Blackwell?" I set the cup down on the table beside me. "What do you want to know about him?"

Nicholas switches his attention from John back to me. "I want to know about your relationship with him."

"Relationship?" The word, in conjunction with Blackwell's name, confuses me. "I don't think I understand."

"When you trained with him, did he single you out in any way? Did he train you differently, or treat you differently? Did he provide you with anything—weapons, advice, warnings even, about what was to come—and not the other witch hunters?"

"No." Then I reconsider. "Not really. But I do remember something he said to me once, after I completed a test. It was toward the end of training and by then, I knew what he was like. And what he said was so unlike him, it was hard to forget it."

Nicholas is watching me closely. "What did he say?"

I hesitate. I don't like talking about training. I didn't then, and I don't now. Not only because reliving it forces me to remember things best left forgotten, but because it forces everyone in this room to remember who I really am.

I don't want them to remember they should hate me.

I hope for a smile from John, or a look of reassurance, something to let me know it's all right. But he's drifted away again, head bowed, hands clasped tightly together. Closed off.

So I go on without him.

It was the maze test, the second-to-last test before our final. Those who were left—there were eighteen of us then—were given four days to get through it. We had no supplies. No food, no water, no weapons, no provisions except our wits, our knowledge, our courage, and our resourcefulness: better news for some than for others.

We were led to the test at midnight; they always began at midnight. The night was thick with fog; it was like walking inside a cloud. Then we saw them: massive hedge walls, stretching too far and too high to see where they ended. The fog clung to them like wisps of snow, twisting and curling around the branches, making them look alive, as if they were breathing. As if they were waiting to devour us.

Three days. That's how long it took me to get through the maze. I'd been attacked, twice, by things inside; things I couldn't name. Creatures that looked like wolves but snaked around corners like serpents. Things that flew like hawks but looked like bears, wearing their teeth and claws and size. My clothes were in shreds, as was the skin on my right arm. I lost a boot along with a big chunk of my hair when something, I still don't know what, grabbed hold of me and almost didn't let go.

When I finally made it out, it was morning. Dawn, or just before it. There was dew in the grass, pink in the sky; there were birds and sun and freedom and success. I crawled out on all fours, bloody and sweaty, hungry and thirsty, and so, so tired. I got as far as I could manage—ten feet, twenty maybe—before flopping to the ground. I wanted to cry; I wanted to sleep. Instead, inexplicably, I started to laugh.

Maybe it was joy, maybe it was madness. But to know I was sent in with the expectation that I wouldn't come out— the feeling went beyond relief.

That's when I heard it. The tiniest noise, footsteps in the

grass, the heel of a boot on a twig. I rolled to my back and there he was. Blackwell. He stood over me, a shadow between me and the sun. Turning light to dark in the way only he could.

"My lord." I scrambled to my feet and dipped into a clumsy curtsy.

"Elizabeth."

I waited. His eyes, cold as wet coal, looked me up and down. Took in my tattered clothes, my missing boot, the hank of hair missing from my scalp. I swiped a lock of what was left behind my ear, to try to hide it. My hand came away red.

"You did well," he said finally.

"Thank you, my lord." My voice was a hoarse whisper, leagues away from the wild, shrieking laughter of just moments ago.

He stepped toward me; I willed myself not to back away. He took another step, then another, until I was staring directly at his doublet: fine cloth of gold and trimmed in emerald velvet, sleeves slashed to show the white of the fine linen beneath.

"Look at me," he said.

I did.

Tall. Dark hair, shaven nearly to his scalp. Short, closely cropped beard. Well over six feet. Attractive, if one could get past those hard, cruel eyes.

"You were a mistake," he said.

I didn't know what to say to that, if I should say anything to that. Finally, I settled on "Yes, my lord."

"Yet with all that, here you are. Again. Still. Here." He began to circle me, the way a wolf does its prey. It took every ounce of control I had to stand in place. "Why do you think that is? Why are you here, Elizabeth?"

I had a thousand replies, none of which I could voice. *Because of you? In spite of you? No thanks to you?* Instead I said, "To learn, my lord."

"To learn," he repeated. "And what, pray, are you learning?"

He was behind me now; I couldn't see him but I could feel him, and every hair on the back of my neck stood on end, shrieking their warning. His words were mild but I could hear the pique behind them. I didn't know how I'd displeased him but then, I never did.

"How to serve you."

He stepped around me so that he was facing me again. But I didn't relax. And I didn't look at him, either. I kept my eyes on his golden tunic, the still-rising sun glittering off the fabric.

"How fortunate am I to have such a servant in you."

He was taunting me, I knew that. Once again I didn't know how to respond, so once again, I repeated myself. "Yes, my lord." It had become a mantra.

Blackwell looked toward the maze. I didn't know what other recruits were inside, or who had already returned. It occurred to me to wonder: Was he waiting for me? Was that why he was here? Or was he waiting for someone else?

"Do you think, Elizabeth, that you will make it through training?"

This, I knew the answer to. I didn't have to hunt around for what to reply and I didn't hesitate when I did.

"Yes, my lord."

Blackwell nodded. "Yes. I see that you believe that. And I

can see you wish me to believe it, too." He smiled, or at least gave the nearest approximation to a smile I'd ever seen from him. It transformed him. It turned him from someone you would fear into someone you could almost trust.

Almost.

"And do you know? From what I saw today, I very nearly do believe it."

My heart swelled, and I felt a flush of pleasure race through my limbs all the way into my cheeks, burning bright with what was, from him, the highest of praise.

"I think, in time, you'll either be my greatest mistake or my greatest victory."

"Then what?"

Nicholas's voice snaps me back to the present. For a moment I'd been there, at Blackwell's, at the mouth of the maze. I could almost feel the dew on my hands, the smarting in my scalp, the burn of sunlight in my eyes.

I look up to find everyone watching me.

"Nothing," I say. "He walked away, and that was it. I didn't see much more of him, and I didn't talk to him. Not until the night of the final test."

"The test in the tomb," Nicholas clarifies. "After which you received your stigma."

"Yes." I rub my eyes. The weight of the evening is bearing down on me, and all I want is for it to be over.

But Nicholas presses on. "Elizabeth, do you know how stigmas are created?"

There's a shift then, a tension that springs from his words and coils around the room. I feel it in the way Fifer stiffens beside me, see it in the way Schuyler moves to stand behind her. The way John jerks his attention from the flames, past me to settle on Nicholas.

The front door opens and Peter emerges from the entry hall into the room. "My apologies for being late." He shrugs off his cloak, holds it out. It's plucked from the air by an invisible hand—Hastings, Nicholas's ghost servant—and disappears from the room. "The ground is harder to dig into, what with the cold. Nearly broke my spade on that second grave—" He stops himself. "How are things here?"

"Enigmatic," Nicholas says mildly. "Though we're working to change that." Peter pulls up a chair beside John, who doesn't acknowledge his father's presence.

"I don't know how stigmas are created," I answer Nicholas's question. "No one had them before us, so there was no one to tell us how it was done. A lot of our guesses were ridiculous and most didn't make sense, but we all agreed that it had to be some kind of spell."

Nicholas nods. "Magic—all magic—works the same way. It is the direction of a witch or wizard's power into an external object, be it a person or thing. A love spell placed on a slip of parchment. A healing enchantment planted within a potion. A protective charm embedded into a ring. A curse placed onto a tablet. A stigma given to a witch hunter."

The hair on the back of my neck prickles in warning.

"Magic, the order that is magic, is to seek unity and balance within all things," Nicholas continues. "The power that is inherent in your stigma: that of strength, of healing, of preventing death or in some instances the death of others"—a glance at John—"disrupts that balance. It is to give power to do what no human, magic or non-, should be able to do. To attempt a spell of this consequence would deplete their magic. All their magic."

"Magic can be depleted?"

Nicholas nods. "When a witch or wizard casts their magic into an object, say, a letter intended to entice, a potion meant to heal, it decreases. How quickly it is restored, and the degree to which it is restored, depends on the spell, as well as the witches or wizards themselves. For an old wizard, or a wizard compromised in some way, their magic may never fully return. The same is true of a curse. My own magic was depleted somewhat by the curse Blackwell set upon me. And while I am not fully restored, I am quite close." He looks to Fifer, who manages a small smile.

"If the spell to create a stigma requires so much power that it could deplete a person's magic entirely, how could it be done?" I say. "There were sixteen of us. Sixteen stigmas, which means sixteen spells, sixteen witches or wizards giving up their power to give us ours—" I stop as I realize. "They didn't give up their power, did they? Their power was taken from them. Stolen."

In the silence that follows, I come to understand the remainder of Blackwell's plan. The first, I already knew: to take the witches and wizards we captured for him and turn them into an army in order to overthrow the kingdom. And now, I know the second: to steal the magic of those who resisted in order to empower his men so they could never be defeated.

"But it still doesn't explain why Blackwell wants my stigma," I say. "There's nothing special about it. Its power isn't any greater than anyone else's. Griffin's, Fulke's, Caleb's—"

"No?" Nicholas breaks in. "Are you sure about that?"

I hesitate. Think of the things I can do; used to do. I think of my strength, my speed, the way I could hunt better and fight fiercer than anyone. How I rose to the top of the ranks, how I was Blackwell's best witch hunter, second only to Caleb. But that was because I wanted it, because I fought for it. It was because of me.

Wasn't it?

"You said yourself there was no precedent," he continues. "No one to tell you how stigmas were created. Did it occur to you that someone had to be first? Someone had to be a test subject in Blackwell's experiment?"

In time, you'll either be my greatest mistake or my greatest victory.

"A wizard's power is not cumulative," Nicholas says. "Magic is not cumulative. Blackwell could not take power from one man after another, or one woman after another, in order to increase his own. Again, the laws of magic, and that of balance, do not allow for it. You only take on the power, the magic, that is greatest of the two. He would not risk diluting his own power, as it were, with that of a lesser witch or wizard. So, no. He is not trying to increase his power." A pause. "I believe he is trying to restore it."

There it hangs: the truth on a knife's edge. The dawning realization of what Nicholas knows, what he's been trying to get me to piece together on my own.

I leap to my feet. Peter jumps to his, too; he turns to John as Fifer snatches my hand, saying something to me in a soothing tone but I can't make out her words through the rush of blood in my ears and the words Nicholas says next:

"I believe your stigma came from Blackwell. And for reasons I cannot begin to fathom, he needs his power back."

10

THE FOLLOWING WEEK IS NOTHING short of agony as we pick apart what it means, what it could mean, for Blackwell to be after the stigma.

Arguments between Peter and John are an almost hourly occurrence. Instead of being frightened by possessing Blackwell's power, by possibly becoming a target of that power, John is determined to use it. He wants to do what Gareth kept me in Harrow to do: He wants to kill Blackwell. Peter, once heartened by his son's desire to throw himself into this fight, has since turned tack, pleading with John to leave Anglia, for him to take me on his ship—the one Peter gave him when he left pirating—and sail away from Anglia, as far as it will take us.

But John won't quit; he can't. The stigma won't let him. The balance of magic is tipping, and not in John's favor. I have a cause for the change in his behavior now. The distance, the violence; every day he heals less, every day he fights more. Blackwell's magic has taken hold of him, and every day that passes it grows stronger.

For now, his secret—and mine—is still safe. But for how long? Each day I train with Schuyler and Fifer, and each day I get stronger, more agile, more battle ready. But John trains alongside me now, and whatever improvement I make he outpaces tenfold. The disparity between us cannot be ignored, and it can no longer be hidden.

It's a problem without a solution, at least, not one I've been able to land on. And I'm running out of time. This morning a pair of fat, creamy envelopes arrived at Mill Cottage, sealed with wax and stamped with a double quatrefoil, Lord Cranbourne Calthorpe-Gough's badge: our summons. John's duty to the Watch has officially come to an end and he and I are to report to the camp at Rochester within twenty-four hours.

Rochester Hall is located in the northernmost part of Harrow, in a town named for itself: Rochester. It's a two-hour walk from John and Peter's home, down a pretty country lane bordered by hedgerows and bramble-covered wood fences, the landscape dotted with trees, red-roofed farmhouses nestled in low-lying valleys, and fields littered with clusters of sheep in their dirty, tangled winter wool coats.

We've been on the road for an hour, Peter leading the way, John and I falling behind, each of us laden with a hastily packed bag filled with clothes and weapons. I've not seen much of Harrow, just a map John drew for me once. But I understand the landscape enough to recall that Rochester is surrounded by hills on the north, Anglian territory to the east, and the country of Cambria to the west. It's an odd place to set up camp. If Blackwell and his men somehow managed to breach the barrier en masse, we would be landlocked, and there would be no escape.

"I've been thinking about the spy," I say. It's the first thing I've said all day so far. "The one letting Blackwell's men inside Harrow. I think we can all agree it's someone still living here. It has to be. They know too much. Enough to tell them exactly where to go, how to get there, and in some cases, when to be there."

I think back to the first breach: the archer found halfway between Nicholas's home and Gareth's. The second breach at the Mudchute, the third at my trial, the fourth in my bed, the fifth on the high street a day later. And now this: the camp.

"What if it's him? Lord... Three Surnames?" I can't continue calling him Lord Cranbourne Calthorpe-Gough, it's ridiculous. "And what if that's why he's setting up camp there? It's so remote. What if he's leading everyone into Rochester with the plan of locking us inside with no means of escape, and handing Blackwell the key?" I flinch at the thought of it. How easy it would be, were it true. How fast. One traitor, one battle, no survivors.

Peter opens his mouth, but it's John who speaks first.

"He's not the spy." John turns to me. "Look, I know how he seems. I know he seems privileged and arrogant and, well, an ass." He smiles a little. "But I've spent a lot of time at Rochester. With Fitzroy—sorry, I call him that, his surname is just too long—and with his family. I've known him a long time and he'd never turn traitor. He would never put his family in danger, no matter what the gain."

106

I want to tell him that sometimes people don't do things for gain, they do them to prevent loss. That sometimes people fall into something, get in over their heads, and the hope is never to get back up, only to do whatever is necessary to keep from falling further.

"John is right," Peter says. "There's nothing Fitzroy wouldn't do for his family, for his daughter. He's as loyal to Harrow as Nicholas. I'd trust him with my life, and I do." Peter's tone is placating, eager to keep the uneasy peace between him and John. "As for why the camp is there, it's simple. There's no other place big enough—or safe enough—to house an army. Southern Harrow is naught but open fields and forests, hamlets and cottages. Rochester Hall is the largest and safest home in all of Harrow, a castle in its own right."

"And there's a benefit to it being remote," John adds. "If anything were to happen, there are plenty of means of escape. There are tunnels that run beneath it, straight across the border into Cambria, and an inlet that runs in about a mile from there, with access to the sea. But most of all, Rochester has as many protective spells on it as Nicholas's house in Crouch Hill. Though a lot of them are—*stop.*"

John holds out an arm, and Peter and I halt in our tracks. John breaks away from us, looking along the ground until he spots a fist-sized rock. He tosses it down the center of the road, as if he were playing a game of lawn bowls.

From nowhere comes a roaring sound, then a sudden drop in air pressure like that before a storm. A thundering gust of wind hurls its way toward us, picking up debris from the road as it goes, whirling into a gray, dusty cyclone.

I take an involuntary step backward, but John moves

toward it, his hand outstretched. "Field of Bulls. The Mount Inn. Snows Hill Arms."

Like that, the wind dissipates, exploding into a cloud of dirt, leaves, and twigs. John starts off down the road again, motioning for us to follow.

"What was that? That you said?" I'm coughing and wiping grit from my eyes. "They sounded like taverns."

"They are." John swipes a hand through his hair, shaking debris from his curls. "To get past the cyclone, you have to list three pubs in Harrow. Three pubs you've been to." He shrugs. "Fitzroy said that if someone wanted to see him but they couldn't name three places they've had drinks, then he didn't want to see them."

Peter explodes into laughter and I smile, the first real smile in days.

As we continue down the lane, the countryside yielding nothing more than what I've seen all day—hills, valleys, trees, sheep—I begin to have my doubts about the supposed grandness of Rochester Hall. If it is as large as Peter says, I should have seen it by now. It should be visible for miles, the same way Greenwich Tower lurked in the horizon, a stalwart blight on the vista of Upminster.

John raises his hand again. He snaps his fingers twice, fast, then lets out a short whistle. I begin to grow irritated at the theatrics of this place, for all its show but very little substance. Until it happens: The air before me shimmers, goes blurry, and at once the hills, valleys, trees, and sheep—there not just seconds ago—disappear, an illusion in tapestry. And in their place: Rochester Hall.

I feel my eyes go round.

Peter called it a castle in its own right, but in truth I expected a home like Gareth's or even Humbert's, with its many gardens and waterways, protected by a moat and a portcullis. I wasn't expecting a fortress.

It's massive. Made entirely of deep red brick and ringed by hundred-foot-high curtain walls, its many spires and towers are cut with arrow slits and connected by parapets. It's surrounded by a large, algae-choked lake, and the only access to the entrance—a heavily fortified gatehouse on the other side—is via a footbridge, easily a half mile long. Beyond the lake the grounds stretch on and on, farther than I can see, all the way into the densely wooded hills.

Peter smiles at my grudgingly impressed silence.

John leads us across the bridge, our footsteps the only sound under the blue, eerily silent sky. "Where is everyone?" I say. "It's so quiet. And how are we to get in? That doesn't exactly look welcoming." I wave my hand at the iron gate looming before us, closed and forbidding.

"At Rochester, you can't believe everything you see," John tells me. "And you can't believe everything you hear, either."

My earlier irritation is back.

John steps up to the gate, places his palm flat against the iron. I expect it to creak upward on its hinges, or to disappear, or perhaps some ghostly ministration to arrive and usher us inside. What I don't expect is this: for the arrow slit that was not a second earlier eight feet above my head to now be in front of me. And for it to be no longer small, nor an arrow slit, but a door-sized opening.

Peter whistles his approval as John steps through, gesturing for us to follow. Inside, a tunnel winding into darkness.

John navigates it with ease, leading us left, right, up and down corridors as if he's done it a hundred times, which he no doubt has, until we're outside again. It takes a moment for my eyes to adjust once more to the bright sunlight but when they do, I see a camp so large it seems almost a village in and of itself.

The park stretches out for miles, every inch of it occupied by people, tents, supplies, wagons, dogs, horses. Smoke fills the air from a thousand small campfires; tents and marquees of every shape and size rise from the ground, some striped and multipitched, others white and single-poled. Crates are stacked everywhere, spilling over with cookware, flatware, lanterns, linens.

Past the park and down a long, sloping incline lie the training fields. Two jousting pits lie side by side, filled with sand and lined on one side with wooden stands, covered by a canopy. Beside them, the archery butts, rows of meticulously racked bows and arrows, colorful targets painted on canvas and wrapped around bales of hay. Next to that, an open meadow bare of anything save for several dozen fat wooden chests filled with weapons—knives and chains, sickles and maces, daggers and axes.

I also see, though perhaps I'm not meant to, the carcasses of several dozen catapults, lurking at the edge of the woods, to be loaded and sprung, then moved to strategic points around the camp in the event of a siege.

Once again, Peter whistles his approval. "Fitzroy's outdone himself."

"There must be a thousand people here," I say.

"He says just under, yes," Peter replies. "We've petitioned Gaul for two thousand troops, and they'll fit."

"What about the rest of Harrow?" We pass a trio of wagons, a dozen men still hauling out supplies. "How many are there? Do we have room for them, too?"

"Three thousand, give or take," John replies. "Not all of them will move here, though, not even under threat of war. But there's space for them if they do."

Six thousand people. It seems impossible that Rochester could shelter them all. Once again, my thoughts go back to the spy, the enemy, the traitor in our midst. What would happen if Blackwell were to gain access. I know what John said, what Peter said, that it isn't Chime's father. Maybe they're right. But I also know what Blackwell always said: *Warfare is based on deception.* To win, you must present yourself to the enemy in a way that makes them believe what they want to believe. I should have listened then, when he all but laid out his secret in front of us.

What am I not hearing now?

As if on cue, he appears then: Lord Three Surnames himself. Up close, he's taller and more attractive than he was at the trial. Finely dressed in brown leather breeches, a steel-gray-and-green harlequin jacket over a steel-gray doublet, and a brown leather scabbard fastened about his waist, only it's empty. He's commander in chief of this army, but he looks like a man playing at war, not planning for it.

He slaps John on the back, gives his hand a hearty shake. Does the same to Peter. Then he turns to me, blue eyes brightening as he takes me in. I watch them closely, as if I could spot deception swirling along their surface.

"Miss Grey." He extends his hand to me; I take it.

"Lord Cranbourne Calthorpe-Gough."

"Please, call me Fitzroy," he says. "It's lovely to see you again, outside the confines of the council. And it's a pleasure to have you join our forces. You're one to be reckoned with, as I understand."

I open my mouth to respond, but Peter speaks for me. "She's quite skilled with a knife," he offers. His grin is broad but I can see the strain behind it. "Her swordplay is nonpareil, and I'm eager to get her to the archery butts. She's far too modest to claim it, but I daresay she's a better shot than you, Fitzroy."

It's uncomfortable, this: Peter extolling virtues learned in order to capture and kill the people of Harrow, now repurposed to save them. Virtues that nearly no longer exist. But Peter has his part to play in all of this, just as I do.

There's a roar then, the sound of men cheering and laughing, coming from the jousting pits. I can just make out a dozen or so men, watching two others circle each other in the sand, their sword blades flashing in the early-afternoon sunlight.

"Sparring," Peter says with some satisfaction.

"Every day," Fitzroy replies. "They'll make their way through their own ranks, then they'll start looking for opponents." He gives my shoulder a clap. "They're throwing away a small fortune down there. But I'd be willing to place my own on Elizabeth."

He smiles. John scowls. Peter swallows.

I smile back.

Fitzroy lifts a hand and from nowhere, a young boy in

white livery scurries up. "Take their bags to their tents, if you please. Elizabeth Grey and John Raleigh. They're both inner ring five, I believe." The boy nods, takes our bags, then dashes away.

"Those fighting are in the white tents," Fitzroy says as we make our way to the jousting pit. "The circles increase by rank. I'm in the center, along with the field marshal, the captain, the lieutenant. You'll meet them later. The company makes up the outer rings." He glances at me. "Does Blackwell employ a similar ranking among his men?"

I allow a smirk. "I'd say he favored a more 'first among equals' type ranking."

Fitzroy throws me a smile; it lights up his face. He really is breathtakingly handsome. "I wager he did."

"Elizabeth!" A familiar voice cuts through the noise around us. "John!"

I turn to see Fifer waving at us through the crowd, Schuyler behind her.

"What are you doing here?" John says as she pulls up before us.

Fifer jerks her thumb at Schuyler. He's got four bags slung over his shoulder, wearing an expression that's equal parts amused and annoyed.

"It's his fault," Fifer says. "He told Nicholas he didn't think it was safe for me to live at home. Not with all the attacks, and not after what happened to you, Elizabeth. So Nicholas sent me here." She looks around, grimacing as she does. "It's the last place I want to be, living in a tent. With all these men. It's unseemly and barbaric."

"I'm going to be living in a tent," I say.

"As I said." Fifer grins. "Barbaric."

We gather at the edge of the jousting pit, watching the bout until it ends: a thrust forward, a jab to the chest that would have been fatal in a real fight but instead ended with a nick to the skin, a bloom of red against a white linen shirt.

The losing man swears; the winning one laughs. The rest of them join in, tossing around coins and insults. The victor, tall and broad and pock-faced, looks around the pit. Finally, his eyes land on John and light up.

"Come on, son. Let's see if your swordplay is as pretty as your face," he calls out. He snatches the cutlass from the losing man's hand and tosses it to John.

John catches it easily, a smirk breaking out on his face again—the same smirk I've come to know and dread. "It's certainly not as ugly as yours," he calls back.

The men all laugh and jeer; even Peter joins in. A dozen or so others, attracted by the noise, wander over to watch. Fifer and I exchange a rapid glance.

"John," Fifer whispers. "I don't know if this is a good idea. You can't win, you really shouldn't even try, not with all these people watching...."

He glances at her, an unmistakable look of contempt crossing his face. "Not you, too." Fifer's eyes go wide. I don't know if he's ever looked at or spoken to her that way before.

John shrugs off his coat, tossing it into the grass. Spins the cutlass once, twice in his hand, and steps into the sand. The man who challenged him, a pirate by his clothing and his attitude, walks forward, flips him an obscene gesture. In return, John kicks up a spray of sand, dousing him with it. The crowd laughs and catcalls.

"Here we go," Fifer mutters.

John and the pirate circle each other, swords held high.

The sun is bright today: too bright. I turn to shield my eyes from the light and as I do, I see a riot of color opposite the pit from me. A cluster of bright girls in even brighter gowns, cerulean blue and emerald green and cardinal red, Chime among them. Her dress, in canary yellow, is the brightest of all. She sees me watching her, but her eyes skim right past me and land on John, and there they stay.

I look back to the match. The gambling has begun in earnest now, men throwing around coins and barbs, catcalls and challenges. John ignores it all, focused entirely on the man before him, who advances blow after blow, all of which John deflects. I know what he's doing; it's what I was taught to do: Allow your opponent to expend all his energy on showing off while conserving yours.

The crowd around us continues to grow. Soldiers in red-and-blue color-blocked surcoats, pageboys in white livery, servants in brown muslin, and one man in black: Gareth. He stands down the line from me, arms folded, eyes fixed on the fight.

John takes a blow from his opponent's sword, parries it once, twice, then ripostes. He makes as if he's about to lunge but stomps his foot instead, a feint. The pirate strikes and John steps aside; there's a shiver of metal on metal before John thrusts his blade forward.

Gareth looks from John to me and back to John again, as if he's beginning to understand something. And he's not the only one. Chime has stepped away from her group of friends to stand beside her father. She tugs his sleeve; they exchange a word, two, before turning back to John, matching eyes narrowed in suspicion.

"He's too good," Fifer mutters. "He needs to stop. They're going to figure it out."

Without a word, I edge away from the pit. Wander to the one beside it, some twenty feet away. There's no one here but two small boys, wrestling in the sand. They take one look at me, scramble to their feet, and scamper away.

I glance again at John, who is circling the man before him, ready to attack.

News travels fast in Harrow, you know that. It's what Gareth said at my trial, to account for the hundreds who showed up to watch it. If he figures out there's more to account for John's skill than his father's tutelage, how long before he tells the council? Before the council tells everyone else? How long before that news reaches the ears of Blackwell's spy and he sends his men after John? I shrug off my coat, toss it into the grass.

Schuyler, I think. *Hit me.*

11

SCHUYLER'S HEAD JERKS IN MY direction from across the tiltyard; he was as focused on watching John as everyone else. Even from here I can see his startled expression, but it quickly gives way to understanding. We need a distraction. Something to take the attention off John and onto something else and it may as well be me.

What are you waiting for? I think. Then, for good measure I add, *Scared?*

I barely have time to blink before he's slamming into me with the force of a battering ram.

I'm knocked to the ground, my breath knocked from my lungs. I'm momentarily stunned at the pain of it but I shake it off, just as I've done every other time he's caused me pain these past two weeks. Get to my feet. There's a murmur from the crowd nearest us; someone saw, someone is paying attention. It's not enough. I need everyone to be watching.

Again.

Schuyler digs his feet in the sand like a restless lion and crooks his finger at me, a mocking gesture. I lunge for him. Catch him around the waist, rear back, then knee him in the place all boys are vulnerable—even hundred-year-old revenants. Schuyler groans and staggers backward. He lobs a fist at me as he goes, a halfhearted swing I duck easily. He's going easy on me; he can't go easy on me. Already our fight has lost interest from the crowd, they're back to watching and cheering for John.

I reach for my weapons belt, for the line of knives I keep there. Schuyler's already recovered, coming for me again. Before I can think better of it, I slide one out, take aim, and plunge it into his chest.

He sucks in a nonexistent breath, a darkness stealing across his face. That smirk he wore before now turns menacing, and I see it: that feral, wild look revenants get when they're in the heat of battle, when they sense blood. The instinct they get when they return from the dead, the one that wants to put others in their place.

Schuyler yanks out the knife, tosses it aside. Then he's on me, smacking me across the face, hard, the force of the blow turning the world black around the edges. I pull my leg back and slam it into his left kneecap. I hear it crack and Schuyler groans and crumples to the ground, his handsome face twisting in pain, lunging for me as he falls. I leap away but I'm not fast enough; he catches my foot in his hand and yanks and I land with a thud in the sand.

He gets to his feet, kicks me in the ribs. I twist and dodge his second attempt; I'm not so lucky with the third. His heavy, black-booted foot lands squarely in my gut; the force of it knocks the breath from my lungs and sends me flying. I tumble across the sand before finally stopping on my back, arms and legs splayed, eyes unwillingly closed. I feel the rumble of feet along the ground. Schuyler, he's coming for me again. I need to move; I have to move.

But when I crack my eye open I see that it's not Schuyler. It's John.

He slams into Schuyler with the same force Schuyler used on me, knocking him into the sand. John pulls back and punches Schuyler in the face once, twice, then jams his thumb into the spot in Schuyler's chest where I stabbed him with my knife.

Schuyler grabs John by the front of his shirt and pushes him off, or tries to. John yanks from his grasp, then rears back and knees him in the stomach.

Damnation, John. Everything I was trying to achieve he's about to undo, and possibly make it worse.

"John! Schuyler!" I throw myself on top of both of them. "Stop!" We tumble together in a tangled heap of arms and legs and obscenities.

"Elizabeth, get off!" John grabs my arm and shoves me off him. I lunge for him again, this time wrapping my arms around his neck, pulling him on top of me, forcing him to look at me. His face is inches from mine, he's breathing heavily against me, his dark curls plastered to his face with sweat. He's staring at me, so intense, and for a moment I forget what I was going to say.

He's hauled off me then, none too gently. Before I can register what's happening, I'm wrenched to my feet, too.

"Move." It's Peter and Nicholas. "Now."

Peter, still grasping my arm, gives me a little shove. Nicholas is holding John, and together they push us across the grass like scolded schoolchildren, Schuyler and Fifer trailing behind us. I glance behind me and, to my horror, a crowd of people stand behind us, watching. Not a dozen, or two, or even three. No, this crowd numbers into the hundreds. I wanted a distraction; instead I caused an attraction.

We trudge across the field, away from the tents, away from the noise and the smoke and the bustle and the crowds. Through a nest of trees to a stretch of wide, flat grassy ground that leads through a long, yew-tree-lined alley and straight into the large inner courtyard of Rochester Hall.

Were I less angry, less worried, I might be able to appreciate the beauty of it. The carefully planted gardens, the fountains, the marble statues, the walls crawling with ivy and bejeweled with stained glass windows that sparkle in the sunlight. As it is, all I can do is look at John. He's long since shrugged off Nicholas's grasp, his face like thunder as he storms ahead of us, looking at and speaking to no one.

"The solar, I think, John, in the west wing?" Nicholas says. "We'll have privacy there."

John doesn't respond, but leads us through one of a dozen archways into an exterior hallway, to a closed but still guarded wooden door at the end. The guard sees John coming and immediately steps aside to let him in. A few turns down a corridor lands us in a cozy room overlooking the courtyard we just came in through.

Nicholas hails one of the maids bustling nearby and motions her over. He looks at John expectantly.

"What?" John throws his arms up. "For God's sake, what do you want from me?"

"Herbs," Nicholas replies, his voice soft, his eye contact direct. "For Elizabeth? For her injuries. What do you need?"

John throws me a half-appraising glance, then turns to the maid.

"Arnica for the bruising. Calendula or chamomile for swelling. Water. One bowl hot, the other cold. Clean cloths." A pause. "Bring some passionflower, too, if you've got it. That should help calm her down."

"I don't need calming!" I shout.

The others look at me.

"Then what in God's name did you do that for? Fighting Schuyler—have you gone mad?" John swings an impatient hand. "Look at you! Your face. *God's nails.* How the hell do you expect to hide that? Never mind that. He could have killed you."

"I wouldn't have killed her," Schuyler says at the same time I say, "He wouldn't have killed me."

"I had it under control," I continue. "We were just ... practicing." I resist an urge to press a hand to my rapidly swelling eye.

"Why, Elizabeth?" Peter's calm voice is a stark contrast to John's rage. "You're not ready. Not for a match like that. Swordplay you could have managed, and I had Fitzroy ready to wager on your archery. Something noncombative. You didn't have to do this."

"It was Gareth." I glance at the solar door to make sure it's shut. "He was watching you fight, John. Chime was, too, and Fitzroy. They could see how good you were."

"So what?" John snaps. "So I was good. Why does that matter? It doesn't have anything to do with you."

Beside me, Fifer lets out a small squeak of protest. "It has everything to do with her."

"Goddammit." John paces the room, threading his hands through his hair. His shirt is untucked and ripped down the front, his trousers are coated in sand and blood—not his own, but mine. "If you two don't shut your mouths about that stigma—"

"John." Peter's voice is firm. "That's quite enough."

"Then I don't want to hear another word about it," John retorts. "The stigma is mine. You gave it to me." He flashes me a look, not one of gratitude or affection, but one of anger and entitlement. "If you want it back, it's the same as wishing I had died. Is that what you're saying?"

The way he's manipulating me in this conversation, boxing me in to get the response he wants, it feels familiar. It's the way Caleb used to speak to me.

"No," I reply, and I wish to God we were having this conversation in private. "I'm not saying that, of course I'm not—"

"Then stop trying to protect me!" he shouts. "You act as if I need you to swoop in and save me at every turn. I don't. I don't need you."

I feel as if I've been punched in the gut. My mouth goes dry and my face fills with the heat of embarrassment and humiliation, of having others witness it. I try one more time, one last time.

"You don't know what having it means," I say. "I know the strength you feel, I know you feel invincible. But you're not." I pause, measuring each explosive word as if it were gunpowder. "I never regret giving you the stigma, I told you that. I also told you it has to be earned. What I didn't tell you was what earning it does to you." I'm aware of my voice echoing through the room, of everyone's eyes on me. "It takes away your compassion. Your humanity. It will take everything that makes you a healer. Everything that makes you who you are."

John shrugs. "And I told you, things are different now. As for my compassion, I have none. Not for Blackwell. Killing him has nothing to do with humanity, it has to do with revenge. I'll be damned if you or anyone else is going to stop me from getting it." He turns and pushes through the door into the hallway, Peter on his heels.

"He doesn't mean that." Fifer looks at me, her face waxen with horror. "He's just angry. He needs time to calm down. I'll go talk to him; maybe he'll listen to me." Even I can hear the uncertainty in her voice. She gives me a weak smile before following John and Peter out the door. Schuyler goes with her, and I'm left alone with Nicholas.

"What is happening to him?" I sink into a soft, golden chair and drop my head into my hands. "I don't understand what is happening to him."

"Blackwell's magic is taking over," Nicholas replies. "John's magic, the magic he was born with, gifted with, it cannot exist in the same plane as Blackwell's. The stigma is simply too powerful, and the balance that magic requires cannot be maintained." He eases into a chair beside me, as if that will ease the words that come next. "It is destroying John's magic."

"Then transfer the stigma back." I jerk my head up. I don't know why I didn't think of this before, but I'm desperate now. "Your magic did it once before; it can do it again. Give it back to me."

"I cannot do that," Nicholas says. "For one, John would not allow it. For me to force it from him would be the same as Blackwell forcing magic from all those other wizards without their consent. Even if I could," he adds above my objections, "it would not work the way we'd want it to. Blackwell's magic is too entangled with John's now. There is no way to separate the two."

"What if I kill Blackwell? If he's dead, if the source of the stigma's magic is gone, will it disappear from John?"

Nicholas shakes his head. "The stigma's magic is not attached to the source, the way my curse was attached to the Thirteenth Tablet. Were the stigma to operate the same way, it would be dependent on that source. Which is to say, if the witch or wizard who gave up their power were to die, a witch hunter would lose his or her power. You know, as I do, that Blackwell would never allow his machinations to fall upon the chance of others."

I drop my head back into my hands. The only sound in the room is the pendulum on a clock somewhere, ticking off seconds.

"I still have to kill him." I say the words not in anger or desperation, but in manufactured calm. "And I have to do it before John makes good on his threat to do it himself and gets himself killed."

"You're not ready to face him."

"The hell I'm not!" I lose the hold on my composure, tether it down again. "I think it is he who is not ready to face us. Why the knights, why the archers, why this spy? If he needs the stigma so desperately, why isn't he coming after it himself?"

"Have you ever known Blackwell to do something when he could send others in his stead?"

"No," I admit.

"Blackwell not being here himself is not indicative of a lack of readiness," Nicholas says. "Our sources confirm that he's marshaling troops in Eastleigh and Spellthorne, Portsmouth and Somerset, and, of course, his own county of Blackwell."

"That's the whole of the southern counties," I whisper.

"Yes," Nicholas replies. "He is moving exceedingly fast, even in winter; especially in winter. He is more than ready to face us."

"Then all the more reason for me to stop him before he gets here," I say. "You have to help me do it, I don't care how. Spell me, curse me, give me an army, or just give me your blessing. But give me something. Give me"—I stop as it occurs to me; I can't believe it hasn't occurred to me—"the Azoth. I wounded Blackwell with it once; this time I can finish the job. I can sneak into Ravenscourt, I can kill him in his sleep—"

"You will not," Nicholas says, stern as the father I barely remember. "The Azoth is magic beyond you, beyond me; it is beyond even the stigma. Were you to use it, it would curse you. It would take you over, take every ounce of your power, until there was nothing left."

"I thought you said I didn't have any power," I mutter.

Nicholas throws me a sharp look. "I said this before at your trial, and I meant it: There is much for you to do to help us, but it does not entail you throwing yourself into death in order to achieve it. I understand you are accustomed to this being expected of you, but we do not expect it of you. *I* do not expect it of you."

"But John—"

"You cannot help him if he doesn't want to be helped," Nicholas says. Then he is gone, his red cloak billowing behind him as he sweeps from the room.

"The hell I can't," I whisper. My eyes begin that familiar, uncomfortable burning that always seems to follow that familiar, uncomfortable feeling of pain.

The maid comes back into the solar with a silver tray full of the things John requested and sets it down beside me. Three tiny sachets of herbs; two bowls of water, one hot, one cold. I don't know what to do with any of it so I do nothing with it. I'm about to tell her to take it away when a soft, musical voice speaks.

"He left without healing you."

I look up to find Chime standing in the doorway, watching me. Up close, her yellow dress is even more beautiful, the skirt iridescent and shimmering, the bodice thickly sewn with seed pearls. But her face is shadowed by worry and beneath that, fear.

I swipe a hand across my eyes. "Yes."

"That's not something he would do."

"No."

"And you're not healing on your own."

"No," I repeat, my voice cracking on the word.

With a swish of silk and a patter of slippers on stone, Chime steps inside and shuts the door, moving to sit in the chair beside mine. With a sweep of her hand, she dismisses the servant and gestures at the tray between us.

"Start with the calendula, for swelling. That's the orange flowers. You'll need to steep them first, but not in the hot water. It'll burn the leaves. Use the cold instead."

"What do you know about healing?" I'm suspicious, remembering Fifer saying Chime's specialty was love spells.

"Not a lot," she admits. "But I've watched John work often enough that I know more or less what he would do. And anyway, I don't think I can make you any worse than you already are." It was meant as a joke, I know, but neither of us smiles.

It occurs to me, in a sickening, resigned sort of way, that Chime is the only one who cares for John the same way I do. She sees the difference in him now. She doesn't even know about the stigma but she knows enough to know he's not himself.

There's nothing Fitzroy wouldn't do for his daughter.

Chime is not my friend, nor will she ever be. But maybe she can be something more than that. Something that, in the end, will be more valuable. Maybe she can be my ally.

We sit together in the solar, empty and silent now but for the flutter of Chime's hands in water and the whisper of herbs as she steeps sachets and I dunk and wring out cloths, holding them to my eye, my cheek, my nose.

And I tell her everything.

12

TONIGHT, AS IT HAS DONE each night in the week since I arrived, the iron bell in the mess tent clangs three times, calling us to supper.

It's a different experience, living and training at Rochester, than it was in Greenwich Tower. There, we had our own living quarters. Warm beds, roaring fireplaces, fragrant rushes on the floor, linens smelling of lavender and changed daily. We ate formally: five-, even six-course meals on plates of silver with flatware made of pewter, wine in crystal goblets. We displayed our table manners, part of our education and a requirement foisted upon us at mealtimes, one we all abided unless we wanted the disgrace of being made to dine in the kitchen with the lesser servants.

Here at Rochester we sit at crowded tables, eat meals off trenchers of wood, often with no flatware at all. No goblets, either; we drink from shared wineskins. Dinner is not quail, or roast lamb, or even chicken: It's porridge and beans, cabbage and turnips, bread and cheese. Once a week, on Sunday, we're served meat, whatever is caught and killed from the surrounding park. It's not what I'm accustomed to, but I don't fault it. Feeding a thousand people is no small feat, even with the fleet of volunteers and servants Fitzroy has on hand. Not just that—these supplies have to last for who knows how long, and be enough for several thousand more.

I'm pushing my barley and onion stew around with a hard piece of millet bread when John appears, surrounded by a group of boys in uniform. They squeeze in around and across from me, all of them dirty and sweaty from yet another sparring match. I know them by sight but not by name: tall, well-built, attractive boys around John's age, laughing and confident. Some of the girls farther down the table watch them as they settle into place and begin reaching for their trenchers, cramming down bread and stew as if it were a delicacy.

John slides in beside me and gestures at the boys around him. "Elizabeth, this is Seb, Tobey, and Ellis." The boys look at me appraisingly. One of them winks. "And this is Bram." He points at the boy across from me. Dark hair, dark eyes, a twisted nose that looks as if it's been broken a few times. "His father's one of Fitzroy's lieutenants."

"I remember you." Bram looks at me across the table. "From Winter's Night. Remember? I congratulated you on your and John's wedding."

I don't say anything to this, but the other boys laugh and catcall John. Accuse him of being henpecked, of being smitten, wife-ridden.

"I'm not getting married," John says. "Never was. It was just a joke." The tone in his voice, the dismissal in it, makes my throat close up and my cheeks burn. I look down at my plate, whatever little appetite I had now long gone.

The way John has treated me this past week, since the incident in the solar, it's wearing on me. He's always surrounded by these boys, always fighting. He doesn't seek me out anymore, not the way he used to. If anything, he's avoiding me. I saw him just last night with his new group of friends, Chime among them. He saw me, too, I know he did. But he didn't invite me over, and I didn't go. I just walked on by.

"Right," Bram says. "But joke or no, I enjoyed talking to you anyway. I remember your dress, the white one with the flowers. It was quite lovely."

I look up at him then, and the smile he gives me drops into the pit of my stomach and makes me feel even worse. He pities me, and to be pitied is the worst kind of humiliation. But I stay quiet. It's a trick I learned from training: If I make myself as invisible as possible, danger may just pass me by.

John and his friends continue eating, devouring everything in front of them. Seb, a tall boy with ginger hair and an unpleasant smirk, pulls a flask from beneath his jacket and uncorks it, the harsh scent of whiskey wafting over the table. He passes it around and when it comes to John, he takes an enormous swallow. I open my mouth to remind him he doesn't drink, at least not while he's healing. Then I remember he's not healing at all and shut it.

"You're not eating," John says finally, nudging my shoulder with his. It's coming up on four in the afternoon, but the sun is already making its way into the horizon, spilling red across the grounds. The short and bitterly cold days of winter have taken hold, despite the warmth of a thousand fires—some real and rooted in kindling, some magical and free-floating—that heat the camp.

"I guess I'm not hungry." I wait, with useless hope, for him to tell me I should eat. That I need to in order to keep my strength up, or to prevent illness, or to stay healthy.

Instead, he says, "You don't mind if I have the rest, then?" He slides my plate in front of him before waiting for my response. "Fighting makes me so hungry. Seems like there's never enough." A pause. "Maybe you should train more. You might eat more, if you did."

With a clatter, the boys rise to their feet, pulling on cloaks, strapping on weapons, snatching last-minute bites of bread off the table. John finishes the last of my food and turns to me.

"We're going to the tiltyards, see if we can't get in on the last matches of the day. Those pirates, they've got more money than sense. There's a fortune to be made off them, and you barely have to try." He shakes his head. "Idiots."

The other boys laugh. I wonder what Peter would say if he heard John speaking about his friends that way.

"I don't suppose you want to come, do you?"

His words, they're so similar to ones Caleb used to dismiss me, the way he'd invite me to things out of habit instead of desire. It hits me hard as a slap.

I shake my head.

"Suit yourself." John unfolds himself from the bench and that's when I see them: A brace of men making their way through the narrow aisles between the tables. Not the

Watch, but members of the guard all the same. Black cloaks, silver pikes, the red-and-orange Reformist badge, stubborn on their lapels. There may not be Persecutors, not any longer; Blackwell took that away. But there are still lawbreakers to persecute.

The crowds around us, they pull back to let them through, following them with bemused looks. The men stop in front of me, but I know they're not after me.

"John Raleigh," one of them says.

"Yes?" John looks down at the guard; he towers over him by at least three inches. "What d'you want?"

"By the order of the council, we are sent to arrest you for possession of materials herewith banned within the parish of Harrow-On-The-Hill."

John opens his mouth, then snaps it shut, a muscle twitching in his jaw.

"What materials?" The boy called Tobey steps to John's side. His hand strays to his hip where his sword is hilted, an aggressive gesture.

"Leave it, son," the guard says to him. "You'll only make it worse."

Another guard pulls out a slip of parchment from his cloak, unfolds it, and begins to read. The gesture is so familiar, so like what I did for all those witches and wizards I arrested not so long ago, that I begin to tremble.

"Aconitum, a known paralyzing agent," the man starts. "Belladonna, which causes convulsions. Mandrake, which arrests breathing. Foxglove, also called deadman's bells, which causes tremors, seizures, delirium, and death."

Tobey turns to the red-haired boy, Seb. "Go fetch John's father. Peter Raleigh. He's at the tiltyards with the rest of the pirates. Now."

Seb pushes from the table and disappears into the crowd. Beside me, John pales; I can actually see the blood draining from his face. And slowly, slowly, he turns to me.

"You," he says, the disbelief evident even in his hushed voice. "You found them, didn't you? In my room. And you told them." He swipes a hand across the table then, sending trenchers and wineskins scattering. The crowd around us, they've fallen so silent I can almost hear my own heartbeat, pounding wildly in my chest.

I wish I could deny it, but I can't: Every word he says is true. I told Chime, and I struck a deal with her father, and now John is to be arrested and charged and thrown in prison. And there he will stay. He will not go to war, he will not fight, he will not try to kill Blackwell, he will not be forced to give up his stigma and be killed himself. He will be safe. And he will hate me.

That was the other, unspoken part of the deal.

John and I continue to stare at each other—him in anger and betrayal, me in grief and agony—as the guard continues speaking.

"According to the laws of Harrow, possession of any one of these materials carries a mandatory punishment of a year in prison."

There's a rustle and a collective murmuring as Peter appears, pushing between the tables in the tent. "Now see here!" He steps between John and the guards. "You cannot arrest my son. He's a healer. The things he had, he used them to cure, not to harm. To put him away for a year—"

"Four years," the guard corrects. "He was in possession of four poisons. Per the rules of the council, that's a term of four years."

He takes John's arm; John yanks it away. Turns back to me, fury turning his hazel eyes nearly black. It's not the same look he gave me when I lay on the table before him all those months ago, injured and bleeding, when he found out I was a witch hunter, when he made the decision whether he was going to save me or let me die. No, it's not the same.

The look he gives me now is worse.

"You cannot do this." Peter lunges for the guard and with a flick of his wrist disarms him in an instant. He points the sword into the guard's chest. "You will not take my son."

"Unless you'd like to find yourself in a cell in Hexham beside him, you'll lower your weapon," the guard says.

"It's your weapon, you idiot," Peter mutters.

"We're to escort Mr. Raleigh to Hexham prison, where he will officially receive his sentence and be given the opportunity to enter in a defense, if he wishes."

"He'll enter a defense," Peter snarls. "And I daresay you'll be needing to enter one before this is all over."

"Father." John turns to him. "Let's go. The sooner we get there, the sooner I can be back. This is all a mistake." One final glance at me. "Nothing but a mistake."

The guards reach for John again; this time he lets them. They clamp his wrists in iron bindings and escort him through the mess tent and across the field, Peter at his heels.

John's friends, the girls at the end of the table, everyone in the tent, they all turn to watch them go. And when John passes out of sight they all look back to me, some with anger, some with confusion, some with bright, greedy eyes as if the scandal unfolding before them were their dessert, sorely missing.

I grab my trencher, and John's. Step through the aisles and the people who don't give way for me, forcing me to push through them so they can push back, vaguely threatening.

At the entrance I glance over my shoulder, just once, and see her. Chime. She's surrounded by her friends, now aflutter with whispers and gasps and poorly concealed smiles. But Chime's face is unhappy, and it, unlike Bram's, is not pitying. She holds my gaze and for a moment, we are united in shared misery.

I step from the mess tent and make my way to the adjoining kitchen tent, where a group of women huddle around vats of water, washing up. I drop the trenchers in the pile at their feet and make my way across the field. I don't know where I'm going, not really, but I find myself pushing through the rapidly darkening sky and into the yew alley, making my way up to Rochester Hall, retracing the steps I took a week ago, following John into the solar.

I don't go there; I'm not allowed into the west wing of the house—no one is, save for council members and Fitzroy's friends, family, and, of course, John. But Fitzroy opened the east wing and a few of its many rooms up to the camp: the library, the music room, the chapel, the dance hall. The library and chapel get much use; the music room and dance hall do not.

The guard posted at one of the doors that lead inside

moves to let me pass. Like the rest of Rochester, the east wing is lovely, if not a bit gaudy. Walls covered in rich yellow brocade. Black-and-white-tiled floor covered in an expansive, deep-blue-and-red carpet. Gold chandeliers, dripping with crystal, hang from arched ceilings. There are even suits of armor mounted on ledges set high upon the walls.

I pass room after room but enter none of them. Not the library with its spiraling towers of books; not the frescoed and gilded dance hall, so like the great hall at Greenwich Tower where the masque was held; not the music room, empty save for a girl and boy who stand entwined in a darkened corner. They all remind me of John.

The last room I try is the chapel; I know it by the yellow cross etched into the stained glass door. I push it open. Marble floors, oak pews; a constellation of stars painted on the ceiling against a midnight-blue backdrop. A thousand candles, set in brackets along the walls, spring to life, magically alerted to my presence.

I crawl into an empty pew—they're all empty—and draw my knees to my chest, wrap my arms around myself, rest my head. I don't cry; it seems too insignificant, too selfish for what I've done. And I had to do it. But it doesn't mean I'm not sorry for it, and it doesn't make it any easier to bear.

There's a rustle then, the whisper of a door on its hinges, the soft sound of two sets of footsteps on the threshold but only one breath. I tilt my head to see Fifer standing there, Schuyler behind her.

She slides in beside me, saying nothing. She doesn't have to. Because after a moment, she moves closer, reaches for my hand, then drops her head on my shoulder, sighing deeply.

Schuyler sits on my other side. He cups the back of my head, just briefly, before leaning forward, head bowed, his forearms resting on the seat back in front of him.

We sit together, a silent trio of misery, until the last of the candles burns out and there's nothing left but darkness.

13

"WE'VE COME TO SEE JOHN RALEIGH."

Fifer and I stand before the entrance of Hexham. She tells me it was once a stable before being converted into a prison: long and low and built from stone, inset with squared windows and rounded doors. The only sign there are criminals inside is the high wall that surrounds it. Even so, it's not like Fleet: not meant for torture, or a place for holding until a death sentence is carried out. I winced when I saw a platform in the yard, but Fifer assured me it wasn't for executions but a holdover from auctions, selling off animals to merchants. There's no one dangerous here. Most of the prisoners are debtors, the occasional petty thief or miscreant, a drunk or two.

And a healer who did nothing except make the terrible mistake of getting involved with a witch hunter.

The guard, armed and dressed in black, that red-and-orange Reformist badge emblazoned on his chest, glances between us.

"I can only permit one visitor at a time."

"You go," Fifer tells me. "I'll wait for you here."

My stomach squirms with dread. The guard checks me for weapons; I have none. Then he unearths a key and unlocks the gate, the creaking hinges echoing across the courtyard. He leads me inside, into the wide, empty corridor, light spilling in through unbarred windows. But for all that it is unlike Fleet, it still smells the same: mold and moisture, anger and abandonment.

We wind up a flight of stairs then down another hall. There's no sound of death here, no bodies bruised and battered and dying in the corner. But it is cold, several of the windows open wide to the frigid winter air. And, as most prisoners in Hexham serve short sentences for their relatively minor crimes, Fifer says it's entirely empty.

Not entirely.

The guard leads me past cell after cell until we reach one at the end, the barred door closed and firmly locked. Inside, on a cot pushed against the wall, is John.

He's sitting with his back to the wall, his boot heels on the edge of the mattress, arms draped over his knees, head down. He's dressed in gray trousers and a long gray cloak, the hood pulled over his head to keep away the chill.

He heard us coming, he must have; it's deathly quiet and there's no one around but for us. Still, he doesn't even look up. Not even when the guard clears his throat: Once, twice. Finally, the guard speaks.

"You have a visitor."

John looks up then. But not at me, at the guard. He still says nothing.

The guard clears his throat again. "You have twenty minutes."

John mutters something under his breath I don't hear. The guard walks away, back down the hall and the stairs, the same way we came, leaving us alone.

"How are you?" I say, awkward.

A scoff. That's his only reply.

"I wanted to see you," I continue. "Talk to you. And to bring you these." I open the bag slung across my shoulder, pull out a pair of books: *Physika Kai Mystika* and *Monas Hieroglyphica*. Both alchemy texts I borrowed from the vast library at Rochester Hall.

"I don't want to see you, and I don't want to talk to you. You had me arrested," John says. "Don't bother telling me you didn't. You went through my stores in my bedroom and you saw them, and you turned me in. It was you."

"Yes," I confess. "I did have you arrested. But I did it to help you. I know you don't see that now. I only want to help you."

He fires off one obscenity, then another.

"The books, I think they will help you, too," I go on. "To remember your magic, the magic you were born with. Gifted with." I use Nicholas's words not to manipulate him, but to remind him. "You're not yourself right now. I know you don't see that, either, but we do. Your father. Fifer. Schuyler. Even Chime." He frowns a little at the mention of her name. "This isn't the John I know."

"You don't know who I am," he says. "You don't know me at all."

"That's not true." I lean forward, touch my forehead to the bars. "I do know you. At least, I did."

I think of the stack of notes he wrote me. Every last one I have with me, tucked carefully into my bag. Notes I've read and reread a hundred times, for the comfort I needed when he was no longer there to give it to me, and to prove to myself that what we had wasn't just something I imagined.

"Blackwell's magic. The stigma. It's part of you now." I tell him what Nicholas told me. "It will take you over, if you let it. It is taking over." I squeeze the bars to steady myself. "But I want you to fight it. I want you to use the time in here to try to remember who you are."

John charges across the cell then, so fast I don't have time to react. He reaches through the bars and snatches my wrists, gripping them hard.

"Do you know what you've done?" He gives me a little shake. "Do you have any idea?"

"Yes!" I try to pull away but his grasp is too strong. "I know exactly what I've done. I've kept you from harm. I've kept you from harming others. I've kept people from learning your secret, and from discovering mine. I've saved your life, again, only you're too far gone to see it."

"It's not your right to do that," he shouts back. "Don't you get it? You aren't my mother. You aren't my sister. And you sure as hell aren't my friend." His eyes narrow into cruel, hard slits. "You don't get to say what happens to me."

I close my eyes, just for a moment. Try to remember his breath on my cheek, his lips on mine, the warmth and the love he once felt for me. But even those memories are slipping away now, insubstantial as a ghost.

"You aren't who I thought you were," he continues. "The girl I thought I knew, she would have been pleased for me. She would have helped me to fight. Not shut me away in a cage as if I were an animal she was trying to tame."

That's not what I did, I want to say. Only I don't, because it is exactly what I did.

"I did it because I care about you," I say instead. It's more than that, so much more. But the words that should be said in private, in whispers and in love, don't belong here.

"Funny things happen to the people you claim to care about," he says, the words cruel and sharp and cutting deep. "You cared about Caleb, yet you killed him. I suppose I got off easy, didn't I?"

I jerk away from him, flinching as if he'd struck me. He doesn't try to hold me back.

"How dare you throw Caleb in my face," I say, my shock turning quickly to anger. "You know what happened that night. You were there. You know I didn't mean to kill him."

John shrugs, utterly careless. "You had me thrown in jail for no reason. You've lost the right to be indignant. And now, I want you out. The sooner you leave the sooner I can put this behind me. Whatever the hell it was." He lunges for the door again, and again, I flinch. But he only bangs the heel of his hand against the bars.

"Guard!"

The man arrives quickly, too quickly. No doubt he's been lingering at the top of the stairs, listening to every word we've said.

"Get her out of here. And make sure she never comes back." He turns his back on me.

"John," I start. But then I stop. I won't plead for him. I won't make him take back the words he said to me. I won't make him turn back and tell me he didn't mean them. *I love you*, I say. Only it comes out as "Good-bye."

Fifer waits for me at the entrance. She's pacing back and forth, gnawing a fingernail. At the clank of the key in the door she stops midstride and rushes over.

"How did it go?" She tosses the guard a nasty look before taking my arm and pulling me across Hexham's empty court-yard, toward the gate.

"He told me to leave," I say. "He said he never wanted to see me again." My voice cracks as his words, the reality and the finality of them, sink in.

"Elizabeth—"

"Don't," I say. "Don't tell me he's not himself. He is. This is who he is now."

"That is what I was going to say," Fifer replies. "But better this way and alive than any other way and dead."

We step through the prison's open gate and onto the narrow dirt road that leads north to Gallion's Reach, past Whetstone, and, beyond that, Rochester. It's desolate here, nothing but frozen fields decorated by clumps of barren trees, fences, and the occasional lone farmhouse, their chimneys sending up fat, erratic plumes of smoke as if they were distress signals.

A mile or so on I catch sight of a group of a half-dozen men standing a few hundred feet off the road. They're members of the Watch; I recognize their gray cloaks, that aggressive orange triangle on the lapel. I can't see who they are, though, not from this distance. But I can see they're having trouble with what looks like prisoners they've captured.

Two men in gray hold up a third man in black. By the way his head hangs limp and his feet drag along the ground, he looks to be unconscious, possibly dead. Two more men in gray are wrestling with yet another man in black. He's not unconscious, but he's well on his way—he stumbles, falls to his knees, gets up, stumbles again. Their grunts and expletives cut through the still, frigid air.

Fifer and I exchange a rapid glance.

"More of Blackwell's men," Fifer says. "And look. Is that Peter?" She points to a dark, curly-haired man in gray, dragging the still-conscious captive across the field.

"Yes." I step off the path into the grass, making my way toward them.

"Wait." Fifer snatches at my sleeve. "I don't think we should go over there. It could be dangerous."

I shake her off and don't reply. I'm too busy watching the man Peter is holding. He's got manacles clamped around his wrists and ankles, and he's been beaten, badly. His movements are jerky, erratic, and as he falls to his knees once again, he groans and coughs out a mouthful of blood.

He's one of Blackwell's men, that much is clear. I know by his familiar black cloak and the emblem on the front—that damned red rose, strangled by its stem and pierced with a green-hilted blade. But there's something else that's familiar, too. The way he moves, the sound of his voice, the way his dark hair falls across his forehead. Something stirs in my chest then: dread and a dawning recognition.

Peter shoves the man to the ground; he hits the dirt with a groan. Peter then reaches for his sword, the sing of the blade against the scabbard echoing across the barren field. As if in response, a flock of birds takes flight nearby, screaming their retreat into the dull gray sky.

I break away from Fifer. Move across the frozen grass, picking up speed as I go. Peter grabs a fistful of the man's hair and yanks him to his knees, the other men of the Watch urging their approval. Peter grips his sword in two hands, swinging it high above his head. The man before him tries to hold himself steady. But even from here I can see him trembling, his body swaying like a stalk of wheat in the wind.

It's Malcolm. The king—former king—of Anglia.

"Peter." His name comes out a choked whisper. I try again, louder, my footsteps pounding to the beat of my heart as I run across the field. "Peter, stop!"

But Peter doesn't hear me. He's too entrenched in the violence of what he's about to do, too caught up in bloodlust, too caught up in the justice he's about to mete out. I scream his name again.

"Elizabeth, stay back." Peter lifts one hand from his sword, holds it out in warning. The other men see me sprinting across the field, Fifer on my heels. Some of them draw their own weapons, unsure of me, of what I'm going to do.

"Don't!" I shriek. But my plea is ignored as Peter turns

from me, places both hands on his sword again, and turns back to Malcolm.

Malcolm shuts his eyes.

Peter raises the blade.

And he swings.

14

I LEAP IN FRONT OF PETER, pushing Malcolm out of the way. Malcolm's not expecting it; he lets out a grunt and we both hit the frozen ground with a muffled thud. I feel the blade swish the air above my head, the hair on my neck prickling at the near miss.

Somewhere behind me, Fifer shrieks.

Malcolm utters something then; I can't make it out. But the sound of his breathless voice brings back a thousand memories and they all come flooding in along with a thousand other sensations: the feel of him beside me, lean and strong. The smell of him, a curious mixture of soap and fir trees, now mingled with the sharp metallic tang of blood. The sight of his dark, rumpled hair, his hands, his neck, and his unshaven face fills me with repulsion, just as it's always done. But just as I've always done, I push the feeling away, and I stay by his side. I'm afraid of what will happen if I don't.

"By God and his mother!" Peter bellows. "What the devil are you doing?"

"You can't kill him." I disentangle myself from Malcolm and climb to my feet. "He's not who you think he is." I look around at them, at the men advancing on me. At Peter looming before me, his cutlass poised like an ax, ready to strike.

Malcolm turns his head toward me: slowly, as if he's afraid to call attention to the fact that it's still attached to his body. Finally, he sees me. At once his eyes go wide, pale gray and bloodshot and wild.

"Elizabeth. Oh my God, Bess." I cringe at his nickname for me, too intimate to be said aloud in front of a crowd, too intimate to be said at all. "It really is you. I heard your voice, but I thought I was imagining it." He staggers first to one knee, then the other, looking up at me. "What are you doing here?"

"My lord," I say, the old habit of deference slipping into place, smooth as bed silk. "This isn't the time—"

"I heard you'd escaped," he continues. "But Uncle didn't tell me what happened to you. I asked—demanded—but he wouldn't tell me." Malcolm shakes his head. "I didn't know you were in prison until after you were already gone. Still, no one would tell me anything. I should be told everything!"

Malcolm is babbling now, a combination of shock, fear, of being beaten half to death before nearly being executed. He talks as if he doesn't realize we're not alone, as if he's forgotten there are men around him, listening to every word he says.

"My lord." I keep my voice low so no one can hear. "Please, stop—"

"I don't know if anything he said was true," he continues. "About your being a witch. It doesn't matter if it was. I would have stopped it, if I'd known. You know that, don't you? That I wouldn't let anyone hurt you?"

Malcolm takes my hand then, curling his fingers around mine before bringing them to his lips. This time I don't grit my teeth and bear it, this time I flinch from it and this is what finally gets his attention. He drops my hand and sees—finally—the men around us, their weapons pulled and poised. It jerks him into the present: shock and understanding first coloring his face, then paling it.

"What is the meaning of this?" Peter steps before me, his eyes dark and angry. "Elizabeth, who is this man?"

I start at the realization: Peter doesn't recognize him; the Watch doesn't, either. They don't realize that the man they captured, the man they nearly executed, the man on his knees before them, is the king—the deposed king—of Anglia.

"He's—" I start. Then I stop, thinking quickly. Is it better if they don't know it's Malcolm? Worse? Would they dare to kill the king? Or would it only make them kill him faster? Malcolm doesn't seem to know, either; he hasn't moved, not an inch. I can hear his ragged breathing, mingled with my own.

It happens so fast then. The man beside Peter lunges forward, snatching my arm and yanking me from Malcolm's side. Peter raises his sword once more, and we're back to where we started.

"He's the king!" I shout. "You can't kill him. He's not one of Blackwell's men. He's the king."

A terrible silence falls then, as weighty as an ax to a block.

"You're lying." The man holding my arm gives it a savage shake. "This man is not the king. He's a witch hunter. He's one of your friends, and you're trying to save him."

"I'm not lying." I turn to Malcolm. "Tell them your name. Tell them who you are."

Malcolm looks at me, uncertain. He doesn't know if this will save him or condemn him.

"If you want to live, tell them."

Malcolm lurches to his feet, unsteady, what little color he has left draining from his face. He's in no condition to stand, or even sit, but that doesn't matter. Malcolm would never state his elevation from his knees.

"My name is Malcolm Douglas Alexander Hall." He glances at the men, his earlier hesitation gone. "Son of William Hyde Alexander Hall, House of Stuart, and Catherine Johanna Louise Hesse-Coburg, House of Saxony. Titles: Duke of Farthing in Gael. Duke of Cheam in Southeast Anglia. Supreme Head and Lord of Airann." A pause, then: "First in line to the kingdom of Anglia and Cambria. Interrupted."

Interrupted from his own throne, by his own uncle. Thomas Charles Albert Louis Hall, also House of Stuart in Anglia, officially titled Duke of Norwich, but who styled himself Lord Blackwell after his principal holding in Southwest Anglia.

Interrupted from certain death, by me.

"Oh my God," Fifer whispers. "Elizabeth, what have you done?" Voices erupt around me, from all the men in the Watch but one: Peter. His mouth has gone slack, as has his weapon, as he stares at the man responsible for the death of his wife, his daughter. He could have had justice, he could have avenged them. He almost did. And I stopped it.

"He is the king of Anglia," I tell him. "To kill him is regicide. That's against the law. It's a treasonable offense, punishable by death."

At once, I know this was the wrong thing to say.

"The law!" Peter's voice, never spoken to me in anything other than honeyed tones, even after I had his own son arrested, rises to a pitch. "Punishable by death!" He rounds on me, dark eyes lit by anger but something else, too: grief. "His laws are nothing but death. He killed my wife, my daughter. He killed them."

"He's done that, yes," comes a voice, thin with pain. "And he's a blackguard, no doubt, and it's a puck to spare him. Even so, the worth of his trouble is still more than the trouble he's worth."

The men whip their heads around and I do, too. The man in the field. The one we'd forgotten about, the one I thought was dead. Only he's not dead, and he's not a man.

It's a woman.

By all rights, she looks like a man: tall, broad-shouldered, well muscled, even; a shock of pale red hair cut above her ears. Early twenties, if I had to guess. But the tell is her voice: sweet and high and girlish. She's on her knees now, and I can see the hilt of a knife protruding from over her shoulder.

The men of the Watch look around at one another, puzzled.

"Who are you?" Peter steps toward her. He lowers his

sword, raises it, then lowers it again, as if he's unsure whether to pull a weapon on a female.

"Keagan Hearn." The woman extends a shackled hand to him. Peter doesn't take it; she lets it fall. "From Airann, 'course, the lovely river city of Dyflin."

"That's all very well and good, Keagan from Airann," Peter says. "But what are you doing here in Anglia? And with him?" Peter jerks the point of his sword at Malcolm.

"I reckon that's clear enough, no? Sprung him from prison, there in Upminster. Fleet. Wretched place." Keagan sits back on her heels, grimacing. "Taking him back to Airann. Was, until we ran into you lot. No chance you could let us on our way—no." Peter's sword is against Keagan's throat now, his decision made. "I suppose not."

"Why would you rescue him?" Another man of the Watch steps forward. "Are you a sympathizer? Traitor? Persecutor?"

"No, sir," Keagan replies. "None of those things. But then, none of those exist any longer, do they? They, like everything else, exist under a different rule now."

"Don't play games, lass," Peter says. "You're in enough trouble already." He glances at Malcolm, still swaying on his feet. "Why were you taking him to Airann? What are you planning to do? Gather troops? Invade Anglia? Take the throne?"

"You can't take what already belongs to you," Malcolm says. "The throne is mine. It was taken from me, and I have every intention of getting it back."

"*Ach.*" Keagan turns to him. "What have I told you about that? Don't lead with that. Never with that."

"I only speak the truth," Malcolm says, a haughtiness to

152

his tone. "A king and his words are divine. You would do well to heed them both."

"That attitude is precisely why you are here"—she points to the ground—"instead of there." She jerks her thumb behind her, vaguely toward Upminster.

"Your lack of respect offends me," Malcolm says.

"And your lack of humility offends *me*," Keagan snaps. "My God, man. If you expect to live through this, you'd best learn to read a room."

Malcolm opens his mouth, then shuts it. I feel my eyes go wide. I've never heard anyone speak to Malcolm that way. Not his councillors, not his advisors, not even his own uncle, who hated him and wanted him dead. But Keagan clearly cares for none of this: the deference nor the consequence.

"Looks as if we've got company." She jerks her head toward the road and straightens her posture, the slightest wince the only giveaway to the knife still lodged in her shoulder blade.

Striding across the field are Nicholas, Gareth, and Fitzroy, their robes flapping in attendance. On their heels is Schuyler. I glance at Fifer, who nods: It was she who summoned Schuyler, told him what happened, told him to come and to bring Nicholas.

Malcolm seems to recognize Nicholas immediately. He'll know him from when Nicholas was in his father's council, from once charging him as the most wanted man in Anglia. He draws himself to his full height—not considerable, as Malcolm is only a few inches taller than I am.

The three men pull up short, take in the scene before them.

"Ye mus' be the cavalry." Keagan's brogue is thick and sarcastic.

"Schuyler's been so good as to inform us of what's happened here," Fitzroy says. "But we've not heard why. Or how. And who you are." He steps in front of Keagan.

"Some lass from Airann," one of the Watch says. "And a traitor."

"*Ach*," Keagan mutters again. "I told you, I'm no traitor. I'm a militant. A member of the Order of the Rose."

The men exchange rapid glances; even I'm surprised. The Order of the Rose is a resistance group comprised of students at the university in Airann, founded four years ago—just after Blackwell became Inquisitor—in response to his antimagic laws. But it makes no sense that this girl, Keagan, is here in Harrow; even less that she's with Malcolm. The Order, at least as I know it, is an intellectual organization. They distribute pamphlets, write scathing treatises for underground journals. They don't kidnap kings.

"The Order," Fitzroy says. "Of course. A fine group. I've been following your movements since you began. I always did enjoy your tracts." He rocks back on his heels. "*A Tale of a Tub* was my favorite. When the brother relied on inner illumination for guidance, then walked around with his eyes closed after swallowing candle snuffs? Amusing."

Keagan grins.

"Your protestations of late have certainly moved beyond satire, though, haven't they?" Fitzroy continues. "Rudimentary explosives. Burning effigies. Defacing buildings. And, most recently, bridges."

Keagan lets out a girlish peal of laughter. "Defaced is right. Did that one myself. Crawled up onto Upminster Bridge, stuck pamphlets on the spikes through those severed

154

heads. Reckon they don't mind, though. What with being dead and all."

"Heads?" Gareth says. "Whose?"

Keagan shrugs. "Some of Blackwell's, some of yours, some just in the way."

Gareth doesn't reply.

"And now you've taken a king captive."

Keagan nods, all earlier levity gone. "That's just the start."

"A student group," Peter repeats in a mutter. *"God's blood."*

"No need to invoke," Keagan says calmly. "Now, much as I'd like to chin-wag all day long, I've got a bit of a pressing matter." She lifts her chained hands, points her thumbs over her shoulder. "This dagger you clapped in me, she stings diabolical."

Fitzroy starts toward her.

"Wait a moment." Gareth holds out a hand. "You don't know who she is. She said she's part of this Order, but we don't know that. She could be one of Blackwell's. She could be lying."

"I told you—" Keagan starts.

"She's not lying," Fitzroy finishes for her. "Her actions prove that. Were she one of Blackwell's, she wouldn't have broken his nephew out of jail, she would have killed him. Hold very still." He places one hand on Keagan's shoulder, the other around the hilt of the dagger. "On three," he says. "One, two—" Before he can get to three, Fitzroy rips the knife from her back.

Keagan lets out a soft groan, pitching forward onto the ground. Fitzroy fishes a handkerchief from inside his doublet and presses it against the wound to stop the bleeding.

"You said taking the king—Malcolm"—Nicholas glances at him; Malcolm has wisely kept his mouth shut since Nicholas's arrival—"was just the start." He steps to Keagan's side, touches a finger to her back. A soft white glow emanates from his hand and at once, the cut is healed. Keagan shuts her eyes, briefly, in relief. "The start of what, exactly?"

"The plan to knock Blackwell off the throne, 'course," Keagan says. "What else?"

I could laugh—I very nearly do—at the idea of a student group believing they can overthrow Blackwell. But Nicholas doesn't look amused at all.

"I see," he says. "And you've taken Malcolm because you believe he should remain as king?"

"Him? No. I mean, he had his chance, didn't he?" Keagan glances at Malcolm, a look of utter disdain on her freckled, ruddy face. Malcolm stares back at her, jaw and fists clenched; I've never seen him look this angry and I almost—almost—feel sorry for him.

"Didn't do much with it," Keagan continues. "If he had, we wouldn't be here, would we? No." She answers her own question. "But he does have his uses. If Malcolm is dead, Blackwell's no usurper: He's the rightful heir to the throne of Anglia, and no country in this world would support overthrowing him. The only chance we have is to keep Malcolm alive. Dead? We're no longer resisting. We're contending. You'll find, I think, we won't last long if that's the case."

I hadn't considered this. And judging by the way the men of the Watch look around at one another, shifting uneasily in their gray cloaks, they hadn't, either.

Nicholas nods, his dark eyes intent. "So you were planning on holding him as a political prisoner. Have you facilities for that? Guards? Troops?"

"In a manner of speaking," Keagan replies.

"To take custody of a deposed king puts you, your university, your city, and your country at terrible risk," Nicholas says. His voice is firm, but it is not unkind. "You risk attacks from Blackwell, once he discovers you have Malcolm. You risk attacks from those in Airann who oppose his being there, and from those in Anglia who want revenge. You risk retaliation from opposing countries. Retaliation from supporting countries. Interest from neutral countries hoping to profit from the chaos, sending in spies and bounty hunters."

For the first time, Keagan's bright eyes flicker with uncertainty.

"He can't stay here," Gareth says. "We cannot risk this falling on us. We are enough of a target as it is. First her"—he glances at me—"now this."

"We cannot kill him," Fitzroy says.

"No," Nicholas agrees. "We cannot. But we can detain him for the time being, until we determine the best course of action."

"You're not suggesting we keep him here," Peter says. "You're not suggesting you put this man in the same prison where my son is." It's too much, then, for him. Too much that his son is in jail because of me, too much that Malcolm still breathes air because of me. Peter sheathes his sword, spins on his heel, and walks across the field toward the road.

"Fitzroy, could you and Gareth escort our two guests to Hexham?" Nicholas says. "And Schuyler, could you please accompany them? Schuyler is a revenant," Nicholas adds.

"With all that it means. So I very much advise against an escape attempt."

Malcolm swallows. Keagan's eyes go wide again.

Nicholas turns to the remaining five men in the Watch. "I'd like you to go with them to Hexham, and to stay as additional guards there this evening. And I would request that you not speak of this to anyone else." He looks at Fifer and me. "You're dismissed."

The men of the Watch step forward, grasp Keagan and Malcolm by their shackled arms, and lead them away. Keagan goes without protest. But Malcolm twists in their grip, as much as he can, looking over his shoulder at me. In his face is a plea: for me to speak to him, to speak for him. For me to stay with him.

But he is not the king anymore and I am no longer his mistress, so I do neither. Instead, I turn on my heel and, for the first time, I walk away.

15

"DISMISSED!"

I'm halfway across the field before Fifer catches up to me.

"Nicholas hasn't dismissed me since I was twelve," she goes on. "Since the time I was angry at him and cursed him and made his eyebrows fall out. He looked ridiculous, he was furious with me but it was so funny—" She stops. "Either way, I'm going to hear about this later, we both are, and it won't be pleasant." A pause. "It's always trouble with you, isn't it?"

I don't reply.

"What do you make of all that?" Fifer switches tack. "That girl, Keagan. Bold as brass, going into Upminster like that, breaking into Fleet. I wonder how she did it."

Still, I don't reply.

"And the Order of the Rose. I've heard of them, of course, we all have. There've been a fair few from Harrow who are supposedly members, but no one really knows. Their membership, their magic, it's all shrouded in secrecy. I suppose it has to be, doesn't it? Otherwise it's just more names for the Inquisition."

I step from the field onto the road and keep walking. I don't make it more than a few dozen yards before I feel a hand on my sleeve.

"Elizabeth." Fifer's breath comes short. "Rochester is this way."

I spin on my heel, begin walking in the other direction.

"Elizabeth!" Fifer steps in front of me then, takes me by the shoulders. Leans into me, her eyes searching mine. "What is it? It's him, isn't it? Malcolm?"

I open my mouth, close it. Fifer heaves a sigh.

"I thought as much." She takes my arm and tugs me back down the road. "That must have come as a surprise."

I'd laugh at the understatement, were I in a laughing mood.

"I never thought I'd see him again," I say. "I never wanted to. But I did, and then I went and saved him. I don't know why I did that."

"I don't know, either," Fifer says. "But it's a good thing you did, isn't it? I hadn't thought about what it would mean if he were dead, not until Keagan said it. I don't know if any of us had thought about that."

I wasn't thinking about that when I pushed him out of the way of Peter's sword, but I don't tell Fifer that.

"Blackwell must have," I say instead. "Otherwise he wouldn't have put him in Fleet. He meant for him to die eventually. No one gets out of Fleet." *Unless it's to the stakes.*

"You did," Fifer says shortly. "And now Malcolm has, too. The Order must have some strong magic, not to mention strong connections inside Upminster, to manage that."

"I suppose."

"I'll admit, though, he's not what I imagined he would be," she says. "The way he looked at you. The way he spoke to you. I guess I expected something different."

"Which is?" My tone takes on a bite but Fifer continues undeterred.

"I imagined him being rather cruel. Summoning you, dismissing you. I imagined he treated you as, well"—she pulls a face—"a servant. But the way he looked at you today, the way he took your hand. He tried to kiss you, for God's sake. He called you Bess."

"He was in shock." I stop to relace my boot. It doesn't need relacing, but it hides my face and the uncertainty I know must be showing. "He thought he was going to die. People do and say strange things when they think they're going to die."

I rise to find Fifer watching me, eyebrows raised. "Seemed to me a little more than that."

"There's nothing more than that. Nothing at all." I throw that last bit over my shoulder, already making my way down the road again. She catches up to me in an instant.

"What do we do now, then?"

"Same thing as before," I reply. "Same as always. Kill Blackwell. Looks like I have to do it even faster now. With Malcolm here, how long do you think it'll be before those guards shoot their mouths off to everyone they know? Before the spy inside Harrow finds out and Blackwell sends in yet more of his men?"

"Nicholas told the guards to keep it a secret," Fifer says.

I look at her.

"Nicholas said you're not ready." She tries again. "He wants you to focus on training. On getting stronger. He told you to let the council sort out what to do about Blackwell. Schuyler told me," she adds hurriedly. "He heard what Nicholas said to you in the solar."

"Nicholas doesn't have to know everything, does he?" I pull my coat tight against the gust tunneling toward us, hardening my already frozen cheeks. "You don't mean to tell me you've never done anything without his permission. Never disobeyed him. Never done the direct opposite of what he—"

"I get the point," Fifer snaps. "But you don't see mine. You're not ready."

I stop. Turn to her. Whatever she sees on my face is enough to make her reconsider.

"Fine." She holds her hands up. "Be a fool. Kill Blackwell. Get yourself killed in the process. By all means, allow me to help."

"That's more like it." I gleam at her. "I want the Azoth. And I want you to help me get it."

"I don't know where it is." She says this fast—too fast. I smile; she glowers. "You'll never get it," she continues. "It's hidden inside Nicholas's house; not even I'm allowed near it. It's protected by spells, and then there's Hastings. Even if you do get in, he'll never allow you to take it."

"You seem to forget who I am."

"Who you were," Fifer corrects. "And I never forget that."

Since we became friends, it's the closest Fifer and I have come to an argument. The road before us, the fields around us, the wind whipping against us, none of it is as cold as the look that passes between us.

"I'm going to take the Azoth, and I'm going to kill Blackwell with it," I say. "And while I'm at it, I want Schuyler to come with me."

This time it's Fifer who walks away from me, the wind carrying the stream of expletives over her shoulder. "You won't stop until everyone hates you, will you?"

"I won't stop until he's dead," I reply, but she's too far away to hear me.

In the three days since John's arrest—and since Malcolm's capture—I've kept to myself, in a virtual state of hideout. It wasn't long before the news spread of my betrayal, how I tipped the guards to John's illegal herbs, how I was jealous of his attention to Chime, how I allegedly got my revenge.

It was enough of a scandal to bury the real scandal: that the deposed king of Anglia, once Harrow's greatest enemy, now resides in prison not ten miles from camp.

I no longer sleep in my tent, not after I returned the first night and found it unpoled, trampled, and slashed. I don't join the others at mealtimes, not after the second night I cleared an entire table as if I had the plague, the air full of mutterings: *traitor, liar,* and worse. Instead, I've spent all my time training, resting in the chapel, planning, and waiting: for the opportunity to steal inside Nicholas's home, take the Azoth, get Schuyler, go to Upminster, kill Blackwell.

Waiting for tonight.

I choke down another meal of oat, pea, and barley stew with a slice of brick-hard bread, hand off my trencher at the mess tent, weave through the sea of soldiers in the field. It's mostly empty now, as everyone is either at supper, the sparring pitch, the library, or, in Nicholas's case, at Gareth's in a private meeting, held to determine what's to be done with Malcolm.

My bag, already packed with what few things I own, is at my side. I carry it with me everywhere now, as I have nowhere safe to leave it. It doesn't arouse suspicion—I look no different this night than I have the past two.

The sun dips over the horizon as I slip over the bridge across the lake, pausing to give Rochester one last look before starting out for Nicholas's. Somewhere inside the grounds is Fifer, still simmering with anger at me, made worse by Schuyler's enthusiasm for my plan.

"Blackwell already tried to steal the Azoth once," Fifer shouted at me last night, before turning the full force of her fury on Schuyler. "If he gets his hands on it again—which he may, if you die"—she glared at me—"he'll be invincible. That will be on you."

"If Elizabeth's going to try to kill him, the Azoth is the best option." Schuyler tried to reason with her. "It's her only option."

"And you wanting to help her has nothing to do with you wanting to get your hands on it."

"Not in the slightest."

Fifer crossed her arms, unrelenting. "Then swear it."

That was how we reached a compromise. Schuyler would accompany me to Upminster and to Ravenscourt, acting as my scout, my guard, and my protection. But he would not help me steal the Azoth, nor would he touch it once I had it, by pain of death or Fifer's wrath, whichever came first.

Three hours later I reach Nicholas's house, following to the letter Fifer's reluctantly given instructions. A fresh bundle of sage and pine tucked into my pocket, pulled out and set alight when I reach the front door. As it begins to sputter and spark, sending up plumes of thick, fragrant smoke, I wave it before me in two long, sweeping diagonal lines. The smoke hangs in the dark evening sky: an X.

I count to sixty, then enter the house.

It's empty inside—and not just because Nicholas is gone. There are no ghostly hands to pluck my bag from my shoulder, or to take my coat and ferry it from the room. Hastings is gone, and would stay gone, until the last of the herbs turned to ash. Sage and pine, burned together, interferes with a ghost's energy, dissipating it into almost nothing. I didn't ask Fifer if it was cruel, but I didn't have to. Forcing someone from his or her home always is, no matter what the reason.

I recall the rest of Fifer's instructions. "Walk to the third beam, beside the painting of peaches in a silver bowl," she'd fairly spat at me. "Kick the bottom—what I'd like to do to you—to release the hinge. Then push. It'll lead you to the wizard pit, and to the Azoth."

Wizard pits. Small, secret chambers built into homes throughout Anglia to protect men and women from the Inquisition, from the witch hunters, from me. Some I'd seen accessed through gaps in staircases, some through false chimneys, others through the privy. Most were skill-less, easy to find. This one is masterful.

I pluck a candle from my bag, light it with another one of my matches, and slip through the narrow gap beneath the beam, finding myself in a small room, maybe six feet square. There's nothing here—no furniture, no adornments. It's completely bare, save for a wooden panel built into the brick wall, narrow and shut and locked.

Tucked into the seam is a note from Nicholas.

Elizabeth, it says. *If you're reading this, I ask you to reconsider what you're about to do. There are some matters that are too great, even for you.*

This stills me.

The care he's taken of me since I entered his life, it's more than I expected of the man who was once my enemy, a man I once would have killed. He has not become like a father to me, not like Peter; he would never be that. But he is a protector and a savior, both of which I am in exceedingly short supply of as late. Even so, his warning falls short.

It is not enough to stop me.

I fold the note back up, tuck it in my bag alongside all of John's, and fish out a cluster of silver thistles. Fifer assured me there would be magic on this panel, a spell or curse to keep me out if Nicholas's words failed, and thistle would help to reduce the harmful effects. It'll still be painful—she assured me of that, too—but I can endure a little pain to get what I need.

I drive my thumb deep into a barb at the tip of the stem, drawing a drop of blood to ignite the thistle's magic, and reach for the door. The moment my hand touches the latch there's a spark, a white-hot flash of blue flame, and a sizzling noise as whatever curse it's imbued with leaps into my skin, up my arm, and into my head, ringing and shaking and vibrating and deafening. I feel as if I've got my head stuck inside a cathedral bell. I grit my teeth against the sensation—I've felt worse—and twist the dials on the lock: 25, 12, 15, 42. December 25, 1542. Fifer's birthday.

The door swings open. With some trouble I wrest my hand from the latch, the ringing in my head subsiding enough to allow me to see it, in the shallow depths of the dark cabinet, lying there, alone: a steely corpse in a wooden coffin.

The Azoth.

I reach in, wrap my hand around the hilt. At once I feel it, surging through my skin as if greeting an old friend: the heat and energy of the Azoth's latent curse, dripped into me the last time I used it—when I tried to kill Blackwell and killed Caleb instead. It hums, erratic at first, a flickering beat in my blood before finding its rhythm, one that matches my own heartbeat. A rapid thump that, as the seconds pass, grows slower, steadier, and surer.

A grin steals across my face.

I slide the Azoth into the scabbard beneath my cloak, snatch up my candle, then retrace my steps through the house until I'm outside once more. I step over the bundle of still-smoking herbs on the threshold, and pull a single mint leaf from my pocket, dropping it in the center. Mint increases energy, and it will help make Hastings's return easier. It wasn't part of Fifer's plan, but I do it anyway: a weak apology.

I'm meant to meet Schuyler in the early hours before dawn, at the desolate crossroads between Theydon Bois and Gallion's Reach, before making our way south through the Mudchute, east out of Harrow, and on to Upminster. But it's not yet midnight, and it's a short distance to our meeting place, maybe forty-five minutes. I've got hours before I need to be there. So I start off on the second part of the plan, thought of and devised by me but wholly unbeknownst to Fifer.

I will go to Hexham to find Malcolm and that student, Keagan. They both just came from Upminster, and they were both just inside Fleet, managing to make it out without detection. They may know things about the city, about Blackwell, about his guard, and about his protection. It could mean the difference between me returning victorious or never returning at all.

16

AT HEXHAM, A COMPLEMENT OF guards mills about the door, six that I can see: four in gray cloaks, two in black. I take note of their posture, the way they walk, shift their weapons. Listen to snippets of conversation that echo into the still night sky. The men are tired but not exhausted, bored but not frustrated—at least not enough to become restless. Restlessness can lead to gambling, sparring, or fighting, that burst of energy making them jumpy and nervy, alert to things that aren't there.

Or that are.

I move north along the wall, cutting left at the junction, until I'm facing the back of the prison. I run my hand along the wall: rough, knobby, and dry, not at all like Fleet. The walls there were always damp and slick with black mold. I sling my bag across my back, secure the Azoth at my side. Plunge my hands into the dirt along the ground, gathering grit for traction. Then I dig my toes into the grooves in the stone and begin to climb.

The walls are high, thirty feet at least, but it's not a hard climb and I reach the top a few moments later, perching along the narrow ledge. I look around, listen. No guards heard me, none of the Watch saw me. There's a certain irony in that, and my earlier grin is back.

Below me is a clearing between the wall and the prison, maybe six feet wide, running the length of the building. There are no doors on this side, only a dozen or so windows, large and unbarred. There's a possibility one of them is unlocked; the day I visited John I recall a few of them were open, filling the hall with frigid air.

I scurry down the wall. Pause, dash across the clearing to the first window. Locked. The second window is also locked, as is the third. And the fourth. My heart speeds up, my breath comes fast. If the guards were to come around the corner, they'd see me, and I'd have to explain what I'm doing here in the dead of night. They could detain me, they could learn where I'm going, they could take away the Azoth.

I run to the last window, the sixth one, slip my fingers under the ledge, and pull. It opens. I nearly laugh with relief, hauling myself in and over the ledge. Inside, an empty cell. Locked, but that poses no problem. I tug a pin from the knot in my hair—tucked there for just this reason—and slide it into the keyhole. A click, a twist, and a pull, and the barred door swings open. I shake my head. The magic on Hexham exists to keep those marked as prisoners inside and visitors, guards—and in this case, intruders—kept out. Even so, it really is a most unsecure prison. If I survive killing Blackwell, I'll have to bring this up with Nicholas.

I search the corridor for Keagan and Malcolm. They're not on the first floor; every last cell is empty. I find the stairs, take them quietly, and make my way down another wide, moonlit hall. I pass cell after empty cell, confusion rising with every step.

Were they not taken here? Did Peter convince them to place them elsewhere so as not to be near John, somewhere like Gareth's? Did Nicholas have them removed—knowing, the way he knew I would go after the Azoth, that I would come here looking for information?

Or, worse: Was tonight's council meeting a ruse for yet another trial, an excuse to put Malcolm in that hard-backed chair, chains on his wrists and snapping lions at his feet, subject of an interrogation and a scryed, watery verdict? Malcolm is nothing to me. But he is the king of Anglia, the rightful king. Not a common criminal, not a traitor.

Not like me.

I keep searching. But as I approach the end of the still-empty hall, my footsteps slow. Because every cell that ticks by brings me closer to the one at the end. John's. Finally, I stop, unsure whether to continue or to leave.

"I know you're there." That girlish, Airann-accented voice calls from the end of the hall. "No sense hiding it. Come on, then, show yourself."

I hesitate a moment longer, then step in front of the cell the voice is coming from, two from the end. Keagan stands there, leaning into the wall beside the cell door. "Well, well. If it isn't the little sparrow. Bess, is it?"

I glance in the direction of John's cell, then back at

Keagan. She's watching me closely, a grin pressing dimples into her cheeks.

"Elizabeth," I say. "If you don't mind."

"Why should I mind? It's your name." Keagan shrugs. "I was just going off what Your Former Highness calls you."

"Bess!" Malcolm's face appears then, pressed between the bars of the cell between Keagan's and John's. His dark hair is mussed, the way he looks when he wakes. I turn my head from it, and from him. "What are you doing here? How did you get in?" He looks around me into the corridor. "Where are the guards?"

"The guards are occupied," I say. "I let myself in."

"Did you now?" Keagan says. "Why would you do that? It's late, and this is a prison. You should be home, asleep."

"You've just come from Upminster," I say, going straight to the point. "I need to know what's happening there. How the city is being guarded, and by whom. What Blackwell's doing. How you got in and out of Fleet without detection."

The grin Keagan has worn since I arrived slides from her face. It ages her like a spell, the amused girl at once becoming a suspicious woman. "And why would you want to know that?"

"Tell me the information I want to know, and I'll tell you what I plan to do with it."

Her bright eyes rake over me. They take in my tight black trousers, tall black boots, my hair pulled tightly back, the bag slung across my shoulder. Then they land on the bulge beneath the folds of my cloak, where the Azoth is hitched to my waist.

"What are you up to, little sparrow?"

"Fine, I'll bite," I say. "Why do you keep calling me that?"

"You're a little thing, aren't you? Too little to pay mind

to, some might say. Some might even take you for granted. But I say different." She cocks her head. "I think the things people think you can't do are what gives you your advantage." A pause. "Why do you want to know what's happening in Upminster?"

"That's my concern. Not yours."

"Another thing about sparrows," Keagan continues conversationally, "is that in some cultures, they're seen as harbingers of death."

I glare at her; she grins back.

"Have you come to break us out?" Malcolm's face is still pressed against the bars, his eyes still on my face. He doesn't see what Keagan sees, what's right in front of him. But then, he never did. "You are, aren't you? I knew you would come for me, I knew it."

"Shhh." Keagan waves her hand in Malcolm's direction. "You're going in, aren't you?" she says to me. "To Ravenscourt. You're going to find him." Her eyes once more land on the sword beneath my cloak. "You're going to try to kill him."

"What? No." Malcolm reaches for me and without thinking, I step away. Keagan's eyes follow the movement, her teeth catching her bottom lip; an incongruous gesture. "You can't do that. It's too dangerous. You don't know what Upminster's like now."

"Which is precisely why I've come. To find out." I step closer to Keagan; she steps closer to me. "Blackwell's after us now, you know that. He's after—" I stop. I nearly say *me*, I nearly say *John*. I nearly say *the stigma*. "Them. And he won't stop until he gets them, unless someone stops him first."

"Interesting." Keagan wraps her hands around the bars.

Her fingers are long and slim, but her nails are short and ragged; they look bitten off. "First you said *us*, then you said *them*. Which is it, sparrow?"

"I don't have time to play games," I snap. "You can tell me what I want to know, which helps you, which helps your Order. Or you can keep this information to yourself, which helps no one. You've got sixty seconds to decide, or else I'm leaving."

She hesitates only five.

"I'll tell you what you want to know," Keagan says. "But first, you tell me what I want to know. Anything I want to know."

There's something sly about Keagan. She wants to trade in information, the way all watchers, players, spies, and operatives do. But something tells me the information she's looking for isn't political.

"Fine. Ask me what you want. One thing," I stipulate.

"What are you doing here?" Keagan says. "And I don't mean here, in this prison. I mean here, in Harrow. With them. *Us.*" Her smile is once again gone, the woman once again returning. "What is a witch hunter—former witch hunter—doing sleeping with the enemy?"

I scowl at her words, forked as a serpent's tongue and no accident.

"I was arrested," I say shortly. "Nicholas rescued me."

"I know that," Keagan says, impatient. "Everyone knows that. Your little story is becoming quite the legend in our world. But as with all legends, there are untruths. I want to know what they are."

"Why?" I say. "What does any of this have to do with what I'm here for?"

"Because I need to know if I can trust you," Keagan replies. "I can't trust you with what I know unless I can trust you."

I turn around then; I almost leave.

"Your debt was repaid," Keagan says to my back. "A life for a life, so they say. But you're not liked here, you can't be. Yet you stay on, and now this." A pause. "I know you'll say Blackwell is after you, but I also know that's only part of it. I want to know the rest of it."

"I stayed because I thought I belonged." I don't look to him, but I think of him anyway, at the cell at the end of the hall, poisoned by the stigma I gave him and hating me for it.

"And now?"

I don't know. The answer belongs to me, but it also belongs to him: John if he can find a way to forgive me, Blackwell if he'll allow me to live; Schuyler if he'll help me to return, Nicholas if he'll permit me to stay if I do.

"I told you what you wanted to know," I say instead. "Now you tell me. A deal's a deal."

"This wasn't about a deal. It was about trust. It's always about trust, sparrow. Don't ever forget that." She smiles then. "And I trust you. You're tough, and I like you. Lose that sweet, fresh-faced-daisy look, you could be a real warrior."

I step to the bars, grip them hard. The Azoth, sensing my anger, fires its solidarity hot and fast against my side.

"You think you know something about me; you know nothing," I say. "And I don't give a damn either way. You tell me what I want to know or I swear to you, imprisonment will be the least of your problems."

I reach beneath my cloak, place one hand on the hilt of the Azoth, pushing the fabric aside just enough for her to see the emeralds glinting in the dim light. If she's heard my story, she'll have heard of the Azoth's, too: No legend is complete without a legendary sword.

Keagan's eyes widen. She goes quiet and she stays quiet, a goddamned prodigy.

"Troops," she says finally. "Blackwell's got them, of course, mobilizing in the south. Your old contingent. Witch hunters. Knighted now, but hunters nonetheless."

"I knew that," I say. "Continue."

"They keep guard at Ravenscourt around the clock. West, at the gate. North, where it meets the Shambles. South by the Severn River has no physical protection, but it does have magical. The gargoyles embedded in the walls? They're enchanted now. If they see an intruder, they screech."

I think rapidly, turning over the layout of Ravenscourt in my head. The south garden by the Severn River was going to be my route in. Unless...

"How far do they see?" I say. "All the way to the Severn? Beyond?"

"We've not gotten close enough to find out," Keagan replies. "Fleet is full of people who got too close."

"Is Blackwell there full-time?" I ask. "At Ravenscourt, I mean? Has he left Greenwich altogether?"

She nods. "We've been tracking his movements. He's not been back to Greenwich since the night of the masque. No one has seen him. He's not made any public appearances; well, except the one. Where he was crowned at Leicester Abbey."

So he's done it: made it official. Malcolm swipes a hand across his dark jaw, not in resignation but in anger.

"I can help you." Keagan's voice is low, persuasive. "I could help you get in and out of the city. I've done it before. I could help you kill him."

I step back from her cell. Rearrange the folds of my cloak over the Azoth.

"You can't help me. I wouldn't want your help, even if you could. You got yourself caught." I allow myself a small, recriminating smile. "Perhaps you can tell me more about being a real warrior another time."

"Sparrow, crafty as a magpie." Keagan's smile is nearly feral. "Stand back."

"What?"

"Stand back, Bess." At the sound of Malcolm's voice, at the command in it, I do.

Keagan raises her hands, palms flat, toward the cell door. Mutters something, an incantation by the sound of it, only I can't make out the words. Intrigued despite myself, I watch the skin on her hands turn orange, then red, then white. The air around her palms shimmers with light, with heat; I can feel it, even from where I'm standing.

Then: fire.

A rope of it shoots first from one palm, then the other. They meet in the middle, twisting and turning together before hurtling toward the door. The bars turn the same color as her hands—orange, red, white—and with a small sizzle, like fat in a frying pan, they simply disappear, collapsing into a molten pile of smoking metal.

"Come on, little sparrow." Keagan steps over the rubble into the hall. "Time to fly."

17

I STEP IN FRONT OF HER, blocking her path. "You're not coming with me."

"Considering I've already broken out, I really don't have much choice," she replies. "If I hang around here, I'll just get tossed back in and I'd rather not go through that again." Keagan snatches her borrowed black cloak from the bench and pushes past me into the hall.

I scowl. This situation is rapidly spiraling out of control.

"You'll never get out of here," I say. "Hexham's guarded by more than just men. There's a spell on it. Only those who aren't prisoners are free to come and go. You can't leave."

"One problem at a time, sparrow."

"If they find you, they'll catch you."

"Which *they* is this, now?"

"All of them!" I lower my voice to something resembling

reason. "If you're caught again, I can almost guarantee prison will be the least of your worries. I may have pushed him out of the way of a sword"—I jerk my head toward Malcolm's cell—"but I'm not doing the same for you."

"They won't kill me," Keagan says. "And they're not going to catch us, because there's no chance they'll think we're going right back to the place we just escaped from."

"There's no *we*," I say. "There is no *us*."

Keagan moves to Malcolm's cell. A single hand held out this time, aimed at the lock. Before I can utter a word of protest there's a sizzling sound, a clank, and the door swings wide open. But before Malcolm can exit, I slam it shut.

"Bess!"

I ignore him. "What are you doing?" I say to Keagan. "He can't come with us. You're supposed to make sure he lives. Remember? That's what you said. If he dies, Blackwell is rightful king."

"Aye, I said that," she replies. "But if you're going into Upminster to kill one king, you need another to take his place. Killing a monarch has repercussions, you know. If Malcolm's not there, one of Blackwell's men will take over as regent, and we'll be in this all over again. It's not what I planned when I started this, but sometimes plans have a way of making themselves."

"Is that what you want? What the Order wants?" I cannot voice the traitorous words that come next; I cannot ask her if she wants Malcolm back on the throne, not while he's standing right in front of me.

But I don't need to.

"It doesn't matter what they want," Malcolm says. "They don't have a choice."

"He's right." Keagan pries my hand off the cell door. "Current King Thomas or former King Malcolm, that's all the choice we've got. Scylla and Charybdis, to be sure. But things would be different this time." She swings the door open, sweeps her arm in an ushering gesture. "Malcolm takes the throne again, he won't forget who saved him, and who got him there. Isn't that right, Your Majesty?"

Malcolm's expression is cut glass. "It's one of many things I won't forget." He spins on his dusty boot heel and strides down the prison hall as if it were an aisle to the throne. Keagan raises a pale eyebrow, then starts after him.

I don't follow, not right away. Because I can feel John's eyes on me, as certain as if it were his hand on my shoulder. I turn around and see him standing by the door to his cell, half lit by shadows. For a moment we stare at each other; I still can't reconcile the change in him. His eyes dark and cold, shadowed as if someone's smeared dirt beneath them; the furrow between his brows no longer a guest but a resident.

I don't give him a chance to turn from me first. I don't give him the chance to throw one last barb at me, as if the sting from the others weren't painful enough. So even before Malcolm can whisper another "Bess!" from the end of the hall, I walk away.

Keagan, Malcolm, and I huddle together at the bottom of the stairs. From where we stand we can make out the door that leads into the courtyard, locked and guarded by the same man I saw earlier. He's leaning against the bars, watching the others play some kind of game. There's the sound of something heavy hitting the dirt, one after the other, then laughter and cheering.

"Are they playing bowls?" Malcolm whispers.

Keagan kicks the wall once, twice. The guard idling by the door turns at the noise, frowns, pulls out a sword. Unlocks the door and steps inside, blade out.

"What are you doing?" I hiss. "He may not know any magic. Not everyone in Harrow does, you know. He may not be able to let us out."

"Shhh."

The guard draws near. He's three feet away, two, when Keagan leaps out from behind the wall, pulls him into a headlock, then drags him into the stairwell. His eyes go wide with recognition.

"Lift the spell," Keagan orders. "Let us out."

"I can't," the guard whimpers. "I don't know any magic."

"Untrue," she says. "You cast a spell on that guard to make him miss his target, because you have a wager with the other guard across the yard."

"How...how do you know that?"

Keagan's neat white teeth are bared in a grin. "When a man watches bowls as if it were blood sport, it's always down to finances. Now. Let us out and I'll let you keep your secret. And your winnings."

The guard curses under his breath. In the next he utters some kind of spell, an incantation. A wasplike buzz stirs the hall, then goes silent.

"You've got ten minutes," he says.

Keagan grabs the back of his cloak and shoves him down the corridor. She finds an empty cell, pushes him inside, and fuses the lock with a blast of heat from her hand.

"Show us the way, sparrow."

I lead them to the cell and the open window I came in through. We climb up and over it and, once outside, make our way across the short clearing to the outer prison wall.

"I scaled it," I tell Keagan. "To get in. I don't think we can do the same to get out. You might be able to, but I don't think he will." I nod to Malcolm.

"You'd be surprised at what I can do," he says.

"I'm sure I would not, my lord." Keagan pulls a face at my servility. But formality is the only weapon I have against him, the only weapon I ever had.

He approaches the wall with the same arrogant posture with which he approaches everything. Spits in one hand, rubs it together with the other, and places both along the stone, feeling for a hold. Keagan throws me a glance; I shrug. Maybe he can do it.

Malcolm begins to climb. To my great surprise, he does it easily, makes it three feet above the ground, five, ten. I move to the wall, too, hoisting my bag over my shoulder before swiping my palm cautiously along the sand, lathering my hands with grit. Beside me Keagan does the same, then starts up the wall beside him. But I don't go, not yet.

About twenty feet up, Malcolm's foot hits scree. He shifts his weight to compensate, but the stone doesn't hold and breaks from the wall in a soundless fall, hitting the ground below with a thump. Malcolm hangs by his hands, his feet dangling in midair, reaching and stretching for another hold. He doesn't find one.

In a breathless moment he falls, silent; I think of the things he's going to break when he lands: a foot, a leg, his knee, or even his back. But he lands on his feet, dropping and rolling to absorb the impact, the way I know to do but had no idea he did.

Malcolm rises and brushes the dirt from his trousers. He doesn't look hurt; he doesn't even look embarrassed.

"You could have broken something," I say. "How did you learn to climb like that?"

Malcolm shrugs. "I spent nearly every night of my thirteenth year inside taverns in the Shambles," he tells me. "I assure you they were not sanctioned visits."

"An enthralling tale." Keagan drops to the ground beside him, nimble as a cat. "But now you've cost us time. And if you had broken something, you'd have cost us even more. And I assure you, I'm carrying you nowhere." She bites her lip in thought. "I'll just have to create a distraction."

We tread along the prison wall until we reach the edge. The guards' laughter and the thudding of rocks echo across the empty, shadowed courtyard. Keagan points to a small guard building posted along the front.

"I'm going to set it on fire," she says. "A small one at first, so it doesn't look intentional. Just know, though, it won't be long before they figure out it is."

"And then what?" I say.

"Look for my signal," she replies. "You'll know it when you see it. And when you do, run. Straight for the front gate, as fast as you can."

"Don't hurt anyone," I tell her.

"I won't." Keagan runs across the courtyard, disappearing into the shadows. I can just make out her crouched figure edging toward the guardhouse. I keep my eye on her but I'm acutely aware of Malcolm edging up behind me, his shoulder pressed against mine.

"Bess." His voice, whispered in the dark, sends a rope of tension up my spine.

"My lord?" I don't turn around.

"Are you really going to kill him? Uncle?" A pause. "I can't ask you to do that for me."

"I'm not doing it for you." The words come out before I find the sense to stop them. "It has nothing to do with you."

Silence. A shoulder that goes stiff beside mine.

"Majesty." I spin around, dip into a hasty but always clumsy curtsy. "My apologies. I did not mean to speak out of turn. But these are..." I fumble around the foolish niceties, unpracticed of late. "Trying times."

Malcolm blinks at me, twice and fast, as if he's clearing something from his eyes. "No apologies necessary." Then he nudges my arm and points behind me. "Look."

A single tiny bird made of flame flits through the sky, zigzagging its way to the prison gate before alighting upon the square iron lock. The metal begins to glow a faint red: It's melting. With a wink, the bird disappears and though I can't see, I know the gate is now unlocked.

"Was that our signal?" Malcolm whispers. "She doesn't mean run now, does she?"

I hesitate. The guards are still playing bowls; they're not thirty feet from the gate. If we run now they will see us, but we may not get another chance.

"My lord," I say. "Run."

We make it five steps, maybe ten, when it happens: A

rumble, a crack, and the front door of the guardhouse is blown wide open, flames pouring from within.

"Ho!" a guard shouts. They all drop their stones and rush toward the building. But they don't know what to do, not really; they stop halfway there, heat and confusion making them wince. They don't see us so we keep running.

Twenty feet from them. Ten. A glance at Malcolm confirms he's slowing down. I reach for his sleeve, yanking it hard just as a wall of fire erupts beside us, tall and wide and crackling hot. The entrance is free and clear in front of us. There's a pounding of footsteps as Keagan appears and the three of us sprint through the gate. She pulls it shut and with another handful of red-hot flames, she melts the lock, trapping the guards inside. I can see the fire rising higher and higher into the sky.

"We can't leave them there," I say. "They'll burn, the prison will burn. John—" I turn around; I start to go back. Keagan swipes her hand through the air and at once the crackling red sky turns black once more. I can't see it but I can smell it: the lingering scent of smoke, the acrid stench that reminds me of Tyburn, and of death.

"I said I wouldn't hurt anyone." She snatches the back of my cloak and pushes me into the field, away from Hexham. "And I'm of my word."

"But the smoke—"

"Will clear. It's not enough to incapacitate. But I can't have you running back in there. We've got fifteen minutes, I wager, before they figure out what's happened. We need to be long gone before then."

I lead them over dark, sloping meadows and through

brackets of trees to reach the crossroads where I'm to meet Schuyler. We have to stop a few times for Malcolm to catch his breath. He said the fall didn't hurt but the way he favors one leg tells me different.

Judging by the position of the moon, already beginning to dip west, it's maybe two in the morning. I'm not due to meet Schuyler until five. But when we come upon the intersection of two small roads and the low, broken stone wall nearby, I'm not at all surprised to see him lounging there, a pale silhouette against the night sky. He sees us approaching and hops off the wall, his boots crunching against the frozen grass.

"Well, you've really done it now, bijoux," Schuyler says by way of greeting. "Breaking this lot out of jail, practically burning the place down. I don't recall this being part of our plan."

"Believe me, it wasn't."

His eyes land on Keagan, bright and menacing. "You're trouble," he says. "I don't like trouble."

Keagan laughs, not afraid of him in the slightest. "You're a revenant, are you not? By my measure, I should think you live for it."

Schuyler turns from her laughter to face Malcolm. But Malcolm does not flinch, does not step away.

"And what of you?" Schuyler says. "Do you plan on causing me trouble, too?"

"I don't answer to you," Malcolm says levelly. "In the future, I'll thank you to address me as sire. Or lord. Or Majesty."

"I'll be in hell first."

"You're a revenant, are you not?" Malcolm repeats Kea-

186

gan's words and the sarcasm in them. "By my measure, I should think not even hell will have you."

"Enough." I step between them. "If this is to work, and God knows that's question enough, it'll be without your childish bickering."

Malcolm blinks, that bewildered look again. He's never understood me, that's true, but he understands me even less now, outside the palace and outside his rule; outside the part he's written for me that I no longer play.

Schuyler reaches down, picks up several canvas bags I didn't see before. He tosses one to Keagan, who catches it with ease, and the other to Malcolm, who doesn't. The bag hits the ground, spilling its contents all over the grass: clothes, a waterskin, a bundle of linen filled with food, and a cache of weapons.

"Fifer's idea," Schuyler says, before I can ask. "I told her what happened. She's still angry with you, so don't get it in your head that she's not. But she said you couldn't very well take these two into Upminster looking like that. So she packed some provisions." He pulls out another carefully wrapped package from his bag and hands it to me.

"Your lady did this?" Keagan's already rifling through her bag, grinning as she pulls out bread, cheese, and an array of fruit. She crams an apple into her mouth, groaning as she chews. "She is kind, delightful, an angel."

"She is absolutely none of those things," Schuyler says shortly. "Now hurry up and eat. We need to get as far as we can tonight, in case the Watch decides to come after us."

Fifer may still be angry with me, but it doesn't escape my notice that she packed my favorite foods: strawberries and cold quail and soft bread and hard cheese. It didn't come from the camp at Rochester, that's for certain. I'm filled with unexpected warmth at the lengths she must have gone through to get it.

Malcolm, Keagan, and I eat quickly—revenants don't need to eat—then repack our bags before making our way through the Mudchute and its wide-open fields, broken only by the occasional farm or cluster of livestock. We walk until the sun begins to rise, the gray sky turning orange and yellow around the edges, until our eyes and backs droop with exhaustion and cold.

We come upon a small, recessed valley near a small brook, under a copse of trees. It's enough to shelter us from the wind and the rain that's beginning to leak from the leaden skies. Schuyler pulls a tarp from his bag and strings it across two trees. Keagan conjures a blast of heat to dry the damp grass, then a low, smokeless fire that heats the space to the warmth of a summer's day.

We stretch out along the ground, tucking our bags beneath our heads. The warm air, the crackle of the fire, and the patter of rain on the tarp soothe and relax me. My lids droop, and I'm nearly asleep when he whispers my name.

"Bess."

My eyes fly open. Malcolm's voice, soft and close to me, even in daylight, makes me stiffen. Across the clearing, Schuyler watches me carefully.

"Are you awake?"

I could say nothing; I could say *Go to hell*. He's no longer the king and I'm no longer his mistress: I am no longer beholden to him and I owe him nothing. But the habit of obeisance is too ingrained now; the pattern too set. I don't know any other way of interacting with him.

"I'm awake." I pull to a sit beside him. His arms are wrapped around his knees, and he's shivering despite his woolen cloak and the warmth of the air. "Is there something the matter?"

"No," he replies. "Not entirely. There's just something I want to ask you. Something I need to know."

The uncertainty in his tone makes me cautious. "Of course."

"Why didn't you tell me about the herbs? The ones you were arrested with," he clarifies, as if he needs to. "I could have helped you, if you'd told me. I could have done something."

As if he hadn't already done enough.

"What could you have done?" I say instead. "You were the king, a persecuting king. I was a witch hunter. I made my living enforcing your laws. I wasn't going to lay them at your doorstep."

"You were more than a witch hunter to me." His eyes and his words are pleading. "You are more than that. And I thought—hoped—I was more than the king to you. You could have told me," he insists. "I would have done everything I could to save you."

There's a world of malevolent naïveté in his words. He couldn't save his throne, he couldn't save himself, he couldn't save his own wife. How could he have saved me?

"You could have saved me by leaving me alone," I say, honest at last. "I was fifteen when you first summoned me. I was frightened, and you were king. I had no business being your mistress, but you left me no choice."

Malcolm opens his mouth, closes it. Across the fire, Keagan's eyes join Schuyler's, the pair of them watching us in mute fascination.

"It's not true," he says finally. "I invited you to my chambers, yes. But you were free to say no. You were free to go anytime."

All I can do is look at him. Because the idea of me saying no to him, to any of it, is so impossible that I know not even he can believe it.

"I knew you were hesitant," Malcolm admits. "But I thought, at least at first, that you were simply nervous. I wanted so much to put you at ease, and I thought I did. I thought we were becoming friends. And then I thought—" He breaks off, swiping a hand across his jaw. "It's something else I didn't see, isn't it?" He says this last part more to himself than to me.

"Your Majesty—"

"Don't call me that."

"But you're the king." He says nothing to this, so I add, "You are the king."

"Then as the king, I dismiss you," he says. "You're dismissed." He gets to his feet and walks from the clearing into the rain, away from Keagan and Schuyler, and away from me.

18

THE NEXT TWO DAYS ARE a blur of walking at night and sleeping during the day. Since he dismissed me, Malcolm has said little, if anything, to me or to anyone else. He keeps to himself: sleeping alone, eating alone, walking alone. But his silence is a warning to me, and I'm always alert to where he is, what he's doing, what he might do next.

Through Fifer, Schuyler tells us that the Watch knows we're gone, but they don't know where. They suspect Keagan and Malcolm have made off for Cambria, and they've sent a contingent of men after them. Most of Harrow believes I've defected, that after what I did to John I saw my opportunity to leave Harrow and took it. They believe Schuyler simply deserted, and neither Fifer nor Nicholas stands to correct them.

By the morning of the third day, we've passed the barrier

of Harrow, marked by a dozen signs graffitied with etchings of skulls and crossbones, flames and crosses. From here it's a single day's walk southeast through Hainault and the southern tip of Walthamstow into the city of Upminster. We reach the outskirts just as the sun begins to dip below the horizon, and here we make camp for the night.

At dawn, we eat the rest of Fifer's carefully packed food, drink the last of the water. One by one we dash behind a copse of trees and change into clothing packed especially for this part of the trip.

For Schuyler and Malcolm there are coarse woolen trousers, muslin tunics, scuffed boots, and unshaven faces. For Keagan and me, threadbare brown woolen dresses and plain leather slippers, our hair stuffed beneath white linen caps. We look simple, as nondescript as servants. Specifically, Ravenscourt servants.

Underneath our clothing, though, we're anything but. All four of us are strapped with weapons: knives in our boots, tucked in belts beneath our dresses and tunics, and for me, the Azoth, secured in a sheath tied around my waist under my skirt. I can feel it calling to me, the invitation to violence hot and thrumming against my skin, not an altogether unpleasant sensation.

"We've been lucky thus far." Keagan grimaces as she adjusts the ties on her cap. Without her short, wild hair on display, she looks more like a girl, a young girl at that, and she knows it. "Since we left Harrow, we've seen and heard nothing. I don't mean to be alarmist, but this doesn't seem right to me."

Schuyler, standing off to the side checking and rechecking his weapons, looks to me. "You think Blackwell knows we're coming?"

I consider it. I thought we had the element of surprise when we snuck into Greenwich Tower all those months ago, dressed as guests for the masque. I thought we had him fooled when all along, he knew. He was just waiting for the right opportunity.

"I don't know," I admit. "I thought we'd run into something, at least. Troops, guards... when I was a witch hunter, Blackwell had us patrolling every night, in every village within a fifty-mile radius of Upminster."

"Well, the laws are different now, aren't they?" Schuyler says.

"Not that different," I reply.

We pick our way through tiny hamlets, down the varying mud-soaked high streets lined with half-timbered buildings and stone cottages that grow progressively larger and more densely packed together the closer we come to the city. Still, nothing seems out of the ordinary. Men and women going about their daily lives: merchants pushing carts, laundry maids lugging baskets, doors and shutters open in each tavern and shop we pass. So far, it would appear that we're not being followed. But I think of the masque again, how everything seemed welcoming then, too.

Upminster seems the same as it was the last day I was here, the last day I walked free. A good deal better, actually, because today there are no protests, no crowds, no burnings. The air is filled with the scent of mud and dung, leather and livestock; the sound of shouts and laughter, wheels on cobblestone.

I glance at Schuyler. I know by the set of his shoulders, rigid and tall, that he's listening, picking through the minds of those around us, trying to pluck danger from the air as if it were petals on a breeze. Keagan, too, is on guard; her dress and her cap and her girlish, freckled face belie the hunt in her eyes, the way she looks to every corner as if she expects to be ambushed.

"I hear nothing," Schuyler says, before I can ask. "Everyone around us, they seem calm. No anger, no deceit, at least not above and beyond the usual. See that bloke over there?" He jerks his head at the merchant on the corner leaning on his broom handle. "He's trying to figure how to tell his wife of twenty years that he's leaving her for a boy of twenty years. Meanwhile, his wife"—he flicks his finger at a woman across the street lounging against an empty door frame, eyes closed and looking vaguely ill—"she's working up the nerve to tell him she's fifteen weeks gone with her fifth baby, only this time it's not his."

"Trouble won't appear before us," Keagan says. "It'll creep behind us, in shadows and around corners. It'll show itself the moment we look away, believing we're safe."

"Where to, then?" Malcolm asks. "If danger is everywhere?"

"A secret's safest place is in the open. So that's where we go: into the open." Keagan lowers her voice. "We're going to walk straight through the front gates of Ravenscourt."

"Excuse me," Schuyler says. "I was listening for sound advice. But what I really heard was the ramblings of a lunatic."

"There's no sense in subterfuge," Keagan says. "There's magical protection all over this palace, everywhere we turn. You don't see it because you're not meant to. The lanterns atop the gates? The flames are enchanted to flare green if they detect deception. The statues that line the promenade? They're hexed to come alive and attack."

I think of them: the stone knights on horseback bearing swords, the gryphons carrying staffs, the horses fitted with horns on their heads as pointed and deadly as lances.

"I've seen them jump down and skewer men through the chest," Keagan goes on. "I've seen them take to the sky, only to plunge down and pluck men from the street, carrying them God only knows where."

Schuyler and I exchange a rapid glance.

"You didn't tell us it was like this," I say to her. "You only told us about the gargoyles."

"If I'd told you, would you have changed your plan? No." She answers for me. "It would have changed nothing."

We walk along the Severn River, the waters frothy with activity: wherrymen carrying passengers on skiffs close to shore; fleets of larger ships clogging the deeper waterways, masts high, sails fluttering in the salty gray sky. Cut through the Shambles, a bankside maze of narrow, dark alleyways full of taverns and tabling houses, drunks and bawds. Malcolm draws his cap over his eyes to avoid recognition.

Finally, we emerge onto Westcheap Road, the large, main thoroughfare that leads directly to Ravenscourt, teeming with people and livestock, merchants and patrons. We pass the once-crowded square at Tyburn, now empty—no people, no scaffolds, no chains—all the way to palace gates, wide open but hardly welcoming.

Ravenscourt is large, the biggest of Malcolm's—now Blackwell's—royal palaces. Built from red brick and stone with depressed arches, elegant tracery, soaring stained glass windows, and its many flag-topped towers and spires, it sprawls across fifty acres alongside the banks of the Severn, a forty-bedroomed home to the over one thousand members of court.

The last time I stood here it was among men and women protesting, shouting against the king; they even had sledge-hammers, breaking apart the stone tablets that hung from the iron posts, tablets that declared the laws of Anglia. Those tablets are gone now, along with the laws, along with the king, along with reason.

"Keep moving," Keagan says without breaking stride. "Don't slow down, don't hesitate, don't look around. Keep your mind blank, as empty as you can. Whatever you do, don't think anything violent."

"What about the lanterns?" I look at them lining the promenade before us, the flames within stirring softly, each a different shade of yellow, pink, red. "You said they turn green if they pick up deception. They'll change color the moment we walk through."

"If you're walking into Ravenscourt, your mind is already set to deceive," Keagan says. "It's the degree of deception it's attuned to. Cheating husbands thinking about their mistresses will get a pass. Would-be regicides posing as servants won't—unless they're not thinking about it. So think about something else. Anything else."

"How do you know this will work?"

"I don't," Keagan says. "Now stop talking, stop thinking, and move."

We pass through the gates, our pace quick with false confidence. Two red-bricked columns, each four feet wide and ten feet tall, are capped with a stone capital and, atop that, a stone lion. They're still; sentinel, all but for the eyes: They roam the crowd around us, all-seeing and unfeeling. Magic crackles around me everywhere I look. The flags atop the spires flap merrily against the gray sky, although there is no breeze. Ravens circle through the air, dipping and wheeling above us like storm clouds, their eyes not yellow but bloodred: hexed and knowing.

Keagan clenches her hands into fists, the only sign of her distress. Schuyler hums something off-key, a song I don't recognize. Beside me, Malcolm whispers. I can't make out the words, but something about their rhythm sounds familiar.

We reach the main entrance and step through the arched door into the central courtyard. The danger here is palpable. I can smell it in the air, sharp with smoke from the kitchens that smells like a pyre. I can hear it in the march of boots on cobblestone; the footsteps of courtiers, petitioners, pages, and servants that sound like the Inquisition. Trouble is everywhere, surrounding us. We are drowning in it.

A fountain lies in the middle of the courtyard, white marble and inset with spouts in the shape of lion heads. When Malcolm was king, the fountain poured red wine all of the day and night; he thought it would be amusing. And it was, with the crowds and the laughter and the constant merriment that surrounded it. Now the merriment is gone and the fountain runs empty, the lees of the wine dried into the marble like rails of blood.

Schuyler abruptly stops humming. Before I can think to wonder why, I hear it: shouts, a thunder of heels, a low

197

murmuring of panic from the men and women around us that rises to a shrill. I whirl around to guards, a half dozen armed and in black, marching toward us, the crowd parting around them like ants before a boot.

Malcolm fumbles for his knife. Schuyler's song turns to a rapid litany of whispered curses while Keagan stands rooted to the spot, her fists curled tight. Only I can see their marbling: orange, red, white; fire at the ready.

The guards descend on a man beside the fountain standing not more than five feet from us. He starts to run. The men give chase but before they reach him, a cloud of the ravens I saw earlier pour from the sky in a swirl of oily feathers, the air rent with their shrieks and dusty, foul stench. They knock him to the ground, rending his navy robes to tatters before turning their claws and beaks to his eyes, his mouth, his face; his screams adding to theirs.

"Go." Keagan's voice is a hiss in my ear. *"Now."*

We walk—nothing draws more unwanted attention than a run—through the crowds who watch the scene before them in horrified fascination, to the archways that line the four sides of the courtyard, four to each wall. We pass through the third opening that leads into a dark shadowed hallway.

None of us speaks as we delve deep into the labyrinth that is Ravenscourt—past the lodgings, the offices, through the gate yard, and finally into the kitchen wing. We pass the cofferer, the wine cellar, the spicery, the pastry house, and the meat larders until we emerge outdoors again, into the narrow, dark, cold alley I was steering us toward: Fish Court. It runs directly beside one of Ravenscourt's many kitchens, where fresh fish caught from the Severn are brought and stored, hence the smell and the name. Schuyler and Keagan throw their hands over their noses, and Malcolm clamps a hand over his mouth to stifle a gag.

"Stop that," I say. "You're meant to be servants. You're used to this." I turn to Malcolm, now slumped against the cold brick wall. His hand is no longer over his mouth, but he's bent over at the waist, staring at the ground. He looks as if he's going to vomit, but I don't think it's because of the smell of fish.

"That man the birds attacked," I say to him. "Was that who I think it was?"

"Uncle's chaplain," he confirms. "He's known him since he was a child. I don't know what he could have done to deserve that."

"He got in the way," I say, because that's all it ever comes down to with Blackwell. Malcolm nods, silent; he's beginning to know it, too.

"We're being circled." Schuyler's watching the blur of black wings wheel above us, those hexed red eyes searching the shadows below. "Where to next?"

I motion them down the alley, to a green painted door at the end. On the other side of it is the flesh larder. It's where meat goes to be cured, and it's always, always empty. For good reason: It smells like a slaughterhouse in here.

In the center of the room is a large grate set into the floor, where the blood drips from the butchered parts of at least fifty carcasses hanging from hooks in the ceiling. I lean down and unfasten it from its sticky moors. The smell that greets me from below is worse than the one that surrounds me.

"I knew you had a plan." Keagan turns up her freckled

nose, an expression that reminds me of Fifer. "But I didn't think it would turn out to be so foul."

"Not as foul as getting your eyes plucked out by crows," I tell her. "Now get inside."

She reluctantly lowers herself down, Malcolm and Schuyler following behind, Schuyler spitting out obscenities at the smell. I'm unwittingly reminded of John then, of the way he would swear often and with glee, making me laugh. I wonder if he's still in Hexham, or if they let him out after our escape. I wonder if he is still free with his words, or if he tempers them for her. I wonder if he wonders about me; if he ever thinks of me, in hatred or at all.

"Sparrow." Keagan peers up at me through the opening, breaking into my thoughts. "Let's go."

I fold myself through the grate. Inside, it's rancid. Sticky puddles of blood stagnate beneath our feet; cockroaches scurry up the walls, maggots writhe in the dirt. The tiny space branches off into a network of tunnels, and I lead them down one after another—the four of us crawling on our hands and knees, filthy and damp—as we wind beneath the palace.

It is foul down here; Keagan is right. I've only ever been down here once, the night I crept from my room to the docks where I hailed a wherry to take me to the stews, to a ramshackle room in a narrow, timbered building set high above the river. There was a wisewoman there; I heard the kitchen maids talk about her. A woman who could speak to the dead, who could make a boy love a girl, who could bring a baby to a woman, who could keep one away.

She was the one who gave me the pennyroyal and silphium, told me how to stew them for three days under the darkness of a new moon, to mask the pungent smell with peppermint. The one who looked at me as I left and said, "These herbs, they'll keep you out of trouble. But they won't keep trouble away."

A wise woman indeed.

Soon enough light begins to squeeze through the darkness, a halo around damp edges. Voices and the sound of footsteps filter down to us: the roasted smell of meat, the sweet scent of pie, and the yeasty warmth of fresh bread as we pass beneath the main palace kitchen, just where we're meant to be.

We set our bags down and prepare to settle in for the night. Keagan warms our clothes with a quick blast of heat, but we don't allow her to start a fire for fear a current will waft its way upward, warming the air and alerting someone to our presence.

The evening hours stretch out before us, made longer by the cold air, the damp, and the lack of food, made worse by the scent of dinner that lingers long after the kitchen closes. I whisper the plan laid out for tomorrow, every detail and amalgamation of it, nothing left to chance: for me to step into the tiny royal pew, no bigger than a closet, overlooking the chapel with its dark-paneled walls, lush red silk curtains, and richly painted ceilings. Where Blackwell takes matins every morning, where I will wait for him to arrive. Where I will pull out the Azoth and plunge it into his chest and watch his life's blood drain from him, along with his magic, along with the hold he's got on me, on John, on Anglia.

Rest comes uneasy for all of us. Keagan lies along the ground, shifting and turning for hours before finally going still. Schuyler sits against the wall, arms folded across his chest, eyes closed. He's not sleeping; revenants don't need to, but it's the closest thing to it.

Beside me, Malcolm fidgets: crossing and uncrossing his arms, pulling his cloak around his shoulders, raking his hands through his hair. He's shivering but I don't know if it's from nerves or cold. His distress puts me further on edge than I already am, and finally I can't take it any longer.

"What was it you were whispering?" I say. "Earlier, when we passed down the promenade. It sounded familiar. What was it?"

At the sound of my voice Malcolm jerks his head toward me and, as I'd hoped, stops moving.

"It's the Prayer on the Eve of Battle," he says. "Do you know it? *To know you is to live, to serve you is to reign, be our protection in battle against evil...*"

He recites the words and at once, that cadence I recognized before becomes a pledge I wish I hadn't. Frances Culpepper, another of Blackwell's witch hunters, the only other female recruit and my only other friend besides Caleb, used to recite it before our tests. She said it brought her luck; she said it kept her alive. It was the last thing I ever heard her say: Frances didn't make it through our final test.

"I know it."

"I used to recite it before meetings," Malcolm continues. "With the privy council, with parliament, diplomats, councillors, chancellors, pensioners, petitioners, parishioners..."

"So, everyone then."

He laughs a little. Malcolm's always been free with his laughter, but his voice cracks on it this time, making him sound boyish and vulnerable, as if all his other laughs were just an imitation. Or maybe this one is the imitation.

"It gave me courage, I suppose, and I needed all the courage I could get," he says. "Those men, Bess. Elizabeth. They were awful, I can't tell you. Each meeting felt like a battle, it felt like they were after my blood. Who knew? Turns out they actually were."

I don't say anything to this. Because it's true, because I don't know how he didn't see it before. Blackwell was expert at deceiving Malcolm, yes. But by then Malcolm was already expert at deceiving himself.

"How will it go tomorrow?" Malcolm cups his hands around his mouth, blows into them, rubs his palms together. "Your plan. Do you think it will work? Or..." He breathes into his cupped hands again.

"It will work," I say. "Blackwell will die tomorrow, even if it kills me."

By my side, the Azoth thrums its approval.

19

INSIDE THE DISTANT CLOCK COURT, a bell chimes three times.

Schuyler nudges my foot but I'm already awake. Three in the morning. Time for us to go. My stomach curls around itself, lurching and tumbling in a dance of anxiety and anticipation and finality.

We pull on our weapons belts and fill them, the sound of metal scraping on stone as we pick up dagger after dagger and stow them inside. They're all but useless against Blackwell, against his men and their magic, but it's all the protection we have.

Not all. I have the Azoth, but it's meant to be used only once: on Blackwell, to finish what I started. I don't need to use it any more than that; any more than that and the curse would set in more than it already has, and I would not be able to stop.

I slide the blade into the belt under my dress. Almost like a whisper, a call, words fill my head and my heart.

You will know the curse of power, it vows. *The curse of strength, of invincibility. The curse of never knowing defeat. Of flaying your enemies, of never knowing another one. As long as you both shall live.*

Schuyler jerks his head in my direction, his eyes wide in alarm. Shakes it once, hard. The voice and the warmth of the Azoth wink out, leaving me cold and uncertain.

"You're sure we'll be alone?" Keagan asks me the same question she asked at least a hundred times last night.

"We won't be alone," I remind her. "The scullions and pages will be there, stoking fires. Emptying chamber pots. Strewing rushes. They won't be paying attention to anything but that. Dressed the way I am, I'll blend right in."

"Are you sure they won't recognize you?" Malcolm's voice, raspy with exhaustion and fear, cuts through the abject darkness.

"At this hour, they'll all be half asleep," I reply. "Plus, they're children. They've never seen me before. I haven't worked scullery in years." Not since I was nine, not since I worked my way up to cooking and serving. The senior servants, were they to see me, would recognize me. But that's not the plan. The plan is to be long gone before they arrive.

"When it's safe for you to come up, I'll tap three times. We'll sneak up the back stairs, into the pages' chamber."

"What about the pew?" Malcolm says. "Are you sure Uncle won't be there already? And the magic. Are you sure—"

"I'm sure," I say. "And I need you to be sure of it, too. We can't have any doubt, any hesitation. That will kill this plan, and us, as sure as anything. Do you understand?"

The three of them nod in mute agreement.

With a small clank, Schuyler pops the grate open. He holds out a hand and I step into it; he boosts me up and through the opening with ease and at once, I'm in the kitchen. It takes a moment for me to adjust to this: *I'm in the kitchen*. Where I spent my childhood, where I met Caleb. Where this story began and where, if all goes the way I've planned, it will end. The sight of it—cold stone floors, warm brick fireplace, wide expanses of smoke-blackened, white plaster walls—combined with the smell—flour and spice, fire and hearth—is enough to fill me with happiness and sorrow, longing and regret.

It all looks the same. A row of low, rounded bread ovens. Stacks of pots and kettles. Cords of wood stacked high beside the fire. Trestle tables laid with food in various stages of preparation: loaves of bread draped with linen and ready to be baked; a boar carcass impaled with an iron skewer, waiting to be roasted.

I slip into my old morning routine the way I'd slip into an old coat. Sweeping the floors, collecting the old rushes and placing them in a basket beside the back door, dragging in a bundle of fresh ones. A maid no older than ten pokes her head in the door. She sees me doing the work she should be doing but if she's surprised, she's too sleepy to show it. She stifles a yawn with the back of her hand and turns away, off to another chore.

I tap my foot against the floor once, twice, three times. There's a shuffle and a clank; the grate disappears and Schuyler, Keagan, and Malcolm reappear. I start for the darkened flight of stairs at the far end of the kitchen and gesture for them to follow me.

Upstairs, the pages' chamber. A long, narrow room with an unlit fireplace on one end, a single, closed door on the other. In the center, a long wooden serving table stacked with goblets and trenchers, linens and cutlery, for the servants to use in preparing Blackwell's breakfast. The room is near black but for a blade of moonlight piercing the bank of square-paned windows, illuminating the pale plaster walls and turning them yellow.

As we pass the table, I run a finger along the rim of a cold pewter goblet and think, just for a moment, how easy it would be to drop in some poison. A salting of Belladonna in a cup or on a plate, just a single taste and it would be over in a five-minute show of spasms and screams, a slowing breath and a stopping heart. It would be easy. Easier, anyway, than what we're about to do.

Schuyler glances at me then, no doubt reading my thoughts. But he shrugs, knowing as I do that poisoning is a faulty plan. Firstly, because we don't have any. But secondly— and most importantly—Blackwell never eats without a page tasting his food first. A man like him knows his enemies, by nature if not by name.

One by one, we file out the door into a long, winding stretch of hall called the gallery. It leads from the pages' chamber on one end of the palace to the king's chambers— now Blackwell's chambers—on the other. I've walked this hall a hundred times, a thousand, when I was summoned to Malcolm, when I was summoned to Blackwell, and it was then as it is now: quiet, empty, dimly lit; only a few flickering torches set into brackets along the wood-paneled walls.

We creep into the silence. Forty, sixty, a hundred paces, passing portrait after portrait, gilded frames filled with oils not of Malcolm or his father or his father before him, not as it was before. Now there are only portraits of Blackwell. On the throne. On the battlefield. Sceptered, crowned, and ermined. I wonder: *When did Blackwell have those painted? And how many months did he store those paintings, so sure of his success that he dared to have them commissioned?*

The gallery turns right, and here we stop. Carefully, I peer around the corner. To the right, a bank of windows overlooks the courtyard below. To the left, a small fireplace with flames burning low, illuminating still more golden portraits of our tarnished king. Beside it, two closed doors lead into the royal pew, a dark-uniformed guard standing sentinel before them. Pike in hand, propped lazily against his shoulder. He's been on shift all night, and he's tired. Even now I see his eyes slip closed, stay closed for a beat, two; then crack open again.

He's easy prey.

I turn to the others. Hold up a hand. They nod; they know what comes next. I round the corner and at once, the guard sees me.

"Halt!" he shouts.

I pretend not to hear him. My eyes are downcast, focused on the carpet, on the way my leather-clad toes peek from beneath the folds of my brown woolen dress. But my hand is restless, slipping beneath my apron to the Azoth beneath. I wrap my hand around the hilt, violence like the rush of fine wine warming me through.

"I said, halt!" The guard's voice draws closer and finally I lift my head. Slow, past his black uniform, past the strangled rose on his chest to his face, eyes now round with recognition.

"You!"

"Me," I reply. And with that, Schuyler appears beside me. In an instant he's got the guard's head between palms pressed flat and, with a savage twist, breaks his neck with a snap. The guard slumps, Schuyler catches the body, I catch the pike.

Malcolm appears then, Keagan on his heels. He walks straight for the fireplace; Keagan to the portrait on the opposite wall, one of Blackwell on a coal-black steed in the heat of battle. Malcolm kneels before the hearth and, after wrapping his hand with a linen napkin filched from the pages' chamber, reaches inside. He slides his hand up the brick, feeling for a lever that, when released, will pop the latch on a panel hidden behind the portrait Keagan has lifted off the wall. It opens to a circular staircase that runs downstairs and opens into the clock court. This was Malcolm's contribution to our plan. Later, it will be our means of escape. Now, it's our means to hide the guard's body.

"It's stuck." Malcolm rattles his hand inside the hearth. "The handle won't lift all the way."

Schuyler snatches the pike from my hand, rushes across the hall, and jams the tip of it into the crack of the panel's barely visible seam. With a snap and a creak, the panel swings open. He steps back, a grin on his face, his foot knocking against the heavy gold frame of the portrait resting against the wall.

It begins to fall. Keagan, in her haste to stop it from hitting the floor, shoves it back against the wall, but too hard, and the frame slams against the paneling. In the soft pre-dawn silence, the sound travels the hall like a shot.

We freeze.

A beat passes; two, three. I start to relax, I almost do. But then I hear it: the tread of footsteps on carpet. Slow, then fast. The clink of pikes, the murmur of voices. Then they arrive: two guards rounding the corner, followed by two more.

Damnation.

I snatch two, four, six daggers from my weapons belt and send them flying, aiming for necks, eyes, hearts. Two hit, but two miss. Schuyler leaps forward, snapping necks one after the other. But he can't get to them fast enough, not before two of them shout a warning: the last thing they'll ever say.

Two more round the corner. One more dagger, one more snapped neck.

As fast as Schuyler and I kill them, Malcolm and Keagan drag the bodies to the passage in the wall, pushing them inside. But we planned for only two dead guards, maybe three. Not six, now eight.

We are surrounded by bodies and blood. It's everywhere: soaking into the carpet, black as ink, spreading among the rug's woolen vines. It spatters the gilded edge of the painting on the floor, of Blackwell in battle. Only now do I see that he's holding the Azoth, the emeralds in the hilt twinkling in the canvased daylight. As if in response, the blade of it fires hot against my leg, daring me to pull it out. Daring me to use it.

As the guards keep coming, the sounds of shouting, pikes clanking, necks snapping, and gurgled whispers of death filling the hall, I think of it. Think of moving past them down the hall to Blackwell's chambers, where he lies waiting—not sleeping now, not with this madness that's spun out of control—but rising, perhaps dressing, perhaps strapping on a weapon. Perhaps even knowing I'm here, readying to face me.

The Azoth whispers at me to do it, taunts me to use it. And though it is the bearer of curses and bad advice, I heed them anyway: pulling it from its bindings, the sing of the blade against leather more like a scream.

That's when it happens.

Keagan is locked in a fight with a guard, tangled together on the floor. The guard wrests the knife from Keagan's hand. But before he can attack her with it, she rolls toward the fireplace. With a sweep of her hands and a muttered incantation, the nascent flame in the hearth roars to life. It leaps from the brick and hurtles down the gallery, a fiery rope growing larger and larger, twisting and turning and suffocating. It crashes into the guard and sets him alight, his black uniform going up in black smoke.

She kicks him away from her. He smashes against the wall beside the windows and at once, the draperies catch fire. Flames devour the velvet and turn them to smoke that fills the hall, thick and noxious. Malcolm appears then, pulling me to the floor where the air is clearer but not by much.

"What do we do?" His words are barely audible through his coughing.

I think fast. This assassination attempt has gone well beyond even what I had planned for. But I refuse to retreat, refuse to walk away from what I set out to do. The Azoth won't let me and, besides, I won't let myself.

"You need to get out," I say. "All of you. Not through there," I add, when Malcolm twists his head in the direction of the panel, lost now in the smoke. "There's too much blood leading to it. Once the air clears they'll see it, and they'll follow you. Go through the kitchen. It will be chaos by now; no one will notice you."

We paw our way back toward the pages' chamber, smoke obscuring our view and our breath. I snatch the cap off my head, press it against my nose and mouth before passing it to Malcolm, still choking and retching.

We're almost to the end of the gallery.

Five feet, four feet.

Three.

A fierce wind rattles down the hallway then, shrieking and whistling, a blast so frigid and cold it blows out the entire bank of windows above us. Glass explodes into shards, raining down on our backs, our necks, and our arms, splintered and sharp. Blood drizzles down my skin, hot and dire. Flames dance along their moorings, then begin to break, winking out one after the other like candles.

"What's happening?" Malcolm's voice is a panicked hiss in my ear.

"I don't know." But it's not true. I do know. I'm just too afraid to say.

The smoke swirls above us, shifting into fog, then into clouds, lifting high into the coffered ceiling. They hover there a moment, a warning. Then a clap, a reverberation, that thunderous sound of a storm, and those clouds open up and begin to pour, a relentless lash of rain.

There's only one person I know who can manipulate the weather this way, who can summon a storm where there was none, bend the skies to his will, bring down rain and wind and dark and light. The way he did the last time I saw him, at the masque I nearly didn't return from:

Blackwell.

"New plan." Schuyler's voice appears somewhere above me. He yanks me to my feet, the force so great it nearly dislocates my arm. Keagan grabs Malcolm. They push us back the way we came, toward the panel in the wall. Through the receding smoke and the rain, through my hair that's come loose from its knot and streams into my eyes, I see it: wide open and beckoning.

And then...

And then...

And then.

I hear it. Music. Dirgelike, the strains of it leaking beneath the door to the royal pew from the chapel below. It's coming from the organ, all music and no words but I know the lyrics anyway:

> *Sleep and peace attend me, all through the night.*
> *Angels will come to me, all through the night.*
> *Drowsy hours are creeping; hill and vale, slumber*
>   *sleeping,*
> *A loving vigil keeping, all through the night.*

The song I sang to myself in my final test, the lullaby my mother used to sing to me. The song that kept me alive inside the tomb that tried to kill me; the one that broke the spell before it could kill me.

I turn around, face the sound. Raise the Azoth.

Schuyler is before me in a moment, his blue eyes wide, his

grip on my arm fierce. I'm in awe, just for a moment, at the power Blackwell wields, so strong that it could cast fear into someone as fearless as Schuyler.

"Forget it, bijoux. It's too much. He's too strong—"

"I know." I twist out of Schuyler's iron grasp. "And that's why I have to do it." I push Malcolm toward Keagan. "Get him out," I tell her. "If you're caught, you won't escape this time. They will kill you on the spot. It's the Order's job, it's your job, to keep him safe."

But Malcolm jerks away from her and rounds on me.

"Don't do this." He takes my shoulders, grips them hard. Leans into me, his face inches from mine. For a moment, I forget to be afraid of him. "As king, I ask you—no, I command you—to come with me."

"You are not king," I say. "Not unless I do this."

"*Goddammit.*" I've never heard Malcolm swear before; the word comes out a frustrated groan.

> *Moon's watch is keeping, all through the night.*
> *The weary world is sleeping, all through the night.*
> *A spirit gently stealing, visions of delight revealing,*
> *A pure and peaceful feeling, all through the night.*

A shadow appears through the smoke then, dark and looming and figureless: a specter in a foggy cemetery, a boggart in a dusky swamp. I can't see who it is, but then, I already know.

"Go," I say. "Let me do this. I need to do this."

Schuyler growls one last curse before tearing Malcolm away from me, nearly lifting him off the ground with the force of it, shoving him toward the passage in the wall.

Through the fog and the driving rain I can just make out Keagan hauling him inside and the final look Schuyler gives me before crawling after him. The panel door closes, a spark in the smoke as Keagan fuses it shut, the three of them making their way down the winding stairs into the clock court and the still-dark skies and, I hope, to safety. I am alone.

Not alone.

He walks toward me, and even in the swirling coalescence I know his height, his strength, his black clothes; I know the wink of the weapon he holds in his hand. How long has he been waiting for me? Since yesterday? All night? He knew I would come. He knew what I would do.

And deep down, I knew it, too.

The Azoth fires hot in my hand, the energy and the strength, the latent curse and the manifest hate coursing through me: sparks before a bonfire, drops before a storm. It is dangerous ground. But I don't care about drowning, and I don't care about burning. I only care about ending him, ending it all, once and for all.

Like a monstrosity lurking from the depths of the dark lake surrounding Rochester Hall, he emerges, and at last I see him. But it's not Blackwell, as I was expecting: It's someone—something—else entirely.

Dark blond hair, falling in waves above his eyes. Tall, pale, dressed in black with that damned strangled rose fixed to his sleeve. And the scent of him: a hint of earth and loam, mold and decay.

I never thought I'd see him again. I thought I had killed him. Yet here he is before me; the shock of it would bring me to my knees if terror weren't holding me up.

Caleb.

He is alive.

He is dead.

He is a revenant.

"Hello, Elizabeth."

20

THE AZOTH GOES WILD IN my hand. Searing, coursing, trembling, cursing; the power of it threatening to unhinge me if the sight before me doesn't. All I manage is his name: "Caleb." The music has ceased, and my voice echoes through the destruction of the gallery, a haunting moan.

He steps toward me. His gait unsteady, his eyes fixed not on me but on the Azoth, the emeralds in the hilt dull and lifeless now, as if they know they're caught. He doesn't reach for it but he looks at it, something like distaste but also fear crossing his cold, white face.

I should say something. I should do something. I should thrust the blade into him and I should run; I should find Blackwell and do the same to him. But all I can do is stand there and look at him.

Caleb a revenant. He didn't die after all, didn't die after I sliced him in the chest with the Azoth, spilling his heart and his blood and his life onto the ground, didn't die, didn't die...

"I did die," he says. His voice is strange, murky. It's his but it isn't, the tone the same but the tenor gone. Not gone: *dead*. "I died. I'm dead. Because you killed me." Caleb tilts his head, an odd, unnatural angle, and fixes me with those eyes. Once blue and sparkling with life and mischief and ambition, now lifeless, pale, and gray, no soul behind them at all.

"I didn't want to kill you," I whisper. "I didn't mean to, I didn't. I cared about you. I loved you—"

"Funny things happen to the people you claim to care about," Caleb says, and I freeze. He's reached into my head, plucked out the very thing John said to me inside his cell, the very thing I can't stop thinking about, can't stop turning over and over in my head.

"Caleb," I whisper again. I think to plead with him, to ask him to spare my life when I know he stands before me to take it. But as soon as I think it, I dismiss it. Caleb didn't spare me when he was alive. He will not spare me now that he is dead.

This is what I know about revenants: I know that they are more dead than alive. I know they have no connection, no anchor to this earth. I know that they are little more than ghosts, the person they once were now just a wisp of cloud in a storm.

Revenants can learn to be human again, a facsimile of their former selves. They can learn to feel, to love; they can even begin to appear human again, the way Schuyler has—the soul he's rebuilt evidenced by the color regained in his eyes. But it takes many years and an unwavering desire to attain it, along with an unshakable connection to someone,

218

such as the one Schuyler has with Fifer. Revenants need a living, breathing being to keep them in the light, when their very nature is to live in the dark.

This is what I also know: Caleb has always lived in the dark.

"You knew I was coming to Ravenscourt," I say. "You read my thoughts, and you heard me coming. You told Blackwell, and that's how he knew to do this." I wave my free hand at the rain-soaked gallery, at the pew in which I meant to meet him, in which I meant to end him.

Caleb nods, once.

I think of Malcolm then, and of Keagan and Schuyler. If Caleb knew I was coming, he must have known they were with me. Did they get free? Or did they simply wind down that staircase and into greater danger than they left?

Caleb only shrugs, a wholly human gesture, stiff and awkward now in the replicate.

"Blackwell doesn't care about Malcolm," he says. "If he did, he wouldn't still be alive. Malcolm can't stop Blackwell from becoming king. Nothing can. He *is* the king." Caleb gazes at me, eyes hard and unfeeling as flint. "You know what he needs."

I nod, because I do. He needs the Azoth for its curse and for its power, and now he needs me, for reasons I still don't understand, to take back what he believes is his: my stigma. It flashes through my mind then—a thought so swift it takes flight again before it can land, before Caleb can seize on it— how can I give Blackwell what I no longer have?

With a confidence I very nearly feel, I squeeze the Azoth's hilt, long since gone cold, and I step toward Caleb, surrendering myself to him. His blank gray eyes go wide just for a moment, and I feel a fierce jolt of pleasure. Caleb may be able to read my thoughts, but I won't let him read my deeds.

"Take me to him."

Down the wet, smoky, bloody hallway we weave around bodies: guards in black with twisted necks and punctured eyes, one charred and black and unrecognizable. Blackwell knew we were coming and he sacrificed his men to us anyway. For the sport of it, for the game of luring us in to see what we would do, how we would play it.

And I don't know how to play it. Not yet.

The hallway ahead ends in a row of double oak doors, closed. I can just make out the shadows of two men standing in front of them. Not guards, no, because they're all dead, but as I get closer and I see them—one tall, black-haired, brutish; the other medium height and reddish, from his hair to the freckles that spatter like blood against white skin—I see that they, too, are dead:

Marcus and Linus.

Witch hunters once, now both Knights of the Anglian Royal Empire. Both revenants. I feel their gray, dead gaze track me with a hate that turns to wariness as they catch sight of the glittering blade in my hand, the very one that brought them to the ground before Blackwell hauled them out of it. As Caleb steers me past, I turn my head. As with any monster, it's best not to look it in the eye.

Through the doors, the privy chamber. Where the king

receives petitioners, where courtiers gather in sycophantic attendance, where musicians come to entertain. Now, it's empty; bare of everything save the throne, upholstered and canopied with a rich crimson cloth of state bearing the royal coat of arms: a crowned lion and a chained steed on either side of a red-and-gold quartered shield. Etched below, in Latin, a motto. Not Blackwell's old, steadfast motto: *What's done is done, it cannot be undone.* A new one now, for a new ruler and a new kingdom: *Faciam quodlibet quod necesse est.*

I will do whatever it takes.

In my wet woolen dress, I shiver.

Next, the presence chamber, the king's innermost private room. Bare and dark, just one shuttered window and one small fire burning in one small grate. No tapestries and no throne, only a desk in the center flanked by two chairs, with a single book lying page-up on the surface. And there, sitting in the chair closest to the fireplace, facing the flame, his back to us, is Blackwell.

Whatever calm I'd forced myself into, whatever illusion of control I once had, now threatens to abandon me. My heart begins to race, my stomach to churn, my palms to sweat. That old feeling of dread, the one I always feel when faced with him, rushes toward me like a tide. Beside me, Caleb shifts; he must feel my turmoil. But I take a breath and push it down, as far as I can, away from his grasping intrusion.

Finally, Blackwell speaks.

"Elizabeth."

This is all he says. He doesn't rise, he doesn't turn, he does nothing but stare into the fire in front of him, the flames crackling and spitting in the grate. At once, I know something is wrong. Maybe I should have known it when he didn't greet me in his privy chamber, on his throne, for me to witness the spectacle of his power.

Keagan's words come back to me, what she said in Hexham: *He hasn't made a public appearance since he was crowned. No one has seen him.*

"You didn't make this easy, did you?" Blackwell goes on. "Coming here. You ruined my gallery, my paintings; you killed my guards."

"You knew we were coming," I say. "If you'd wanted to protect your men, you could have."

He shrugs, dismissive. But he doesn't reply.

"You want your power back from my stigma," I continue, going straight to the point. "It's why you sent Fulke and Griffin after me, why you sent the others the day of my trial." I pause. "I killed them, you know. All of them." It's a lie, but it's what he would expect me to say if I were still who he thought I was. "If you wanted them to bring me back to you, you should have presented a real challenge. I'm almost insulted."

A strange huffing noise, something between a hiss and a laugh. Then: "You always were one of my best witch hunters."

Abruptly, Blackwell rises from his chair, the legs scraping against the wooden floor. He looks every inch the king: dressed in crisp navy trousers and a matching coat embroidered in rich gold thread. Knee-high black boots, a black velvet cape around his shoulders, the collar and sleeves trimmed in ermine. Moments pass and, still, he will not turn around. My neck prickles in warning: a distant rumble of thunder before a storm.

"Do you know what you did?" he says. His voice is measured. But beneath the calm I hear a note of something else: an undercurrent of fury.

Blackwell turns to face me, and I see what I have done.

He is every inch the monster.

21

HIS FACE—WHAT'S LEFT OF IT—IS completely ravaged. A scar runs a diagonal path from his temple, across his right eye, and over his nose and lips, ending at his jaw. His right eye is useless, frozen half open; the eyeball underneath it white and cloudy and unseeing. His nose is split in two, his mouth ripped and twisted, half his jaw visible. Someone stitched him up—someone tried—and did a sorry job. The scar is raised and raw and horrible, and I can see the crooked marks of the needle and the indentations in his flesh where the sutures were tied. This is the damage I did, the damage the Azoth did.

Unflinching, I stare at the horror. As if it recognizes a job well done, the blade fires to life in my hand.

"Caleb said that you, too, were injured by the Azoth." A pause. "I assume it doesn't look like this."

I don't reply. The wound I received was terrible; I would have died were it not for John. But after he was sure I wouldn't die from every other injury I received the night of the masque, he made certain I wouldn't be scarred by them, either. He spent weeks applying herbs, making tisanes, doing everything he could for me. It was a labor of love, I know that now. But now that love is gone, just like my scar.

Blackwell lets out a short, barking laugh, that twisted, gaping mouth glinting in the room's dim light. "Perhaps I should have spared myself a healer after all."

I shift toward the fireplace. If I'm to do it, it's to be done now. Can I do it now? Are the Azoth and his fear of it enough to repel Caleb, enough to keep him away to do what I came here for?

In one fell motion this could all be over.

"Taking my stigma back won't heal you." I inch forward another step. "Its power is no match for the Azoth." I remember the way the blade sliced into me, the way it hurt, the way it bled. The way my stigma did nothing. "It won't do anything."

Blackwell's mouth twists into a shape that almost passes for a smile. "And I'm sure your warning is in my best interest and has nothing to do with self-preservation."

I adjust my grip on the hilt. Fingers curled loosely, firm but not tight, my thumb pressed against the cross guard. All the while the Prayer on the Eve of Battle marches through my head, keeping my thoughts engaged so Caleb can't besiege them.

I'm almost to his desk now, almost halfway to him. I slide to the far side of it, putting as much distance between me and Caleb as I can, as if a mere wooden desk could keep him from me.

As I do, the book on the surface catches my eye. Red leather-bound with gilt-edged pages, open to a page dense with scrawling text surrounding a single image, an image I know well but didn't expect to see here. A glyph used in the Reformist symbol, representing unity, infinity, wholeness: a snake devouring its own tail.

"The circle closes its end."

The words slip from my mouth; I didn't intend them to. It's a line from the prophecy given to me all those months ago by a five-year-old seer, her recitation holding the cryptic instruction that opened the gate to the path I stand on now, between one dead man and another cursed one, holding a sword.

"The Ouroboros," I continue. "It's a symbol of resurrection, continually reborn as it sheds its skin. It represents the cycle of birth and death, the eternal harmony of all things. The unity of opposites."

Blackwell raises a ruined eyebrow. "Been studying alchemy, have you?"

Not really, no; but in a way, yes. For a moment my thoughts slip from the battle prayer to the alchemy books at Rochester, the ones I brought to John at Hexham. How I flipped through page after page to choose one he'd like. Studying the words to try to get close to him, to try to understand what he was going through when Nicholas told me the magic I gave John was at war with his own.

"The stigma is a manifestation of invincibility." Blackwell speaks the words as if they were wine, something to savor. "While the Azoth is pure destruction: the opposite of invincibility. Alchemists believe that if you were to combine a single element together with its opposite, uniting them, you could transcend them. Move beyond the power of either in order to become the power of both."

I can almost picture the pages before me in that dark and shadowed library. The words etched on yellow parchment, the drawing of the serpent devouring its tail, the words *One is all* scrawled beneath it.

"The power of both," I repeat. "What would that power be?"

Blackwell watches me, his expression hungry. "I think you already know."

I don't answer right away, because he's right. I do. But if I say the words, if I allow them to form shape, then they become real: an abdication of sanity.

"Immortality," I whisper at last.

That is when the fire goes out.

The room falls dark. And the air around me, once warm and still, drops by degrees and begins to swirl, great gusts of wind from nowhere whipping my hair around my shoulders, into my face, flaring my skirts around my knees. A cloud of breath snakes from my mouth, and I feel it against my cheek: the first flake of snow that within moments turns to a blizzard.

My dress freezes in place, the skirt ballooned around my knees in statuesque attitude. My hair freezes, too, strands sticking to my cheeks and my lips and eyelids that feel at once numb and sharp and heavy. The wind howls around my ears, bringing with it still more snow; the presence chamber has become a winter wasteland.

Blackwell appears before me, untouched by the cold, as if it exists for me only—*does it exist for me only?*—his coat and his face and his skin bear not a trace of it. I will myself to move. To pull away, to hold fast to the sword, to raise it and to lay it into him, to finish what I set out to do. But my commands fall on the deaf ears of my immobile body. Blackwell reaches forward and with a twist and a tear of metal against hardened skin, he pries the Azoth from my hand. I'm frozen solid as winter: I can do nothing but watch it go.

At once, the snow and the storm disappear, swirling upward into the pale plaster ceiling and into nothingness, a terrible silence descending on the room. Just the sound of Blackwell's strange, whistled breath, the dawn chorus of birds in the eaves outside the window.

"Take her away."

Away: to Greenwich Tower. Where I am to be held until Blackwell can assemble his retinue of alchemists in preparation for the spell. When he will take the Azoth and run me through with it, when he expects my stigma, his power, to be absorbed by the blade. For the power of both to be transferred into him, making him whole before uniting those opposites, transcending them, allowing him to live forever.

These are the words he uses to describe what will occur next. I use but one word, simple but final.

Execution.

I sit shackled in a wherry, floating down the murky Severn River. The waters are quiet at this hour, save for a few idling ships not wanting to risk getting moored in the morning's low tide. They wait in the middle, still as a raft of mallards. I find myself watching them, allowing myself to hope, just for a moment, that one of them is Peter's. A galley, maybe, with a hundred rowers at the helm to chase us down, pull up alongside us and whisk me away, saving me again the way he saved me before. But as we drift on by and there are no shouts, no anchors pulled, no row men and no pirates, I know that I am on my own.

Ahead, Upminster Bridge. Two dozen brick archways spanning the length of the water, topped by rows of leaning shops and taverns and lodging, some nearly four stories high. Like the waters, the bridge is nearly empty now, too early still for buildings to open their doors. But by noon, it will be madness: the pathway clogged with pedestrians and carts and carriages, stinking of mud and filth and people and waste. Caleb and I attempted to pass, just once; it took us an hour to get halfway. That was when he suggested we take to the river and swim our way across.

I wonder if he still remembers. How he jumped onto the low wall and stood teetering on the edge, arms wide as if he were flying, laughing. I laughed, too, because it didn't matter if he fell. He thought nothing could touch him then; we all did.

I glance at him, sitting behind me. I half expect to find his muted gray eyes on me, watching me the way Schuyler does when he's listening to me, hearing my every thought. Instead, he's looking above me. I turn to follow his gaze, and I see it: them. A dozen heads impaled on a dozen pikes, set on top of the southern gatehouse, their faces frozen in a mask of defiance, fat carrion crows with their black legs tangled in bloody hair and Keagan's shredded pamphlets, pecking away at what's left: skin, sinew, eyeballs. I don't recognize them but that doesn't matter; they are traitors and this is what happens to traitors. If I do not find a way out, it is what will happen to me.

Greenwich Tower looms into view, casting a long, dark shadow, black with ever-present mold. Beyond that, the castle itself, four flag-topped spires marking each corner. The iron gate slides open as we approach, as though it were expecting us. The boat slips through and bumps against the bottom of a set of stone steps, the same steps I climbed the night of the masque, the night John danced with me, the night he first kissed me.

Today no footmen take invitations, no roses bloom in the gardens, no guests arrive dressed in finery or wearing masks. It's only Caleb and me standing at the top of the watergate, staring across the landing, across the now-bleak landscape to the park beyond. Guards in black teem from a nearby tower and make their way toward us, their footsteps crunching in the gravel. They pull me from Caleb's grasp, make a show of checking my bindings around my arms, my feet.

While the Prayer on the Eve of Battle continues to run through my head, I tick through my options of escape.

I think of unshackling myself, but I can't without my stigma: I don't have the strength to break through the iron on my own. I spy a rock, two, scattered along the path. Consider snatching one up, smashing the guards with it before smashing my chains, then reject the idea immediately. It would take too long and be too loud.

I could try to escape the grounds. But how? I could probably outmaneuver the guards; they've never been much of a challenge. Then what? The river? I could scale the wall; even chained, I could still manage that. I'd have minutes—ten at most—before the other guards were alerted to my absence. It would be better to hide somewhere on the grounds, wait for cover of darkness to sneak away. But by then they'd have every guard, revenant, and Knight of the Anglian Royal Empire after me. And they would find me.

Of course, then there's Caleb. He would stop me before I could take the first step in any one of these plans. But I've got to figure out something. Because when Blackwell comes for me, when he tries to retrieve my stigma and discovers I don't have it, he will turn Caleb on me. He will turn Marcus and Linus on me, he will force me to tell him what happened to it. I will never tell him; I swear it on my life. But it is not only my life I am concerned about.

We pass the guards' station, the servants' quarters, and the lieutenants' lodgings, built back when Greenwich Tower was a defensive castle only. They could almost be mistaken for Upminster town homes: white plaster and dark-timbered facades, thatched roofs, rough-hewn wood doors painted in a charming shade of robin's-egg blue.

We reach the house at the end. I've never been inside before—I had no reason to be—but unlike the others, this one is no lodging: I know this by the heavy, barred door. The guards unlock it, and Caleb pushes me inside and up a set of circular winding stairs, through another and yet another locked, barred door into what looks like a holding room. It's strangely large, bright, and clean: high walls inset with leaded glass windows, fresh rushes strewn along the floor, a wide wood bench along one wall, and a fireplace along the other, though it's unlit.

The door shuts on me; the lock clicks into place. The guards turn and leave. Only Caleb remains: standing at the door, hands wrapped around the bars, watching me. It's a familiar scene, so reminiscent of the time I stood behind bars at Fleet, when I still believed in him, trusted him; when I still believed we could get through anything as long as we were together.

I start to turn away when Caleb's strange, murky voice breaks the silence.

"I have to tell him everything now," he says. "Everything he asks. I have to do everything he demands."

This is typical. Revenants are always beholden to the witch or wizard who returned them from the grave. The magic that binds them together requires it. I don't know why he's telling me this, but perhaps there's a way I can use it to my advantage.

"Yes," I say cautiously. "You will have to do everything he demands as long as he is alive. And once he has my stigma, he will always be alive."

"Don't manipulate me." Caleb's words turn quick, sharp; maybe I'm imagining it but I think I see a flash of blue behind his cloudy gray eyes, but then it's gone.

I nod, acknowledging the accusation. "Even so, it's the truth. You know it is."

He says nothing, at first. Then: "You don't know what it's like." His voice is quiet, hesitant; a whispered secret in a barred confessional. "I feel nothing. I know everything. I exist, yet I do not. I am no one but who he tells me to be. I want to escape. I don't know how to escape. I don't—" Caleb stops himself. "I have to go. He needs me." He releases the bars and backs away. "I would not," he adds, "turn your back."

"What?"

Caleb shifts out of sight. And in his place Marcus appears: black cloak, black hair, those gray eyes black with hate and want for revenge.

22

I SPEND THE NEXT FOUR nights in a cold, dark, tomblike room in the presence of the dead.

I don't sleep for long; I don't dare. Instead I sit perched on the edge of the bench, pinching myself to stay awake, succumbing to five-, ten-minute snatches of rest when I can't. Every waking moment is devoted to the Prayer on the Eve of Battle, a liturgy on a loop, keeping Marcus from my thoughts. He finds them anyway—not all of them but some—taunting me with carefully buried memories of childhood and of training, of my time spent with Malcolm, my parents' deaths and Caleb's, whispered in his loamy, rotting voice.

Not once does he mention John.

Not once do I turn my back.

I don't have to wonder why Marcus was given the job of guarding me. Caleb could have kept me from escaping just as well, but he would not have kept me awake for the purpose of unhinging me. He would not have stared at me all through the night, unblinking, seeing everything. Almost everything.

The only thing left to wonder is what will happen.

Days pass slowly, murky light breaking through quilted clouds each morning, escaping on dust motes through leaded glass each evening. I'm light-headed with exhaustion, my limbs and eyelids heavy with vigilance. The only sounds in the room are Marcus and his malignant mutterings, me and my mitigating prayer.

In the tower outside, bells chime out the hours. Then, on the fifth chime of the fifth day, Marcus finally stops speaking. Rises to his feet. I still don't move, rooted to the bench with manifest fear, watching how he cocks his head, a lupine gesture, toward the window. Listening to something I can't hear. Then he turns to me, a slow, sly grin crossing his face.

Today is the day.

I have to escape.

I don't know what to do.

I hear the echo of a clank, a key in an iron lock, the creaking of a door hinge. Footsteps on a stone staircase. Guards appear at the window of my door then, two of the same men that escorted me here. They let themselves in. It's not difficult to spot the caution on their faces; I don't know if it's directed toward me or toward Marcus.

The guards don't give an order, they don't have to: Marcus lurches for me, rips me off my spot on the bench. I struggle against him, against the chains still bound around my ankles and wrists; useless. Then, with Marcus on one side of me and the guards on the other, they march me out the door. My heart taps fast against my rib cage. I've got to do something, and time is running out.

We wind down the stairs until we reach the door at the bottom. One guard pulls out a key and unlocks it, the other holds it wide for Marcus to step through, keeping a wide berth. For a moment, just a moment, I'm left alone with them.

But a moment is all I need.

I swipe my hand through my hair, snatch the hairpin from the knot at the nape of my neck, still tucked there from nearly a week before. Jam it into the locks in my bindings, feel them catch, hear them snap open. Marcus hears it, or senses it; he spins around just as I reach forward and slam the door shut, jamming the bolt into place.

The guards advance. I throw my elbow up and back, hard, catching one in the nose. It cracks, breaks; blood spurts onto the floor as he bends over, groaning. I take him by the back of the head and slam it into my knee; he drops to the ground. The other guard turns to run, but he's not fast enough. I grab his arm, whirl him around, my fist is at his mouth before he can utter a sound. He joins the other guard on the floor in a heap.

Marcus batters himself against the door like an enraged wild animal.

I run like hell.

Up the twisting stairs, back to my cell again. Throw myself through the door, slam it shut, and lock it, yanking more pins from my hair and cramming them into the latch so it can't be opened from the other side.

I've got seconds, if that, before Marcus escapes and reaches me. I snatch the apron from my soiled woolen dress, wrap it around my fist as I've done before, and smash it through the window that overlooks the back of the lodging house, the opposite side from where Marcus still hammers on the door. Shards of glass fall from the frame and crackle to the floor. I move around them carefully in my worn leather slippers; I cannot cut myself, I cannot bleed.

I step onto the narrow window ledge, peer into the dawn and the darkness below. I don't know what might be down there; I didn't get a chance to scout it before, not with Marcus watching my every move. Likely it's a stone path. But what if it's an iron gate? A pitched roof? I could impale myself, I could hit the heavy, shale slats and knock myself unconscious; roll to the ground and break a leg, condemning myself to capture.

I'm willing to take the chance.

I don't get it.

The door to my cell explodes open, and Marcus is through it like a battering ram. He's fast—I cannot get used to his speed—and he's on me, fisting the collar of my dress with an iron, unforgiving hand. I'm yanked from the ledge, hard, thrown to the floor. I land on my stomach, the wind knocked out of me. I scramble to my back but immediately wish I hadn't. To look him in the face is to be terrified: He looks furious, vengeful, and worst of all, amused.

He grabs me, grasps my head between both palms, and begins to squeeze. The pressure of it lifts me off my feet; it splinters my vision, at once going white, then red, then black. He's going to crush my skull. He's going to kill me with his bare hands. He mutters obscenities at me; his breath is in my face and it is not human. It is dark and black and oily; it smells of dirt and death and decay.

"Marcus." Caleb's voice breaks into my screams. He stands at the door, hands curled into fists, either in anger or restraint. "Release her."

Marcus starts like a scolded dog, pulling his hands from my head. I don't expect it and I slump in a heap to the floor, my head knocking against the stone.

"Now go." Caleb points to the door, blown open on its hinges. "I'll have to tell him of this. You know what will happen when he hears."

"I was told to prevent her escaping," Marcus says. "Using whatever means necessary. That is what I did."

"Make your excuses to him," Caleb replies. "I don't have the time or the use for them."

Marcus glares first at Caleb, then at me before stalking from the room. I don't know what to say to him: Thank him for stopping Marcus from killing me? Rail against him for it? Because wherever he's taking me, it's no better than where I am now, and the fate is the same.

But I don't get to decide because in an instant Caleb is beside me, pulling me to my feet. In the space between one breath and another my wrists are bound once more, a blindfold strapped over my eyes. He marches me back down the stairs, no chance of escaping this time.

Outside, the sound of gulls wheeling overhead, the gust of cool wind on my face, and the brackish scent of the Severn River are my only sensations. I begin to struggle, but I know it's no use and I stop. Whatever strength I have left for whatever happens next, I'm going to need it.

The scent and the damp, velvety feel of grass give way to the crunch of gravel; the gravel gives way to pavers, then the dank smell and sudden coolness of a tunnel. I try to sort out where he's leading me. It could be any number of places, none of them good: This is Greenwich Tower, after all.

A slight stumble as we cross a threshold, the creak of a door, then the sensation of falling. Stairs. They go on and on. I've counted sixty, yet we keep going, deep beneath the Tower, into the ground. Into the earth.

The earth.

I begin to struggle again, bucking and twisting against his grasp. But it's as though I'm wrestling with a stone pillar. My skin chafes and burns, and I wind up nowhere.

Finally, we reach the bottom of the staircase, hitting solid floor. I start a little at the cold smoothness of it, at the ringing echo of our footsteps.

"Where am I?" I don't bother to hide my fear; Caleb knows it anyway. "What is this place?"

Instead of his reply, there's a low rumble of chuckles in the room, not from just one man but from many. It makes the hair on my neck stand on end, the kick of buried fear taking flight in my chest. Caleb's hand fumbles to the back of my head, pulls away my blindfold.

I'm in a small circular room that I've not seen before. The floor underfoot is marble, the same that lines the walls and the ceilings. Brown, veined with white; an elegant tomb. Glittering stones inset into the floor form a star with eight points, marking the cardinal and intercardinal directions. In the middle, a table. Narrow, long, shining wood.

It's a ritual room.

I've seen them before, rudimentary versions of this. Dirt or brick walls, never marble. Twigs or rocks to mark the directions, never inlaid with precious gems. Rough-hewn candles made of tallow and stinking of fat instead of elegant oil lamps, cut glass hung from brass brackets along the walls.

Eight men stand in a circle around the edge of the room, surrounding me. I spin around, looking at each of them in turn. They're cloaked and hooded, so I can't see their faces or tell who they are. They all look the same. But I know one of them by his height, his presence; I know him by the sword at his side, emeralds on the hilt glittering like a pulse.

I know it's useless, but I run anyway. Spin on my heel and sprint toward the door that Caleb just led me through, the door that not sixty seconds ago was there.

Only now it's gone.

At once, the eight men converge on me. I duck past one, knock into another. Jam into one with my shoulders, get past him only to run into another. I kick him, my hands useless and bound before me.

Someone grabs me from behind. I buck and I twist, gnashing at his arms, his hands, my teeth sinking into his flesh and drawing blood. He thanks me for it with a slap to my face, hard enough to rattle bones.

They throw me onto the table, faceup. Someone procures a length of rope and wraps it around me, around the table, binding me to it. I'm completely immobile. I twist my head around, side to side, watching as the men produce candles from beneath their cloaks, lighting them from the oil lamps before setting them along the edge of the eight-pointed star. A small wooden bowl of salt is set on the cardinal point north. A larger candle, also lit, set on the point south. A bundle of herbs east, a chalice of water west. Four directions, four elements, four virtues, four phases of time, all leading to a single, final end.

There's a rustle, then a squawking sound. A rattle of bars. A tall, hooded man steps forward; in his hands is a small black cage holding a huge black raven. He pulls out the bird as Blackwell holds up the Azoth. There's a flash of green, a caw, a rustle— then silence. A dripping noise, the scent of iron, a wet thud as the dead bird is thrown into the center of the star. A sacrifice.

It all happens fast now. Blood smeared on the wall, shapes and figures I can't decipher. Herbs held over the flames, catching fire, then quickly put out, still smoking, the scents mingling with the blood. The swish of robes. All the while murmuring, chanting, an incantation.

I twist against the rope, my head whipping from side to side, when suddenly the room disappears. No marble, no glittering compass, no candles. No dead raven and no hooded men. Only a dark room. A hole, a tomb. No way in, no way out.

The room flickers back to marble, then back to dark. Over and over again. The chanting grows louder, drowning out my shouts that give way to my screams. Marble, dirt. Men, no men. Light, no light. Faster, faster.

Blackwell appears before me then, the Azoth held high. Something flares inside me at the sight of it, the heat and pull and desire of the curse.

My pulse thunders now.

A swish of air as the blade is lifted. I take a breath, likely my last, wait for the point to impale me, for me to bleed onto this table, to die; the only solace is knowing that if I do, Blackwell will never get what he wants.

He pauses. I think, maybe, wildly, that the blade recognizes

241

me, knows who held it these last weeks, refuses to turn against me. But the Azoth has no loyalty. It would just as soon kill me as anyone else, as long as it kills someone.

"What is this?" Blackwell's voice in my ear; his palm to my head, twisting it this way and that. "And this?"

I don't answer, because I don't know what he's asking. Then he answers for me.

"Bruises." The room falls silent, all chanting stopped. "On your face. Neck. How, Elizabeth, do you have bruises?"

I go still. Witch hunters do not get bruises. That is, witch hunters still protected by their stigmas do not bruise. All the care I took not to be cut, the care I took not to allow my secret to leak, now undone by the smallest of things: the imprint of Marcus's palms against my face as he tried to squeeze the life out of me.

"Where is your stigma?" Blackwell leans forward. Presses the tip of the Azoth against my cheek; it's still dripping with raven's blood. "What have you done with it?"

"I'll never tell you." Somehow I find the courage to look into his ruined face, one last defiance. "I will never tell you what happened to it."

This, to him, is no threat. He simply looks to Caleb, who steps toward me, hood lowered and eyes narrowed. He will try to read me, he will burrow into my head and he will try to find the answer to Blackwell's question. Once again I recite Malcolm's prayer, over and over, I fill every crevice of every thought with it; I will not let him in.

After a moment, Caleb shakes his head.

"There are other ways to retrieve this information." A smile crosses Blackwell's split face but it shouldn't: He does not know the lengths I will go to in order to keep it from him. He jerks his head at his men. "Take her."

The same tall, hooded figure who held the caged bird now clamps his hand around my wrist; unseen hands fumble with the rope. I stop my prayer long enough to direct one to Caleb to end me first, before they do. Blackwell has many avenues of making me talk; roads littered with the dungeon and the rack, eye gouging and tongue cutting, split knees and sawed limbs and irons and screams.

But Caleb remains still, mute to my pleas.

The rope slithers to the floor. I'm hauled to my feet, wrists still shackled, and dragged to the door that has now reappeared. I begin to imagine the things they will do to me, but I don't imagine this: a scuffle, a startled shout; a squeeze of my arm and a flash of light before the room once more goes dark. I'm being crushed, my lungs don't draw breath. I can't see. I'm moving, flying, yet immobile, going nowhere.

Then, finally, silence. Vast. Endless.

Complete.

23

THE FIRST THING I NOTICE is warmth.

The smell of carbon: flames, but not ritualistic or stinking of oil, or of death. These flames are friendly: the rosemary-scented fire of holiday and family and life. The grip on my arm is still there, joined now by a hand on my shoulder, firm but gentle. This, too, feels friendly, but I'm unsure. Too many things that started out as one thing have too quickly turned to another, and not for the better.

"Elizabeth." A whisper in my ear then, a voice I know. Quiet, reassuring. Fatherly. "You're safe now. You can open your eyes."

I do.

I'm kneeling on a soft rug, and I know it, too: flowers and vines woven in yellow, orange, and green. The fire I smell roars in a familiar hearth; woodland tapestries draped across white plaster walls, wide-open ceilings.

Before me: Peter, crouched on his knees, smelling faintly of tobacco and something sharper—whiskey; brandy, maybe. He fumbles with the bindings around my wrists, my ankles, they unlock and he throws them aside; they land across the room with a clatter. Then he pulls back to look at me, his eyes dark and red-rimmed, his skin pale, his clothes rumpled. He looks so much like John I have to turn away.

Someone hovers beside me. Slowly, I turn to face him: a tall, dark-robed figure from the ritual room, no longer holding a candle but a stone. A lodestone, still giving off a faint, pulsating glow, a thin veil of white smoke. Slowly, he lowers his hood.

Nicholas.

"You," I say. My voice is hoarse from screaming. "How?"

"Keagan," he replies. "And Schuyler. They told me what happened at Ravenscourt, then Schuyler told me where you'd been taken. Keagan helped me devise a way in; Fifer helped me devise a way out."

So Keagan made it back from Ravenscourt alive. "And what of Malcolm?" I say. "Is he safe, too?"

"Yes," Nicholas replies. "They are both alive, and they are both well."

"They're at Rochester." This from Fifer, standing in the shadows by the fireplace, Schuyler by her side. She's wearing a dressing gown pulled over sleep clothes, but she doesn't look as if she's been sleeping. "Waiting to hear word of you."

I don't say anything to this. I shouldn't be here, I shouldn't be alive; there should be no word of me because I should be dead. But I can think of none of this now, not after what I know.

"Blackwell's plan." I look to Nicholas. "What he intends to do. Is it possible?"

Nicholas discards that hateful hooded robe, carried off by Hastings's unseen hands, and doesn't answer right away.

"Perhaps," he says finally. "If you'd told me before, I would have said it was but a lark, a far-fetched scheme on his part. He required the Azoth to achieve it; he never would have gotten to it. Not hidden behind my walls, not protected by my spells. Now he has it."

He says this not in accusation but in fact; guilt sickens me anyway.

"And now he needs but one thing to reach his goal, this one far more attainable."

He means John, of course.

"We've got to get to camp," I blurt. "Fitzroy needs to know what's happened so he can rally his men. Protect John. I need to tell him; it's my fault, I'll go—" I get to my feet but stumble as I do, exhaustion pinning me to the floor.

"You will not." Peter takes one arm; Schuyler steps forward to take the other. Instinctively, I flinch from them; their grasp like those of the guards, and of Marcus and Caleb. At this thought Schuyler releases me, but Peter holds fast. "Let's get you upstairs," Peter continues. "Cleaned up. Rested."

"I can't rest," I tell him. "Not now. Not after what I did."

I look to Fifer then, remembering how angry she was with me before I left, how she tried to stop me, how I all but blackmailed her to help me. How she was a friend to me and I was no friend back. To Peter, for once again failing to save his son. To Nicholas, because he put himself in great danger—once again—to save me. This after I lied to him and stole from him, after I lost the Azoth, a great asset that has now become a great threat.

"I'm sorry," I say finally. "I thought I could end this. I thought I could kill Blackwell, but I was wrong. I overestimated my abilities," I add, and it shames me to admit it.

"Perhaps," Peter says with a squeeze to my arm. "But not as much as you underestimated his."

"I don't know what to do," I whisper, as much to myself as to them.

"You are going upstairs with Fifer, as Peter suggested," Nicholas says. "Get some rest. We will speak later, after I've had time to piece through all that has happened."

I don't argue with him; I don't dare. But before I turn from him I say, "Thank you. For coming after me. For risking yourself to save me. Again."

Nicholas rounds on me, swift. Places his hands on my shoulders, his expression grave as he looks at me. For a moment, I fear his anger, his recrimination, all of which I deserve but none of which I want to hear, at least not right now.

"If I have any wish for you," he says, "it is that you understand the value of what you risk. What you do is no longer about you alone. There are no longer people who will simply turn their heads if misfortune were to befall you, no matter how true that may have been in the past. You are not," he adds, in that way of his that makes me think he can read my mind, "replaceable."

Fifer's hand appears on my elbow then, soft and guiding, Schuyler close behind. Peter murmurs to me in a low, comforting tone as Nicholas's words burrow into me, finding their way to truth.

They lead me up the stairs: more plaster and wood, soft floors and tapestries, the occasional oil portrait of rough seas and prancing horses and vases of blooms—no painted kings or battles or weapons here—until we reach a door and the bedchamber beyond, welcoming in pale green and white, too bright for the darkness in my heart.

In the center is a tub already filled with water, steam floating from the top. Beside the bath is a chair stacked with bath sheets, a nightdress, a blanket, and a bowl of what looks like bath salt. That was fast. *One of the benefits of a ghost servant,* John said to me once.

"I'm going to see about food," Peter says. He smiles, but the strain still shows. "I'll be back soon." Then he and Schuyler step into the hallway, closing the door softly behind them.

"Fifer, I don't—" I start.

"Save it," she says, but there's no malice in her voice. "I'm still angry with you, but I'm more relieved you're not dead. You could have died. You should be dead."

"I know." I drop into a chair beside the fireplace, warm and crackling, and press my head into my hands. "I know."

"Yes. Well." She goes quiet and when I look up at her, she's watching me with an expression I'm not used to seeing from her: worry. "Let's get that dress off you," she says finally, extending a hand and pulling me to my feet. "The stench and the sight of it are unbearable."

It takes a moment; five days of accumulated filth sticks the fabric to my skin. I watch as Fifer drags it to the fireplace and shoves it inside. With a savage thrust of a fire poker, the grimy brown fabric goes up in flames.

I step into the bath. At once, the water turns dark and

murky with dirt. Fifer tosses in a handful of bath salt—what I thought was bath salt—and the grime disappears, winding backward in the water in tendrils before vanishing entirely. Magic. Then she reaches into the neck of her robe and pulls out her necklace: brass chain, ampoules filled with salt, quicksilver, and ash.

"I think it best we keep Caleb out of your head from now on." She slips it over my head. "Or anyone else who might be poking around in there. Schuyler told me about that prayer you kept reciting," she adds. "I figure you might be tired of saying it."

I lean back in the bath then, sinking into the warm soothing water. The fatigue I've held off for days rushes back in force and it's a struggle to keep my eyes open.

"What happened?" I ask after a moment. "After Caleb found me and everyone else got out? Did they run into trouble?"

"Schuyler said it was chaos." Fifer clears off the chair and pulls it beside the tub. "Guards pumping water from pipes in the courtyards, staff running around with buckets, people screaming. Everyone thought it was a kitchen fire, so no one was suspicious, at least not at first. But once they saw the blood and then found the bodies..." She pulls her robe against her, tight, as if warding off a chill. "By then, they were far enough away to avoid being caught. They ran full tilt for nearly two days to get here—Malcolm was near vomiting when the Watch found him."

"Were they arrested again?"

"No, although it was close. Malcolm, he was completely out of control. Demanded they go back for you, shouting at people, ordering weapons, horses; he even ordered Fitzroy to give him his army." Fifer tsks. "You'd think a deposed king would be less demanding, but you'd be wrong."

I nod. I don't find this behavior surprising, on or off the throne.

"Eventually, Nicholas had to give him something to calm him down. He slept for twelve hours, only to wake up and start his demands all over again." Another cluck of displeasure. "After you broke in and out of Hexham so easily, Fitzroy and Nicholas decided it was potentially unsafe to send him back, so they put him in Rochester under house arrest."

"What about Keagan?" I say. "Is she being detained, too?"

"Not entirely," Fifer says. "We thought she might be, but the council decided there was no cause to keep her. They released her to go home, back to Airann, but she asked to stay on to help us fight. But she's still an outsider, and a dangerous outsider at that. The council thought it best to restrict her to the grounds at Rochester. She's turning out to be a good ally," Fifer adds. "She's already sent word to the rest of the Order, asking them to join us. Keagan says they're as powerful as she is, if not more. We could use that."

I nod but say nothing, my thoughts already moving on to another prisoner at Hexham. Wondering where he is, if he's safe.

"John is at Rochester, too." Fifer guesses at my silence. "He's being held in a room somewhere in the west wing, but I don't know where. They're not allowing visitors. I haven't seen him, not even Peter has seen him. Only Nicholas and—"

She stops herself, but I already know what she was going to say. The only visitor John has besides Nicholas is Chime.

"Do you know if he's any better?"

Fifer looks down, her long, pale fingers plucking at the hem of her dressing gown. "I don't know." She shrugs. "I keep asking to see him, but Nicholas says it's best if I don't. So I assume not."

I shake my head. At the utter failure of my plan, at the danger I've put everyone in again: even more danger than they were in before.

"I should never have stayed in Harrow." I close my eyes. I don't want to see Fifer's face, her acknowledgment of this truth. "If I'd left, Blackwell would never have found out I didn't have my stigma. I could have kept the secret, and I could have kept John safe. I could have kept Blackwell on the run until the curse and his weakness eventually killed him."

"Do you really believe that?" Fifer's tone is so fierce I have to open my eyes and look at her. "Do you really think it would have been that easy? Knowing Blackwell's goal now, do you really believe you would have been able to outrun him on your own? Alone? With no power? That Caleb wouldn't have picked your mind clean and eventually led Blackwell here?"

"I don't know," I say.

"I think you do."

I take a breath then. Everything I know, and everything I don't, war with each other until I'm left with the casualty of knowing nothing at all.

"What now?" I say. "What happens now?"

"I think you know that, too."

I do. Blackwell will learn the truth about my stigma, he will come after John, after Harrow. He would have anyway, but now, with this provocation, it will be different. The attacks we've had, they were coquettes compared to what's coming. They will not be skirmishes; there will be no delay.

"It was always going to come to this," Fifer says. "And there's nothing you can do to stop it."

24

I MOVE BACK TO ROCHESTER. Nicholas wanted me to stay in his home, for a few more days at least, to recover. But you don't recover from Blackwell's devices. You absorb them. Shuffle them around, make room for them within a catalog already full of horrors until, eventually, you find a place for them. A place that is never hidden, but one day you hope will be just out of reach.

Nicholas escorts me back to camp, a silent guard against the stares and whispers of the others who fall still when they see us. Me, wrapped in a long green velvet cloak but still shivering under a cloudless blue sky; and Nicholas, a soothing but stalwart presence in robes of gold and ivory, threading us through the grounds.

Despite efforts to contain them, the details of my disappearance—and subsequent reappearance—spread like a virus through the camp. Everyone knows where I went, what I did, what happened to me, how I was brought back. News travels fast in Harrow, just as Gareth said.

Rings of white tents stretch out before me, flapping in the breeze like canvas sails. I veer toward mine, inner ring five, when Nicholas holds out a hand to stop me.

"Malcolm has requested your presence," he tells me. "It is your choice to refuse, of course, and I have made him no promises either way. We have passed along the message that you are here, and you are safe, but I think part of him won't believe it until he sees it for himself."

I hesitate. It was my plan to install myself back in my tent, then back in the pits; to run myself ragged with training both to atone for the things I've done and to prepare for the things Blackwell is about to do. But a visit to Malcolm is inevitable, and a small part of me wishes to see him for myself, too, to make sure he is as well as I've been told.

"Yes," I say. "I'll see him."

Nicholas takes me to the west wing of Rochester Hall, even grander than the east. Golden coffered ceilings, red-and-gold-brocaded walls fixed with miles of gold-framed oil paintings. Marble busts of Cranbourne Calthorpe-Goughs stare at me from pedestals, all of them awash in light from floor-to-ceiling windows framed by swaths of rich red velvet.

Guards line the many doorways, but I already know which door leads to the room where Malcolm is being held: Five men mill before it, none of them looking pleased. They snap to attention as we approach, pikes clanging to let us through.

Inside, Fitzroy and Malcolm sit at a small table by the

window overlooking a garden and the lush forest beyond. Silver trays, crystal goblets, and pewter plates filled with food line the surface. Malcolm looks up from his untouched plate, sees me, and scrambles from his chair.

"Elizabeth." His linen napkin flutters from his lap to the floor. "You're here."

In the past, when he would greet me this way, I would always curtsy. I almost do at present. But the impulse passes and I dip my head instead.

"I was told you wished to see me," I say. I'm aware of every eye in the room on us both.

"I did. I do," Malcolm says. He seems unaware of anything but me. "Would you care to eat? You must be hungry. Or perhaps drink…" He looks around as if he's expecting servants to leap forward to do his bidding, still surprised they don't.

Fitzroy saves us both from embarrassment. "Today is Sunday." He untucks himself from the table and turns to Nicholas, standing firmly by my side. "I understand they're roasting boar today. Not just one, mind, but an entire herd caught only last night, a spectacle I wouldn't mind seeing for myself. Perhaps you'd care to join me, Nicholas?"

Fitzroy gestures toward the door, but Nicholas smiles, apologetic. "Would that I could say yes! But I am Elizabeth's servant today, and I wish to see her settled safely in her tent."

"It's all right," I tell him, warming at his protection. "I can see myself there shortly. Or perhaps I'll meet you at the boars? I'd like to offer my thanks—and condolences—to the cooks who had to dress them."

Nicholas smiles at this, then glances at Malcolm. His

255

dark gaze holds Malcolm's pale one, and if I'm not mistaken, I see a flash of warning there. Then he and Fitzroy step out into the hall. The door slips shut and Malcolm turns to me.

"You're here." A faltering smile. "I know, I said that already. Are you well? Do you care to sit?" He rushes to Fitzroy's chair, holds it out for me.

"I'm fine," I say, a slender and abridged truth. "I'll stand."

Malcolm nods, his smile disappearing. "It was a frightening moment, there in Ravenscourt. So much magic. And to see Caleb like that..." He shakes his head. "I get news slowly here, you know. No one is rushing to tell me anything, which is understandable, of course. But Fitzroy told me everything regardless. Everything you went through..." Malcolm breaks off and I break in; I don't wish to relive it, not at all, but especially not with him.

"I see you and Fitzroy are on a first-name basis." I change the subject. "Is that because you're familiar, or because you've grown tired of saying his surnames? Or perhaps you've forgotten them."

"As someone with three given names, I understand what a disadvantage that can be. But to answer your question, we settled on first names mostly because Fitzroy didn't know what else to call me." His smile is back. "Although I suppose he could simply call me captain."

"Captain?" I repeat. "You?"

"Indeed. Of my very own fledgling army." Malcolm steps back, sweeps a hand toward a table on the other side of the room. It's covered in maps and parchment, chess pieces scattered across both. "Turns out a deposed king can come in handy, particularly when said deposed king learned battle strategy from the very king who usurped him." A pause. "That wasn't too maudlin, was it?"

I almost smile. "Not at all."

"Good. I've been working on it. Fitzroy said I was irritating when I got that way. Called me stroppy! He's as bad as Keagan. No respect." He says this last part in a put-on, lofty tone, and now I do smile.

"He's taught me a great deal about Harrow, and the people who live here. I'm glad for the knowledge, more so than the embarrassment of not having it before."

"Such as?"

"Reformists," he begins. "I thought they all practiced witchcraft, or at least had magical leanings. Not so. I'd say half the troops at camp are without magic. Neutral, Nicholas calls them. Funny word. In any case, since they don't have any magic to rely on, and since half of that half have never held a sword in their life, they've offered them to me to train."

"So you're in charge of all of them?"

"Oh, no. Half of that half doesn't want anything to do with me. That leaves just over one hundred men who can stand to be in my presence. Half of *that* half—"

"Malcolm."

"Sixty." Malcolm shrugs. "Sixty soldiers out of one thousand. But it is, as they say, a start. All things considered, I'm grateful for it. Fitzroy thinks if I do well enough by them, if I can turn metal into gold as the alchemists say, more will join in. That's what I'm planning right now." Another gesture at the table.

"When do you run drills?" I ask. "Maybe I'll come join you. Then you'd have sixty-one soldiers."

His expression is sunshine. "Yes. I'd like that. It would be nice to see a friendly face." He pauses, considering. "Well, a face, at any rate."

I do something then I didn't think I could: I start to laugh.

In the early days of training, when Caleb and I were new to the tests, when even he couldn't have imagined what we'd be asked to face or the things we'd have to do, he devised a way for us to manage the toll it was taking on us.

He showed up outside my dormitory at Ravenscourt one morning, dressed for the outdoors and carrying a bag, but he wouldn't tell me what was in it or where we were going. The sun was still rising, but the streets were already crowded and Caleb pulled me through them, cobblestoned and wide until they became gradually narrower, the smoke- and dung-scented air giving way to cottages and trees and grass, the scent of a village.

We traipsed up a hill; at the top was a cemetery. The gravestones tumbled over one another like pirates' teeth, jumbled and cracked and stained. Headless statues scattered throughout, fighting for space among the trees. There were no people around, no paths, no flowers; it was a place that had been forgotten, just like the dead that lay there.

Caleb found a flat patch of grass nestled in the center of a half-dozen tombstones and sat down. He pulled his bag off his shoulder and opened it, pulling out food wrapped in linen: bread, ham, cheese, fruit he'd filched from the kitchen.

"What are you doing?"

He looked up at me. I expected him to tease me, as it was obvious what he was doing. But for once, his blue eyes were serious. "Eating," he replied. "It's been a while since you ate, hasn't it? I know it has for me."

I thought about it. It had probably been days since I ate, but who could know? It had probably been days since I slept, but who could know that, either? I sleepwalked through them; it was the only sleep I would get.

"How did you find this place?" I settled onto the ground across from him. He tore off a piece of bread and handed it to me. It was still warm from the oven.

"I don't know," he replied, chewing as he talked. "It was sometime after the second test. You know, the one at the Serpentine."

I swallowed. Blackwell had taken us to Serpentine Lake, a forty-acre lake inside Jubilee Park where the royal family spent their summers boating and fishing. He commanded us to swim across it—it was December; freezing and snowy—and none of us knew how. We were forbidden to help one another. It was an agonizing day spent listening to two of the recruits slowly drown: their pleas rending the frozen air, then all at once silent. One of them was only twelve.

"I couldn't stop hearing their voices," Caleb continued. "So one night, after three with no sleep, I just started walking. I had no destination in mind; I just wanted to move. I found myself here after several hours. Ironic, no?"

I managed a small smile.

Caleb took another bite of bread. "I sat here for I don't know how many hours. Looking out at all these gravestones, these markers, these people... They're all dead, Elizabeth.

More than that: They're forgotten. When was the last time someone thought of them? Enough to come see them? Look around. It's been a while."

Years, at least, by the look of it.

"It hit me then," he said. "No matter what's happened to us, what we've been through, what we've had to see, at least we're not them. At least we're not dead. We're not like them, Elizabeth. We're alive."

It was a small comfort, but it was the only one we had. So we spent the afternoon in that cemetery, both of us eating, Caleb leaning against a tombstone and napping. When I got back to Ravenscourt, I slept for the first time in four days.

We were alive.

Despite the chain around my neck, the soft pallet beneath me, and the relative safety of my tent—guarded now, for I've made more than a few enemies—I still can't sleep: Visions of Blackwell and his ruined face, of Caleb and his ruined life, haunt my nightmares. After my third sleepless night, I rise, dress, sling my bag over my shoulder, and step into the cold predawn morning, silent and still around the edges. I stop by the food tent, still waking up; the pair of cooks inside yawning as they measure grain into a vast, bubbling kettle. When I appear in the doorway they say nothing. But after a moment the older cook, a woman dressed in gray, steps forward and presses a bundle into my hand.

"It's not much," she says. "The cheese is a little hard, the bread's gone a little stale. But you look as if you could eat."

I thank her, place the food inside my bag, then thread my way through the sea of sleeping tents, across the field and over the bridge, out of Rochester.

Three hours later, I find myself in Hatch End, standing before the black gates of the cemetery that lies beside Gareth's home. They're locked, but only about seven feet high, and even as tired as I am I scale them with ease. I skirt along the side of the chapel, through the flat patch of grass with neatly lined gravestones. Then, just as Caleb and I had done so many times so many years ago, I tuck beside an obelisk, unpack the food from my bag, lay it before me. But it is not the same.

I am alive, yes. But Caleb is dead, and it is not the same.

I don't know how long I sit there, my back against the stone, a flat of bread in my hand, before I see him. He creeps toward me, silent as a ghost.

"You followed me?" I look up at him, his hair quicksilver-bright in the nascent sunlight. "Why?"

Schuyler shrugs. "Wanted to see how you were coming on. Haven't seen you around much, and Fifer's worried about you. You've been keeping busy."

Since I returned to camp, I've spent much of my time with Malcolm, as promised, helping run his men through exercises, showing them things I've never shown anyone: things no one should see. Ways to injure, ways to maim, ways to kill. We managed to add some twenty-odd soldiers to Malcolm's retinue after a demonstration in which I took out a band of wolves—magically conjured by Nicholas—with nothing but a pair of knives and a handful of coniferous tree branches.

"You think it's a good idea?" Schuyler continues. "Coming here?"

"Why not? Gareth isn't here." I shrug. "He's been locked up in council meetings. Malcolm said he's not left Rochester in a week."

"Not what I meant." Schuyler brushes aside a pile of leaves and settles down beside me, leaning against a mossy tomb. "You sure it's wise, convening with the dead like this?"

"I'm convening with you, aren't I?"

"Point." Schuyler raises a hand.

I glance at him. At those almost unnaturally bright blue eyes, slightly dimmed today by worry or trouble or both. My thoughts run to Caleb again.

"He told Blackwell I was coming," I say. "Caleb. He said he has to tell him everything he knows, everything he thinks. He said Blackwell demanded it of him."

"Yes," Schuyler says. "Blackwell is Caleb's pater—the one who brought him back—so Caleb must do what he orders. Everything he orders."

"But he didn't tell Blackwell I didn't have my stigma."

Schuyler shrugs. "He probably couldn't hear you clearly enough to figure it out. I had a hard time hearing you through that damned prayer, and I've got years of practice. Caleb is new. It's hard to focus on a single person's thoughts, when there are so many others to hear."

"I suppose," I say. "But in the ritual room, I wasn't saying the prayer. Not at first. I was too tired, too worried about what was about to happen. Caleb could have dug in, he could have heard everything. But when Blackwell asked him where my stigma went, he said he didn't know." I pause. "Do you think he did, and that he lied to Blackwell about it?"

"I don't see why he would." Schuyler breaks off a piece of

bread, tosses it into the grass. A pair of birds flutter to the ground beside us and begin pecking at the crumbs. "He didn't do anything to stop what was happening to you. At any rate, it's not a matter of choice. A revenant's will is completely subordinate to that of his pater. He doesn't—" He stops, abrupt.

"You don't have to talk about it," I say quickly.

"It's not that," he says. "It's just that it's hard for me to recall. It's been a few hundred years since I thought about it. I don't even remember how long it actually has been. Do you know I don't even remember my surname?"

"You don't?" I don't know whether to be amused or horrified. I decide on the latter. "I'm sorry."

"I'm not." Schuyler grins, wicked. "Feels rather legendary, having only one name."

I fall silent a moment, recalling the way Caleb spoke to me, the way he whispered to me through the door, as if he were telling me a secret. The way he seemed at turns angry and defiant, then almost contrite.

"Caleb cannot physically disobey Blackwell." Schuyler interrupts my thoughts. "But it doesn't mean he has to be loyal. There are a thousand ways to show disloyalty besides disobedience."

"Such as?"

Schuyler shrugs again. "Revenants are very base creatures," he says. "The word itself means 'to return.' When they do, they're like infants, in a way. They know only base desires."

I note his use of the word *they*, as if revenants are a separate entity from himself.

"It's an indelicate balance," he continues. "They are beholden, but they don't want to be held. Some—most—simply bide their time, obeying in simmering resentment until their pater dies, until they can finally be free. Others, shall we say, take matters into their own hands, inasmuch as they can."

"How do you know this?"

Schuyler fixes me with his bright, knowing gaze. "Because I had my pater killed."

I open my mouth; nothing comes out.

"He asked me to buy a ship; I bought him a ship," Schuyler says. "What he didn't ask was for me to buy him a sound ship or a competent crew. The ship was full of weak timber and shoddy sails; the crew not a crew at all but beggars and vagabonds looking for coins and drink; they didn't care how they got it. Nor did he ask me to ensure the weather would be clear when we sailed. So when we did, we hit a storm, the ship fell apart, every last man on board died. Except yours truly."

I swallow a lump of bread that's somehow turned to stone.

"It's the things a pater doesn't ask that can be taken advantage of." Schuyler throws me a look, a half smile on his face. "You can exorcise a revenant with salt all you want, bijoux, but the devil inside still remains."

He stops then, his hand frozen midthrow, the bread still poised between his fingers. Then he's on his feet in a blur, snatching my cloak and hauling me up. The bread tumbles from my lap; the birds converge. He hauls me behind the obelisk.

A second later, the door along the side of the cathedral opens—the same door I let myself out of the day of my trial, the day Blackwell's attacks came—and Gareth steps out. He's accompanied by another man, dressed in all black like a councilman, only I don't recognize him at all.

"I thought you said he was at Rochester," Schuyler whispers.

"I guess I was wrong," I whisper back. "But does it really matter? He won't like our being here, but it's not as if he'll arrest—"

"*Shh.*" Schuyler clamps his hand over my mouth.

"I understand things have changed. But I cannot be expected to settle all my affairs in one week," Gareth says.

"And what affairs would those be?" asks the man.

"I—" Gareth stops. "My home."

"Provided you have one left," the man says. "At any rate, there are plenty of fine homes to be had in Upminster."

"That was not the plan," Gareth says.

"Ah, but that should not faze you." The man holds up an appeasing hand. "You are, if nothing else, a master planner. I should think this is nothing to you. Even so, it is our role, is it not? To do whatever it takes?"

Gareth considers this, then nods. *"Faciam quodlibet quod necesse est."*

Blackwell's motto.

Schuyler's hand is back over my mouth, stifling the gasp and the realization:

Gareth is the spy.

25

THE MAN IN BLACK VANISHES then—disappears into nothing, seemingly into thin air. Gareth glances around, furtive, before striding down the path, out the gate, and onto the road leading toward Rochester. Schuyler keeps his hand pressed to my mouth, waiting for him to pass out of earshot. Minutes pass. Finally, he lets go. Snatches my bag from the ground and darts out from behind the obelisk.

"One week?" I say. "Does that mean Blackwell and his men will be at Harrow in one week?"

"I presume." Schuyler's on his knees, stuffing my things into my bag, ruffling the ground to scatter the bread crumbs, erasing evidence of our presence.

"What are we going to do? Schuyler." I grab his arm to stop his frantic and pointless tidying. "Stop that. You need to listen to Gareth. Find out what else he knows."

"I can't." Schuyler rounds on me. "I already tried. Can't hear a thing. My guess is they were both wearing a barrier. Mercury, ash, like that damned necklace Fifer has. But I don't need to listen to know what they mean. One week until Blackwell sends his men to take Harrow, to take John, to take that stigma, and to go through with his bloody insane plan."

One week.

"We're not ready," I say. "The troops from Gaul haven't arrived yet, the Order hasn't arrived yet, Malcolm's men aren't trained yet... What are we going to do?"

"Tell Nicholas. Fitzroy. Prepare." Schuyler throws my bag over his shoulder. "It's all we can do."

"Do you think we should—"

"Kill Gareth? No." Schuyler picks up on my thought before I can voice it. "Can't go around killing councilmen, bijoux, even if they are traitors. No, we need to tell Nicholas and let him decide. After that, if he's looking for volunteers, I'll be first in line."

We start back toward Rochester. I wanted Schuyler to go ahead of me, to try to reach the camp ahead of Gareth. But Schuyler doesn't know the path he'll take, and neither of us can risk being seen.

Walking at turns fast and cautious, we reach Rochester sometime before noon. Smoke rends the air, the scent of food being readied for supper. People cluster in groups at the tables; stand in line at the bathing tents, the laundry tents, the weapons tents; sit around multiple fires that spring in rows along the ground. In the distance, men scatter along the jousting pits, either sparring or watching, some at the archery butts, others running drills in the adjoining fields.

Schuyler and I look through the crowds, searching for one man taller than everyone else, one man dressed better than everyone else, and one man more traitorous than everyone else.

We don't see Nicholas, Fitzroy, or Gareth anywhere.

"Let's split up," I say. "I'll stay here, search the tents. You go inside. Check Malcolm's quarters, too," I add as an afterthought. "Fitzroy may be there."

Schuyler nods. "I'll fetch Fifer first. She needs to know what's happening, and she can help me look. If we don't find them, or even if we do, we'll meet you in an hour in the chapel."

He slips into the crowd then, and I turn and make my way toward the tents, flipping the hood of my cloak over my head as I go, pulling it down low. I don't want to be seen, I don't want to be stopped, and right now, I don't want to speak to anyone but Nicholas or Fitzroy.

The crowd thins as I reach the ring of officer tents. Men in uniform, men carrying weapons, men poring over maps and endless lists of inventory. I'm spared a glance, two, as I thread through them, but still no Nicholas, and no Fitzroy.

I leave the relative safety of the inner ring and make my way to the jousting pits. Nicholas won't be there, but Peter might, and he might be able to tell me Nicholas's whereabouts. I'm squinting under my hood into the bright sun and I don't see him until I'm nearly on top of him: a boy in a navy-blue cloak standing beside a girl bright as a winter rose in a crimson gown, her hand clutching his arm.

John.

"Elizabeth." His eyes, still shadowed but not as deeply as last I saw him, grow wide at the sight of me. My heart, running rapid before, launches into a sprint.

"You're back," Chime adds, when John falls silent and I don't reply. "I was so pleased to hear you were safe," she adds, but the pique behind her words tells me different.

"Yes." I dart my eyes left, right; I look for an escape but there is none. Not from John's intense, searching gaze, and not from the three other boys, John's friends—some I recognize, some I don't—who walk up and encircle me. I feel vaguely hunted.

"I see you've returned," one of them says. "Returned, recovered, and now helping one king to try to kill another."

"Yes," I repeat. I think if I don't speak too much, they will grow tired of whatever game they're setting up for me and leave me be.

"Speaking of kings, I heard you faced Blackwell." Seb, the ginger boy, looks me over, that unpleasant smirk I've seen before crossing his face. "What was that like?"

I remember Marcus's hands against my skull, Blackwell's scarred face, the dead raven in the center of the ritual room. Caleb and the legion of dead guards; the prowling, all-seeing lions, the vengeful, red-eyed crows.

I look away and don't reply.

"I heard you lost the Azoth, too," another boy says. He's attractive, very much so, blond, blue-eyed, and tall like Caleb and Schuyler, though this does little to endear him to me. "You went through a lot of trouble, didn't you, only to create more."

I don't reply to this, either. Instead, I look at Chime, the only one of this company I can stand to look at, and then only barely.

"I'm looking for Nicholas. Have you seen him?" The courtesy in my voice, you could choke on it.

Chime opens her mouth, but John steps forward and answers before she can. "I have. He's in the solar, but you'll need an escort to the west wing. I can do that, if you wish."

I don't wish it. But I've asked for Nicholas, John knows where he is, and at the very least it leads me away from this uncomfortable gathering.

I turn away from them without replying and make my way to the yew alley and Rochester Hall beyond. I think, for a moment, John has decided against going with me, or was talked out of it. But then a fall of footsteps and the flutter of a dark cloak beside me tells me I was mistaken.

I reach the exterior hallway and the guarded door leading to the west wing. John nods to the men; they move to let us pass. Soon enough I'm standing in the solar—a place I have no fond memories of—looking around at the settees, the fireplace, the window embrasure, and the round mahogany table set with chairs.

It's empty.

I push the hood off my face and whirl around. John steps before the door, blocking my exit. His eyes are trained on my face, watching me closely.

"What are you doing?" My confusion mingles with apprehension. "Where is Nicholas?"

"I don't know," he confesses. "But I heard you were back at camp, and I wanted to talk to you. I've been looking for you all day." John pushes his hair back in a gesture that's familiar, his dark curls longer than when I saw him last. He looks more like himself.

But he is not himself.

"I tried the tiltyard, the archery, the training meadow, and the park, which is a mistake too early in the morning. I was almost trampled by a herd of deer."

"I'm sorry to inconvenience you," I say. My words are casual, indifferent, but the tremor in my voice betrays me.

"I don't care about that." He shakes his head. "It's not what I meant. I just meant I wanted to see you."

Latent anger flares up inside me. "The last time I saw you, you said you never wanted to see me again," I fire back at him. "Do you recall that? I do. You said you wanted to put this— me—behind you. And then you told me to leave, and to never come back."

"Elizabeth—" He steps toward me.

"While I appreciate the heroic effort you went through to find me, it wasn't necessary," I go on. "You don't need to tell me not to bother you, or get in your way. You're on your own now. Just like you wanted." Then, out of spite, I add, "But from what I saw, you're not so alone, are you?" Seeing John, talking to him, it's more painful than I thought it would be. I start for the door.

"Elizabeth, please, just listen." He reaches for me, but I pull away.

"Don't touch me." My eyes begin their telltale burning; my voice cracks. I am dangerously close to tears now. "Get out of my way." I push past him for the door again.

"Goddammit, listen to me!" John snatches my arm, turns me around. I start to tear away from him again, until I see

271

his face. Pale skin, eyes red, brows creased in an expression I know, or at least I used to: part pleading, part sadness, all misery.

"I was angry with you," he says. "I said things I wish I hadn't said. Stupid things I didn't even mean. And when I thought those would be the last words you ever heard from me—" John releases me and turns to the door. For a moment I think he's going to walk through it; I don't know if I'll stop him or let him go.

"The stigma." He turns back to me. "It does things to me. It makes me violent. Irrational. Not myself. But you know this already."

I nod, cautious.

"If I was unstable before I was put into Hexham, I was even worse after," he continues. "I got into fights with guards. Repeatedly. After you left, after you broke Malcolm and the other one out and you left, I was so angry. I injured one of them so badly they had to take him to a healer." He winces at that. "I was completely out of control. But you know this already, too."

I nod again.

"Nicholas came to release me from Hexham," John goes on. "Told me Fitzroy petitioned the council for custody of me, that he needed me to tend to his mother. It was a lie; I knew that much. I was told I'd be kept under house arrest, but that was a lie, too: Nicholas and Fitzroy had me quarantined. I was not allowed out. No visitors were allowed in, except Nicholas. I was allowed nothing but herbs and tools, books and potions. He wouldn't even give me an alembic at first; he was afraid I'd burn the house down."

John allows himself a rueful laugh, but I don't laugh at all.

"Within days, I started to feel better," he says. "I understood why they shut me away. Because the more I practiced my own magic, the magic of the stigma seemed to go away. And the more I returned to myself, the more I thought of you. I wanted to know what happened to you, if you were safe. But Nicholas wouldn't tell me anything, and I thought..." He flinches, stops. "The day he brought you back, he came to see me. And he told me everything."

"Why did he finally allow you out?"

John reaches out a hand for me, then lets it fall.

"Because he said you needed me," he says. "If you don't, tell me. I'll do my best to understand. But I need you. And I'll never stop trying to prove that to you."

With that, my resolve breaks. I take a step toward him; he closes the distance between us in three strides. I reach out and he crushes me to him. His arms around me, his hands in my hair, his lips on my face and his words in my ear: *I love you, I love you, I love you.*

Nicholas is silent as Schuyler and I tell him about Gareth.

The chapel is empty but for the five of us seated in the front pew: John to my right; Fifer, Schuyler, and Nicholas to my left. Light from the flickering candles set along the wall casts our blue shadows onto the marble floors.

"One week." Nicholas looks skyward, to the stars painted on the ceiling. "That will be because of the moon, of course."

I frown; everyone else nods.

Nicholas turns to me. "The day of the ritual, and of your rescue, the moon was in first quarter. Half light, half dark; in balance."

I think back to that morning—up until now I've tried not to—and I remember it as I perched on the sill of the window in my holding room, on the edge of my escape: hanging low in the still dark sky, striking in its half light.

"A moon phase is not required for his spell; the magic he is attempting is far beyond that of the sky," Nicholas continues. "But Blackwell is leaving nothing to chance, and that explains the timing. The next half-moon, the third quarter, will be in—"

"One week," Fifer says.

Nicholas nods. "It is likely Blackwell now knows John has the stigma. If not from Caleb, then from Gareth, who has no doubt pieced it together by now." A pause. "I would not have believed it was him. That Gareth would turn to Blackwell, that he would sacrifice all he held dear for what I can only assume is an elevated position in a new regime."

"He has always been ambitious," John says.

"Yes," Nicholas says. "And it will be his downfall."

Once again, I think of Caleb: of his unwavering ambition, how it drove him onward and upward until, eventually, it drove him into the ground.

"I don't understand," I say. "If Gareth has aligned himself with Blackwell, why then, at the trial, did he order me to kill him? And why did he send his scouts into Harrow? The information they were looking for, Gareth could have given him. He tipped his hand. If his men had never arrived, we wouldn't have known there was a spy within Harrow. Not until it was too late."

"When Gareth ordered you to kill Blackwell, he was no doubt following orders," Nicholas says. "Blackwell knew you would rise to the occasion; what better way to get you in his path? As for the scouts, I believe they were sent to confirm the information Gareth passed on to him. Traitors cannot be trusted, as Blackwell himself knows."

"What do we do?" Fifer says. "Do we alert the rest of the council? Have Gareth arrested? Detained at Hexham, or somewhere else within Rochester?"

Nicholas steeples his fingers together. "I think not," he says after a moment. "I think that would only hasten Blackwell's arrival into Harrow. If Blackwell discovered we knew the truth about Gareth, he would have no cause to delay his attacks. As I say: The quarter moon is not required for his magic, simply preferred. I do not believe he would sacrifice his military advantage for it."

"You know that I would never question you," Fifer says. "But the idea of Gareth walking freely around camp, listening to our strategies, hearing our secrets—more of our secrets—I can't stand the thought of it."

Nicholas looks to Schuyler. "Will you monitor him? As closely as you can? I know you said you cannot hear him, but I wish to make certain he has not ensnared anyone else, councillor or soldier, in his plans. And I wish to know who else he meets with, and who else he allows inside Harrow, within these next seven days."

Schuyler nods. "I'll shadow his every step."

Nicholas turns back to Fifer. "I know it is difficult to imagine, but sometimes it is best to let a plot run its course until the full extent of involvement is known. On both sides."

He gets to his feet. "In the meantime, all we can do is prepare. John, I ask that you tell your father; he will know to keep it silent, and he will want to know the danger you are in. I am going to find Fitzroy. He'll need to begin preparing his troops in a way that doesn't alert Gareth. The sooner, the better, I think."

26

ROCHESTER SPRINGS INTO ACTION. Troops begin arriving from Gaul, a thousand in the last twenty-four hours alone, another thousand due in the next twenty-four, over the safe, protected borders of neighboring Cambria and through the tunnels hewn beneath the Hall. Fitzroy leads drills. Malcolm spends dawn until dusk with his men, running them through exercises. And I've begun training again, too: mornings at the archery butts, drills in the afternoons, sparring with Schuyler in the evenings.

On the morning of the fourth day—three days until Blackwell's troops begin their attack—I slip from my tent and into the deep gray, cloudy morning light, eager to get started. Already I hear the trumpets in the distance, calling us to order. The sight of three thousand men marching in uniform over the hills sends a thrill through my veins.

Halfway to the training yard I spot John walking toward me. He stops before me, offers me a quick, tentative smile.

Unlike me, he's not dressed for drills. He's in brown trousers and a black cloak, the strap of his worn brown leather bag thrown over his shoulder. He takes me in, his eyes warm but also a little wary. We stand there a moment, looking at each other but saying nothing.

"How are you?" I say finally.

"I'm well," he says. "You?"

"I'm well, too." I shift a little at this awkward exchange.

I'm unused to being around John now. Unsure of how to act, what to say, or how to be with him. It was easy when he first came back to me, in the way that a crisis can charge down walls between two people. But in the days that followed, those walls were built up again, every word and every action calling attention to what raised them in the first place: the betrayal and the lies, the things he said, the things I didn't. I don't know how to knock them down again.

"Are you going somewhere?" I nod at his battered bag.

"I...yes," he says. "The apothecary. I haven't been in a while."

Of course he hasn't been in a while, because he was in prison. Because I put him there.

"What I mean to say is, my stores have run a bit low." John tries again. "So I thought I'd go in, pick some up. Do you—" He stops. Clears his throat. "I know you're busy and have things to do. But I'd love your company, if you're up for it."

I hesitate. If I don't report into drills, I'll have to answer to Fitzroy. He'll assign me to a menial task for punishment, dishes or laundry or weapons detail. But it's not just that. It's that I need to keep training. I don't have room to step back, not even a little. I start to say no, but then I see John's hands clenched into fists at his sides, the set of his jaw. The way his eyes dart around the camp, watchful and wide.

"Yes," I say. "Of course I'll come with you."

He reaches for my hand, cautious; I take it. Together, we start toward Rochester Hall, to the only entrance left open for us now, the heavily guarded and magicked front gate.

If we were trying to leave the camp unnoticed, we chose the worst time to do it. The trumpets sound their final, frantic call as men stagger from their tents, tugging on coats and tunics and boots, and leap to their feet in the meal tent, knocking over goblets and snatching the last of the food from their trenchers, spilling into the grass around us.

I don't miss the stares leveled in our direction, or the whispered disapproval as we pass. John sees—he's far too astute not to—but he holds on to me as if he might protect me from whatever they might say or do. And when he smiles at me and squeezes my hand, I know his protection is a promise.

The wall edges down.

Until I see Chime in the courtyard, sitting on a stone bench, the brightest thing under today's dull gray sky. She's surrounded by friends: The girls in rainbow-hued gowns I recognize from that day in the meal tent when John was arrested, and some of the boys, too; the same ones he sparred with, who encouraged his violence while at the same time discouraging me. The girls are playing some sort of dice game, the boys choosing sides and placing bets. But when they see us they stop: A roll of black dice hits the stone and stays there, no one bothering to pick it up.

"John." Chime greets him, ignoring me completely. "Are you leaving camp?"

"Just for a little while," John replies. "To pick up some supplies."

Chime arches a perfectly shaped eyebrow, then looks away.

"Back to healing, are you?" the boy beside her says, the blond one who harassed me a few days ago. "If you ever get tired of nursing old women and delivering babies, you're always welcome to join us again. Well, one of you is." He glances my way, nose flaring in distaste.

John lifts his finger to the air a half second before the trumpets blast their final call. The boys scramble to their feet, yanking on cloaks and holstering weapons.

"Enjoy wash duty," John says, tugging me from the court-yard.

The apothecary lies in the center of Harrow's high street in Gallion's Reach, nestled between the cobbler and the baker. It's nearly empty today: one or two merchants pushing carts along the road, a few standing in vacant doorways, watching as we pass.

John steers me into a side street that leads to the alley behind the shops. We cut through the mud and puddles of stagnant water until we reach a narrow, unassuming wooden door. He fishes a key from his cloak and unlocks the latch.

"The lock on the front door is broken," he says. "I've been meaning to fix it, but never got around to it."

We enter the back of the apothecary, into what looks like a storeroom. It's dim inside, the light from the one small window set high beside the door just enough to see by. There are great wooden barrels, baskets on shelves, crates in the center of the room. Set into a nook on the other side of the room is a bed, somewhere between a cot and a pallet. It's made up with clean white linens, unruffled and smooth, as though it hasn't been slept on in some time.

"My mother put that there," John offers. "She thought it might be useful to have an infirmary. It's not terribly welcoming, but it's away from the street, and quiet. Though as far as I know, no one was actually infirm enough to make use of it." He smiles, gestures to another door. "This way."

I've never been inside an apothecary before, but it's just as I imagined. The back wall is lined with shelves, crowded with bottles in all shapes and sizes, murky glass of green, amber, and red, wrapped in labels of yellowed parchment and scrawled with John's illegible handwriting. A few jars, presumably hazardous in some way—I smile at his elaborate rendering of a skull and crossbones—sit on the topmost shelf. A single large, opaque window of ochre glass bathes the room in a golden, almost otherworldly glow, and the battered door leading to the main street is bolted shut with a beam, the broken lock hanging by its hinge.

The rafters bristle with flowers and herbs in various stages of drying. I recognize a few by scent alone: lavender and anise, rue and cypress, hazel and marigold. The shop smells exotic, a mixture of sharp spices and tangy herbs along with something softer, candles or soap. It smells like him.

"I would say have a seat, but . . ." John looks around. "There doesn't seem to be one, does there? I don't usually have visitors, just customers. I could bring in a crate from the back for you to sit on, if you'd like."

"That's all right." I hop onto the countertop, littered with books and tools and parchment and pens, brushing aside a few as I do. "I'm fine here. Comfortable. It's nice."

He gives me a wry smile. "It's a mess. I would·say it's because I haven't been here in a while, but that's not really it. It pretty much always looks like this."

"What supplies did you come for?" I ask him. "Maybe I can help you collect them. I'm good at recognizing things; if you just give me a list I can—what?"

John's face, arranged in a careful expression of control, falls. "I didn't come here for supplies. I came here because I had to get away from camp. From the people, from training, from everything. I just...had to get away."

He crosses the room to an enormous cabinet standing beside the front door. Inside are shelves lined neatly with volumes of leather-bound books. He runs a hand along the stack, pulls one out, and walks it back to me.

"Remember how I told you that when I first came back to Rochester, Nicholas gave me books and supplies, in the hopes I would start practicing magic again?"

I nod.

"What I didn't tell you is that at first, I refused to touch any of it. I told myself I wasn't interested, but in truth, I didn't want to know just how far gone I really was. But when I finally forced myself to pick up one of the books, I saw what they were. Remedial texts. For children."

He smiles at me, but I can't bring myself to smile back.

"I went into a rage. Threw them at walls, I nearly threw them out the window. But before long, in the absence of anything else to do, I began to read them. There's not much to them, really: just pictures and descriptions of herbs, botanicals, flowering plants. It was magic I already knew, just buried inside the violence and the anger of the stigma.

"Now, when I feel it start to take hold, I go back to this." He gives the book in his hand a little shake. "Back to the beginning, to remind myself of what matters. It's starting over, I know that now. And I suppose, what I really brought you here for, is to ask if you would start over with me."

I hold out my hand. He passes me the book; the title written in gold on the brown leather cover: *Phytologiae Aristotelicae Fragmenta*. A text on botanicals.

"What do I do?"

"Just read me the names of the plants," he says. "And I'll tell you their indications."

I flip it open to the first page. "Hawthorn."

"*Crataegus laevigata*." He pulls himself up onto the counter across from me. "Parts used: leaves, flowers, fruit. Improves shortness of breath, fatigue, and chest pain. No known precautions."

I turn the page. "Skullcap."

"*Scutellaria lateriflora*. Leaves, stems, flowers. Used to relieve anxiety, insomnia, nervous tension." A muscle in his jaw clenches. "Known precautions: May cause drowsiness, and when combined with germander; may cause toxicity."

"Goldenrod."

On we go. Page after page, herb after flower, plant after root. Eventually, John's posture begins to droop, his eyes begin to close. His voice grows softer, deep and hypnotic.

I flip the page one more time, and what I see makes me smile.

"Jasmine."

His eyes fly open. They find mine and they hold them, so full of longing my breath catches in my throat.

"*Parsonsia capsularis.* Parts used: petals and stems. As a tincture for abrasions, a compress for headaches and fevers."

He slides off the counter then. Steps in front of me. Takes a strand of my hair, coils it around his finger, tucks it behind my ear.

"Precautions: May cause rapid heartbeat, shallow breathing, nervous stomach."

Being this close to him I finally see—really see—what the stigma has done to him: the toll the fight against it has taken. The sleepless nights in the redness of his eyes. The worry in the dark shadows beneath them. His face, shaven though not carefully, a quick swipe with a razor to say it's done but not with much care. His shirt, too clean and too unwrinkled to be of his doing.

In that moment he lets his guard down: He places his hands on the counter on either side of me, leans forward, rests his head on my shoulder. He's still, so still, as if he expects me to pull away, to tell him no. I feel the sweep of his lashes on my cheeks as he closes his eyes, the weight of his chest as he takes a breath and lets it out, a slow, long exhalation.

There are different kinds of strength, I know this now. The kind that wields swords and slays monsters but there's another kind, too; one that comes in quiet but in the end is stronger and harder and more powerful: the kind that comes from inside. For all the time I've needed him, I never understood the extent to which he needed me, too.

I slip a hand into his hair, thread my fingers around his

curls. Lean forward, brush my lips against his, soft. I linger there a moment, my lips on his, but he doesn't kiss me back. He's gone still, and I know he's thinking if he moves, breathes, speaks, anything, this spell will be broken and I will be gone.

But I keep going.

I'm pressed against him now, and I can feel his heart hammering beneath his shirt, the tension in his arms as he grips the edge of the counter. My lips move back to his, then away again, feather-light, across his cheek to his ear, then down his neck. I flick my eyes to his just for a moment, just long enough to see them close.

"You don't know what you're doing." His voice is a whisper, a breath against my skin. Not an admonishment: a warning.

I allow myself a smile, just a small one, my lips curving into the warm, spicy skin on his neck, kissing it once, twice, before slowly trailing my way back to his ear only to whisper:

"Yes, I do."

He yanks me toward him then, one hand in my hair, the other gripping my waist before sliding me off the counter and onto his hips. I let out a little gasp of surprise and then his lips are finally, fiercely, on mine. I'm breathless, but he's not through. He kisses me again, still. My feet slip to the floor; we stumble away from the counter.

It's him who pushes me against the door; it's me who pulls him through. It's him who yanks off my coat; it's me who takes off his. It's him who slips off my tunic; it's me who unfastens one button on his shirt, then another, before sliding it off his shoulders. It's him who pushes me into the room with the small bed in the corner, me who pulls him on top of it, wrinkling the smooth, carefully made sheets.

285

When the only thing left between us is a question, he pulls away from me, as far as I'll let him, enough to look me in the eye and say without saying it: *Are you sure?*

It's not enough to say yes. It's not enough to answer not with words but with a kiss. I do both of them but I do something else, too: I say it. After feeling it for so long, I finally find the courage to say it.

"I love you."

He twitches the blanket over us both, then he kisses me.

And the walls come down.

27

I WAKE TO THE FEEL of John's hands in my hair, running the ends of it through his fingers. I crack open an eye to find him watching me, his eyes half closed and half asleep, but the smile on his face wide-awake.

"What time is it?"

He rolls to his back, lifts his head up, and glances out the window by the door. "I'd say around seven or so."

"Oh." I think a moment. "That's later than I thought. We'll have to come up with some excuse why we were gone all day. Maybe we can say we ate in town."

John rolls over to face me, his grin now a smirk. "Seven in the morning."

I let out a gasp; he starts laughing.

"I'm in so much trouble," I groan.

"You are," he agrees. "You'll be washing dishes for a week."

"Just so you know, I'm blaming it all on you."

"You can blame me for whatever you want, any time you want." He grins again. "Even so, I suppose we should get back. My father will be frantic." He pauses, considering. "Although if he's figured out you're with me, frantic probably isn't the right word."

We collect our things and step from the back door of the apothecary, John locking it behind him, then thread through the alley into the cobblestoned main street. It's gray and early still, the air cool and calm. It was quiet yesterday, too, but today it feels almost abandoned. The doors to all the shops are closed tight, the windows shuttered, no one to be seen at all.

"Do you think something happened?" I whisper. No one is around, but it seems important to whisper.

"I don't know." He releases my hand, moves down the street. Tries the door for the cobbler, lifting the shoe-shaped brass knocker and letting it fall once, twice. Next he tries the bakery, the fishmonger, the bookseller, then the tavern, aptly named the Shaven Crown. Knocks on their locked doors, waits for them to be opened.

They don't.

"I don't like this," I say. But there's nothing not to like. No sounds of an attack, no screaming, or smoke, or horses whinnying. No stomping of boots or clashing of swords. No copper-scented wind, the smell of fresh blood hanging in the air.

"Let's go." John is by my side again. "If something's happened, someone at Rochester will know."

We make our way past the apothecary again and the rest

of the empty storefronts. We're nearly to the end when a man appears around a corner, rushing past as if he were being chased.

"Ho!" He throws up a spear, a shoddy-looking thing, the rusty rough-hewn arrow broken from its shaft and lashed onto a knobby stick by a piece of leather. His eyes go wide when he sees John, and he lowers his weapon immediately.

"John Raleigh. What're you doing here? And you?" The man looks at me. "Our troops came through here and rounded everyone up last night, took us into Rochester whether we like it or not." By his scowl it's clear he doesn't. "Blackwell's men got in again."

"What happened?" John demands. "Was anyone hurt?"

"Don't know." The man shrugs. "It's chaos. Rumor is people have gone missing, but it's hard to say who just yet. They're doing a head count now."

John and I exchange a rapid glance.

"Best get back," the man continues. "Your father's no doubt worried."

"If they took everyone to Rochester, what are you doing here?" John says.

The man nods toward the cobbler. "Realized I forgot to lock up shop—stupid, really—"

The arrow pierces his eye before he can finish. The man sways on his feet, blood pouring down his face, before slumping to the ground, facedown. Dead.

It all happens in less than a second.

From the corner of my eye I see the archer. Black-cloaked, his hood up so I can't see his face, poised at the corner of the same side street the cobbler came from. He's reloading, and he's aiming right at us. John snatches the pitiful weapon from the man's death grip, takes my hand, and we run.

An arrow chases us; I can hear it whistling through the air. We don't dodge it; instead John grabs me and throws us both to the ground. We fall, hard, onto the cobblestones as the arrow sails by us. John's up before I am, pulling me to my feet again, and we run, again.

More arrows. They fly at us from every direction now: front, behind, from the side. We're surrounded. An arrow grazes John's shoulder; I gasp as he pitches forward, clutches his hand to his arm; it comes away with nothing but a small smear of blood: It's already healed.

We skirt into the alley, back to the apothecary. We reach the back door, the key already in John's hand. He jams it into the lock, flips open the latch, pushes me through.

"We need to hide." I look up, down, around. "Can we get into the attic somehow? Climb onto the roof?"

"We're not hiding." John pulls me into the front of the shop. Pushes me behind the counter, then dashes around the room, opening drawers, turning in circles, muttering to himself. Then he drops to his knees and throws open a cabinet.

There's a crash, then a shower of ochre glass as a rock flies through the window. They've found us. After a moment John leaps to his feet holding two masks; they look like executioners' masks. He hands me one.

"Put it on."

"John, I don't—"

"Put it on!"

I do. It's tight, with only slits for eyes and nothing for

my nose. Just a tiny hole where the mouth is, not enough to speak, just enough to breathe. Barely.

John ducks down, his head disappearing into the cabinet again. When he reemerges, he's holding a small leather pouch. He quickly unties the leather strings and upends it onto the counter. Inside is a white block, only slightly larger than a sugar cube, wrapped in parchment. It's stamped with a red skull and crossbones, this one not drawn in his hand.

"John...what is that?" My voice is muffled.

Another crash; another rock sails through the window. The shouts out front grow louder. John turns to me, his face pale under his dark hair.

"It's *Ricinius communis*. Derived from the castor bean plant. Heard of it?"

I shake my head.

"It's poison. A single breath of it kills instantly. It's not just outlawed in Harrow, it's outlawed everywhere. I keep a bag for patients who are dying and don't want to prolong it, who want a quick end. If anyone knew I had it..." He doesn't finish the sentence; he doesn't need to. If the council had known about this, it wouldn't have meant prison: It would have meant death.

"I'm going to use it on them," he continues. Even his lips are pale now. "I'm going to blow it into the air, they're going to breathe it, and they're going to die."

I feel sick. All the time he's spent to gain control over the stigma will now be undone in a single breath. I step forward, place my hand on his.

"Let me do it."

"No. It needs to be me." His voice is quiet but sure.

I nod.

"Keep that mask on, you hear me?" His words come fast. "You're okay to breathe through it, but don't take it off until I tell you to. Don't touch anything, either. Don't do anything until I tell you to. Got it?"

I nod again.

He slips on his gloves: thick, heavy black canvas. Yanks the mask over his own face, pulling it tight around his nose and mouth. Plucks a long glass pipette off the counter. One end broad, the other narrow, like a trumpet. He unwraps the block of poison from the parchment, pinching and crumbling it between his fingertips before shoving it into the widest end of the pipe. He presses his thumb against the other end, creating a vacuum to hold the powder inside.

There's an enormous crashing noise. The front window has shattered, shards hanging by the frame, yellow and glinting like cats' eyes in the weak morning sun.

John points to the corner of the room, to the left of the door.

"Get down. Wait for them to come in," he says. His voice is muffled behind the mask.

Another smash and they're here; they're inside the shop. Two, six, eight of them crawl in through the open window, and they converge on us, all black cloaks and choking roses, their arrows pointing right at us.

"Your armor won't do you any good," one says, taking aim at John's forehead.

"Neither will yours," John says.

And he blows.

Powder fills the air like mist. Finger-shaped white tendrils coil from the pipette, almost predatory, floating their way toward the men. For a second, the air is filled with the sounds of their laughter, but between one breath and the next, that laughter stops.

Their skin turns white; it's as if they've been doused in powder. Eyeballs turn red, veins dilating wider and wider until they're nothing but crimson. They jerk and shake like puppets until the strings are cut and in unison, all eight men slump to the floor in a bloody heap, a catastrophe of a grotesque tragedy.

I'm hauled to my feet. Elbowed, none too gently, over and out the broken window and into the street until we reach the other side. John shakes off his gloves, then spins me around, fumbling with my mask, pulling it off before ripping off his own.

He looks at me closely. "You didn't touch anything?"

I shake my head. "No. Nothing."

John tugs me toward the water pump in front of the fishmonger's. Draws it a couple times until the pipe runs clean, then rinses his hands and face, sucking in mouthfuls of water and spitting it onto the cobblestones.

"Your turn," he says. "Even if you didn't touch anything, it won't hurt to make sure." I reach down and cup my hands beneath the cold stream, rinsing my mouth and splashing water on my face until my cheeks are numb.

I dry my face and hands on the folds of my cloak, then look to him. I fear I'll see hostility in his face again, the violence from the stigma swirling through his veins, wreaking unseen havoc. But instead of aggravation, I see only caution.

"You're all right?" I say.

John glances back at his ruined apothecary, at the shards of yellow glass littering the cobblestones, the heap of black cloaks visible inside.

"Not quite," he says. "But I will be."

I don't want to ask him, but I do. "What about the bodies?"

John offers a grim smile. "They'll take care of themselves. In six hours or so, they'll be nothing but bones."

We keep a quick pace back toward camp, our heads swiveling right to left and back again, searching the meadow, the forest, watching for more archers in black lurking behind trees.

I barely see Rochester as we approach, hazy and blurry behind what must be a new barrier. I almost don't see the man standing just behind it, either; a figure in cloudy gray, a blaze of orange triangle on the lapel, a man of the Watch. He sees us coming and waves his hand; the air around us turns opaque, like fog, a clear opening in the center.

"Were there more behind you?" He waves us through. "Theirs, or ours?"

"Theirs, yes," John says. "But we took care of them. There was one of ours, too, but he didn't make it. He told us there were people missing. Have they been found?"

"Two of them have." The guard nods at us. "Best be off so they know you're safe."

We continue down the road into Rochester, across the bridge into madness. Horses, men, soldiers, pages running everywhere; voices shouting orders. John and I push through it all, looking for Peter, for Fitzroy, for Nicholas, for anyone we fear has gone missing, for anyone who could tell us what's happening.

Soon enough there's a roar and Peter appears, wrinkled and disheveled. He tackles John, pulls him into a rough embrace, ruffling his hair. He mutters in his ear; I can't make out the words but I can hear the tenderness behind them. Then he turns and does the same to me.

"I thought the worst." Peter pulls back, his dark brows furrowed. "Blackwell's men, they got in again. We rounded up all of Harrow, but people are still missing. I thought you among them."

"We know," John says. He fills Peter in on the archers, on the man they killed, on the poison and what happened afterward.

"God's blood," Peter exclaims. "You were at the apothecary? I went there myself after I couldn't find either of you here. The lights were off and the doors were locked. I didn't have a key, but when I knocked, no one answered."

"We were there," John says. "We just…didn't hear you." I flush a little at this and so does he, but he doesn't look away.

"But why—*oh*. Ah. I see. *Ah*." Peter swipes a hand across his beard, looking discomfited.

"You mentioned people were missing." John swiftly changes the subject. "Who?"

"A few soldiers. A woman and her son from the Mudchute. From what you saw in town, we can add the cobbler to the list. And Gareth."

"Gareth?" John and I exchange a rapid glance. "Was he taken against his will? Or were Blackwell's men meant to be his escort out of Harrow?"

"There's no way to know for certain," Peter says. "But Nicholas believes he was abducted. Fitzroy went to Gareth's home and his door was unlocked, his belongings where he left them."

"Why would they take him?" John asks.

"Hard to say," Peter says. "Could be because Blackwell discovered we know he's the spy, could be because Gareth had a change of heart about defecting, and we know what Blackwell does to traitors." A pause. "It doesn't much matter. He's gone, and though it's a small consolation, it saves us from having to arrest him ourselves. At any rate, we've got a larger issue at hand. A few members of the Order of the Rose arrived last night. Said Blackwell's men were beginning to mobilize in Upminster, earlier than expected. We believe they'll be here sometime tomorrow."

"How many?" John asks.

"A conservative estimate is ten thousand."

Ten thousand. Against our four thousand.

"Some of Blackwell's army—perhaps as many as half—are fighting under duress," Peter continues. "They will defect the moment battle begins. They'll either escape, or Blackwell will waste his troops to hunt them down. Even if this leaves us more evenly matched, he's still got his revenants. The strength of one is equal to that of ten ordinary men, and they'll be loyal to him."

I think of Schuyler's words and wonder if that's not entirely true.

"Let's get you to your tents," Peter says finally. "You'll need to pick up your uniforms, and your weapons, and we're doing a last rally tonight. Tomorrow will be—" He breaks off. "Tomorrow will be here soon enough."

John places his hand on Peter's shoulder, but there's nothing he can say that will ease the worry on his father's face. Peter knows there's a chance John won't make it through this battle. I know it, too, despite everything I will do to make sure he does.

We start across the crowded field, weaving through the circle of white tents toward mine when I hear it. A shout, a laugh, and then I see him, bounding toward us in a streak of stripes and feathers and smiles:

George.

28

"Oi!"

He bounds across the grass toward us, bright as the afternoon sun in a green-and-blue-striped coat, blue hat with a yellow feather, and matching yellow cape. He hurtles into John, nearly knocking him over. They're both laughing and shoving each other; then finally George steps back and looks us both over, a smirk on his face.

"Well, well. If it isn't my favorite star-crossed couple." He looks from John to me, then back to John again. "Though it looks like the stars have finally aligned, conspiring now to blind us all."

George steps forward and pulls me into a tight embrace.

"I really am glad to see you." He looks me over carefully, his smile faltering for a moment. "Fifer's been writing me, telling me what's been going on. All of it. You..." George trails off, uncharacteristically at a loss for words. "You're going to be all right. I think we all are."

He falls into step beside us as we thread through the crowds.

"When did you get back?" John asks him.

"Last night, late. It was a bit rough crossing the channel. But we're here now, and just in time, too. They came for a fight; it seems they're going to get one."

John nods, then turns to his father. "What's the plan for those not fighting?"

"After midnight tonight, the women and children will be inside." Peter waves his hand at Rochester Hall. "George has been placed in charge of them, and of their evacuation into Cambria, should it come to that. Regardless, they'll be safe. Nicholas and some councilmen are working on the spells now. No one will be allowed out until the council—minus Gareth, of course—gives the instruction."

I don't ask what will happen if none of the council is left to give that instruction; I know I don't have to.

We look around the grounds at the thousands of Gallic men, their tents decorated with a fluttering flag of Gaul in stripes of red, blue, and white, chatting and laughing, some sparring, others reclining on the grass smoking pipes or drinking deeply from crystal goblets.

"I see they're making themselves comfortable," John notes wryly. "By the looks of it, you'd never know they were going to war."

"They brought their own wine and their own glasses," George says. "They're the damnedest. Deadly as hell, but terribly high-maintenance. I can't tell you how many of them asked me where the ladies' tent is. We're at war, and they want a ladies' tent."

I roll my eyes. John and George laugh.

"Not that it would be difficult to do," George continues. "Anglian women always did have a thing for Gallic men, and the women of Harrow are no different. So later tonight there'll be music, wine, food, no doubt as much flirting since I was at court. And speaking of court..."

I look up just as Malcolm comes striding in our direction. He's dressed in Reformist colors: black tunic, black trousers, the orange-and-red Reformist symbol blazing in a crest along the front, a sword at his side. To see him dressed this way, free and armed and walking through the camp as if he owns it, is both a shock and an expectation.

George steps forward, sketches a quick bow. "Sir."

Malcolm waves it off, a smile crossing his face. "I told you to call me Malcolm. I think we're well beyond formalities now."

George turns to us. "He's a rounder, this one, as I discovered last night. He took all my money in a single game of cards. Then, after ensuring I was thoroughly distraught, lost it all in one hand. A hand I do believe was skillfully thrown."

"The skill was not mine but yours," Malcolm says graciously. "But I'm happy to arrange a rematch, if you'd like to test your theory."

"I've got no plans tomorrow evening," George says.

"You do now," Malcolm says.

George laughs and extends his hand; Malcolm takes it, grinning. His eyes flick to me then.

"Glad you're back. We were worried." He looks at John

and nods. "For both of you." The silence hangs a moment. "Elizabeth, may I speak to you?"

John turns to George. "You seen Fifer?"

George nods. "Last I saw her, she was terrorizing some poor Gallic soldier. Cursing at him before *actually* cursing him. She gave him some kind of rash and now it's spread. All over the man's face and lips and tongue."

John laughs. "Why, what did he do?"

"He called her '*un peu fig mignon.*'"

A cute little fig.

John rolls his eyes. "Mind leading me to them both? I want to let her know we're all right. And it sounds like I've got a pox to treat." He turns to me. "I'll find you later?"

"Of course," I say.

John nods at Malcolm, squeezes my hand, then he and George walk away, the breeze carrying George's chatter and John's laughter back to me. It makes me smile.

Malcolm turns to me. "How are you?"

"I'm fine," I say. "Had a run-in with some of Blackwell's archers, but they came out of it worse than I did."

"Good. But I didn't mean just that. How are you feeling about tomorrow?"

Tomorrow. It stands on a knife's edge: victory and defeat, life and death, joy and sorrow. It will be one or the other; there will be no half measures.

"I'm ready," I say, and this is the truth. "I've lived beneath the shadow of your uncle's rule for so long, I'll do whatever it takes to overthrow him."

He surveys the field, his eyes squinting against the setting sun in a way that makes the wrinkles around them deepen. I think of how he became heir at twelve after Blackwell killed his parents and unsuccessfully tried to kill him. How at sixteen he became king. Then, at twenty, how he went into a Yuletide masque a king and came out a prisoner, stripped of his title, his wife, his country, his life. He's experienced enough life for a man twice his age, and now, for once, he looks it.

Malcolm looks back at me, his mouth curving into a smile as if he knows exactly what I'm thinking. "Did I ever tell you what I did my first day as king of Anglia?"

I shake my head.

"I turned the country over to someone else to rule." He grimaces. "To Uncle. I told him I didn't want to do it, that I couldn't do it. I should have known then, how quickly he agreed, that something wasn't right. He said he'd hand the reins back when I was ready. But drinking, gambling, roistering, hunting, well." Malcolm laughs, a short, derisive sound. "I thought I was doing the right thing, turning my head from whatever Uncle felt was his duty to do. Apathy became a habit; now it's all I'm known for."

"You're here. You're fighting," I say. "You're helping to save the country, and you're putting yourself at risk to do it. That's what you'll be known for."

"If I do this right, I won't be known for anything at all."

"You're the king," I say. "You can't die."

"I can, I might; I will, I won't. That's not what matters. What matters is that I'm ready. Like you, I'm ready to be out from underneath his shadow. I'm going to get Anglia back."

He extends his hand to me. "May I?" he says, and I nod. Then he presses my fingers to his lips; a formal, courtly kiss.

"I'm glad you're here with me," he says. "I don't trust a lot of people; I don't trust anyone. But I always trusted you. And now I need to apologize to you."

I wait.

"I knew you didn't feel about me the way I felt about you. I simply chose not to listen." He lets my hand drop as his expression falls; he looks as vulnerable as a boy. "It was self-ish and wrong, and I am sorry. I know they're just words but they're all I have. Can you forgive me?"

And on this, the eve of the final battle from which we may not return, I know that it's too late to withhold forgiveness, too late to hold grudges. Too late to punish him for playing by the rules when the rules were stripped from both of us, turned inside out before being served back to us on a poisoned platter.

"I do," I say, and I'm not at all surprised to find I mean it.

"Now I've got a battle to win." His grin is back; it lights up his face and that's the Malcolm I know: loud, brash, confident, the world at his feet and everything to hope for. "This time tomorrow, we'll be celebrating. Mark my words." He spins on his heel, throws me a wave.

I watch him go. As he walks off into the last of the dying light, it swallows him. And I think he'll come out brighter, untarnished, or the blaze will devour him, as it will all of us.

Night comes. And with it, a celebration. The Gallic soldiers insisted on it—to their way of thinking, it was the only thing to do. If the battle was to go poorly, if we were to fall, if they weren't to return to Harrow tomorrow, at least they'd have had tonight. Better than the alternative, they said: huddled in their tents, alone and afraid.

George was all for it. And no one can organize a celebration better than he: Within the hour we had wine, both from the soldiers who brought their own from Gaul, and from Lord Cranbourne Calthorpe-Gough's private reserve. Someone conjures fairy lights, tiny and white and nestled in the trees surrounding the camp, twinkling in the moonlit night.

Music fills the air: pipes and tabors, harps and drums. People laugh and they dance; they chatter in Gallic and flirt in Anglian. And none of us talks about it at all. The chance we won't return, the chance that this will be it. The very real chance that come tomorrow, there will be nothing left.

At midnight, the music ends. The fairy lights go out; the laughter stops. With little fanfare and even fewer words, the celebration disperses. The women and children are led inside Rochester Hall. The Gallic soldiers retreat to their side of the grounds, drunk with laughter and wine not moments earlier, now sober and stoic.

The armorers retreat to finish the task of preparing weapons for the three thousand that make up our army. We don't have many horses, a few dozen, perhaps. A handful of coursers to lead the initial charge, some palfreys for signaling. But this won't be a cavalry charge; it never was going to be. This will be an infantry battle: face-to-face and hand-to-hand, bloody and vicious and personal and deadly.

As abrupt as the others, John steers me back to my tent. Wordlessly, we huddle together on my narrow camp bed, his arms around me tight, my head pressed against his chest.

I breathe him in, that same, soothing scent of him: lavender and spice; the same warmth and comfort I always feel around him.

I don't tell him I'm afraid of tomorrow. I'm afraid of what will happen if we lose, what will happen if we win. I'm afraid of the heartache and the loss and the wait, the interminable pause between the start and the finish to know how it ends. I don't tell him any of this. But by the way he holds me and kisses me and says he'll always love me, he tells me he already knows.

29

IN THE MORNING, THE AIR is cool and still. Muted sunlight filters in through the white canvas, bathing it in a yellow glow. Outside, the rustle of activity has already begun, frantic and loud. The knot, already coiled tight in my belly, turns tighter.

John and I dress in silence, both of us in the same thing: brown trousers, white tunic under a thin layer of mail, blue-and-red color-blocked surcoat—traditional Anglian colors in a battle to restore Anglia—topped with a breastplate of armor. I help him fasten the leather straps at his shoulders and sides. When I'm finished, he does the same for me. And for a moment we stand there, face-to-face. I can read the look of dark finality in his face, hear the men shouting outside the tent, their footsteps and the thundering of hooves, and I know it's time to go.

But still, we don't move.

Finally, I step away from him, reach for my bag stuffed beneath my cot. Pick through it until I unearth it: the dark green length of ribbon I pulled from the bodice of the pale green linen nightgown Fifer gifted me with, the one I wore the night I climbed up the trellis into John's bedroom, the last time we were together before everything went terribly wrong.

I hold it out.

John's eyes skim the length of it, then flick back to me. "I never thought you were one for ribbons," he says. "But I remember this. I remember everything about that night, including what you wore. I wondered why that color. Why green when your best color is easily blue. Then I wondered where you got it, and if you had others like it."

"You thought a lot about it," I say.

"I think a lot about you," he corrects. "Most of the time, though, it's not about ribbons."

That makes me smile, but only for a moment.

"I want you to wear it," I say. "And I want you to think of me when you do. Whether green is my best color, or whether you'd rather be thinking about something else." My words are coming fast, but we're out of time and I need him to hear them. "But however you think of me, I need you to know that I need you. I need you to come back to me."

I hold up the ribbon, and with a shaky hand I tuck it inside his armor. It's something a maid would do, giving a knight her favor as he enters a joust. But this is no joust, and I am no Queen of the May. I am what I am: A killer and a traitor, a sometime liar and a forever troublemaker, but he somehow found a way to love me anyway. "Please think of me," I repeat. "Please come back to me."

John reaches for me, captures my hand in his. There's nothing left for us to say so he kisses me, hard, crushing me against him, maybe forgetting we're wearing armor, maybe not, not caring either way. We kiss to the sound of drums, to the sound of trumpets and hoofbeats and heartbeats, we kiss until there's nothing left but to stop or go on, so we go on. He tugs at my armor, impatient, and before I know it it's on the ground, his hand sliding beneath my tunic as I start to pull on the fastenings of the armor I only just put on him.

There's a flash of sunlight and a cool draft of air and from the corner of my eye I see Schuyler, standing in the mouth of the tent, shaking his head and smirking.

"You're about six hours too late for this kind of send-off," he drawls. "You should have done this last night, along with the rest of camp." A pause; another smirk. "Did you know there's a twenty per centum increase in the number of children born in wartime than in peacetime?"

"Get out," John murmurs against my lips. He doesn't turn away from me, doesn't release me. But Schuyler continues.

"It also nearly doubles the average number of infants born to a single couple. Frightening, considering this one"— he jerks his head at John—"already wants six."

I push away from John then, my mouth dropping open. "You want six children?"

"Quit that," John snaps at Schuyler.

"I'm not listening in. I swear it." Schuyler holds up his hands. "Fifer told me."

"Six?" I repeat.

"I thought it sounded like a nice, even number." John shrugs. "Maybe we can talk about it later? Because as much as I'd like this to be a group discussion, I really don't think now is the best time."

"That's right," Schuyler says. "Because ten minutes before going into battle is the best time to unsheathe your sword and—"

John fires off a stream of curses, all of them aimed at Schuyler. But they're both laughing, and so am I.

"Save your endearments for the bedroom," Schuyler says with a grin. "It's time to go."

John plucks my armor off the ground, helps me back into it. He starts to lead me out of the tent, but I stop him.

"I'll catch up with you in a moment," I say. "I'd like to speak to Schuyler first."

John leans forward and presses his lips against mine, holding them there. Then he leaves, mouthing something to Schuyler as he pushes past. I catch the gist of it, and it isn't pleasant. It makes Schuyler laugh anyway. The tent flap falls, blocking out the sun, a shadow falling across us both.

"How is this going to go?" I say. "Are we marching into victory or into defeat?"

"I'm no seer, bijoux." Schuyler's voice is uneven with honesty. "I don't know what's going to happen. And I wouldn't dare try to read what anyone else thinks will happen, either. I'm prepared for it to go any way. I've made my arrangements."

Revenants rarely die; rarely die again, that is. But it can be done: most often a savagely broken neck, something only another revenant can do, or by fire, something anyone can do. And I know that somewhere, ensconced inside Rochester Hall, Fifer waits with the knowledge that he may not come back.

"What about John, then?" I say. "I'll do whatever I can to keep Blackwell from finding him, we all will. But what if John decides to go looking for him first? He says he's got the stigma under control. Does he?"

"He thinks he does," Schuyler says. "And as much as he's thinking of that, he's thinking of you. That's all I get from him, and it's all I want to know. Don't ask me to listen for any more."

"Schuyler—"

"You can't stop what's going to happen," he interrupts. "For all that you tried, you never could. It was always going to come to this." Fifer's words in Schuyler's mouth.

We slip outside into the bright sunlight. Make our way across the green while a thousand others do the same: filing from their tents, armor glinting in the sun. Squires number in the hundreds, boys in white scurrying behind weapons masters, fitting men with longbows and quiver belts, spikes and knives, axes and swords. A dozen or so men and women, members of the Order of the Rose, carry no weapons. Their magic is enough for them.

I spot Keagan standing in a small group near the jousting pit, her long white tunic bearing the black embroidered outline of a rose. She sees me and waves me over.

"This is Odell and Coll," she says, introducing the boy and girl standing beside her.

"We heard about you." The girl, Coll, looks me over and smiles. She's small, like me, with short dark hair, dark skin, and a bright smile. "Keagan says she calls you sparrow. I like that. It's fitting."

"What magic can you do?" I ask.

"Oh, me?" Coll holds up a hand, wiggles her fingers. Within seconds a red-crested bird alights on her shoulder. It cocks its head and watches her closely.

"You can summon animals?"

"And speak to them." Keagan glances at Coll, who seems to blush under her gaze. "We're so lucky to have her. Power like that is exceedingly rare. It comes along only once every ten years, and only to a tenth female born from a tenth female."

"You have nine sisters?"

"Twelve, actually." Coll's grin is as white as her tunic. "There's one now." She points to a girl no older than ten ducked behind the yew alley, half her face poking out from behind a tree. "Her name is Miri. You should see what she can do."

The bird careens from Coll's shoulder into the air just as a wall of water from the nearby lake rises up, twisting and turning and hurtling toward us. It slams to a stop, hovering above our heads like a shimmering pane of glass, then squirts a single stream of water into Coll's face. Keagan flicks her wrist and the entire wall of water explodes into mist. Across the field, soldiers break into laughter and applause.

"I haven't seen you around," I say to Keagan.

"Rochester's a big place, is it not? Thousands of people, only fifteen of us. At any rate, they've kept us sequestered. Thought it best for others not to know too much about what we do, so it wouldn't get out."

The trumpets begin blowing then. Calling us to ranks,

calling us to orders. The noise stills the air, dissolving the tense exuberance of three thousand men and women armed with magic and weapons into silence.

"See you on the field." Keagan turns and strolls away, her cropped red head held high.

"Keagan," I call after her, but I don't know what to say. I want to tell her to watch out for herself, to watch out for the Order. For Malcolm, who I know despite everything she's grown fond of. "Be careful."

"I will." She turns around. "You be careful, too."

I dive into the crowd, make my way to my company. Soldiers fall into formation around me, bright in their red-and-blue surcoats and Reformist badges burning yellow and orange against the bright blue sky and looming walls of Rochester, the browning hills and greening trees. Horses and shields, pennants and pikes, courage and fear, all of it stretching in front of me, farther than I can see. It's so much more than I thought it would be.

But when John appears by my side, the brightness of his armor tempered against the shadow in his eyes as he surveys the men around us, I know he's wondering, like me, if it will be enough.

We see Nicholas then, cutting through the swath of men, dressed not as a soldier but as a wizard: ivory robes to distinguish him from Blackwell, who will surely be wearing black. Nicholas has no armor, no weapons. He pulls up short before us, glancing at each of us in turn.

"He's vulnerable," Nicholas says. I know without asking he means Blackwell. "But he is still powerful. And he is desperate, which makes him formidable. He needs only one of you, but he will be looking for you both. If he finds you"— Nicholas looks to me—"he will not let you go."

"I know."

Nicholas looks to John then. For a moment they look at each other, something passing between them, something I'm not privy to.

"He will not hesitate," he says. "He will not take you back to Upminster, he will not risk the time because he does not have it. He will kill you as quickly as he can."

Caution and premonition tug at me: Nicholas's words don't sound like a warning as much as they do instruction. But John only nods.

Nicholas steps away from us then, takes his place along the front, between the line of men and the barrier. John and I find our place along the middle, behind the spearmen, in front of the bowmen. Between the formations, each of the councilmen sits atop a horse, sheathed in armor, ready.

We march under the Reformist banner: a small sun surrounded by a square, then a triangle, then another circle; a snake with its tail in its mouth. Each symbol has its own meaning: the sun the dawn of a new existence; the square to represent the physical world; the triangle is for fire, a catalyst for change; and the snake—an Ouroboros—for unity.

Today, we fight for all of it.

We march to the barrier, to the edge of it all. I can't see Blackwell's men, but I know they're there. I can feel it the way you can feel an oncoming thunderstorm. The air, still and pregnant with tension, waiting to crack open and rain destruction on us all.

At once, the councilmen raise their hands and begin whispering an incantation, no more than a breath, but then it happens. Dissolving like mist, like clouds in the morning, thick then thin, there then gone.

30

AT ONCE, THERE'S SOUND. Like a curtain that's been lifted, I can suddenly see and hear everything: every leaf on every tree, every bird in every nest, every man on every horse.

Every enemy in front of me.

They stretch for miles, ten thousand of them in all black, an endless, roiling midnight sea. *God, they're everywhere.* The darkness on the ground stretches into the skies: rolling clouds of black, swirling with unleashed menace and peppered with murders of crimson-eyed crows. They press down on us, dissolving the sun and the blue above Harrow.

I don't know who draws first. But someone does, a blade pulled from a sheath, steel singing against leather, a roaring command, a rustled footfall, a shout. And then, with a booming roll of thunder and a flash of lightning, the battle begins.

I lose John immediately. Men push between us and I shout his name once, twice, but my voice is engulfed by the chaos unfolding around me. The skies open up and freezing rain floods the air, pouring in sheets around us, obstructing our view like a veil.

For a moment I freeze, overcome by what's unfolding in front of me. The enormity of it; the finality of it. But then something takes over: years of training, years of anger, years of fear. I plunge into the seething mass of bodies, knives yanked from the belt at my waist. I fling one after the other, the scent of blood filling the air around me, red and hot and copper, the sound of men dying.

I need to find Blackwell; it's the only thing I need to do. I know he's here, somewhere. Too cowardly to show himself now, he'll hold back until we're weakened, until half his army is dead and we begin to grow tired and weak, until he can take our advantage and turn it into his.

I don't see her, but Miri makes herself known: The rain abruptly stops, holds unmoving in the air, and with a sound like an incoming tide, roars up and back across the plain. I can't see it, but I hear the water hitting, crashing onto the sea of men in black.

The reprieve isn't long and the rain starts up again, this time coupled with streaks of white-hot lightning. It strikes where the water falls, at the feet of men on both sides: black and blue and red. I watch as they jerk and sizzle, rooted to the spot before slumping to the muddy ground, charred and unrecognizable and dead.

I keep moving, threading through the mass until I see Malcolm, his dark hair plastered to his face, his skin covered in blood and mud. He's surrounded by his men, locked in battle with the crows that rain and swirl around them, lashing out with beaks, talons, and beating wings, knocking them one by one to the ground.

"Coll!" My shouts disappear into the rain and the screams, but somehow she hears me. In an instant, a mob of owls appears as if from the clouds, a hundred of them feathered in tawny brown, inky black, snow white; each with blazing yellow, enchanted eyes. They dive into the crows, their bodies flapping and screeching; the noise is deafening.

Malcolm rolls away from the fray, gets to his feet. Blood mixed with rain runs down his face; he snatches his blade from the mud and plunges into the fight again. I move alongside him and his men, an eye on what's in front of me and always, always an eye on what's not.

Arrows fire indiscriminately around me, some iron-tipped, others blazing with fire, the latter no doubt Keagan's. They slam into man after man, all of them in black, their cloaks catching ablaze and the stench of burning wool and skin adding to the miasma already in the air. Malcolm, clashing swords with someone, is caught in the crossfire and gets hit: the arrow slicing into his unprotected forearm, the sleeve of his tunic turning into flame.

Malcolm twists to try to put it out, the distraction opening up an opportunity for his attacker to end him. He doesn't get it. I yank another dagger from my belt, take aim, and let it fly. The blade impales the man's eye; he drops to the ground in a heap.

I'm at Malcolm's side in an instant, slapping the flames out, examining his wound. It's deep, but it's clean.

"Hold still," I say. "I'll pull it out on three. One, two—" I yank the arrow out. Blood soaks his tunic, but he'll live. "Go," I say. "Your men need you. They—" My words are cut off, along with my air.

I can't breathe. Malcolm pulls at his armor, at his mail; his mouth is open and he's gasping for air but there's none for him, either.

A soldier in black stands before us, his index finger twirling idly in the air, his face twisted in a grin as all around us men drop to their knees, to the mud, holding their throats, gasping, their faces turning blue. Dizziness overcomes me and I stagger to one knee, then the other, my lungs screaming. I claw at my throat, fall to the ground and into the soft, cold mud. I can't breathe, I can't breathe...

Keagan appears from nowhere, and it happens before I blink: the flash of a knife blade, a line drawn across the throat. A fountain of blood and a gargled moan and the wizard slumps to the ground, eyes open, staring unseeing into mine.

"Get up." Keagan reaches down, snatches my arms, pulls me to my feet. "Elizabeth. Get up now."

Malcolm is already on his feet, pale and breathing hard. Men lie all around us, some gasping for air, some so still I think they've died. The owls and the crows have all taken flight, only a few feathered bodies strewn in the mud. Rain continues to pour around us, all of us soaked down to the tunics beneath our mail, cold and rough against our skin.

"Let's move." Keagan grabs the back of my tunic, shoves me across the field. Malcolm's men fall in beside us, still breathing hard but weapons out.

At once, a pack of soldiers step in front of us—no, not soldiers, revenants—weapons and malice bared. Caleb, Marcus, and Linus are not among them, but still I know that's what they are. I can tell by the gray in their eyes and the ferocity on their faces. I can tell by the way the human soldiers in the field give them a wide berth, pouring around them as if they were stones in a river.

But for all I don't know them, Malcolm does. He steps in front of me, hand out as if to shield me. His other hand holds out a sword, useless against them.

"Majesty." One of the revenants dips a clumsy, false curtsy; the others laugh, deep and throaty.

"Bray."

Now I remember who this is, was. Bray, a nickname for Ambrose Courtenay, once one of Malcolm's most trusted courtiers. Malcolm told me he was banned from court after Bray's gambling and drinking and violent behavior became too much for even Malcolm to bear.

"I'm not called that anymore. At least not by you." He breaks from the pack, begins to circle us. He's not armed— doesn't need to be—but his hands, flexing in and out of fists at his sides, promise as much violence as a cannon.

"When did this happen?" Malcolm gestures at him with his sword. "When did you come back to court? When did you..." He trails off. I don't know if Malcolm knows how revenants are created.

"I returned when he summoned me. The king." The other revenants shift around him as he speaks. I know their movement and posture well: They're falling into formation; they're preparing to attack. "The true king."

He's baiting us, I know this. But I can't stop myself from saying, "Summoned you, then killed you."

"Do I look dead to you?" Bray was handsome once, this I can tell. Not by his looks, no; I can tell by the way he is like Malcolm, the way Malcolm was. Confident, as if the answer to everything simply lay around every corner, under every stone, just waiting to be discovered. "We are all very much alive."

"We?" I say. "And how many would that be, exactly?"

"One hundred." Bray grins, his teeth flashing in the dark gray air. "More to come. More every day. Men line up to serve, to serve an eternal king for all eternity."

My heart sinks. One hundred revenants, with more to come.

"*Ach.* I've had enough of this." Keagan throws up her hands. Palms out, skin already red.

"Down!" Malcolm shouts to his men before snatching the back of my armor and throwing me facedown into the mud. I hear it, even before I lift my head to see it: twin ropes of fire blazing from Keagan's hands, coiling and twisting into knots around the revenants. Their robes erupt into flames, black into red. The rain, still falling, has no effect on them: The water turns to steam around us, the air filled with white fog and gray smoke and unending fire.

But the revenants, they don't scream, they don't fall to the ground, they don't cease. They continue walking, aflame and charred, skin melting into bone, hair singeing from their scalps. They hold their weapons high, and they keep coming.

"Goddammit." Malcolm pushes himself away from me, onto his feet. Pulls his sword. Swings. The blade slices through one revenant's burning neck, then another, then another.

Keagan drops her hands, the fire sputters out. The air is a

cloud of burning stench, like Tyburn, smuts floating around like charred snowflakes, the scent of burning skin so sickly sweet I could gag on it. A few of Malcolm's men do, retching into the mud.

"Well done, Your Highness," Keagan says.

Malcolm nods by way of acknowledgment, but he's not looking at her, nor is he looking at the heap of smoking bodies around us. His focus is on the field, at the battle that still rages all around.

"Those men. Those revenants." Malcolm glances at his sword, the revenants' black blood dripping into the mud. "The birds. The elemental magic." He looks into the air. "They keep appearing. One thing after the other."

"As things do in battle," Keagan replies, sarcastic.

"No." Malcolm turns to face us. "Look around. Look at what's happening. Look closely."

I do. All around us, battles wage. But I cannot see what's happening, I cannot see who is making ground. I cannot see retreat, I cannot see advance. All I see is chaos, but now I see that it is orchestrated chaos.

"We are fighting in place." Malcolm continues, "It's as if he's trying to keep either side from moving. Uncle. It's as if he's throwing one thing or another at us to keep us from looking beyond the battle—to distract us."

"Misdirection," Keagan says, sharp.

Malcolm nods. Turns to me. And there, in the field around us full of men and revenants and hybrids, the sky full of black, seething, impenetrable fog, is my clue.

"Blackwell once told us the best way to achieve one objective is to make your opponent believe you're trying

321

to achieve another." Realization drops my voice low. "In a battle, this means chaos, disorder, feints, misinformation. You're so preoccupied with what's in front of you that you don't see what's happening around you. He called it the fog of war."

"What is his objective, then?" one of Malcolm's men says.

"Rochester Hall." Keagan jerks around to look at me, her eyes wide.

I should have sensed it, known it; as soon as I saw Blackwell's men, his creatures, all here in front of me: It was a diversion. A way to concentrate all our men here, too, so he could reach the one place he really wanted.

But not only that.

I think of how John disappeared the moment the battle began.

I think of Nicholas's warning to him, the one that felt more like instruction.

And I think of Blackwell's constant advisement: *Warfare is based on deception.* This time, I wasn't deceived by Blackwell, someone I expected. This time I was deceived by two people I didn't, people I trusted.

Maybe Keagan can see it in my face; maybe she's realized it, too. But she turns to me, her blue eyes wide, the black smuts from the burning revenants stuck to her face.

"Let's go." She gestures to Malcolm, his men. "Stay behind me. All of you. If he's trying to keep us away, he'll try to stop us. I'll burn what I can, but keep your weapons out."

With only a precious few knives left, I yank my bow from my shoulder, an arrow from the quiver at my waist. Malcolm readies his sword. The three of us plunge into the organized disarray, dodging men and arrows and rain, running back the way we came. We don't get more than a few hundred feet before a flapping noise, like wash on a laundry line, fills the air. Dark shapes fill the darkening sky: winged, oily, sharp. I remember them, these hybrids, from training. We killed them once but now they live again, this time en masse. Five, ten, then fifteen of them assault the sky.

At once, they swoop. Onto the fields, claws out, pointed, deadly, snapping up man after man indiscriminately, slashing them open, some of ours, some of his. But I know Blackwell doesn't care. He won't be satisfied until we're all dead and he's the last one standing, because a king over nothing is still a king over everything.

They come with a caw, dipping and wheeling and grasping, picking up men the way birds pluck worms from the ground, wriggling and trying in vain to escape. Keagan holds up her palms and at once the air is filled with threads of fire, wrapping around three of the hybrids, consuming them in flames.

I raise my bow and take aim. As with most of Blackwell's hybrids, their eyes are the weakest spot, and that's where I fire. Once, twice. I miss the first but land the second, then the third. The thing shrieks and plummets to the ground in a jumble of leathery black wings and purplish-black blood. Malcolm finishes it off with a clean slice of his blade to its neck, severing the head from the body.

I reload; Keagan readies her fire. But for every hybrid we kill, three more appear and descend on us, as if they've been sent straight for us. That's when I see it: a mass of white across the sky, as thick as a cloud but faster, denser. And then I see her, sitting in the highest branch in the highest tree, a silhouette of a girl in white against the marbled black sky. Coll, the girl who can control animals.

She sees me watching her and grins, cocky and sure. Coll raises her hand skyward and curls her fingers slowly, as if beckoning. I see her lips moving, muttering, speaking an incantation to that mass in the sky. Then she slices her hand through the air, a blur.

The birds dive. Into the mass of blood and limbs and screams, and unlike Blackwell's hybrids, they attack only black: pecking at faces, ears, mouths, gouging out eyeballs. The air is filled with the sounds of flapping wings, screeching beaks, feathers and leathery skin and death.

We start to run again, Keagan beside me, Malcolm and his men behind me. I need to get to Rochester. I need to find Blackwell, I need to stop John, to stop Nicholas, from whatever it is they think they're doing, from whatever mistake they are undoubtedly making.

We make it a couple hundred yards, maybe, when suddenly the ground begins to buckle and jerk beneath us. It trembles and rumbles, as if something from far beneath is pushing its way through, shaking the trees from the ground, me from my feet, my weapon from my hand. Keagan spins one way, I fall the other, plunging face-first into a damp smear of leaves, Malcolm skidding beside me. There's a crack like thunder, a sway I can almost feel. I snatch my bow with one hand, Malcolm with the other, and roll us both over as an oak tree smashes to the ground with another earth-shattering tremble, where the pair of us lay not a half second before.

"That was too goddamned close." Malcolm's lying beneath

me, his mouth pressed against my ear. "How is he seeing us? How does he know where we are?"

"Don't you know this yet, about your uncle?" I jump to my feet, pull him to his. "He always knows everything."

Keagan screams at us to keep moving, her voice dampened by the smoke that rends the air; somewhere, something is burning, from her magic or from Blackwell's. She directs us away from the trees, into the open field. I turn to follow but as I do, I catch a glimpse of him. Malcolm sees him, too, and then he's at my side, his sword raised as we look at him, standing at the mouth of the forest, alone, as still and rooted as the trees around him.

Caleb.

31

HE WATCHES ME—ONLY ME—HIS EYES as gray and restless as the Severn. And, as the Severn, there is no telling what may lie beneath the surface. I hesitate a moment, studying him as he does me, wondering what he plans to do. I can feel Keagan beside me: the heat shimmering around her, ready to attack him, to kill him before he can kill us.

But I don't think he will. Caleb can hear me, he can feel me. He's known where I've been ever since this battle began. I didn't wear Fifer's necklace, not today; I needed Schuyler to be able to hear me. If Caleb wanted me dead, he would have done it by now; there's nothing or no one that could stop him. So what does he want then, standing there, staring at me, if not to kill me?

I start for him.

"No." Malcolm steps in front of me, to try to stop me.

"It's all right," I say. "I don't think he'll hurt me. I think"—I glance at Caleb, see his slight, almost imperceptible nod—"he wants to talk to me."

Malcolm and Keagan exchange a rapid glance.

"Revenants aren't much for talking, are they? No." Keagan answers her own question. "But if he's got something to say, it might be worth hearing. As long as he doesn't get any other ideas."

A burst of flame leaps from Keagan's palm; she lobs it across the field toward Caleb. He's fast but the fire is faster; he spins out of the way but not before the flame grazes the side of his head. He turns back to us, eyes gleaming with malice.

"Antagonizing a revenant," I say. "That wasn't wise."

"It's wiser than you think," Keagan replies. "Now go, before I change my mind and set him alight like St. Crispin's Day fireworks. We'll be watching from the woods."

I cross the ruined field to where Caleb waits for me. He's dressed in uniform, as the last time I saw him: black tunic, black trousers, Blackwell's badge on his sleeve and the insignia of the Knights of the Anglian Royal Empire on his chest. His blond hair is singed black over his left ear, smoking slightly.

"Elizabeth." Those gray eyes flick over me, empty, but not with hostility. "You're alive."

"Yes." But then, because I can't help it—I never can—I add, "Are you planning to change that?"

Something then, a glimmer behind his cold expression. If this was the Caleb I knew, I'd almost think it was amusement. Then it's gone.

"No," he says. "I don't plan to hurt you."

"What are you doing here?" I say. "You should be fighting. Killing. It's what he wants, isn't it? It's what he would order."

A pause. Then: "That's not what he's ordered me to do."

It's the things they don't ask that can be taken advantage of. Schuyler's words play in my head.

"What did he order you to do?" I ask, knowing as I do he can't tell me.

"Your friends," he says instead. "They know what has to be done. They all do."

"My friends?" I want to ask Caleb what he means, but I know he can't tell me that, either. Instead, I think about why he's here. It's not to help me; Caleb has always only wanted to help himself. It is as Schuyler said: He is beholden, but he doesn't want to be held. He is disloyal without being disobedient. But all of these things are in service of a goal that, for once, is the same as mine. So I try and frame my words in a way that will help us both.

"If I go to Rochester Hall," I say, "what will I find?"

Caleb's eyes flash, an acknowledgment of my guile. "What you are looking for."

I turn then, and I run. I don't wait to see if Caleb follows me, or if Keagan and Malcolm and his men do. It scarcely matters. All that matters is reaching Rochester Hall, to find what Caleb wants me to find, to play my part even though I don't know how it's written.

To confront whatever is happening there before I'm too late to stop it.

I thread through the woods, through the trees until the smoke ends and fire dies and the rain runs out, until I reach the other side, plunging into the open rolling valley and heading north toward Rochester. Now that the battlefield is behind me, I see how little progress was made. So much destruction for so little direction.

Thirty minutes of hard, flat-out running and I finally reach Rochester. Whatever magic Blackwell used to keep us corralled in battle doesn't exist here, where the air is pale blue and clear, sweet and silent. The barrier does not exist here, either: It was altered before the battle to allow our side in but Blackwell's side out in the event of a retreat. But no magic can stop Blackwell, I knew that even then.

And now I know it was never meant to: that the plan all along was to bring him in.

Rochester Hall stretches in front of me, that bastion of red brick and beauty and safety: the safest place in all of Harrow. The surrounding grounds are empty of men, the lake serene and smooth. No shrieking from the monsters above, no crying from the bodies below, only the third-quarter moon, half black and half white, hanging low in the horizon. Even my footsteps across the road sound muffled, a tiptoe instead of a crunch, a sigh instead of a groan. This is a relief to me; it means the women and children—and Fifer and George—remain safe inside. But then, they are not who Blackwell is after.

I peel yet another arrow from the quiver at my waist, and nock it into place before stepping from the main road onto the footpath, then to the bridge that leads across the lake. I'm vulnerable—too vulnerable—and it's in every move I make. My slow, careful footsteps; the way I swing the bow up, down, left, right; the way I control my breath in an effort to contain my careening pulse.

The path ends at the massive iron door, barred shut. There are only three ways, that I know of, to access the grounds from the outside: across the lake on boats, through the main door, and through the tunnel specially allowed for John.

But the tunnel will be closed to me, because John is not with me. I need to find another way. Rochester is so highly protected magically that I think there may be no other way. I turn left, walking along the parapets, searching. Nothing, just an endless stretch of red brick. Then I see it: a tiny stone monkey crouched on a parapet, its head cocked to the side, staring at something directly below it. I remember the gargoyles at Ravenscourt, how they marked secret entrances, passages that led into and out of the castle.

I run my hand along the surface and soon enough I feel it, buried in the tracery, the intricate lacework of stone that decorates the wall. A latch. I hook my finger into it, pull. There's a low, echoing click and a shifting of brick: a door. It creaks open, leaving just enough room for me to slide through.

Inside is a tunnel, perhaps an adjunct to John's, perhaps different; it's hard to tell in the dark. But I push my way through it, a thousand twists and turns and dead ends, until I find another panel that slides open behind a marbled bust, one of a dozen I passed in the east wing on my way to visit Malcolm the week before.

Where could Blackwell be? Nicholas said he would not hesitate. That he would not risk the time to go back to Upminster to perform the ritual. Once he has John he won't need much to perform it: a ritual room and four elements; an eight-pointed star and a sacrifice.

My footsteps are muffled by the thick carpet underneath

as I dash through the west wing, forgoing bedchambers and solars for great halls and music rooms: spaces that are bare enough to allow for adornment, private enough to discourage discovery.

Even disallowing half the rooms in Rochester as options, it takes ages to search them all. There are so many floors, so many hallways, so many twists and turns that I lose my way, only to search the same spot twice.

Still, nothing.

I stop and I think. Try for a moment to put myself into Blackwell's frame of mind, his insane desperation. He's in a place he doesn't know. He doesn't have time to learn about it, to walk from room to room and risk getting lost, as I have.

I walk to the window, staring out at the late-afternoon sky. From here, the trees are blocking my view of the horizon. Nicholas said the moon was not necessary for the ritual, only preferable. But he also said that this time, Blackwell would not take any chances. If I were the gambling type—I'm not, at least not with lives that aren't my own—I would wager that Blackwell will want to see it; to be close to it. He will want the security it brings him, when he's in a place and a position that gives him none.

I turn in place, trying to align myself with the direction where it will be visible. If the sun is to the west, the moon will be directly north. A room facing north could be both in the east wing and the west, but those in the west face nothing but hills; I remember seeing them the day I visited Malcolm. Besides, they're all chamber rooms there, and carpeted: difficult to draw a star upon. The east wing, then.

Keeping an eye on windows as I pass, I race through the massive entryway into the east wing until I reach the stretch of rooms Fitzroy kept open for his troops to visit. I pass the library—a too-crowded space for a ritual; the chapel—too holy; the dance hall—too windowless. Finally, I reach the dark, polished door at the end. Small, quiet, facing due north and banked with windows for visibility: the music room.

I hesitate, just a moment. I fear what I'll find when I open the door; I fear what I will not find. Raising my bow, I shoulder open the door.

Inside: wood-paneled and tapestried walls, a grid of parqueted floors, a bank of stained glass windows casting around fractured, jewel-toned light from the fading sun. In the center of the room stands a group of figures, gradually coming into focus as my eyes adjust to the darkness.

The first I anticipated, tall and deadly and dressed entirely in black: Marcus. The second I expected, slashed and twisted and stitched back together, dressed as a king in crimson and gold, ermine and jewels, sewn with his coat of arms and always, always, that damned strangled rose: Blackwell.

But the third I neither expected nor anticipated, standing sacrifice in the center of the room, his ivory robes ripped and pulled apart as if by a beast, blood blooming fast against his chest: Nicholas.

If they're surprised to see me, none of them shows it. Marcus regards me with gleeful malice; Blackwell with feigned disinterest. But Nicholas doesn't regard me at all, eyes fixed intently at a spot somewhere over my head, as if he doesn't even see me.

I blurt out his name, start toward him, but stop when

Blackwell pulls a knife from nowhere and holds it to Nicholas's throat.

"Let him go," I say, a useless plea.

"You found me," Blackwell says. "Although it's not me you're looking for at all, is it? You came for your healer, didn't you, to bid him one final good-bye before I take back what is rightfully mine? I have to say, Elizabeth, I'm surprised. Giving up your power, your own life, to save his?" He shakes his head. "A pity you didn't show me half that loyalty."

By way of response, I raise my shaking bow and aim it at the gaping hole that holds the remains of a milky, ruined eye.

"Charming, as always." The s whistles serpentine through his cavernous cheek.

I glance at Nicholas once more, to try to get a sense of how injured he is, if he can move, if he can help me somehow rescue him. But he still does not meet my gaze.

"Set down your weapons," Blackwell commands. "All of them."

I don't.

"Do it," he says, "or his blood will be on you." As if to illustrate his point, he slides the tip of the knife into Nicholas's bare, vulnerable neck. A line of blood dark as ink appears, joining the rest on his tunic.

"Don't!" I throw out my arm, the one holding the bow, and it drops with a thunk to the parquet floor. One by one I lay down my sword, my knives, my quiver of arrows, and back away.

"You forgot the one in your boot," Blackwell says.

Unwillingly, I reach into my boot and toss my knife—my last—into the pile. Before Blackwell, before Marcus, I am completely, utterly vulnerable.

Blackwell releases Nicholas then, throws him to the ground. He lands on his stomach; there's blood on the back of his cloak, too. He's injured worse than I imagined; he may even be dying. Marcus—I suspect this is his work—could have so easily finished the job. Why didn't Blackwell order him to?

A breeze of a warning makes the hair on my neck stand on end.

"Nicholas." I keep my voice low to disguise its trembling. "Listen to me. Look at me. Don't let him—"

"That's enough of that," Blackwell barks. "He cannot hear you. Even if he could, he would not reply. Nicholas is under my command now, and he must do what I say. Exactly what I say." Blackwell snaps his fingers and Nicholas rises, puppet-like, to stand by his side. Another snap and his eyes shift to mine, finally seeing me. They narrow to hard, obsidian slits.

Blackwell circles around him, the hard soles of his polished boots a staccato against the floor.

"We have some unfinished business, you and I," he says to me. "And I thought it fitting that the one who once saved you"—a dismissive wave at Nicholas—"should be the one to end you."

Another snap, and Nicholas raises his arm, points a finger in my direction. And with the unseen force of a battering ram, I'm lifted off my feet and thrown backward across the room. I slam into the hard, paneled wall, my breath and half my consciousness knocked out of me.

I drop to my knees, try to breathe. Try to stand. Another snap and I'm thrown forward to the floor. Another snap: backward into the wall. My head rings from the force of the blows, I cannot breathe, and I cannot think fast enough to know what to do. So I do the only thing I know how: I lunge for the pile of weapons on the floor.

I don't make it.

Yet another snap of Blackwell's fingers propels Nicholas once more into action.

He turns to the window, throwing his arms wide, conducting the bank of stained glass panels as they bow and crackle and then, with an explosion like thunder, a kaleidoscope of deadly shards hurtles toward me.

I run—I almost don't make it—to the wall and the tapestry before me, diving beneath it just as the glass shatters around me, a dull thud against the thick, dense wool. A few larger pieces pierce the fabric like daggers, stabbing my cheeks and my arms, drawing hot drops of blood I don't bother to wipe away. Because the warning I felt before, the slight breeze of a caution, has now turned into a torrent with understanding.

In the first, failed ritual attempt, Blackwell offered up a raven as sacrifice: its death an oblation for his own, to be forever withheld. Now, in his second attempt, Blackwell needs another sacrifice. He could have chosen anyone or anything, another humble raven, perhaps; it needs only to be a living, breathing thing. Instead, Blackwell chose Nicholas. An act of revenge, perhaps, or twisted symbolism: to extinguish Nicholas's light in order for Blackwell to shroud the world in dark.

But for him to risk capturing the only man with power to rival his own at a time when he cannot risk anything, that tells me the real reason:

Blackwell is out of magic.

Just as the Azoth gives power, the way it gave to me when I used it, it takes power, too, from those it injures—and from those it curses. *A curse can deplete magic*, Nicholas said. And while Blackwell's got enough power left to control Nicholas, it's not enough to carry out the ritual. Not with whatever magic he used up to be here in Rochester, to control his army, his creatures, his revenants.

Caleb must have known this. It must have been why he sent me, at least in part. Because maybe—maybe—if I'm able to bypass Marcus's malevolence and Nicholas's capitulation to get to my weapons, I can take advantage of Blackwell's weakness. Before he sacrifices Nicholas, before he finds John, before he can carry out his insane plan of immortality.

To do the impossible. Again.

I throw back the tapestry. Yet another snap and Nicholas advances on me, lips curled in something that looks like amusement. I don't look at him, I don't acknowledge him. Instead, I turn to Blackwell.

"Is that all?" I taunt. "You're the most powerful wizard in Anglia, and that's all you can do? Turn puppeteer before blowing out the windows?" I allow myself a wide, feigned smile. "First you send Fulke after me, now this. Once again, you insult me."

Engaging him is a gamble, a liability. But if I can tempt him into using his power, it will show me what he's got left, using up what he's got left. I may be empty of weapons, but I'm not empty of wit.

Blackwell gleams at me. "You always were one of my best witch hunters."

"Yes," I say. "I was."

There's no snap. No ministration. He throws his own arms up this time.

And the sky comes down.

The vaulted ceiling of the music room cracks; massive shards splinter and plummet to the floor. Falling lumber tears the tapestry from its moorings; the heavy cloth falls on top of me and I hold it over me like a shield. Marcus and Nicholas stand watching me, unharmed: The air around them is clear.

I run through the room, dodging falling timber to try to reach my discarded weapons. My tapestry snags on something along the floor; it's yanked off my head. I free it but not before a splinter of wood, sharp as a knife, slices through my forearm, through skin and bone, all the way through to the other side. I gasp, stumble to one knee, rip it out. Blood pours down my arm, drips through my fingers. I press my hand to stanch the wound; press down my feelings to stanch the pain.

The roof is open to the sky now, no longer blue and clear as it was when I arrived, but choked with a swirl of black rumbling clouds rolling in like a band of horses. Blackwell flicks his hand and with a clap and a roar the clouds open up, a waterfall of rain pouring in through the open roof.

I spot a gleam of steel beneath the tinder. A knife or a sword, I can't tell. I drop to my hands and knees, scrabble through the dust, the wood, until finally I reach it. It's a knife, but only one. I grasp the hilt. Spin around. Through the rain I see his outline, as black and thunderous as the clouds above. I pull back, take aim: the space right between his eyes.

I will not miss.

Then: an earsplitting crack, a blinding flash. Lightning.

It tears into me, spears me to the floor; I feel as if I'm on fire. In the middle of the pyre at Tyburn, heat and smoke and lit from within by searing-hot pain that rain does not abate, and I begin to scream.

"Stop."

At the sound of his voice, the recognition of it, everything ceases. The rain, the lightning, but not the pain. I'm pinned to the floor by it. I can't move, I can't think. But I can see. Him. Them. Standing in the doorway of the splintered, broken room: Caleb in black, and in his grip, finally—Nicholas might say inevitably—is John.

32

"STOP," JOHN SAYS AGAIN. He starts toward me, but Caleb holds him back. "Let her be."

"You don't command me." Blackwell's voice has taken on a clipped edge, one of authority and triumph.

"I have something you need," John says. "If you want it, then you'll do what I say."

Blackwell chuckles. "Rather ridiculous request, don't you think? But I'll acquiesce. I'll let her be, until the time it takes to kill you. What I do to her after that will no longer be your concern."

"If you think she'll allow you to do anything to her, you don't know her as well as I do."

A lewd, twisted grin. "I'm sure I don't."

John's eyes haven't left me since he entered the room. To others, his careful expression may read as fear. But only

I know him enough to know it's determination. He's determined to do this. To give himself to Blackwell, to die for him, to allow him to become immortal. I don't understand, and I don't want to.

I turn from him to Blackwell. Get to my feet, slowly. Raise my arm, the one still holding the blade, and once again take trembling aim.

"Elizabeth." John's voice, a whisper, rings through the room like a shout. "Don't make the end harder than it has to be."

This: the end. What John planned for all along, what Nicholas planned. Never mind what I planned: scheming and lying and stealing to make sure it didn't. Even so, I drop the knife and it falls to the floor, a thud among the rubble.

Blackwell's tangled, destroyed eye flicks to John. "Confidence, determination, fearlessness." His voice is a drawl. "You possess all the qualities I value in my men, despite your allegiance. At the very least, you appear to have been a competent steward for my power." A pause. "I'm curious. What did it do for you? This power?"

There's so much John could say to this: too much. But his reply lies only in his disdain. "Nothing," he says. "It did nothing for me."

The levity drops from Blackwell's face, and he turns back to Caleb. "Did he put up a fight?"

"He was trying to escape," Caleb replies. "With the rest of their army. They're retreating."

"Retreating," Blackwell repeats, his voice a satisfied purr. "And my nephew?"

"Dead." Caleb shrugs. "I saw to that myself. He is dead, and you are king."

340

I expect Blackwell to revel in this news. To eat it, to drink it. Instead, his eyes narrow and he says in a voice full of silent rage, "I am king. I have always been king."

A pause. Then Caleb sketches a deep bow. "Majesty."

John, escaping. Malcolm, dead. None of this rings true to me. John wouldn't turn from a fight; he would die before he would do that. As for death, Keagan would never have allowed Malcolm's. Not without some sign of a fight, of blood or of fire, and Caleb shows neither, nothing more than the singed hair he wore earlier.

But then I see the skill in Caleb's reply to Blackwell's questions. He gave him an answer, but he didn't tell him what he really wanted to know. And Blackwell never commanded him to be truthful. *It's the things a pater doesn't ask that can be taken advantage of.* Once more, Schuyler's words echo in my head.

Something is happening, I don't know what. I turn to John, then to Caleb to try to glean something from their faces. But they both look away, ahead, anywhere but at me.

Blackwell snaps his fingers and on command, Nicholas steps to his side.

"Begin the preparations."

Nicholas holds out a hand, murmuring under his breath. Embers begin to glow beneath the rubble strewn along the floor, and as Nicholas waves his hand, his movement coaxes the nascent flame until it begins to roar, cracking and spitting and smoking.

Marcus steps forward, reaches into his cloak, passes the contents to Blackwell. A scattering of salt, a clutch of herbs, a skin of water set to mark the cardinal points north, east, west. A bundle of thin, rough-hewn candles lit from the fire

341

on the floor. A single one set south, four more to mark the intercardinal directions: an eight-pointed star.

I know what happens next.

And it happens so fast.

Nicholas, now immobile in Marcus's grip, dragged to the center of the star. Blackwell beside him, a knife in his hand. A glint of steel, a repressed grunt of pain, and blood—still more blood—to flood the rest of his ivory robes. Nicholas slumps to the floor, dead. A sacrifice.

I'm too horrified to even make a sound.

Blackwell reaches for his scabbard, and with a song against the leather he slides it out, the same damned blade that's etched in duplicate on the badge on his sleeve: the Azoth. This time, it doesn't call to me. This time, it repels me. I want nothing more than to see it—its curse and its power—destroyed.

Blackwell begins chanting. His voice, the only one in the room this time, is clear, and I can hear every word:

I am old, weak, and sick; fire torments me;
Death rends my flesh and breaks my bones.
My soul and spirit have abandoned me;
In my body is found salt, sulfur, and mercury.
Let them first be distilled, separated, purified;
That they will be transmuted and reborn,
Through Opus Magnum; the greatest of all works;
The circle closes its end.

The emeralds embedded in the Azoth's hilt begin to wink brightly, frantically, as if they understand the change that is about to occur.

"You." Blackwell gestures to John, still in Caleb's grip.

"Don't!" I shout, finding my voice. "Don't do this. Don't—" I lunge for him, for them, just as Blackwell raises his hand, and a shard of glass flies across the room and slices into my face.

"Elizabeth!" John shouts my name as I gasp, pressing a hand to my face. The glass, it's only skimmed me: a long cut across my cheek that stings and bleeds but a little, though it stands as a warning. "Don't," he says. "Please."

"Okay," I say. "Okay." I try to be as brave as he is but I am not. Everything I did, all of it, was for naught. Saving Nicholas, only to have him killed in front of us. Saving John, only to have him offered up like a lamb for slaughter. The two of them saving me—not once but twice—but without the charm of the third.

Caleb brings John forward, to the center of the star. John doesn't hesitate; he doesn't stumble. He walks straight to Blackwell, stops in front of him. They stand eye to eye: John's armor is missing, his surcoat is tattered and battle-worn, his face is shadowed with dirt and his hair plastered with sweat. But his posture is ramrod straight and his gaze is direct. He does not flinch from Blackwell's horror.

"You will not fight," Blackwell says. "If you do not want to see her throat slit, slowly, agonizingly, in front of you. You will not fight," he repeats, "if you wish for her end to be merciful."

"What do you want me to do?" John's voice is steady.

"You?" Blackwell scoffs. "You do nothing." Then, without warning or ceremony, he holds up the Azoth.

And he thrusts it into John's chest.

For a moment, nothing happens. Then, a glow: It begins, like the embers in the fire beneath our feet, spreading from

John's chest outward, down his arms into his hands, up his neck into his face. John's eyes go wide, he opens his mouth; nothing comes out but a gasp. His body goes rigid for a beat, two; then he begins to convulse as if someone's shaking him. The light around him turns from white to yellow to red as he burns up with the force of the magic, the force of the stigma leaving his body.

I know this pain; I finally remember it. The heat, the burning, the feeling of being carved inside out and thrust back together. I remember the pain of it, the surety that I was going to die, the pleading because I wanted to die.

Once more I lunge for John, to try to stop this. Caleb is beside me in a blur, his hand clamped around my arm, pulling me back. He's saying something to me but I don't listen, it's drowned out by my screams.

Then, like a torch that's been plunged into water, the light goes out. Red fades back to white and John drops to the floor in a heap, lifeless, his hazel eyes open wide to the ceiling, seeing nothing.

Caleb releases me and I run to John, drop to my knees beside him. I shake him, because that is what you do. I call his name, because that is what you do, too, hoping that somehow this is all a joke, a cruel joke but one nevertheless, that they somehow might groan or cough or roll over or sit up, that they might have cheated death after all.

But this is not what John does. I run my hands across his face, his neck, his pulse points on his wrists, his chest: They are all empty, silent. He is empty. He is silent.

He is dead.

And I have nothing to save him with. I can do nothing for

him. Nothing at all. I knot my fists into the front of his shirt, already gone cold, and I begin to sob. But even as I do, I cannot take my eyes off Blackwell, off what happens next.

Blackwell raises the Azoth to the sky, swirling charcoal above us, faster and faster. The blade is coated in blood, dark red and nearly black. But the hilt, the emeralds... they are no longer green. They are yellow and bright as the sun, not twinkling but flashing, growing brighter and brighter with every passing moment. He continues chanting, his words picking up speed, pulsing in time with the sky and the light from the Azoth.

A hole opens in the center of the clouds, a window into the now-deepening sky. There, in the center of it: the moon. Half light and half dark, heavy and guiding, luring the spell to its completion.

The Azoth explodes into sunlight. It engulfs us, it fills the room with brightness so white and suffocating I close my eyes, bury my head in John's chest. I can feel it pouring into me, filling me with a heat so intense I feel as if I'm being burned from the inside out. I grip John's body tighter, shielding him with my own as if I can protect him from this, even when I could not protect him before, even though he does not need my protection anymore.

As quickly as the room filled with light, it goes out. Black. Silent. I open my eyes, but I can see nothing before me. Not John, not my own arms around him, not anything or anyone. Just the sound of ragged breathing: mine, perhaps Blackwell's. The others do not breathe at all.

Moments pass. I don't move; no one around me moves, not that I can hear. Then, slowly, the room begins to illuminate:

gently around the edges at first, a ring of purple and red fading inward, giving way to lavender and rose until the room is bathed in a haze of pink. It should be beautiful but there is something horrible about it, as if the air itself is drenched in blood. And in the middle of it all, Blackwell.

He stands stiffly, the way John did. His eyes open wide, an expression of something—pain? Fear? I don't know, I've never seen Blackwell anything other than composed—etched into his face, his arms held stiffly before him. The Azoth, held in his hand just moments before, is gone. All that remains is a scattering of stones along the floor, green again now, but a dull green of decay, as if whatever illuminated them before from within is now dead.

It is as if I'm watching time run backward: Blackwell's skin knits together, growing and stretching over his face; his black veins fading to gray before disappearing altogether. The spell is working. The destruction of the Azoth has combined with the invincibility of the stigma. It is repairing him.

This is the end.

And we are all finished.

There's a shuffle beside me then. I turn to see Nicholas moving toward me, a slow labored crawl. I hold John tighter, shield his body with mine. There is nothing more Nicholas can do to him now, I know. But that doesn't matter.

Nicholas ignores me, he keeps moving toward me, toward us.

I pull back my leg, the same way I did in Fleet prison all those months ago. When Nicholas came to rescue me and I almost didn't trust him, when I almost didn't go with him, when I almost killed him.

I stop.

Look at him closely—really look at him. His dark eyes—blank and unseeing before—are now focused on me, full of clarity and pain and desperation and the closest thing I've seen to fear ever come to pass along his face.

Whatever spell Nicholas was under, it's gone now. I don't know how: Maybe Blackwell released him; maybe Blackwell's transformation severed the magic. I reach for him again but he shakes his head—once, hard, and once more I pull away. He crawls closer, close enough for me to see how pale he is, how he trembles, how he's left half his blood on the floor behind him. Close enough to John to touch him, his hand fluttering along his neck.

"He's dead," I say, and I could scream with the grief of it. "This wasn't part of your plan, was it? It couldn't be, not this." The sobbing that never really stopped starts up again.

"Elizabeth. Listen to me. Listen." Nicholas's voice is a rattling breath, a choking cough full of blood. "The unity of opposites."

Abruptly, I stop crying. "What?"

"Everything must have its opposite. Up to down. Black to white. Destruction to invincibility." He speaks quickly, his voice urgent; he wants me to understand something I do not. "Everything has an opposite."

"Yes." I lean toward him. His hand is still pressed to John's neck, his trembling fingers cupped behind it as if caressing him. "I know this. I understand—"

Another sharp jerk of his head. "Immortality. It has an opposite, too. Do you hear me? Elizabeth." More coughing, more blood. "Immortality cannot exist without its opposite."

I turn back to Blackwell, still standing in the center of the room, his empty hands still held before him. He presses them against his chest, a frown crossing his now-pale, unscarred face. He looks as if he was expecting to see something he does not, to feel something he does not. How should immortality feel? What is the shape of it, the breath of it?

Or does it not exist at all?

"Immortality has its opposite, too." I whisper it as I finally begin to understand it.

The Azoth, now dead and dusted and gone, gave up its destruction, just as Blackwell planned. The destructive power of it combined with the invincibility of the stigma to transcend them both, just as Blackwell planned.

But what he did not know, what John and Nicholas somehow did, was that immortality does not exist. That it cannot exist: not without death alongside it. That the powers of both became the power of neither, and here Blackwell stands, empty of it all.

Mortal.

"The circle closes its end. That end is for you to make. His end. Do you understand? Do—" Nicholas slumps to the floor then, his hand still clutched around John's neck. His eyes close, and he falls terribly, horribly still.

The end is for me to make.

I wanted to make it mine, when I swore I would protect John from his. This is not what I would have chosen, but it has been given to me to carry out, to finish what was started too long ago to remember, a history that started without me but somehow entangled me and is now left to me.

Does that still make it mine?

Does it matter?

As if he can hear my thoughts, Blackwell turns to me, and by the look on his face he blames me: for what happened to him, for what didn't happen to him; for not understanding what happened at all. He stands there and he stares at me, the haze of pink still surrounding him like a halo of blood, his eyes dark and his expression even darker.

"You did this." Blackwell flicks a hand and at once Marcus is by his side, drawing his own sword and placing it in Blackwell's hand. Blackwell advances on me, waving the blade before him, a slow, sluggish movement. "You. And him." I don't know if he means Nicholas or John; it doesn't matter.

I climb to my feet. Slowly, painfully; through broken bones and bleeding wounds and burnt, torn flesh. Pull myself from the rubble, from the carnage, from Nicholas and from John, releasing him the worst pain of all.

"You told me once we create our own enemies." My voice is determined, but it is weary: as weary as the end of every battle I've ever fought. "I was never your enemy, nor were they."

"You conspired to deceive me; you colluded to deceive me. You stand here before me, deceiving me still."

"I said I *was* not your enemy." I reach down and gently slide John's sword from his scabbard. It is dirty, stained with blood, ordinary. But if Blackwell is ordinary, if he is mortal, it needs to be nothing more. "But I am now."

"You think you can kill me?" Blackwell's voice, it's different. Not just in tone or timbre but in tremor: the slightest shake that alerts me to the truth: He is afraid. For once, he is like me; he is like all of us. And for a moment, just a moment, I almost pity him.

"You should have left me alone," I say. "If you'd left me alone, I'd be nothing to you. But by pursuing me, you created your own worst enemy. And for that, for what you did to them, to all of us, I'm going to pay you in kind."

I raise John's sword. At once, Marcus starts for me, jerky, hesitant steps as if he's moving against his will, against Blackwell's will. Caleb does not move at all. Blackwell waves a hand to dismiss them both, exerting his control as a pater, the only power he's got left.

Blackwell tries to circle me, tries. But I match his every step. He throws up his blade. It's slow, it's unsure, it's the swing of a mortal man and a frightened man at that. I meet the blow, deflect it, the clash of silver on steel echoing off bare wooden walls, the empty wooden floors.

He strikes again; I deflect again. I can hear him gasping for breath as we whirl across the floor, lunging, parrying, attacking. But he's not landing the blows he should, and he knows it. So he does something I don't expect:

He throws his weapon down.

It spins end over end across the slick wood floor, skidding to a stop against the paneled wall. The shock of him disarming himself is enough to stop me, enough to divert my gaze, only for a second. But a second is all he needs.

Blackwell leaps forward. Snatches my right arm, the arm carrying the sword, thrusting it away from him. With the other hand he grabs a hank of my hair, then kicks me hard, harder than I thought possible, along the side of my knee: a move I learned from him now turned against me.

I crumple to the floor, a sharp shriek of pain escaping my lips. The blade tips from my grip, skittering along the floor into a heap of rubble. I scrabble for it, my leg tangled beneath me, but I cannot reach it.

Blackwell turns to Marcus. "Finish her."

Marcus snaps to attention. Those gray eyes alight on me as he starts for me, grin as bright as his gaze, his steps smooth: commanded. Caleb stands in attendance beside Blackwell, both of them watching, waiting, for the end.

My fingers search wildly in the dust and the timber, and finally they find something: cool, smooth, a handle; not of a sword but of a dagger. I unearth it, twist to a crouched position.

Blackwell's eyes go wide as I pull back the blade, wider still when I fling it. It hits where I mean it to: his chest, two inches right of center, straight to the heart. He grunts, falters to his knees. Blood blooms against his surcoat, flushing the red rose of his house—that twisted, snarled, thorned rose—black and drenched with it.

A roar of anger and Marcus leaps for me, wild as any animal, hate and revenge in his eyes. He never makes it. Caleb reaches him before Marcus reaches me; it happens so fast. A scuffle, a curse—the savage snap of a neck and Marcus slumps to the floor, dead once more; his face frozen in a twisted snarl of surprise.

Blackwell reaches for the blade in his chest, pulls it out. More blood, a stifled gasp of pain, a shocked look at Caleb for allowing this to happen. Yet he is still breathing, still alive, and I have no time. No time until Blackwell turns his command to Caleb, commanding him to turn on me.

I get to my feet. Pitch under the weight of my shattered knee, of the wounds scattered like petals along my skin. Spot Marcus's sword, the one Blackwell so carelessly flung away. A quick glance at Caleb: I know he hears my thoughts, knows what I intend. Blackwell knows, too; he must. I've got seconds before Blackwell orders him to finish me and this time, there's no one to stop him.

I rush forward to grab the weapon. And before I can consider the fear beginning to etch itself along Blackwell's face, the fear of defeat and of death, the fear that defined him and now defies him; before I can stop to regret it or allow sympathy to temper it, I plunge the sword into his chest. It screams into his flesh, smooth; no hitches, as easy as a hand into warm water. And there it stays as his life ebbs out.

There is no pomp in killing a king, only circumstance: no magic, no fire; no ceilings thundering down like rain. The end comes for Blackwell the same way it came for Nicholas, and for John; the way it does for any man: quickly, silently, painfully.

Finally.

33

IT IS OVER.

The magic Blackwell took and twisted to his own purposes—before it twisted against him—is gone. At once, the room is lighter. The clouds, black and ominous before, have scattered, giving way to muted, early-morning skies. It throws the destruction around me into sharp relief: the blood, the piles of rubble, the discarded weapons, the shattered glass. The broken bodies: John's and Nicholas's.

I don't move, I don't speak. Not even when Caleb shifts into motion, moving slowly across the room, footsteps dragging through the ruin. He stops before Blackwell, his body as lifeless and still as the others', but unlike the others', his face is twisted into a grimace of pain and defeat. There's no peace for him, even in death.

"He's dead," Caleb says. That gleam, the one I saw earlier

in the field, in the heat of battle, flares once more into his face. "I feel as if I can breathe again."

"You knew." My voice is dull, emotionless. I have no emotion left. "You knew this would happen. You helped make it happen."

Caleb shakes his head. "I didn't know, not at first. But Nicholas and your healer, they figured it out. They knew what the unity of opposites really meant. It's why they sacrificed themselves to allow Blackwell to attempt it. Your other friend, Schuyler, he knew it, too. He called to me, told me I could help. Him. Nicholas. You."

"Yourself." The word is bitter enough to choke on.

"Yes. Myself." Caleb acknowledges the truth. "But Blackwell is dead now, and we are all free. That's what you wanted, isn't it? To be free?"

Free. Without John, and without Nicholas, the word feels more like *forsaken.* But I know what Caleb wishes me to acknowledge. His role in this, the risk he took; the part he played that no one else could. John, Nicholas, they are not the only ones who had to die in order for Blackwell to die, too.

"Anglia is grateful," I say, "for what you've done." It's all I can manage, the only thing I can manage.

"Maybe someday, you will be, too."

I nod, but I'm already backing away. I don't want to talk to Caleb and I've already stopped listening. I want to sit with John until I cannot sit with him anymore, and then I need to figure out a way to tell Peter his son is dead. It's nearly enough to make me wish Peter were dead, too, so he wouldn't have to bear it.

Caleb glances toward the open, shattered windows.

Frowns, purses his lips, shakes his head. It's a gesture I've seen Schuyler do before, one he does when he's piecing something together from the fragments of thought around him.

"They're retreating," he says after a moment. "Blackwell's men. They're leaving. I can feel them." Another crunch of glass as he moves toward the open window. "I should leave now, too."

I don't ask where he'll go. But when Caleb steps through the window, half in light, half in dark, he turns to me and says, "Do you think we'll meet again?"

I look at him. Watching Caleb leave—again—holds nothing for me this time. There are too many wrongs that have passed between us that can never be set right.

"I don't know," I say. "But I think it's best if we don't."

Caleb says nothing to this, only nods. Then he's gone, slipping through the window like a ghost. And I am alone.

Slowly, as if in a nightmare from which I will never wake, I walk to John's body, resting pale and motionless before me. Nicholas lies prone beside him, looking younger in death. His face is pale, marblelike in its placidity, but arranged in a peaceful expression that looks almost as if he's smiling. His hands are clasped over his chest; he is so, so still.

I kneel beside John, take his hand, cool in my own fevered grip. His eyes, open before, are closed now; Nicholas must have done that. His body has shifted slightly, his head listing toward the window. Nicholas must have done that, too. Unlike Nicholas, John doesn't look younger in death. Nor does he look peaceful. His brow is slightly furrowed, creased between his eyes. He looks as if he's asleep and not having a particularly good dream, he looks as if he could open his eyes at any moment and tell me all about it. But he can't and he won't and the simple, sharp finality of that is more than I can take.

"I'm sorry." I repeat it over and over, curling into him, grasping his tunic and rocking back and forth, whispering and sobbing until my voice gives out and I'm limp with exhaustion and grief.

That's when I feel it: a hand on the back of my head, cupping my neck, fingers feathering my hair. I don't move, not right away. Because when I do, I know I'll see Peter standing beside me, grief etched in his face the way I know it's etched in mine, and I can't bear it. But then, when I hear him say my name, "... beth," in a voice that's not a whisper as much as it is a breath, I jerk my head up.

John. He's turned his head, he's watching me through one eye, barely open, his hand that was just on my head poised in the air. His other eye cracks open and he blinks, dropping his hand to my side, his fingers grasping for the hem of my tunic.

I'm too afraid to say anything. Too afraid to do anything that might take this moment away, that might lift the spell, that might take the possibility of what I'm seeing and turn it back into what it really is: impossible.

But when he says my name again, clearer and louder this time, I'm finally able to utter a single word. "How?"

John doesn't speak. He just turns his head and there, on the skin along the side of his neck where Nicholas had laid his hand, is a tiny fleur-de-lis, no bigger than a thumbprint, no darker than a sunburn. It's all that's left of Nicholas, of his power: given to John, healing him as they both lay dying.

"Oh." It's all I can say. I tuck my head back onto his chest and wrap my arms around him and bury myself into him again. John presses his head against mine and whispers in my ear, his words unintelligible from the tremor in his voice and the tumult in my breath, but I feel the love and relief in them anyway.

Slowly, eventually, I help him sit up and then to his feet. He's unsteady, and he holds to me tight. "How do you feel?" I don't know if I mean without the stigma, or with Nicholas's magic, or after having died. Perhaps I mean all of it.

"It's hard to say." He offers up a tentative smile, as if he knows what I'm thinking. "I'm tired. A little dizzy. But for the most part, as far as I can tell, I feel like me again."

"Caleb said you planned this," I say. "You and Nicholas. When?"

"While I was sequestered in Rochester," John replies. "Nicholas brought me the books I needed to figure it out. It was part of the reason he shut me away. He needed me to know what my part in this was. What I would need to do. What we both would need to do."

"Did anyone else know about this? Your father? Fifer?"

"Fifer knew," John says. "She figured it out even before I did. Even so, she had a hard time accepting it. Especially toward the end." I remember how she was nowhere to be seen the night of the celebration before the battle, how Schuyler was absent, too. "I waited until last night to tell Father, though," John continues. "I almost didn't. But I didn't want him to think I went into it unknowingly."

"But you didn't tell me."

He nods. "Because I don't know if I could have gone through with it if I had."

John takes my hand and we pick our way through the destruction of the music room, out into the hallway. It's quiet and calm here, as is the neighboring chapel. With care, we carry in Nicholas's body, laying it in the chancel and draping it with the heavy, embroidered altar cloth before making our way outside into the courtyard.

It's clear here, unharmed, but that doesn't mean it's safe. And it isn't: As we emerge from the yew alley into the meadow, the battle that began in the fields and farms outside Rochester is before us now, spilling into the tents and the grass, the jousting pits and the training yards. Men running everywhere: men in black, men in blue and red, a few in white.

I yank John's arm, pulling him back into the alley.

"Wait." He peers around the tree line. "They're not invading. They're retreating. Look."

We edge out into the field, cautious. But John is right, and it seems Caleb was, too: Blackwell's men, what's left of them, are rushing across the grounds, desperate in their attempt to escape. The skies above us are clear now, empty of dark clouds and hybrids with wings, a landscape of nothing but dawn and green.

"I want to find my father," John says. "I need to let him know I'm all right. And I want to help, if I can, people who need it."

We make our way toward the bridge that leads away from Rochester, never straying too far from each other, never letting our guard down. We search the scattered felled bodies for those we recognize, but they are mostly Blackwell's men and a handful of Gallic soldiers. We cross to each one, to see if there's anything John can do to help them. But they're all past saving.

The other side of the bridge is a far different story. The road here is littered with men wearing both colors; some of them alive and injured, but most of them dead, including two in white, members of the Order. The first, a boy I don't know, the second a girl I do: Miri, the one who could manipulate water. I feel a stab of sorrow at that: She was only ten years old. John goes to them to see what he can do to help, and I continue roaming the field, searching the maze of men dashing around, looking for Peter.

That's when I see Malcolm, lying in the clearing. He's alone, and I know he's hurt by the way he moves, twisting from side to side, slow; his back arching, his hand splayed beside him, grasping at the wispy, flattened grass. But more than that, I can tell by the pool of blood beneath him, creeping outward, rusty and bright.

"Malcolm!" I sprint toward him, drop to the ground beside him and take his hand. It's slick with blood, his or someone else's. His armor is missing, his blue-and-red surcoat shredded and torn.

"How'd we do?" He squints at me through one half-opened eye, gray and pale against the blood on his face. "Did we win?"

John appears then, slow and a little out of breath. He kneels beside Malcolm, lifts up his surcoat to reveal what's left of the tangled mail beneath. It looks as if it's been chewed away. Carefully, John peels the rest of it off, piece by piece.

"We won," I say.

Malcolm closes his eye, breathes in. When he exhales, he's looking at me again.

"What of Uncle?" He holds my stare. "How did he fare in all of this?"

I debate telling him I don't know. But I know he already does. I can tell by the resigned look on his face, the way he looks at me, holding me to the truth.

So I tell it.

"He's dead."

Malcolm nods, slow. "Did he hurt you?"

"No," I say. "Not today, and not anymore."

He closes his eyes again. When he opens them and looks to me, they're full of sorrow and light, relief and darkness, all of those things all at once, impossibly opposite, like the Azoth but impossibly human.

"I can't say I'm sorry for it," he says. "But I can't say I'm glad of it, either. Ironic, isn't it? He was all I had left, and he wanted me dead, and now he's gone."

"He's not all you have left," I say, only I don't know if that's true. I don't know what waits for him back at Rochester, or at Upminster, what waits for him at all.

"You're only saying that because I'm dying," he says, as if he's reading my mind.

"You're not dying," I say.

"Try not to talk," John says. He reaches forward and gently rolls up Malcolm's tunic. I hiss in a breath. His skin is sliced across the middle in a diagonal line from hip to armpit. His entire chest is coated in blood.

John slides a knife from Malcolm's belt. "I'm going to cut your tunic off, all right?"

Malcolm gives a tiny nod, and John begins slicing the fabric. He examines it before tossing it aside; it's nothing but a bloody rag. John slips off his surcoat and mail before pulling his own tunic over his head, naked now from the waist up.

"What are you doing?" I can feel my eyes go round.

"I need to stop the bleeding." John presses his shirt into Malcolm's chest, the white linen quickly blooming red. "Hold this here," he says to me, climbing to his feet. He darts across the meadow in a stop-start motion, looking along the ground. He disappears into the trees, then after a moment reemerges clutching a handful of bell-shaped white flowers with spiky dark green leaves. I'd laugh if I weren't so confused.

"You really know how to woo a lady," Malcolm says when John drops beside him again. "The bawd in the battlefield, shirtless, dodging certain death to pick flowers…"

John shoots him an exasperated look, plucks the leaves from the stem, then shoves a handful into his mouth and begins chewing.

"I take it back," Malcolm says. "*That's* how you woo a lady."

"Comfrey," John says, his voice muffled. "It'll help stop the bleeding." He spits the leaves into his palm, an enormous green glob.

"That's disgusting." Malcolm looks genuinely distressed.

"If you prefer, I can let you bleed to death," John replies calmly. "Leave you here for the gulls to peck out your eyes, the boars to tear you up, and those red-eyed crows to finish you off—"

"By all means, carry on."

John jams the wad of leaves into the wound, holding them in place with the flat of his palm. Malcolm lets out a stream of curses, twisting in pain under John's hand.

"It'll hurt only a minute," John says. After a moment he pulls his hand away. It's bloody and sticky with green, but just as he said, the bleeding has slowed. John takes the knife, quickly slices his own discarded shirt into a bandage, and wraps it tight against Malcolm's chest.

"We'll need to get you out of here." John glances around. The field is littered with bodies, soldiers still darting around, weapons held high. "We can try to cut through the woods back to Rochester, though we don't know what could be lurking inside—oh, only you."

I look up to see Schuyler step from the trees into view. He's got a sword in one hand, a bundle of gray fabric clutched in the other. He pauses a moment, takes us in.

"It's a good look." Schuyler eyes John's half-naked body. "Bit like a republic gladiator, strutting about the arena. Shall I bring you a loincloth? A pair of sandals? A lion, perhaps?"

John flips him an obscene gesture, and then, to my surprise, he laughs.

Schuyler tosses him the gray bundle—a shirt. "Found this lying around. Thought it might come in handy." John takes it with a word of thanks, then yanks it over his head. "He going to die?" Schuyler jerks his head at Malcolm.

I shoot Schuyler a look.

"No, he's not," John says. "It's a nasty cut to be sure, but it's not fatal. Jagged, though—it'll be hell to stitch up." A look of mild distress crosses his face; at once I know why. John may not recall how to stitch him up, not anymore. He looks back to Malcolm. "What was it? A serrated knife?"

Malcolm shakes his head. "It wasn't a weapon. It was talons." He points overhead. "One of those bloody winged things picked me up and flew me a hundred feet straight up before someone shot it down. I was still fifty feet in the air when it dropped me."

"You're lucky you didn't break something." John pauses, considers. "Unless you did. Can you move your arms and legs?"

"I can move everything but my left leg," Malcolm says. "I can't bend it. I already tried."

John looks up at Schuyler. "You'll have to carry him."

Schuyler reaches down, scoops Malcolm into his arms. He pauses, then nods. "I'll warrant you didn't," he says, and I can guess what Malcolm's thinking: that he never imagined himself to be injured in a battlefield, fighting against his family, tended to by a Reformist, helped by a revenant. "And you're welcome," Schuyler adds.

34

FIFER AND PETER GREET US at Rochester Hall. Fifer rushes up to Schuyler like she doesn't even see anyone else. She looks at him as if she wants to laugh and cry at the same time. Then she turns to John, throws herself in his arms.

"Nicholas." It's all she says; it's all she needs to say. John shakes his head, and Fifer ducks her head into his shoulder again. He whispers to her, his voice drowned out by her sobs.

"Put me down," Malcolm says to Schuyler, cracking open an eye. His voice is barely a whisper. "I can walk—hop, rather—and you should go to her...." He wriggles in Schuyler's grasp, breaks off with a gasp of pain.

"No talking," John tells him. "And no more moving." He glances at Schuyler. "I need to get him to the infirmary. Do you mind taking him? I'll come along. You can drop him off but I'll stay." John turns to me as if to explain, but he doesn't need to. He's going to stay with Malcolm to make sure he's taken care of, because although one enemy is gone, there are still many others who would see him gone, too.

Schuyler starts off across the field, Malcolm still in his arms, Fifer beside him. John tells me he'll be back for me soon, and then he's gone.

It's just me and Peter alone now, alone save for the thousands of men running around us, shouting and screaming, cursing and laughing. I watch them as they pass, some in chaos and in pain, some in triumph and in relief. Perhaps they never expected to win but now we have, and it's a strange, heady sensation to rejoice when so many others have died, to feel that we've won when we've still lost so much.

Before I can say anything, before I can begin to say or even think what it might mean for us, for them, for everything, Peter snatches me in an embrace, patting my back as if I were a child, murmuring words of comfort I didn't know I needed. I let myself sag in his embrace and cry until I'm weak with release and his shirt is wet with my tears.

The battlefield continues to clear off; men continue to stagger back to camp at Rochester, coming in steady streams through the gatehouse. After seeing Malcolm safely installed and heavily guarded in an infirmary tent—with the promise that he would return to check on him soon—John finds me again, Schuyler and Fifer in tow. There were a panic-filled few hours when we couldn't find George, but finally Schuyler finds him huddled around a tent with two dozen Gallic soldiers, all of them drunk as choirboys. We're angry for all of one minute, until one of the soldiers tosses John a bottle of wine. John takes a drink before passing it to me, grinning.

The four of us sit down beside them, and we spend most of the night drinking and laughing and feeling something I've not felt in a long time:

Relief.

Much later, Gareth is found. Back in Harrow, hiding in the cathedral of his own home, huddled beside the pulpit where he denounced me and ordered me to kill the very man he renounced his own side for, a sword in his hand, dead.

Peter reasoned that at some point during the battle he'd had a change of heart, a traitor turning traitor once more. Perhaps he was injured before; perhaps he took a hit on the way back. It wasn't a deep wound, something a healer could have fixed had he returned to Rochester. Instead, he bled to death; he hadn't even bandaged it to try to stop the blood. But perhaps he didn't know how injured he was, not until it was too late.

In the days that follow, Nicholas is laid to rest in a plot beside his home, a home that now belongs to Fifer. Shortly afterward she disappeared from camp alongside Schuyler, keeping to herself and working through her grief in private.

With Blackwell's death, Anglia falls into crisis: We are a country without a king. Upon their surrender, Blackwell's councilmen—once Malcolm's—meet with Harrow's council, led by Fitzroy, the newly appointed Regent of Anglia. And for days they table the unprecedented question: Who is to take the crown? By right, it should revert back to Malcolm. Only, he won't take it.

"I can't do it," Malcolm says. We're inside Rochester Hall, in one of the hundreds of plush bedrooms, most of them filled now with recovering soldiers. I sit in a chair beside his bed, John on the other side, checking him over. It's been seven days since the battle ended; six since Malcolm was installed in a fine room, far different from the room he was imprisoned in. He could have had any one of a dozen healers attend to him, but to my surprise, he only wanted John.

"I couldn't do it the first time. You saw what happened. It led to... all this." He waves his hand vaguely out the window. In the distance, soldiers still mill about the camp. "I thought about what I'd do, if we won. I was going to hand the crown to Margaret, but that was before..." He trails off, turning his gaze to the floor. John and I exchange a glance.

Malcolm was not a good husband, not at all. But when he learned of the death of his wife he took it hard, more than I imagined he would. Her death was not a repercussion of war, but one of neglect: Three days ago she was found abandoned in a cell at Fleet, left to a pitiful death by starvation and cold.

"Someone's going to have to do it, and soon," I say. "Fitzroy can't continue ruling; his claim isn't strong enough. Great-grandson to Edward the First, three times removed—"

"Four times," Malcolm and John say at the same time.

"Fine. Four times removed. He can hold it now, but once someone starts digging—and you know they will—they'll find someone with better lineage. If it's someone the council doesn't like, and whoever it is doesn't give up his claim, there could be another war. We can't have that."

"Were I to claim the throne, there would be a war anyway," Malcolm says. "I'm still the enemy to some. To many. Don't make me do the math again." He hisses in pain as John presses down on his broken leg.

"Sorry," John says. "Your leg looks good, though. You should have full use of it within six months. Your days of jousting and hunting and dancing might be limited for the next year, but that's not too bad, all things considered."

"I was thinking of taking up painting," Malcolm says, his face still a grimace. "Or maybe lute playing."

I don't say anything for a moment. The sight of John and Malcolm talking as if they don't hate each other, as if they aren't enemies, holds me to silence.

There's a knock at the door, then it swings open.

We get to our feet, John and I, nodding our heads in deference. Fitzroy nods at us, then glances at Malcolm.

"Forgive me for not standing, Lord Regent." Malcolm smiles at him, and there's no malice in his voice at the deference. "I seem to be at a disadvantage at the moment."

"No apology necessary." Fitzroy smiles in return. "Do you have a moment? I thought we could talk." He flicks his hand, and a handful of servants appear from behind him carrying trays laden with food and wine; pewter plates and crystal goblets; fine silverware. A feast for a king. He glances at John. "I know this isn't on the approved list of physics, but if you could allow it just for today…"

"It's fine," John says, then looks at Malcolm. "I think I can trust you not to overindulge?"

"I think my days of indulgence are over," Malcolm replies.

We leave Malcolm and Fitzroy alone and make our way down the long, light-filled hallway, out one of many doors and into one of the many courtyards. There's a ring of benches around a fountain, splashing and gurgling in the warm sun, the bushes and hedges around it beginning to show bloom. I sit down on the one closest to the water; John sits beside me.

"You and Malcolm," I say after a minute. "It's an odd thing to see you by his side. Helping him." I pause. "Why did you? Not just here, today, but before on the battlefield. Why did you do it?"

John smiles. "Well, I wouldn't be much of a healer if I left him to die, would I?"

"That's not what I meant," I say.

"I know," he says. "But I don't know if I've got a better answer. Part of caring for people is to try to see past what it is they're showing you. Malcolm was in a cell beside me at Hexham. He showed me a lot about himself there, most of it having to do with you."

I pull a face. I don't want to know the things he said.

"I'll spare you the details," he says. "But if I thought for a second Malcolm ever meant to harm you, that he acted out of malice instead of ignorance, I wouldn't have stood by him. I would have healed him, but I wouldn't have helped him.

"He's spoiled and he's flighty," John continues. "He's ignorant, too, but not about things. About people. He's lived so long with people telling him yes that he can't imagine a world where they say no." A pause. "You forgave him, didn't you?"

I nod. "He asked it of me, and I didn't think I could put it behind me if I didn't. It was right before we went into battle, and I didn't know if I'd ever see him again. At the time, it seemed pointless not to."

"And now?" he says. "How do you feel about the possibility of him being king again?"

"I think it will be different this time," I reply. "I think he's different. I think we all are."

John cups my face with his hand, skimming his thumb along my cheek. "Not that different," he says. And then he kisses me.

"The Gallic king offered his daughter in marriage to Malcolm," Peter says. We're loitering in yet another courtyard outside yet another hall where yet another council meeting is taking place: the fifth one in as many days. John, Schuyler, Fifer, George, and me.

"Not three weeks ago they wanted to ransom him to the Berbers," I say.

"Three weeks ago he was a prisoner," George replies. "Now he's the victor of a battle, the heir to the throne of Anglia. The heir who abdicated to a commoner."

"Fitzroy is hardly a commoner," I say

George shrugs. "To Gaul he is. His line is impressive, to be sure. But it's too removed. Great-grandson to King Edward, three times removed—"

"Four," I correct. "Four times removed." George raises his eyebrows. "Sorry. Go on."

"Not much else to say," Peter continues. "The Gallic king offers his daughter, along with a sizable dowry, including a hundred thousand livres to help rebuild Anglia."

John lets out a low whistle.

Peter nods. "A marriage like that would strengthen our ties to them, unite us against attacks from Iberia, against the Low Countries, should they ever decide to move against us.

As it stands, they see us both as weak. One country without a king, the other with only a daughter to be queen."

"He doesn't want to do it," I say. "He told us."

"Doesn't matter." George shrugs. "Kings don't get much of a say in how they were born, do they?"

Peter shakes his head. "They don't. It's coming to a vote tonight. Fitzroy is prepared to step aside, if he has no one to contest him. If the majority say yes, it's down to Malcolm to refuse. And I don't think he'll refuse. Do you?"

I don't imagine everyone's eyes on me, as if I could guess what Malcolm might do. But I do anyway. And I shake my head.

In the end, I was right.

Malcolm agreed to the council's wishes and he's to be king of Anglia once more, but ruling Anglia in a way that's never been done. He will have a privy council, as before. But he will also have two additional regional councils—the Council of the North and the oddly named Council of the Marches—to oversee the northern and southern outlying counties of Anglia. The divine right of kings—the law that allowed kings to rule as gods—has been abolished. The Twelve Tablets, already abolished, would remain so, new laws drawn up and voted on.

It was all but done.

When the Gallic princess arrived with her courtiers, her ambassadors, her advisors, her plate and her jewels and her livres, I wasn't there. When Ravenscourt opened back up, the gates and the courtyards scrubbed clean of all signs of war and death, hybrids and revenants, I wasn't there.

The week after Malcolm was reinstalled as king, the privy council was installed inside their apartments inside Ravenscourt, now being lavishly redecorated and refitted to erase all signs of ever being inhabited by Blackwell. Once again, I wasn't there.

I can't go back to court; I don't think I'll ever want to.

John helps his father load the last of his trunks onto the wagon that sits in front of their cottage, waiting to take him to Upminster. As a member of the Council of the Marches, his presence is required monthly at court, and although he doesn't need to be there more often than that, he's taken a house along Westcheap, a short walk from the palace.

We watch the wagon tip its way down the narrow lane, the wheels kicking up mud. There would be a wagon for me, for us, if we decided to go. Half the girls in Harrow have already left, eager to be ladies-in-waiting in the court of the soon-to-be-queen. I could do it, too, if I wanted. I could be part of it all, just as I was before.

But I know how close power comes to corruption, how fast good intentions turn bad. I know that despite promises and declarations and even laws, things have a way of turning on their own, of starting down a path, trespassing so far that redress becomes impossible.

I turn to John. He's watching me and I know he's waiting—in that way he does—for me to tell him what he already knows. That I can't be part of Malcolm's court, no matter how much I'm asked, no matter how much it's changed. Because there are some things that never would change, just as there are some things I don't want to remember.

"I can't do it," I say.

He closes his eyes for a moment and for a moment I think I've disappointed him, that I've read his looks and his words wrong, until he opens his eyes, a grin on his face.

"Thank God."

I blink back surprise. "You don't want to go, either?"

John shakes his head. "No. I never did. But I would have, if that was what you wanted. I just want to go where you go." He watches me carefully. "But I wanted you to make up your own mind. For once, I wanted you to do what you wanted, without anyone deciding for you."

"Are you sure?" I say. "You won't mind being alone?"

"I'm not alone," he says. "I'm with you."

I smile. "You know what I mean."

He grins. "We'll hardly be alone. Schuyler is staying. Keagan is staying, too; she and Fifer are starting a new branch of the Order here in Harrow. As for the rest, we can see the others anytime we want. Upminster isn't that far."

"It's far enough," I say.

John smiles. "It's far enough."

He takes my hand and tugs me toward the cottage, the bright blue door still open to the sunshine and the breeze, welcoming us in. It's a good place to start over.

And a good place to continue on.

ACKNOWLEDGMENTS

Ah, the second book. It's a thrill, a challenge, a stressor, and a triumph: It is, much like all of publishing, all the things people tell you it will be but you don't believe until you reach the other side. This book is dedicated to everyone who helped me push through.

My agent, Kathleen Ortiz. I feel like I could thank you every day and it still wouldn't be enough. For your patience, for your perseverance, for always having my back, and for knowing me well enough to know when I need *that* phone call to say, "I think we should talk." (And for always starting those calls with "You aren't driving, are you?" followed by, "Don't freak out.") You are a BAMF, and I adore you.

My editor, Pam Gruber. We made it! I consider this book your accomplishment as much as mine: all those calls, all those emails, all those conversations ("Do you really think she would?" "Maybe, but I don't think she *should*.") and spreadsheets (yes, we plotted spells using spreadsheets). Thank you for your endless patience, guidance, intuition, for making me better at what I do, and for making this story something I am truly proud of. I feel like we are forever bonded in magic.

My agency, New Leaf Literary + Media. You are still the coolest kids on the block, and I'm so proud to be part of your ranks. Special thanks to Joanna Volpe, Danielle Barthel, Jaida Temperly, Dave Caccavo, Jackie Lindert, and Mia Roman.

My publisher, Little, Brown Books for Young Readers. Not a day goes by that I am not profoundly grateful to be part of this imprint. Immeasurable gratitude to my incredibly talented team: Leslie Shumate, Kristina Aven, Emilie Polster, Victoria Stapleton, Jenny Choy, Jane Lee, and everyone at The NOVL. Marcie Lawrence for the most gorgeous cover I've ever seen, Virginia Lawther and Rebecca Westall for making me a book, Annie McDonnell for making it shine, and Emily Sharratt for your spot-on, London-specific notes. Thank you also to Megan Tingley, Alvina Ling, and Andrew Smith. The support, kindness, respect, and enthusiasm you've shown me and my books is in everything you do.

My foreign publishers. Thank you for your support, your beautiful covers, and for giving Elizabeth & Co. the best home in all corners of the world.

Alexis Bass. I could not do this publishing thing without you. Thank you for our long, hilarious, insane conversations, inappropriate crushes, and for sharing the same brain and taste in just about everything. You are the bestest, and I am so grateful for our friendship.

My Secret Society. The ranks have closed, and we are it. KL, JMT, LK, I love our corner of the universe where things are dark, funny, truthful, and supportive. Of all the groups in all the towns in all the world, I am so happy you walked into mine.

Stephanie Funk. For being there from the beginning.

Melissa Grey, critique partner extraordinaire. We're like those two things in chemistry class you should never mix together, yet somehow when we do it shines. Here's to cupcakes, Freixenet, sushi, crying over puppies, hot gay mages, and Mexican Al Rokers. I love the alchemy of us.

April Tucholke. Thank you for your friendship, your mentorship, and for making me laugh so hard it hurts. May we always have stormy coastal writing retreats and Liberace Panel Resting Faces™.

The writing community. Readers, reviewers, bloggers, booksellers, teachers, librarians: Thank you for taking the time to read my words, writing about them, telling your friends about them, and coming to see me talk about them. Thank you for your support. For all my fellow authors: You're all so talented, and such an inspiration. I'm so grateful to know all of you.

My friends and family. You are proof that magic exists. Thank you for your endless patience and understanding with "this writing thing." Special thanks to my intuitive daughter, Holland, when she sees me looking less than happy, for saying, "You didn't go on Goodreads again, did you?" My clever son, August, when he sees me deep in thought, for saying, "Do you need a magic spell? How about one where a wizard steals oxygen from the air?" (Thanks, buddy! That one I used!) And to my husband, Scott, whose words of wisdom could fill an entire book. Thank you for always believing in me no matter what. Because of you I am, quite simply, the luckiest girl in the world.